DEATH
IN
EDEN

# DEATH IN EDEN

A Mystery

Paul J. Heald

YUCCA

Yucca Publishing books may be purchased in bulk at special discounts for sales promotion, corporate gifts, fund-raising, or educational purposes. Special editions can also be created to specifications. For details, contact the Special Sales Department, Yucca Publishing, 307 West 36th Street, 11th Floor, New York, NY 10018 or yucca@skyhorsepublishing.com.

Yucca Publishing® is an imprint of Skyhorse Publishing, Inc.®, a Delaware corporation.

Visit our website at www.yuccapub.com.

10 9 8 7 6 5 4 3 2 1

Library of Congress Cataloging-in-Publication Data is available on file.

Cover design by Yucca Publishing
Cover photo credit © Kirsty Pargeter

ISBN: 978-1-63158-008-6
Ebook ISBN: 978-1-63158-026-0

Printed in the United States of America

For Catharine and Gloria; Jenna and Tera

"What was the sign that Adam and Eve had sinned?
They covered up their nakedness. In a state of grace, clothes
are unnecessary."

Donald Johansson
Director of Eden Studio's *Toys in Babeland*

# Contents

# I.

# PUBLISH OR PERISH

Professor Stanley Hopkins looked at the Greek letters emblazoned on the chest of Slouchy McBallCap and then glanced at the power cord to his laptop. How much time would he spend in jail if he garroted the tow-headed frat boy in front of the one hundred fifty students in Sociology 101? Maybe none when the jury heard that he had been asked once again why the Iraqis had nuked New York on 9/11. Instead, he counted to three, patiently explained the difference between Al Qaeda and Afghanistan, and then watched the class slowly file out of the room. Right after he got tenure, he was going to jump over the podium into their midst and pitch the electronic devices of every laptop-poker-player and Lady Gaga-re-tweeter right against cinderblock walls of the basement auditorium. That is, if he got tenure.

He fended off a couple of questions about the exam (heaven forbid an undergrad should ask a question about the actual material) and trudged back up to his office where he found Victoria Kwon, his favorite graduate student, nervously waiting outside his front door.

"Hi, Professor Hopkins! Did you have a chance to look at my draft?" Stanley had spent two days plowing through her doctoral dissertation, writing a detailed analysis that might help her nail the second draft in time to hit the post-doc market. This part of his job he didn't mind at all: shepherding graduate students from a jumble of ideas and intuitions to a tight, polished, finished product. Seeing his own projects to completion was another story; that was like dancing in a minefield.

He unlocked the door, motioned for her to take the chair across from his desk, and handed her a thick sheaf papers with a smile. "I think this is a great start."

A look of relief washed over her face, and the assistant professor spent the next hour praising the strengths of her history of labor relations in the early twentieth century garment industry and gently suggesting the sort of revisions and additional sources that her dissertation committee chair would want to see.

"I wish you could be my official advisor," she sighed as she got up. "Professor Martin is hardly ever around and he takes forever to read anything. And he doesn't give nearly as thorough comments as you do."

"Until I get promoted and tenured, I can't formally chair anyone's committee." As she left, he considered the two hurdles standing in the way of a permanent contract and elevated status: finishing his book on industrial sociology and not killing any undergraduates, both of which he could accomplish better by shutting his door and studying the "revise and resubmit" letter just received from a potential publisher of his research.

A few minutes later he heard a sharp rap on his door and before he could respond, the Chair of the Sociology Department, Max Kurland, strode in and plopped down on the chair across from his desk. "Gotta second?"

"Sure." As usual, Kurland's timing was unerring. Every time Stanley got his motor going, the administrator or one of his neighbors dropped by for a chat.

Kurland gave his junior colleague a knowing wink. "I saw Vicki Kwon coming out of your office a while ago. With her body, she could always go into modeling if the grad school thing didn't work out. Or maybe pole dancing."

"She is attractive," Stanley replied warily, "and one of the best students I've ever had." He was friendly with Max, but avoided talking with him about women. Before he became an administrator, the darkly handsome Kurland had the reputation of sleeping with some of his prettier students. Stanley was not above fantasizing about someone like Victoria, but he clung to the old-fashioned view that any sort of sexual relationship with a student was unethical, an opinion that his wife of ten years seconded enthusiastically.

"I'll have to take your word for it. I've never had her," Max gave a lecherous little chortle. He stretched out his legs and studied the degrees in sociology and law framed on the wall. "I saw the Dean this morning and she was asking whether I anticipated any close tenure cases next fall." He paused and looked at Stanley over steepled fingers. "Since your book is almost done, I told her no worries."

"Well," he replied slowly, "it is, really. I just got a revision letter yesterday. The publisher is demanding one more chapter, one that focuses on a profession dominated by women." Stanley had completed studies of lumberjacks, carnival workers, insurance adjusters, and pest control people, but his final planned chapter on hair salon workers had just been derailed by a brilliant paper from a professor at Cornell. "I just need to find a proper subject, and I've got it."

"Are your preliminary findings still consistent with your thesis?"

Stanley nodded. Why wouldn't the old sleazebag just get the hell out of his office and let him work? Kurland had no real interest in the content of the book. He just wanted to avoid the embarrassment—to himself and to the department—of seeing a struggling, young professor denied tenure. If Stanley failed to finish the book it would mean a black mark and a lot of paper work for the middle-aged department head.

With a minimal effort to hide his impatience, Stanley explained that all groups of workers he had studied scored similar averages on the factors he was measuring: job satisfaction, self-esteem, drug use, inter-office relationships, and legal trouble related to employment. Much to his father's disappointment, Stanley's law degree had not led to a single billable hour, but rather to graduate school and the study of the sociology of human labor and the workplace. Instead of sucking three hundred dollars an hour from large employers, he interviewed their workers for an assistant professor's paltry salary, a mind boggling decision discussed at every holiday meal since he had decided to stay in school.

Max scratched his head as if he were digesting the information for the first time. "What about adding elementary school teachers? They're still mostly women."

"God, I could fill a room with the existing scholarship on school teachers."

"Nurses?"

"Ditto." Stanley got up in an attempt to get Max to leave. "Don't worry, I'm all over it." When he was finally alone, he slumped back in his chair. Were it not for the mortgage, the car payments, and a deep-seated aversion to disappointing his wife, he would pay a final visit to Kurland's office, hand in his keys and laptop, and leave his manuscript and the loutish undergrads far behind. The irony of his researching job satisfaction was temporarily lost from view.

An hour later, the professor arrived home and deposited a sack of groceries and a briefcase in the kitchen. Hearing the television, he made his way to the living room and buried his nose in Angela's soft, dark hair. He kissed her gently on the top of her head and slipped down next to her. On the screen, two grave pundits were concluding a debate on North Korea's growing nuclear capabilities.

"Lousy day?" Angela asked.

"How did you guess?" He sighed as she leaned against him and told her about Max Kurland's visit to his office. It pained him to see concern etching in her flawless skin and troubling her dark brown eyes. Her father had been a professor too, and she understood the vicissitudes of promotion and tenure. She did not suspect that he was beginning to doubt his own fitness for the academic life.

He turned his attention to the television as she made a suggestion for the final chapter of his book. He barely heard her as he stared at the man being interviewed on the television, racking his brain for the proper reference. The interviewee was tall and wore a casual wool suit and stylish glasses highlighting an animated and intelligent face. Stanley could not quite make out what he was saying. "Turn it up!"

"…hoping to make this the first major national release of a pornographic film since *Deep Throat* and *Behind the Green Door* in the early seventies," the man explained.

"I notice you just referred to *Toys in Babeland* as a pornographic film," replied a pretty Hispanic newswoman. "Don't most people in the industry prefer 'adult film'?"

"They do, Maria," he replied, using the soft Spanish pronunciation of her name. "But that euphemism is not honest, or accurate. Let's face it, *Saving Private Ryan* is very much an adult film, isn't it? But when a director makes *Saving Ryan's Privates*, I should be clear and call it pornography, no?"

"I see," the lovely reporter said as she stifled a giggle.

Stanley leaned forward on the sofa. "Holy crap." He turned with wide eyes. "That's Donald Johansson."

"Who?"

"Shh…" He reached over and turned up the volume.

"…our nation's brief flirtation with mainstream pornographic movies failed for several reasons. First, Linda Lovelace's revelation that she was forced to have sex on the set of *Deep Throat* justifiably revolted critics and viewers alike. Nobody wants to go to a movie and feel like an accessory to rape. Also, the early movies were really boring, with poor production values, lousy scripts, and very amateur acting. Some of them look like bad documentaries on gynecology."

"And how is *Toys in Babeland* different?"

"For one thing, our studio has a very good reputation with actresses. In fact, many of my scriptwriters and directors are women. If anyone isn't comfortable, we stop shooting and make adjustments. It's more time consuming to shoot with a woman's needs in mind, but we get great performances and that draws the most talented stars to our studio. Perhaps your viewers won't believe this, but we really try to have fun on the set, and I think it shows in the finished product."

"I'll have to take your word for that, Mr. Johansson," Maria shot back.

"You've got to come see the movie, Maria. It's a good comedy too." He winked at her and then at the camera. "The test audiences have been rolling in the aisles!"

"Maybe the network will ask me to do just that," she stammered and then recovered her composure. "This is Maria Lopez, with Donald Johansson, aka Richard Ramrod, executive producer of the new 'comedy,' *Toys in Babeland*."

Stanley took the remote control from Angela's and muted the sound. He stared in disbelief at the screen for a minute and shook his head. The porn mogul on the television had been a member of his fraternity in college. They had not known each other well, but there was no mistaking the commanding voice and distinctive profile of Don Johansson. In fact, the tall Californian had been one of the reasons he had quit Alpha Omicron at the end of his sophomore year.

As a freshman at the University of Virginia, Stanley had drifted into fraternity life without really thinking about it. His friends in the dormitory were keen on "rushing," so they went from frat house to frat house, barely able to remember the various concatenations of Greek letters swimming before their boozy eyes. His lack of eagerness proved to be a virtue in the cool eyes of the brothers of Alpha Omicron, for he was soon made a pledge and later moved into the house for his second year at college. He thought the rituals were stupid and the hazing sadistic, but the parties were great and enough of his new brothers shared his cynicism so that life was tolerable.

When Stanley moved in, Don Johansson was a senior and notable for having the highest grade point average in the house, and the most atypical career plan: graduate studies at an Episcopal Seminary. As the underclassman with the best grades, Stanley came to the attention of the older student who made it a point to sit with him occasionally at dinner and poke fun at their compatriots who were avoiding academic probation by plagiarism or professional note-taking services. But it was not the breaking of bread with Johansson that the young professor remembered; it was the breaking of heads by the future seminarian.

Stanley had been playing pool in the basement of the frat house with his roommate when one of the upper classmen had hurried down the stairs and asked if either of them was interested in *pulling a train*. The future sociologist shook his head instinctively and kept shooting, while his opponent scrambled up the stairs. He had heard the expression whispered before and knew that he had been invited to take a turn having sex with some drunk young woman. Several of his brothers had bragged of their exploits and had even suggested with a laugh that any unconscious female in the house was fair game. No one who heard the statement had contradicted his opinion. Given it was a Friday night and a party was raging above his head, anything was possible.

He racked the balls and continued to play, rationalizing his decision to stay in the basement and ignore the warning bells going off in his head. The men involved were undoubtedly bigger than him and drunk off their asses. It wasn't just one guy that he could reason with, but a whole fired up group. And what could he do anyway? Call the cops and get the whole frat closed down? And who was stupid enough to pass out at a frat party anyway? This last uncharitable thought sickened him instantly, for it was surely shared by the men upstairs. But there was probably nothing going on. It was probably consensual.

Two minutes later, that last hope was punctured by excited shouts and the sound of furniture breaking above his head. He rushed up the stairs just in time to see Don push one very drunk frat brother into a walnut trophy case and then throw a lamp at another who ducked around a bookshelf. A sobbing girl was cowering behind him as he cut a furious path toward the front door, throwing punches and shouting obscenities at the small group of young men protesting his rescue of the girl. The star of the house's intramural football team was the last obstacle blocking his escape out of the foyer, but Don was not alone in his anger and disgust, and the way was cleared by two of his friends who wrestled the big lineman with a reverberating thump to the hardwood floor. When Don finally pushed the girl outside, the house erupted into a drunken melee of name calling and accusations of oathbreaking that took hours to subside fully. The hero of the episode never set foot in the house again, and Stanley left for good, several weeks later when the semester ended.

The professor told the story to his wife, sparing none of the details of his own spinelessness. Angela hummed noncommittally, apparently impressed by the story of the rescue, but unwilling to ignore the stain of Johansson's present career choice or brush aside her own husband's shortcomings.

"Tell me more over dinner. Let's put the groceries away and start cooking." She walked to the kitchen, but Stanley stayed seated for a moment, staring at a dog food commercial while an outrageous thought scurried about in his brain.

# II.

# THE IVORY TOWER

"You want to do what?" Kurland narrowed his eyes and repeated his question. "Explain this to me one more time."

Stanley had spent a sleepless night trying to figure out a way to sell his idea to his department chair, to Angela, and to himself. Once the shock wore off of seeing his former housemate talking about pornography on national television, the professor had asked himself a simple question. Had anyone ever done a serious study of women working in the porn industry? Johansson had talked as if having sex on camera were just another type of job. Then couldn't it be studied like other jobs? Could this be the magic last chapter he needed to finish his book? Max presented the easiest hurdle. He had once enthusiastically approved a new course on "Sexuality in the Internet Age" to attract students to the Sociology Department.

Stanley himself felt a fleeting misgiving about possibly legitimizing the porn industry by taking it seriously, but given the number of porn stars cropping up on talk shows and reality television, that boat seemed to have already sailed. Besides, his involvement would consist of professional interviews in a clinical atmosphere. His role would be academic, not cheerleading.

Convincing his feminist wife that his plan was not the ultimate in sleaze would be a more challenging proposition.

Stanley answered the department chairman's question with a sober expression, heightened, he hoped, by the conservative gray suit that he was wearing. He sat in Kurland's office, soft spring sunlight streaming in through the high windows behind his colleague's desk. The spring day was perfect and so, he told himself, was the plan to finish his book.

"You want the University to fund a trip to Los Angeles so you can interview porn stars?" Kurland paused and shook his head in wonder. "It's brilliant! How come I never thought of this?"

"Probably because your specialty is cooperative behavior among Appalachian farmers." Stanley offered his most confident smile. "Does this mean I can do it?" He watched Max open his mouth to say more, but nothing came out. The administrator gave him a quick look and then scanned through a folder on his desk, murmuring underneath his breath and finally nodding affirmatively.

Money was not a problem, given that the audiovisual equipment had long ago been purchased and money had been allocated for travel expenses, but there was one possible hitch. Kurland flipped the folder shut and tossed it to the side. "What are you going to do about the university's human subjects committee?"

Stanley groaned inwardly. He had forgotten that any interviewing conducted by a faculty member had to be approved by the famously obstructive and recalcitrant committee established to protect the rights of interview subjects. They had raked him over the coals and then taken six months to approve his list of questions for the pest control workers.

"Shit, Max, I don't have time to deal with that bunch of assholes." He felt a familiar pessimistic wave pass through him. This was the first promising idea he had had for a long time and a bureaucratic technicality was about to derail it. He had no time to go back to the institutional review board and convince them that interviewing porn stars was an academic necessity.

"Well," the department chair nodded at this assessment of the committee, "let's think about this. Aren't you going to ask the same questions to the porn stars?"

"Basically, yeah. We're trying to measure the same kinds of attitudes, but I imagine the follow-up questions will be different, given what they do."

"Sure, but you can't be expected to get spontaneous questions approved, can you? As long as your initial script is the same, I think we can wink-wink, nudge-nudge the substitution of adult entertainment workers for hairdressers." He gave his younger colleague a broad grin. "Don't want to create unnecessary paperwork, do we?"

"Max, I love you!" He then explained his plan of attack to the fascinated administrator. The biggest problem would be setting up the actual interviews. When he interviewed lumberjacks, he had to go through the union, which had been a bureaucratic nightmare. Both the pest control and carnival workers had been non-union, but the companies that employed them were paranoid that he might be an undercover investigator trying to document illegal practices. It had taken months to win their trust, but the porn industry could potentially be cracked by exploiting his connection to Don Johansson, aka Dick Ramrod. Max admitted knowing the name, and there seemed little doubt that a cooperative producer could make arranging interviews much easier.

As Stanley talked about the project, it became more real, and he began to believe that he could pull it off. The racy subject matter would certainly spice up the rather dry chapters that he had already written. Surely Angela would see the logic of his plan, even if she wholeheartedly disapproved of the profession he would be studying.

"Okay, keep me up to date on your progress." Kurland stood up and his tone got more serious. "I know this is a perfectly legitimate and promising line of research, but let's not publicize it too widely, alright? Almost half the faculty is women now, and I don't know what they'd think about this. And you've already got doubters among those who think all good research has to rest on numbers and statistics." The two colleagues walked toward the door and paused. "Once the book is done, this will look like a serious study and I don't think anyone will question it. But until then, let's not look for trouble. Understood?"

Stanley nodded, shook Max's hand, and suddenly wondered whether he was playing with fire. If he was, he pondered while he walked back to his office, it felt surprisingly good.

* * *

Angela sat in bed with her laptop updating photos on two pieces of real estate where she was the listing agent, and trying to come up with a humorous new subject for her weekly newspaper column. She had just split a large commission with her best friend and colleague, Nanci Nguyen, and the closing day negotiations over a brutally ugly bird bath had the makings of a hilarious commentary on human irrationality. She had just finished describing the seller's frothy billowing ear hair when Stanley slid into bed next to her explained his plan for salvaging his career by diving into a cesspool of porn.

For someone who bought her bathing suits from Land's End and had a hard time distinguishing between *Penthouse* and the *Victoria's Secret* catalog, her husband's proposition was a lot to swallow. While he earnestly explained his insane research plan, she scrambled for a way to push him in another direction.

To avoid being labeled a prude, she tried to explain her reservations using internet poker as an example. Even though online money games were illegal, she had noticed the popularity of televised poker tournaments with well-dressed commentators treating the competition just like it was a sport. Now, all sorts of gear were for sale: visors, hats and t-shirts, and suddenly the general public viewed themselves as poker fans instead of victims of corporate gambling interests. Porn was being mainstreamed in the same stealthy way, from sex toys being sold by pretty "hostesses" on QVC to late night *Girls Gone Wild* ads on the edgier cable networks. She did not want her husband to give it all a patina of legitimacy.

Stanley remained irritatingly calm during her disquisition, insisting that being a neutral observer was different than being a promoter. She was not so sure. After all, his avowed goal was to take the adult film industry seriously, and if he succeeded in making his comparisons with other legitimate businesses, wasn't he part of the mainstreaming process? His response, depressing though it was, was hard to refute. Academic books by sociologists seldom sold more than five hundred copies, mostly to university libraries, so the chance of his chapter having any impact one way or the other was remote. This gave her pause, and she wondered for a moment what had motivated him to become a professor in the first place. Her own newspaper commentaries might be a little fluffy at times, but each one reached thousands more readers than his.

But whether anyone read his book or not, the project still made her uneasy. She had to admit to herself that she simply did not like the thought of him locked up in a hotel room studying voluptuous and uninhibited women who had sex for money. In theory, she trusted him completely, but she had put on twenty pounds since they were married and every year she had felt more out-classed by the lithesome students who flounced over to the house for the class parties he hosted every semester. Her husband was a handsome guy, and she had always felt a little insecure.

"But Stan, no matter how the study is eventually received, I'll be worried sick the whole time you're gone." She pouted as though her only concern was loneliness, but he saw right through her.

"Don't you trust me?" He looked eager to convince her otherwise.

"Of course I do! But I sure as hell don't trust *them*. Why should I trust a bunch of women that I've never met, who do what they do?" She folded her arms across her chest. "I know you think this is a good idea, but it's such a bad idea!" At this point, the conversation started to slip away from her as he took the initiative in a dialogue where she felt like she was one step behind.

He reminded her of how hard he had searched for an appropriate topic and then scooted in front of her and looked her in the eye. "How many times have you shown empty houses to men, alone?"

"A lot of times," she admitted, "but I don't see how that's relevant."

"Well, I trust you to be alone in bedrooms with men who are probably fantasizing about the sexy young broker at their side." He cocked his head and looked up. "Have I ever worried about you?"

"No, but I'm not like Nanci. I don't have guys drooling over me all the time. And you know I have no interest in other men anyway."

"And you know that I have no interest in other women."

"Aaargh!" She pulled the pillow onto her lap and squeezed it. "It's just not the same. I don't show houses to porn stars." She suggested that he conduct his interviews in some public place, but he explained to her that privacy was necessary and probably required by the notorious human subjects committee.

Then she listened wide-eyed as the conversation spun out of control. He outmaneuvered her completely. He took her concerns seriously and found an irritatingly reasonable solution. All the interviews would go more quickly and smoothly if someone were with him in the interview room to work the camera and change the digital memory cards. Why shouldn't she come with him and help out? They could stay in a nice hotel in Los Angeles and kind of have a second honeymoon. He leaned over and gave her a warm kiss to seal the deal even before she assented. While he went on and on about how wonderful it would be to travel with her, she realized she was trapped. She had to let him go, or go with him. He knew that she did not need to stay for work and that Nanci could handle her small number of listings while she was away.

She frowned and worried a lock of hair. "Let me think about it." She reluctantly concluded that whether she went or not, she would have to let him to go to California. The compromise he offered was just too reasonable to reject. She finally gave in with a long sigh. "What does one wear to a porn interview, anyway?"

# III.

# CALIFORNIA DREAMIN'

Stanley leaned against the airplane window on the flight to Los Angeles, wishing that Angela had been able to book the same connection. Although her friend and colleague could handle most of her listings while she was away, a botched home inspection had forced Angela to delay a day in order to hammer out a new sales contract with a pair of skittish buyers.

He studied the familiar emerald topography of America's heartland drifting slowly beneath him. Born in Illinois, in a small oasis of a town in the midst of endless rows of corn and soybeans, he had escaped to the University of Virginia for his undergraduate studies and then on to Penn for law school and his doctorate. Ironically, his best job offer had come from the BFU, back in the flatlands, back in the sea of corn. Even so, California evoked strong images for him. Early in his initial job hunt, he had received an offer from Belle Meade College, a small liberal arts school in a Los Angeles suburb. For two weeks, he had lived there in his mind, idling in a snow-free, laid-back utopia where his Spanish-style townhome teemed with tanned and fit neighbors ready to invite him over for a Margarita or an impromptu salsa lesson. Then, Max Kurland had called from the BFU, and he had done the most sensible and boring thing: taking the job that offered the best salary and the most funding for his research.

Maybe studying the adult film industry would break him out of his rut. A clever Google search had found Donald Johansson's email address buried in a pdf file listing the members of the Outreach Committee of a Los Angeles Episcopal church. His former fraternity brother had replied enthusiastically by phone a few hours later, inviting the professor to California to set up some interviews and introduce him to other major players in the field. They spent over an hour catching up and sketching out a workable plan of attack. Just as helpful, Stanley had found almost no serious research on adult films in the huge BFU library. The shelves were stacked with hysterical diatribes against porn and impassioned First Amendment defenses of it, but for every one hundred firmly-held published beliefs, he found one maybe one piece of actual data.

He brought with him on the plane the only two books of real interest, both written by a UCLA professor of abnormal psychology who concluded, contrary to his initial hypothesis, that adult film stars were not typically mentally ill (or at least no more crazy than the general population in California). This was heartening news. If actresses ended up looking statistically like workers in other professions (maybe with the same levels of STD's as insurance adjustors!), then he would have a publishable book that coincidentally bore out Johansson's assertions in the television interview about the mundaneness of adult filmmaking. The sociologist didn't consider whether the lack of academic interest should be raising any red flags.

He turned his attention back to the book lying on his tray table. His love of reading had made law school surprisingly enjoyable, but once he had experienced sixty hour work weeks and mind-numbing document reviews during his summer clerkships, he had jumped at the chance for a doctorate and a career as a professor. Sometimes he wondered whether he should have figured out a way to practice law without being suffocated in a large law firm. Surely a nerd should be able to sit and read and do serious analysis without having a partner with a large yacht payment breathing down his neck.

* * *

Arriving mid-morning at LAX, Stanley found the expressway northbound blissfully clear all the way to the Van Nuys exit. He drank in the warmth of the sunny spring day and promised to make time to explore the mountains rolling scenically to the northeast. His sightseeing ended abruptly when he left the highway and drove his rental car through the jungle of scarred warehouses and potholed parking lots that led to the headquarters of Eden Studio. The business occupied a huge corrugated steel building with a single story add-on that served as entrance and office space. He frowned at the gritty scenery and was glad he had booked a hotel in an upscale adjacent suburb. Angela would not have appreciated staying in the junky mish-mash at the epicenter of the porn world.

He pulled into the Eden parking lot, grabbed the old fraternity paddle that he had found in his attic, and got out of the car. He wondered once again what his friend was doing there. Nothing in Johansson's past had foreshadowed such a bizarre choice of career. If he had gone completely off the rails, then the whole California sojourn could get really uncomfortable.

Stanley pressed a button next to the glass entryway into the studio office and was buzzed in by a middle-aged woman with tortoiseshell glasses and a grim expression on her face. She did not bother to get up from behind her desk as she motioned for him to sit down in a small furnished alcove. "Mr. Johansson is in a meeting and will see you in a moment."

He glanced down at her name plate and gave her a warm smile. "Thanks, Miriam." If she noticed his courtesy, she was not impressed.

He sat down and looked for something to read. A table next to a sofa held recent issues of *Time* and *Sports Illustrated*, as well as a trade magazine for the adult film industry. He picked it up and thumbed through it, stopping abruptly when he came to the casting announcements.

"Oh my god," he mumbled under his breath, prompting a disapproving glance from the secretary. The advertisements painted a sordid picture. A single production was asking for: *Asian schoolgirl-type, must be flexible; mature brunette for foot fetish sequence; busty blonde for stripper role (dance experience preferred).* Dozens of other ads called for every size, shape, race, age, and hair color of every gender and transgender imaginable. The only thing they had in common was the requirement that each applicant prove he or she or s/he was at least eighteen years old. He was staring open-mouthed at an ad for a production provocatively entitled, *Starsky and Crotch*, when the door to the office down the hall from him flew open and a stunning young woman burst out.

She charged toward him. A thick mane of dark hair trailed behind her, revealing a finely sculpted face and a flawless cocoa butter complexion. She moved with the grace of a pagan goddess, her devastating body worshipped by a tight pair of blue jeans and a half-buttoned sweater. But it was the dark eyes that entranced him—even with a muttered curse on her twisted lips, Stanley thought this was the most compelling face he had ever seen. Her eyes flashed with anger as she swept past him and slammed the door, but the glare did nothing to diminish the impact she had made in the space of five seconds. He was still sorting out his visceral response to her when Miriam announced that Mr. Johansson was ready to see him.

Stanley walked down the short hall to the open office door and peeked inside. Johansson was clearly agitated following the blow up with the woman, and he stood by a book case clenching and unclenching his fists. Stanley cleared his throat and waved hello with an ironic waggle of the Alpha Omicron paddle that he had brought with him. Johansson's mood changed instantly and he strode quickly across the room to embrace his former fraternity brother.

"I didn't know how to thank you for helping me, so I brought this paddle for you to hang on your wall, or burn, or use as a prop in your next movie. Whatever's most appropriate." Stanley shrugged and handed over the paddle. "I imagine you hate these toys as much as I do."

"Boy," the Californian grimaced as he hoisted the faux cricket bat, "talk about some ugly memories." He laid it down on the coffee table and turned back to his friend. "At least we were both smart enough to get out of that shithole."

He squeezed Stanley's shoulder and led him to a brown leather couch that divided the room in half. It was a simple office, but tastefully decorated with modern art and a silk rug with a Mondrian pattern. The walls were covered with autographed head shots of dozens of woman whom he assumed must be actresses at the studio. He did not recognize anyone except for the woman whose picture was prominently centered behind the producer's polished mahogany desk, the same stunner who had stormed out of the office minutes before.

Johansson sat down and explained that the classy headshots were designed to send the message that Eden was a respectable business. He disparaged other studios whose décor consisted of "boobs hanging out all over the place."

The director was a little over six feet tall, lean and fit, with dark hair and a healthy tan. The subtle wrinkles on his face spoke of smiles and sun rather than stress. His bright blue eyes fairly sparkled as he asked Stanley whether he was married or had any children. He seemed genuinely interested in the professor's home life and expressed regret at his own failure to find the right woman and start a family. Stanley was surprised how little he had changed since college. He seemed no different from the serious young man who was so out of place at raucous frat parties. Stanley took another look around the office. It really did look like any other place of business. Take down the celebrity glossies and the volumes of Kierkegaard and Saint Augustine on the bookshelves and it could have belonged to a partner in a law firm. Johansson did not seem unhinged, but that just deepened the mystery of what he was doing in Van Nuys.

The director stood up and retrieved a sheaf of papers from his desk. "Your email was really helpful," he said as he tapped a paper in his hand and got down to business. "I've set up interviews with about twenty actresses from four different studios, including mine. Since you want to cover the mainstream market, I've contacted Boudoir Films, Chimera Productions, and Janus Studios, in addition to Eden. Between us, we've probably got about sixty percent of the mainstream market."

This was exactly what Stanley wanted to hear. He did not want to waste his time talking with fly-by-night outfits with a video camera and just enough money to spend on a hooker. The focus of the book was on mainstream laborers, and he was no more interested in amateur porn than he had cared about amateur lumberjacks cutting down trees in their back yard or running a part-time limb removal service.

He listened with increasing excitement as Johansson explained how he had played to the vanity of his rivals by telling them they were worthy of academic study. The prospect of appearing in a scholarly book had flattered even the most hard-nosed producer. The manipulation had been clever, and Stanley was reminded that Don's violent outburst at the frat house years ago had been an anomaly and that he had usually been able to get his way through a mixture of diplomacy, horse trading, subtle threats, and outright deception.

Stanley was handed a file folder that contained a sheet of names, contact information, proposed interview times, and some basic financial information about the industry. He flipped through the material and his jaw dropped when he saw the gross profit figures. Maybe the conversion from seminarian to porn mogul was all about the money. He would not be the first to be seduced by wealth, even though greed had not been part of his old persona. He was dying to know what made the man tick. What sort of mental gymnastics did it take to reconcile the nice guy persona with the porn guy persona?

"Would you mind me asking how you got into the business in the first place? The last I remember, you were headed off to seminary." Stanley put the papers down and continued, "What happened? I know Episcopalians are more liberal than Baptists, but…"

"It was pretty much an accident." Johansson leaned forward on the couch as he explained, elbows resting on the knees of his gray wool slacks. "I went to seminary and spent two years there, but I felt something was missing. The summer after my second year, I was at home in LA doing some volunteer work and thinking over my vocation, when I met a former high school classmate who needed some help scaring off an abusive boyfriend.

"Well, it turns out she was a small-time porn star and her 'boyfriend' was her agent, a real shithead who had promised someone that she was going to do some oral-anal stuff in a movie that she didn't want to do. He was threatening her and generally being a jerk, so I had a little talk with him." He grinned and Stanley remembered how he had dealt with the would-be rapists at Alpha Omicron.

"As you can imagine, I tried to counsel her and get her out of the business, but she wasn't interested in my efforts at playing social worker. She was making good money and had no skills that could earn her nearly as much as making videos. Talking to her was like slamming my head against a concrete pillar. I couldn't convince her that she was doing anything wrong." Stanley nodded and tried to imagine what he would have done in Don's place.

"Anyway, we stayed friends and had drinks once in a while. As you can imagine, hearing her talk about her job was slightly more interesting than listening to other people's grad school stories." Don got up from the sofa and took a bottle of Pellegrino from a small refrigerator hidden in his credenza. "I became fascinated with the business."

"And so you started your own porn studio?" Stanley asked skeptically.

"Not hardly," Don laughed. "All I could see was rank exploitation, but I came to realize that if my friend wanted to make her living being filmed having sex, then she should be paid a wage commensurate with the risks that are involved."

"I see," he nodded slowly. "So you became her new agent."

"Exactly," he acknowledged the perceptiveness with a nod of his head. "At first I took no money at all; I didn't want to feel like a pimp. But I got good at dealing with the studios, and pretty soon her friends were asking me to represent them. I was not only getting people a decent salary, but also negotiating things like condom use. I felt like I was making a difference, so by the time summer ended, I decided to delay my studies. I started taking a small percentage and moved out of my parents' house."

Stanley did not doubt the story, but it was a big leap from getting young actresses more leverage with exploitative studios to becoming one of the exploiters. "But how do you go from there to making films and running your own business?"

Johansson took off his glasses and polished them slowly. When he put them back on he looked intently at his friend. "This only makes sense if you believe a single crucial fact: if Eden Studio did not exist, every single woman working for me would be working for someone else. That means that if I have the safest studio, the most comfortable studio, the best paying studio, and the studio that treats these women with the most respect, then I'm making a positive contribution." He finished his water and screwed the cap on the empty bottle. "And remember, I'm also putting tremendous pressure on the competition. I've already put several studios out of business, and others are having to adopt our standards, like requiring condom use, in order to stay competitive. Until society evolves, and its need for porn fades, I'm in the business of making the world a marginally better place. That's all."

Stanley nodded. The story sounded horribly logical. Angela would surely have some devastating comments to make but his professional instinct was not to argue, just keep his object of study talking.

"You mentioned your parents," Stanley shifted in his seat and crossed his legs. "What do they think of all this?"

"They haven't spoken to me since." He gestured with his water. "That's the worst part of all this. I can't get them to see it's a ministry like any other."

"A ministry?" Stanley was taken aback. "Uh, I just assumed that you had some sort of religious crisis."

"Oh no! I still go to Saint James' every Sunday." He gave a wry smile. "They're not about to put me on the vestry, but I'm tolerated well enough."

"But how do you reconcile your job and your church? I mean..." He had not been to church since he was a child, so he struggled to find the right reference point. "…what about Sodom and Gomorrah and all that stuff?"

Don nodded and replied confidently, eager to tell a favorite story. "The most important moment in my spiritual life occurred during my first semester in seminary when we were studying Latin." He paused. "Do you know what the word 'religion' literally means?"

"I don't know…to redo something?"

"Exactly. Literally it means to retie. The 'lig' in 'religion' is the same root as 'ligature,' a knot."

Or as in *lien*, Stanley thought, like the legal tie that the bank had on his house.

"In its original sense, the word refers to the attempt to retie oneself to God, to narrow the gap that opened when Adam and Eve were thrown out of Eden." He paused. "True religion is the act of becoming closer to God."

"Okay, so religions are all attempts to reconnect with God," Stanley pushed him. "Sounds good, but how does that get you to *On Golden Blonde*?"

The producer laughed but hung tightly on to his train of thought, "In its original sense, the word religion indicated no necessary association with any kind of organized sectarian activity. Meditation could be religion, helping your neighbor could be religion, even smelling a flower or taking a nap could be a religious act if it brought you closer to God." His hands indicated distance with a graceful eloquence. "And if anything that brings me closer to God is religious, then anything that moves me further away is sinful. That's the compelling part about this understanding of religion; it provides a very nice definition for sin. Sinful activity cannot be captured in some sort of laundry list of condemned acts. Rather, every act must be scrutinized in terms of how it affects our relationship with God."

Stanley nodded and wondered what his third grade Sunday school teacher would have thought. She had been awfully big on the Ten Commandments. But now he thought he understood where the lesson was headed. Don needed justification for his lucrative participation in the sin business. "So that's how you deal with your sin!"

"My sin?"

"Uh, yeah. You know, making all these movies." The director smiled graciously, completely at ease with the accusation. "I don't mean to be judgmental," Stanley backpedaled. "In fact, I never think of things in terms of evil or sin."

"Maybe you should!" Don replied emphatically. "You've struck right at the heart of the matter. Is what I do sinful? It's a serious question. I think that sometimes making a pornographic movie is a sinful act, and sometimes it's not. It depends very much on who is participating and how they're treated."

Don went to his desk and took out a picture of a young blonde woman who looked to be in her late teens or early twenties. She stood next to a backyard swimming pool and filled out her bikini extravagantly. "This young lady came here to interview for a part last week. She was very attractive and very eager to do a film, but when I sat down to talk with her, it came out that she had just been cheated on by her boyfriend and was looking for revenge."

"That seems a bit extreme."

"It is! You'd be amazed by the people I meet." He cleared his throat. "Anyway, my guess was that being a porn star would end up being a humiliating and degrading experience for her. A sinful experience, in other words, so I turned her down. I see too many real exhibitionists to take a chance on someone like her." He smiled. "I did use her story as the plot for another movie, though."

"So, sometimes making porn is sinful, and sometimes it's not."

"In a nutshell."

"But what about the audience?" Angela was convinced that the biggest problem with porn was its effect on its viewers. Something about the former seminarian's passion and conviction made Stanley want to engage him on his own terms, to test the superficial logic of his rhetoric. "What if the videos push their viewers further from God? Wouldn't the movies be sinful?"

Don nodded his head. "Things in and of themselves aren't sinful, but I get your point. What if porn were an ultra-hazardous material like heroin or nuclear weapons?"

"Isn't porn hazardous to the audience?"

"If I were convinced of that, I'd quit. But I've seen no evidence that sexual fantasy drives people away from God. Our sexuality, after all, is a gift from God. It can certainly be misused, like in violent pornography, but I don't think my films have a negative effect on their viewers. In fact, the fantasies I sell are pretty healthy." He stood up and shrugged. "But you can judge that for yourself."

The professor had no immediate response. He was a comparativist by nature. His study would not care whether porn stars used too many drugs, but only whether they used significantly more than lumber jacks and pest control workers. Who was more soulless, the plodding academic, or his old house mate, the passionate porn czar? He realized with a start that he was more of a relativist than the pornographer, who at least purported to have a single reference point against which to weigh the value of his occupation.

# IV.

# PORNO OR PARISH

After a quick lunch at an undistinguished Mexican restaurant, the moviemaker and the professor went to meet three of the producers who had agreed to lend their employees to the study. Don explained his plan as they drove his BMW convertible around Van Nuys and Canoga Park. Stanley stuck his arm out of the car and let the cool breeze prop it up like a wing in a wind tunnel. Nary a touch of smog marred the bright blue sky. The Illinois winter had been a harsh one, and when spring had finally arrived, a freak ice storm and high winds had scoured the landscape of its initial burst of color. For someone who had crunched broken daffodils underfoot only a few weeks earlier, the glow of southern California was ethereal.

The studio owner at his side shone in a different way. Don Johansson was a walking advertisement for the joy of guilt-free living. Although Stanley had escaped much of the guilt laid naturally upon children in the Midwest by their Protestant—or Catholic—or Jewish parents, he still hesitated to live too far outside convention. He thought back to the Eden website. It would have been easy to click a button and satisfy his curiosity, but he had not seriously considered it, and not just because some university computer overlord might be monitoring him. On the other hand, Johansson had faced down convention with reason, or what appeared to be reason, and made the leap all the way from the condemnation of porn to its production with a pious wink. Right or wrong, Stanley was envious of his friend's ability to reconsider basic assumptions and the course of his life.

As Johansson pulled into the weed-choked parking lot of Boudoir Productions, he admitted that he had engaged in a bit of social engineering with the schedule of women he had arranged for Stanley to interview. The first several were veterans who could give him valuable background on the industry. Many actresses were not so thoughtful, so he had front loaded the most interesting people and put the "bubble-headed valley girls" at the end of the process. For added balance, he had included a former starlet who was at present an anti-porn activist. The director seemed to instinctively understand that a skewed sample would taint the sociologist's research.

In the context of his broader research, the question of why anyone ended up in the porn business was not that important, but Stanley could not help wondering what he would discover. Usually, people just fell into their jobs through chance and a wide variety of external circumstances. No one dreams his way through high school hoping to spray poison on termites, or cut down trees. But such pursuits do not require overcoming personal sexual inhibitions and ignoring society's judgments. Could one clear those hurdles by happenstance?

He imagined a group of Swedes or Danes raised on a commune where free love and shared partners were the norm. Someone raised wholly without engrained inhibitions could probably just stumble into a career having sex on camera. On the other hand, how many people fit that unique bill, especially in the U.S.? Of course, some one could be raised traditionally, but lack inhibition due to some sort of anti-social tendencies. He had long suspected that people labeled nymphomaniacs were not suffering from some strange endocrine condition, but were rather non-violent sociopaths. Angela had another theory, insisting porn was not about nymphomania, but coercion. The statistics he had seen on sex slavery were certainly sickening, but he was not going undercover in Eastern Europe. He was studying large scale commercial films in southern California, where sex workers had agents, filled out job applications, and interviewed for roles.

In fact, he had studied something like slavery already. For a paper on illegal immigration, he had interviewed workers whose families were held hostage overseas until outrageous fees were paid for transport to the United States. His present research, however, was focused on people who at least believed themselves to be working under their own free will. None of the questions in his interview protocol would make sense if asked to a hostage. So, he found himself in Los Angeles, looking at a select group of actors, still wondering exactly how anyone other than hippies or nymphos ended up in the porn business.

Before the formal interviews began, Don wanted to introduce the researcher to the studio heads who had agreed to allow access to their personnel. He explained they were a little suspicious and just needed to be assured that Stanley had no axe to grind.

The two men slipped into a waiting room where a pretty blond receptionist told them that Mr. Mulkahey, head of Boudoir Studios, would be with them in a moment. The room was clean, but not as well furnished as the Eden Studio reception area. The secretary's desk was metal, and hundreds of boxed and unboxed DVD's lay stacked in a corner. Sexy movie posters lined the walls, but no breasts were completely hanging out, as Don had implied.

When the receptionist left the room for a moment, Don spoke in a low voice. "I'll be interested to see what you think of Brian. We're not exactly friends, but if you want an accurate picture of the industry, you need to meet people like him."

The blonde returned and pointed them down a short hall before returning to her desk. Don led them to the office and they entered without knocking.

Brian Mulkahey was a red-faced and balding man, with wire-rimmed glasses and piercing green eyes. He pulled up two chairs and then sat down facing his guests on top of a highly polished wooden desk. The shelves behind him were filled with an enormous collection of stuffed animals. Don introduced his companion, and the three men talked for several minutes about the Lakers' chances of advancing in the NBA playoffs.

"So, Professor, you want to write an academic book on adult films." Mulkahey spoke in a blunted New Jersey accent and gestured to his fellow producer. "What sort of bullshit has this guy been feeding you so far? Has he explained that we're not all saints come down to do God's work among the bimbos?" He looked over to see if he got a rise from his rival, but Don remained serene.

Stanley thanked him for his cooperation and was rewarded with a short and mildly obscene lecture on the proper ingredients of adult filmmaking: "Take one part well-hung stud and add one part super-vixen, mix thoroughly and yell action."

The sociologist was surprised. Most bosses took their work more seriously, even when it wasn't glamorous.

"Surely," the Eden director interjected with a laconic smile, "there's more to it than that."

"Yeah," Mulkahey growled in return, "there's all the interesting things that the girls do with each other." He jerked his thumb at a provocative poster of three Asian women outfitted in bondage gear. "Professor, this business is all about creating heat. That's our job: to create heat for our customers. What you're going to learn about the girls themselves, I have no idea." He shrugged his shoulders and turned up his palms. "I honestly don't."

Mulkahey let his glasses slide down his nose and rested the heels of his hands on the edge of the desk. "All they ever tell me is that they're in it for the money, but that don't explain why one pretty girl chooses to make money being a nurse and another chooses to do anal on film."

"I know you have some theories," Don replied. "We've talked about this before."

"*He's* the guy who likes to theorize," Mulkahey tilted his head at his competitor but spoke to Stanley, "but you've probably figured that out already. My pious colleague here thinks that the girls are looking for love and acceptance." He motioned to the stuffed animals behind him. "I'll admit there's an odd kind of family feel to this business. You wouldn't believe how many times I've handed a pooch down to one of my girls or some pathetic wannabe, but the story is about security, not love. A lot of the people in the business come from really fucked up backgrounds. They haven't all been molested; that's a myth. But most of them have been through hell of one sort or another. They come here, and they meet people that accept them for who they are and protect them. There's sort of a circle-the-wagon mentality, and once you're in the circle, you feel safer."

"Having anal sex on camera?" Stanley could not help but counter. "That doesn't sound horribly safe." He had not pushed Don hard enough earlier, but there was no reason to let Mulkahey snow him with his tissue-thin arguments. The producer responded with an indulgent smile and a questioning rise of his eyebrows.

"Tell me, Professor, would you let someone bend you over if you didn't trust them?"

"Uh…well…um."

"Well, you wouldn't. And neither would most people." Stanley looked over at Don and saw with surprise that he was nodding his agreement. "Some are willing to do it; some aren't. We don't force anybody. And that's one thing you need to understand: nobody's got a gun to their head when they go on camera. That's another myth you can bust. Sure, some of these folks need money real bad, and some of them have pretty fucked up lives, but they know what they're doing."

Stanley grinned. "You don't mind doing a little theorizing yourself, do you?"

"Yeah, well, ya gotta be a fuckin' philosopher to work in this business." He laughed and stood up. "Professor, I don't know if you're gonna learn anything other than people are all fucked up, but if you do, lemme know." He led them out of his office into the foyer and seemed ready to send them on their way when he held up his hand and asked the receptionist what was currently being filmed.

"Let's see," she looked at her desktop calendar, "you've got *Tart Wars II: Revenge of the Stiff* going on in Lot Two."

Mulkahey clapped his hands together in delight and asked his guests if they wanted to spend any time on the set. Stanley looked at Johansson with alarm and was surprised when his guide encouraged him to accept the invitation. Eden Studio sets were always closed, so the head of Boudoir was presenting him with a unique opportunity to assess working conditions in the industry he was studying. The professor nodded his head and Mulkahey shook his hand, gave instructions to the receptionist, and headed back to his office.

The blonde led them across the parking lot to a gray steel building accessible only through a key-coded door. The space inside had no permanent walls, only movable dividers, and was open from its concrete floor to the girders under the roof. In a far corner, a klieg light played on two women and one man, each of whom was brightly painted to resemble some kind of colorful alien. Their guide pointed them in the direction of the set and then left them to their own devices. Don put a finger to his lips as they approached the action.

"Cut!" an overweight man in a baseball cap yelled before they took more than a couple of steps. "Let's get Scott and Kayla on the middle of the sofa with Alexis sitting on the arm." Several people sprang into action around the set, moving boom mikes and reflective umbrellas. The sole male actor stood up and stroked himself unselfconsciously in a successful effort to maintain a massive erection.

Stanley stood dumbfounded and then felt his former fraternity brother put a hand on his back and push him closer to the set. The whole scene was unreal. Oddly, it was not sexy at all. Bored technicians in blue jeans and t-shirts dampened the erotic atmosphere, and the actors were too nonchalant in their nakedness to convey the sense that any forbidden fruit was really on offer. The scene was shocking nonetheless. Convention and cultural norms were unhinged but no one seemed to notice, and Stanley felt like a voyeur, not of intimacy, but of its polar opposite. Maybe medical students seeing their first autopsy felt like this.

"I didn't know that Michael Moore directed porn." Stanley whispered in his Johansson's ear and nodded at the chubby director in the Dodger's cap.

"That's John Olson. He's directed hundreds of videos." Don thought for a moment. "Maybe thousands." They walked to the edge of the set, just behind the cameraman. Don waved at Olson and got a nod of approval in return.

"Alright," the director said, his thin, high voice barely audible in the barn-like building, "I want Scott sitting down, with Kayla kneeling between his legs." Once the actor was settled, Kayla got right to work, jerking his member with her right hand like she was shaking a bottle of salad dressing. "Alexis? Let's see you do your finger routine. Sort of hover above 'em and then get off when Scott does his thing."

"He's so predictable," Don whispered in Stanley's ear.

Stanley could not help but stare. Kayla was a surprisingly small-breasted brunette whose enthusiasm seemed authentic. She stared intently in Scott's eyes and gave him a pleading look while she worked her mouth. A middle-aged man with a thinning pony tail brought his camera to within inches of her ministrations. Meanwhile, Alexis, an older and bustier blonde, was perched nearby, groaning like an earth-shattering orgasm was imminent.

"How does she do that?" Stanley looked over at Don with alarm. "Those fingernails must be three inches long! How does she not cut her colon to ribbons?"

The producer shook his head. "I don't know, but it's been her signature move for a long time now. She's almost thirty, I think."

After several minutes of relentless effort by Kayla, Scott arched his back and moaned. Alexis screamed in blissful agony and slumped down next to him on the sofa. Staying in character, Kayla leaned over and initiated a messy three-way kiss with her two partners. The director yelled cut and Kayla immediately stood up.

"Goddamn it," she chided Scott, "could you possibly keep that shit out of my eyes?" She made a face and wiped off with a t-shirt discarded on the sofa.

He grunted in response and tried to get up, but his sweaty back stuck to the stained leather sofa. He rolled to his right with a sound like scotch tape being ripped off a balloon, grabbed a towel from the man working the lights, and stalked off the set.

"Thanks, John!" Don waved at the director and then led Stanley away from the set. As soon as they were out earshot, he asked the professor what he thought about the scene.

"I don't know," he replied honestly, "how the hell can they concentrate with the camera right in their faces?"

He shrugged. "Say what you will, but you can't deny these people are professionals."

Stanley nodded his agreement, but in reality he did not know what to think. He felt unsettled, but no one else seemed disturbed by what they had witnessed. He remembered a similar feeling when he had seen a pest control specialist shoot a family of squirrels in an attic nest and when he had seen a lumberjack cut down an old-growth redwood tree. It was all in a day's work for the people he was studying, but outsiders did not have time to develop any protective armor. He had nothing to say until they emerged into the sunlight.

Stanley sat in the car, grateful that the top was down as they cruised along a busy boulevard. The fresh breeze in his face was a welcome contrast to the sweaty scene he had just witnessed. Johansson stopped by Chimera Productions briefly, but Milton Barkley, its owner, was not in. On the way to Janus Studios, the Eden director explained how he had put a significant dent in the profits of all three of his rivals by attracting the best talent in the business to work exclusively for him.

Eden was one of the first studios to sign women to long-term contracts. The most popular actresses were entitled, "The Women of Eden," and they received special perks and publicity. Johansson was consciously borrowing a page out of the old Hollywood studio employment system. Eden paid them a regular salary, with medical and dental benefits, along with the possibility of getting a small percentage of profits for a starring role in a film. He emphasized that some were eventually given the opportunity to direct. The future of porn, he claimed, was the middle-class couples market, and only women directors would be likely to shoot movies that worked for dubious wives.

He made another left and slowed down as the roadway became congested. "Boudoir is still operating in the stone age. Brian does a video that takes about forty-eight hours to shoot, and the actors get paid in cash at the end of the day. He treats his people as well as anyone, and some really are fond of him, but I'm operating under a totally different business model. I'm getting all the best talent, and I'm making better pictures with bigger budgets. We dominate the major adult cable channels. We've even been talking to iTunes about adding a small, 'classy' porn section to its online store."

"So, Brian hasn't adapted? You're putting pressure on him and he doesn't like it?"

"Exactly," he replied. "He still sees porn as an outlaw art form and himself as a cross between Ken Kesey and Larry Flynt. Kinda quaint, really. Fuck Hollywood! Fuck the Establishment! For him, mainstreaming porn is anathema. It's a contradiction in terms."

Don drove several blocks to a building that looked like it might have been a bowling alley at one time. "Here's where I got my start," he explained as they got out of the car. A small sign on the door identified Janus Studios and Don entered without knocking. "Hi, Christie," he said to a short redhead stuffing DVD's into glossy boxes. "Is Herb around?"

"Donny!" The receptionist exclaimed with genuine warmth as she tottered over on five inch heels and gave her former boss a big hug, letting her breasts linger against his chest as she spoke. Her boss was in the storage room going over inventory and she offered to lead them there.

She walked in front of the two visitors and looked over her shoulder as if to make sure they had noticed how the swish of her miniskirt flashed the bottom edge of her red bikini panties. She pushed open a gray metal door at the end of a long hallway and ushered them into a room several degrees cooler than the rest of the building. At least a dozen large bookshelves held thousands of boxed titles, each bearing the embossed visage of the two-headed god, Janus.

"Donny's here!" Christie yelled and then turned to her former boss. "Who's your cute friend?"

"Stanley, meet Christie." The professor clasped her small, moist hand and smiled. Making eye contact with her produced an alarming sensation throughout his body that refused to subside even when he was no longer touching her.

Before he could respond, Herb Matteson, a rangy fellow in his mid-thirties with an acne-scarred face framed by a head of curly black hair appeared, extended his hand to Stanley and introduced himself. "Don probably told you that we used to be partners here." He pulled down a DVD and pointed at the Janus trademark on the side. "This was one of Don's good ideas. Two men running the company, represented by a two-faced god. I came up with the motto though." He pointed at the fine print underneath the faces of Janus: *Janus Productions. Where you get twice as much head.*

"Nice." Stanley stammered and added nothing more. Matteson sent Christie back to reception and led them to a cramped windowless room with a small desk, a leather captain's chair and a sofa pushed underneath several rows of book shelves. The walls were lined with posters and several framed Adult Film Critics Circle awards. Stanley examined the closest one and Matteson went on a tirade about the pretense of using professional film critics from men's magazines to decide on the winners.

"We need awards based on which movies are best at raising the blood pressure of the average horny bastard off the street." Matteson sat down in the swivel chair while his guests took the sofa. "That would be the best test for the product, not the votes of Roger Ebert wannabes."

Stanly found it hard to imagine the brash owner of Janus Studios ever working together with the thoughtful former seminarian and asked Johansson whether he agreed with his former partner's sole criterion for merit.

"To a large extent, our ultimate goal is 'creating heat for our customers' as Brian put it earlier, but I don't think that means you have to neglect the traditional aesthetic and technical elements of good filmmaking. Get-off-ability and aesthetics aren't mutually exclusive." Matteson rolled his eyes. "In fact, I think that we influence what our viewers want. Eden Studio is attracting them to a new sort of product and away from one that's running out of gas."

"That's such horseshit!" His former partner snorted. "You cannot change people's fetishes. Sexual tastes get set early, and they're not adjustable. Try all you want to turn a leg man into a tit man, but you're just wasting your time." He picked up a handful of DVDs from his desk and flashed them at Stanley. "The key is tapping into what people already want to see. I've got about a dozen different series currently in production. You see what I mean? *Lesbian Sorority Girls 4, My Best Friend's Mom 2, Juggies 15 and 16, Booty-Shaking Beauties 7*…we even mix things up. *Asian Bondage 3* and, here you go, *Biker Redheads*." He set the DVD's down. "We've got a simple philosophy here: Give the people what they want."

Stanley nodded and with difficulty forced his eyes away from a leather-clad redhead bending over a new Harley Davidson. He wondered aloud whether any porn director had ever done a formal survey of the market. In an economic sense, pornography was pretty boring. Consumers had certain tastes and it was no surprise that a market had arisen to satisfy them. But studying the players in that market was his domain as a sociologist and what he had seen so far was anything but boring. Nonetheless, the economist had a tool he lacked, a metric for evaluation. A market was efficient or inefficient and nothing in his own academic tool kit had prepared him to pass judgment. That's okay he thought, anticipating his wife's arrival the next day. Angela will take care of that.

"If you think about it, every film we make and distribute is a survey of the market." Matteson spun his chair around and reshelved the videos. He clearly enjoyed the business side of the business. "If it sells well, then we know we've struck a chord. If a concept doesn't sell, then we junk it. I like to think that we know more about male sexuality than most psychologists."

"Pay attention, Stan" Johansson interjected. "After Chimera and Eden, Janus Studios is the third highest grossing firm in the business."

"So Donnie, why don't we join forces again?"

"Because I'd like to stay friends!" Johansson looked at his watch and shot Stanley a glance that told him they needed to leave. "Besides, I think we're both doing quite well on our own."

"That's not what I hear," replied Matteson. Stanley watched Johansson's face as he got up to leave but saw no response to the provocation. The head of Janus told the professor that Christie would be happy to take care of any scheduling difficulties and referred all further questions to her. He suggested that she herself would be a good person to interview, since she had quit acting just two years earlier.

Traffic was heavy on the way back to Eden, so Johansson put the top up on the BMW and let the air conditioning save them from the ambient exhaust. He drove without speaking for a couple of blocks, preoccupied by his own thoughts. He finally reached over and found the local public radio station. They listened for a while but when the announcement of the annual fund drive began, Stanley asked his guide why he no longer worked with Matteson.

Johansson reached over and turned the radio down. "He's a great guy in a lot of ways and is generally easy to work with. We had our first disagreement over condoms. I wanted the girls to have the absolute right to demand condom use. That's the current policy at Eden, but Herb thought it should be up to the director. You see, some of the guys have problems keeping it up with a condom on, so it makes shooting a scene more time-consuming. According to him, the standard program of monthly AIDS testing and weekly STD screening is enough."

"Couldn't you have just worked with girls who don't demand condoms? Or are they hard to find?" Stanley asked.

"No, they're probably a majority." He sighed. "We could have worked something out, I think." He pulled into the Eden lot and turned off the car. "Our real problem was, uh, creative, I guess you could say." The car slowly warmed up as the director explained what led to the dissolution of a profitable partnership. "Well, you've heard his filmmaking philosophy: Give the people what they want. He really believes that, so he's willing to pander to any kind of fantasy he thinks is out there. One of his series—he didn't show you that one—is crammed full of rape and torture fantasies." Johansson frowned in acknowledgment of the darkest side of his profession. "He films just within the bounds of obscenity law, but it's not a market I want to satisfy. We had a huge argument about it. He thought I was claiming the moral high ground and took it really personally."

Don clicked open the doors of the BMW and walked Stanley over to his rental car in the corner of the Eden parking lot. They shook hands and exchanged notes on timing the upcoming interviews. Finally, Stanley got in the car and rolled down the window. Don leaned over for a final word.

"He called me prude. Get that! A prudish pornographer!"

# V.

# YOUR TAXES AT WORK

Angela arrived in Los Angeles the day after her husband's adult film studio tour. She had never been to California before and had always pictured her first trip out west in the company of young children headed for a Disneyland adventure. Instead, her husband was dragging her out to the San Fernando Valley to talk to porn stars. She sighed as the plane touched down at LAX in mid-morning and made her way slowly to the baggage area in the airport. When she finally walked past security, Stanley was at the carousel already, stacking her garment bag and the black case containing the audio-video equipment on a rolling cart. Her irritation evaporated as she watched his broad back flex, and she snuck up behind him and gave him a tight hug.

He told her that he had booked them a four-star hotel in North Hollywood, close to Universal Studios, but within an easy drive of the epicenter of the porn world in Van Nuys and Canoga Park. They arrived as their room was being cleaned, and Stanley suggested they have lunch first at the chain restaurant across the street. A young waitress with a small butterfly tattoo on her right ankle led them to a booth next to a window in the nearly empty dining room.

Angela focused on the menu and then smiled indulgently at her husband. Stanley had recapped his previous day's encounters during the ride from the airport and surprisingly had spoken of Donald Johansson like he was some sort of philosopher king. He seemed amused by Eden's competitors in the porn business, talking about them as if they were crotchety old men arguing in a barber shop rather than as misogynistic opportunists. When she prodded him to be more critical, Stanley had retreated into academic mode, refusing to pass judgment on the people he had met. Of course, it was entirely possible that he had been snowed under. For someone who was so smart, he could be stunningly naïve. He had zero grasp of faculty politics, for example, and the space under their kitchen sink was filled with no-name cleaning products sold by sketchy young people who knocked on their door claiming to be putting themselves through college. Most of the time, she appreciated his boyish disingenuousness and generous impulses, but did they really need two cases of Girl Scout Thin Mints in the pantry?

Writing a newspaper column about pornography would be much more satisfying than debating her husband about it. When she wrote, she had time to reflect, to choose exactly the proper unassailable set of words to reveal the humor or absurdity or downright wrongfulness of a situation. She could reread to her heart's content and not press the send button until her emotion was surgically directed. Not that her emails were always so well-considered, nor her Facebook postings so coolly composed, but she had never yet fired off a newspaper column in the heat of the moment. Her conversational style, however, was not always so considered. When Stanley was either frustratingly innocent or just playing a part in some kind of Socratic exercise, her verbal response tended toward the slash and burn.

So, she smiled at her husband, ordered a club sandwich and tried to figure out how she was going to survive the dinner party that Donald Johansson was throwing that very night. The producer had invited the couple to a fancy sit-down banquet being held at Eden Studio to celebrate the release of *Toys in Babeland*. The studio head had promised Stanley a chance to see the entire industry at play. The formal interviews with actresses would start the next day. Seeing her husband's reaction to the spectacle would reveal whether he was being captured by the powers of porn or whether he was just carrying objectivity and academic analysis to an annoying extreme.

When the food arrived, she realized how hungry she had become and she dived into a Cobb salad. Stanley took a couple of bites from a colossal hamburger and reminded her that they needed to do a sound check on the recording equipment later.

"I think I've been spending more time on this project than you have," she said with a grimace and a vivid description of the ridiculously pierced Goth media assistant who had trained her how to use the equipment during an interminable two-hour session.

"Hey," he protested, "I've spent the last two weeks boning up on the porn industry."

"God, Stan!" She couldn't help but giggle. "Don't go all Freudian on me! Next thing, you'll be telling me how *hard* this assignment is getting!"

"Well," he replied with a straight face, "I've got some stiff competition."

"Let's hope your research isn't a big bust."

"I'll try not to cock it up."

"That would sure suck." She waited for Stanley to respond, but he seemed to have exhausted his store of innuendo. She suddenly started laughing again. "I guess you're all out of cracks."

"Oh God," he said, putting down his hamburger, "that was terrible. You win. *No mas!*" He popped a French fry into his mouth and tried to change the subject. "See how much fun this is? Aren't you glad I convinced you to come with me?"

"Come with you!" She burst out and then with a mischievous grin pulled a baby ear of corn out of the salad and popped in her mouth. "Maybe this afternoon…if you're lucky."

The hotel room was clean and cheerful, and Stanley lay on the bed while his wife showered away the travel bugs that she claimed made cross-country flying so unhygienic. He grabbed the television remote off the night stand and pushed the menu button. Among the standard movie and television fare, the initial options list promised a wealth of adult titles available for viewing, and he could not resist scrolling through the offerings. One group of movies entitled "Classic Superstars" featured videos with multiple scenes starring Asia Carrera, Nina Hartley, Jenna Jameson, Miko Lee, Gina Ryder, Sydney Steele, and Stephanie Swift. He clicked on a name he had run across in his research and was soon confronted with the still image of Crissy Moran, lounging on the beach, provocatively pulling at the top of her string bikini while gazing languidly in the general direction of his zipper.

He clicked back to the main adult menu and found several movies produced by Richard Ramrod and Eden Studio. He clicked on one of them, *Girls will be Girls,* and his eyes saucered to the image of woman bending over a satin couch in a black bra, panties, and a garter belt. The blurb under the picture promised her in action with any number of glamorous women in the industry, all leading to an explosive final scene where she discovers the most earth-shattering sex is with her husband.

He was contemplating accepting the free preview offer when he heard Angela turn off the shower. He returned to the menu and looked for titles from Chimera Productions and Janus Studios. He had rented a couple of movies before he left town, but it had been a clumsy and embarrassing operation starting with a leering teenage video store clerk and ending with a dirty look from his wife as he emerged from the study with the movies to return. She was unlikely to suggest that he do further research here in the hotel. He had just clicked on the description of a Janus production called *My Best Friend's Mom* when Angela entered the room wrapped in a fluffy blue towel.

"What are you looking at?" she exclaimed as she stood next to the bed and looked over at the television. The "mom," a raven-haired beauty named Porsche Michaels, was gifted with smoldering eyes and a lascivious mouth. As a shy high school student, Stanley would have turned to ash if such a neighbor lady had turned her attention to him.

His wife put a hand on her hip with a disapproving look and suggested erroneously that he was too old for that particular fantasy. He skipped to the next option and was greeted by an ad for *Doing Ms. Daisy,* an interracial feature from a studio he did not recognize. The title at least managed to get a laugh out Angela, which was a good sign, given her sense of humor usually deserted her whenever the subject of pornography came up.

The next offering was a video by the Chunky Bunch Group entitled, *Big Girls, Big Lovin'*. She gasped at the sight of a three hundred pound woman in lingerie and bright red lipstick pouting at the camera. She plopped down next to him unable to take her eyes off the television screen. "Does that do anything for you?"

"No," he answered emphatically. Then he ran his fingers over the small hairs on the nape of her neck. "What about you?"

She slapped his hand away with a disgusted snort and revealed that she had only seen one adult film in her life: a tape played at a slumber party in high school. The male star had been fat and hairy, and the female lead's main talent was her ability to appear completely bored regardless of the orifice being invaded. The small group of girls had watched one scene and a half, declared it gross, and gone on to a much racier game of truth or dare. He wondered if there were any movies in the hotel's vast online library that might change her mind, at least on the narrow issue of grossness.

Angela stood next to the bed and watched her husband flip through the movie offerings. He stopped on a screen that offered several options featuring a stunning biracial beauty. Angela snorted skeptically as he read aloud the description of *Girls Will Be Girls* and struggled to fathom why it was necessary to maintain the pretense of a morality tale where the slutty wife and husband live happily ever after. She glanced at her husband and decided that he would probably have a heart attack if she gave him permission to push the "buy" button.

Normally, she never would have considered the idea, but she had come to California with the kernel of a plan in her head and indulging Stanley's racy little fantasy might be an effective way to nurture it. They had been talking for years about having children, but waiting for tenure had always seemed a sensible reason to delay. With that obstacle about to be overcome, their California vacation would be a natural time to abandon the stringent birth control practices they had clung to since graduate school. She was tired of being alone in the house and was ready for children's voices to fill the void. As the middle child of seven, she had long been eager for a family, and Stanley had managed to put her off for long enough. It was time to deal with his foot dragging.

She nodded her assent. He blinked in disbelief, and when she nodded again, he clicked on the remote. After a few seconds the Eden logo appeared and the movie began with a group of women chattering away at a wedding shower. A pale blonde, a tan brunette, an Asian, and an African American woman sat in a semicircle on a leather sectional couch with presents perched on their laps. The star, an Indian woman with long jet black hair, sat in the middle of the friends. After several minutes of stilted conversation, it became clear that the center of attention was soon to be married. As she opened her gifts of skimpy lingerie and sex toys, the girlfriends questioned her decision to leave her swinging life behind and started to reminisce about the exciting times they had shared in the past. As the blonde regaled the group with a particularly spicy encounter between herself and bride-to-be, the scene faded to a flashback.

Although Angela did not indulge in lesbian fantasies, she was not overly offended by the tender caresses and low moans exchanged by the two beautiful women on the television screen. It was clearly a male fantasy, but at least the immediate goal for the women in the scene was to achieve, or appear to achieve, some level of satisfaction for themselves. Men would love to watch—she cast a quick glance at her husband who was riveted to the screen—but in this scene they did not invade the privacy of the two characters. And the two women really did seem to be getting into it. Either they were honestly enjoying themselves, or they were darn good actresses. Given the unromantic nature of the movie set described by Stanley at lunch, she could not decide which would be more surprising.

As the lovers escalated their encounter, she looked over at her husband again. He knew she was watching him, and he put on his academic face, pretending to be seriously studying the sociological behavior on display before him. Who did he think he was fooling? She knew what he was thinking, and she knew that she could have her way whenever she wanted. With a little creep of her fingers down his chest, she reached over and tugged on his belt. He flinched, but did not say anything as her hand strayed below his buckle. She had his undivided attention now, and after a couple of minutes she took the remote out of his hand, clicked the mute button and crawled on top of him, blocking his view of the movie.

A few frantic kisses later and he was tugging down his pants, trying to pull her onto him. She kissed him again and admitted that she had forgotten to bring any protection with her. The arching of his back and determined expression on his face told her that he was not worried about birth control at the moment.

"Oh shit!" he cried, as she pressed down on him and lost herself in the sweet friction of their bodies. Shortly thereafter she felt him shudder, and she tried to continue on her own but he was too sensitive and grabbed her hips to slow her movement. "I'm sorry," he panted. "That's too much."

She smiled and brushed a stray and sweaty lock from his forehead. He was seldom selfish and it had been a rush to control him so completely. She stayed on top, savoring the touch his skin, still tingling when she finally rolled over to the side of the bed. Stanley let out a satisfied sigh and they both turned their attention back to the frenzied action taking place on the television. Their eyes met and came to instant agreement that sex was about the silliest looking thing that human beings did and then they burst out laughing.

After a short nap, the couple lay on their backs, hands clasped and staring at the ceiling. Angela tried to remember the last time they had unprotected sex and eventually gave up. Stanley was so paranoid about an unwanted pregnancy that he would wear a condom even when it seemed ludicrous. She had guessed right that getting the book back on track would lower his guard, and the stupid movie had not hurt either. She rolled over on her side and spotted the narrow groove in between his eyebrows that meant he was worried. She tried smoothing it out with her thumb, but it kept popping back like a tiny whack-a-mole. He was probably contemplating fatherhood.

Angela sympathized and understood his fear of change. She had not wanted to move to Illinois, nor had she wanted to sell real estate to help make their mortgage payments. But the biggest adaptation for her had been sharing a quiet house with just one other person. If she could survive being parted from the warmth and chaos of her gloriously crowded childhood home, he could handle a linoleum lizard or two crawling around kitchen floor. Of course, having kids would be a challenge for her too. She knew all about midnight feedings and foot bruises from stray Legos, but at the end of the day there would a moment of quiet when she could sit down with her laptop and spin her children's diarrhea and pin worms into comic gold.

She kissed his cheek and lay her head on his chest, comforted by the steady thump of his heartbeat and wondering whether she might be misreading him. Maybe he wanted change. He had complained about being stuck in a rut at the university and having kids would cement him in the job. Fear of kids might be fear of stasis, not a fear of change. She put her chin on his chest and took one more peek at his handsome face. Maybe he was starting his mid-life crisis early? He shifted his weight to the side and grunted as her chin bit too deeply. Would he be the type to take a hot graduate student as a lover?

She lifted her head up and looked at the digital clock on the bed stand. It was time to get dressed for the banquet. Her fingers searched for him underneath the tousled sheets. She nibbled his ear. "Are you sure we have to go?"

He slipped out from under her arm, gave her a quick peck on the cheek, and walked to the closet. "It's gonna be a classy party, Ange. Don said even the mainstream media are covering it." He picked a conservative gray suit out of the closet and brushed a piece of lint off the lapel. "I'll go alone if you want me to."

"No way!" She went to the bathroom where she had hung her dress to steam while she had taken her shower. Finding something to wear had posed a difficult problem. On the one hand, she never wore the sort of daring outfits that the porn queens would undoubtedly be sporting. On the other, she did not want to stand out dressed like a schoolmarm. She finally settled on a stylish black dress with spaghetti straps that plunged into her cleavage further than she preferred but still did not stray outside middle-class cocktail party norms. When she finally got dressed and fixed her makeup, she stood for a while in front of the mirror. For once, her brunette locks were not frizzing up and the new cut looked sleek and elegant. And the dress did a good job of drawing attention away from the weight on her thighs that no amount of dieting seemed to diminish.

She grabbed her pocketbook from the dresser, noticing with a frown that it did not quite match her dress and shoes. Stanley snuck up behind her and gave an approving squeeze. "I know who's going to be the prettiest woman there."

"And I know who'll be full of the most shit," she laughed as they disengaged. "Do you think they'll have a red carpet? Maybe we should have rented a limo."

"I don't think it will be quite that extravagant," he said doubtfully as he led her out the door and down to the elevator.

But there was a red carpet, and she felt more than a little self-conscious stepping out of the rented Taurus first and waiting for her escort to make his way around the car. His face wore a huge grin as photographers' cameras flashed in their faces, and he gave a confident wave as if he were a movie star attending a premiere. "You're really enjoying this, aren't you?" She whispered in his ear as they started down the carpet past the phalanx of cameras and microphones with logos from Fox News, CNN, MSNBC, VH1, Bravo, and the Playboy Channel. She shaded her eyes from the glare of the lights and slipped behind him as he strode toward the studio.

"If anyone asks," Stanley turned and whispered back, "I'm Long Dong Silver, scourge of Pleasure Island." Two more steps and they slipped into the refuge of the studio lobby where they were met by a beaming man in a tuxedo.

She watched him closely as he first took Stanley's hand and then warmly pressed her own. Johansson looked pretty normal for a porn czar who had turned his back on the priesthood and now paid sweaty young men and women to roll around under klieg lights. His smile seemed genuine, and he made eye contact without sending shivers of sleaze into her soul. No wonder Stanley had been seduced so easily. There's nothing more dangerous than a self-confident man.

"Thank you for helping Stanley out with the book," she offered graciously. "You've really saved the day."

"I doubt that," he said, pressing her hand one more time before disengaging and turning back to her husband. "Oh, I've seated you with Layla DiBona and Kristy Page, who are your first two interviews tomorrow, plus a couple of my production assistants." He gave them both a quick smile of dismissal and turned to face two beautiful women in sequined gowns who had just finished running the gauntlet of reporters.

They followed a row of flowers in crystal vases topping mock Greek columns through an open door at the end of a short hallway. Beyond the doors, they found a large room with a polished concrete floor filled with round tables. Although the dining area had been festively decorated, the room itself still had the feel of a warehouse. A large dais had been set up at the far end of the room with a huge promotional poster for *Toys in Babeland* and a large podium. After giving their names to a young hostess in black pants and a white Eden Studio t-shirt, they were led to a table in the back.

They were the last couple to arrive at the table. Two men wearing brightly colored jackets stood up, shook their hands and introduced their dates. Angela promptly forgot the men's names, although she remembered that one was a major league baseball player and the other was a drummer in a rock band she had never heard of. The ball player was sitting next to Layla, a middle-aged blonde with short, thick hair who was wearing a tuxedo cut for a woman. Despite the lack of a shirt underneath the jacket, she managed to convey a surprisingly conservative demeanor.

She smiled and waved at Stanley and Angela as they sat down. Kristy, a petite brunette in a low cut red dress, nodded and passed them a bottle of white wine. The production assistants, their identity obvious from their complete lack of glamour, were engrossed in conversation and barely noticed the new arrivals.

The location was a perfect place to observe the festivities. With her back to the wall, she could watch the whole room with complete anonymity. She laid her napkin in her lap and accepted a generous glass of wine poured by her neighbor. She recognized the bottle and was impressed that Johansson would serve fifty dollar bottles of wine to such a large group. The appetizers that arrived shortly thereafter turned out to be as good as the wine, and she began to relax as she noticed many other couples dressed as conventionally as herself and her mate. There were some, however, who flaunted the attributes that made them top earners. A gorgeous blond wore a toga-like outfit that exposed one breast covered only by a small sequined fabric flower; the brunette next to her kept flopping out of her dress until she finally pulled the top down to her waist and then tugged it up in a vulgar attempt to solve the slippage problem.

The mood at the long table set upon the dais was more subdued than that of the groundlings. Angela watched Johansson, seated next to the podium, sipping a glass of wine and surveying the room as the appetizers were cleared and the main course, lobster risotto and beef tenderloin, was carried out to the tables. She saw the star of the movie, listed as Jade Delilah on the poster, sitting next to him, picking at her food and ignoring his whispering in her ear. Her voluptuous figure was far from her only stunning feature. Her creamy olive complexion was even and unblemished. Jet black hair cascaded down her back and her bright eyes sparkled with intelligence and sensuality. Angela realized with a shock that she had been the star of *Girls Will Be Girls*.

"What are you looking at?" Stanley asked.

"I was just staring at this Jade woman next to Don. Is she on our interview schedule?"

"I think we've got her the day after tomorrow." He leaned back as the waiter put plates in front of everyone at the table. "I saw her for a second in Don's office before I met him yesterday."

"I wonder how she got into this business," she whispered so that only he could hear. "Just look at her. I'll bet she can snap her fingers and get anything she wants. Can you see any employer interviewing her and turning her down?"

He managed a glance up at the dais without drooling. "Not a chance."

For the next hour, they tucked into their food and savored wonderfully crisp glasses of Côtes du Rhone that were replenished as soon as they were half-emptied. To Angela's surprise, the conversation around the table seldom lagged. Everybody seemed interested in the book project, and Stanley's questions prompted a round of scandalous storytelling from Layla, Christie, and the production assistants. I'm partying with porn stars, Angela mused. When Nanci hears this, she'll never believe it.

An hour later, the dinner plates were cleared and dessert arrived. Angela looked up at the dais and was surprised to see that no one had yet approached the podium to begin the scheduled after dinner speech. The guests of honor were talking to each other and casting concerned glances in the direction of Don's and Jade's empty seats. As the invitees finished their sweets and moved on to their coffee, they began to get more impatient, and a trickle of guests began leaving to continue the party elsewhere. After fifteen minutes of growing restlessness, a middle-aged man in a tuxedo approached the podium and began to speak.

"I'm Trent Holmes, associate producer of *Toys in Babeland*. First of all, I know that Don would want me to thank you for coming. I'm sure he'll be here in a moment, but let me take this time to—"An ear-splitting shriek from the hall doorway stopped his impromptu speech in mid-sentence. The entire room turned to see a young woman in a yellow spandex minidress scream again, fall to the floor with a wild sob, and then throw up all over the concrete floor.

# VI.

# A HARD-BOILED DICK

Detective Stuart McCaffrey walked up the red carpet and scowled at the camera crew who dogged his steps until he reached the yellow tape that declared the Eden Studio Building to be a crime scene. As he opened the door, he flicked a cigar butt at the feet of a reporter and nodded at the sergeant who had initially responded to the call that a dead woman had been found in the office of Donald Johansson, aka Richard Ramrod, owner of Eden Studio. The sergeant led him down the corridor to the office. More yellow tape stretched across the entrance to the murder scene, and while the sergeant ducked underneath, McCaffrey lingered outside to check for fingerprint dust on the door frame. He saw none. The idiot local cops had taped over the most likely place a perpetrator would have rested his hands before entering the room.

The detective entered and surveyed the room from left to right, ignoring the body that lay crumpled on an expensive Persian rug. It was several minutes before he spoke to the sergeant. "What has been moved or touched since the body was discovered?"

"The woman who discovered the body," he looked in a small spiral notebook, "a Miss Lanie Watts, says she opened the door looking for a bathroom, took a couple of steps in, saw the body, and then ran right back out. Security heard her screaming and came immediately. They checked the body for signs of life and sealed off the room. It's lucky that we didn't have a bunch of partygoers rushing in to see if they could help."

McCaffrey walked onto the carpet and took a close look at the body. A young woman in a purple silk dress lay in an ocean of blood. The left side of her face was completely caved in, eyeball hanging onto the cheek, teeth glistening in the back of her throat. He had not seen such destruction to a human face since he had stopped working traffic twenty years earlier. He looked up and found spatters of blood and tissue on the wall and curtains behind her.

"The security guards say this is her," the sergeant finally dared to interject. He pointed to the picture behind the large teak desk. "Her name is Jade Delilah."

McCaffrey studied the picture. "Nice."

The sergeant worked his way carefully around to the sofa, and pointed down. "We think this might be the murder weapon." On the floor between a heavy glass coffee table and the sofa lay a cricket bat emblazoned with the Greek letters for Alpha and Omicron. The upper half of the bat was smeared with blood.

McCaffrey bent down and scrutinized the long flat club without touching it. "Wouldn't it be nice to get some clear prints off of that bat handle, Sergeant?"

"I think we will, Detective."

He straightened up and gave the sergeant a curious look. "Why do you say that?"

"Well," he said, cracking a smile for the first time, "when the security guards got here, they found the owner of the studio passed out on the sofa. He was flat on his back with his left hand draped right over the murder weapon. After the guards checked to see whether the girl was still alive, they took him down to the security office."

"Is he still there?"

"No. He's been taken to the station for processing."

"Photogs been through?"

"Yup."

"What about the Medical Examiner?"

"She's waiting for you to finish up," said an impatient voice directly behind the detective. "And I wouldn't mind getting to the body before she goes stone cold."

The detective turned around and saw his ex-wife, Ellen, standing with her hands on her hips, equipment bag hanging loosely from her left shoulder. Fifty years old and still looking nice. He met her eyes and was rewarded with a frown. Bitchy, but nice. The divorce was two years past, but the pain resurfaced every time he saw her, an all too frequent event given their respective jobs. "There ya go," he said, "violating the anti-stalking order again."

She gave him with a thin smile. "Do you mind if I look at her while you poke around?"

"Have at it," he said. "Maybe you can establish a time of death for us."

"No problem there," the Sergeant interrupted. "There was a big party in the studio tonight, bunch of tables set up, catered dinner, the whole nine yards. The victim was seated at the head table along with the suspect. We've only just begun our questioning, but everybody agrees that Johansson left the table around nine, and Delilah left around nine-thirty or so. Her body was discovered half an hour after that."

"Do you have the names of everyone who was at the party?"

"Yes, sir. We checked I.D. on everyone before they left."

McCaffrey walked slowly around the room. He was leery of any murder that looked like an open-and-shut case, but if the handle of the fraternity paddle bore Donald Johansson's fingerprints, then there would be little left to discover except a motive for the killing. He took another look at the victim's picture hanging behind the desk and remembered the film noir adage that where a beautiful woman was concerned, there was usually no shortage of motives.

He looked at the desk and decided to go through it after the room had been swept for prints, fibers, and hair. Ellen was kneeling down over the body, finishing up her initial inspection. "Is the cause of death what it appears to be?"

"You never know until the tox work is done, but there seems little doubt that this is a blunt trauma death. We'll do an autopsy tomorrow and get you a report as quick as we can." She zipped up her bag and stood up. "Is there anything else?"

"No. I think we can leave and let the good Sergeant oversee the transportation of the body to the morgue and deal with the techies." He closed his notepad and walked toward the door. "Let's get out of here."

She followed him out of the office and down the hall to the lobby where several uniformed officers were still speaking to a security guard. An impatient member of the forensics team checked his watch and then dialed his cell phone. McCaffrey held open the door and they walked out into the warm night. A single camera crew remained, but it was occupied interviewing another security guard about half a block away. "Lemme walk you to your car," he said.

They walked silently to a station wagon emblazoned with the logo of the Office of the Medical Examiner for Los Angeles County. "You wanna get a cup of coffee?" he asked nonchalantly.

"Not tonight." She slipped her key into the door and sat down in the driver's seat. She looked up with a blank face before she shut the door. "Not a good idea."

McCaffrey made good time to the local police substation where the suspect in the murder was being held. He parked in the spot reserved for the Captain next to the entrance, walked into a brightly lit lobby, and asked a burly officer behind the front desk where he could find Johansson.

"I'll take you down to him. He was pretty fucked up when he got here, but he's coming around now."

"Has anybody talked to him?"

"No, sir. We were waiting for you or the Sergeant."

"Good." The officer stopped at the end of the hall and motioned toward a gray metal door on the right. Through the interrogation room window, McCaffrey saw a middle-aged man in a tuxedo, slumped forward on a metal chair, resting his forehead on the table in front of him. "What do you mean, he was 'fucked up'? Have you ordered blood work?"

"Yes, sir." The officer jerked his thumb at the detainee and pulled a prescription pill bottle out of his pocket. "We found this in his jacket. He was extremely disoriented. Wanted to know why we were taking him here. When some smart ass told him he had just killed a porn star, he totally lost his shit."

"Totally lost his shit?" The detective had long grown impatient with his colleagues' inability to get beyond common vulgarity in describing simple events.

"I mean, he fell down. He was sobbing, 'no, no,' struggling with his restraints. That sort of thing."

"Thank you, officer." He waited for the young man to unlock the deadbolt. "Now let me have a word with our suspect. And bring us some coffee."

The detective looked down at the figure before him. Johansson looked like he had not slept for weeks, but when he was reread his Miranda rights, he sat up. Both his tie and cummerbund had been removed.

"Could you give me your name, age, and address?"

"My name is Donald Johansson. I'm thirty-six years old, and I live at 457 Deerfield Terrace in Santa Monica."

"Nice neighborhood," the detective commented. "Own or rent?"

"I'm renting it." He took a deep breath and pushed the hair out of his eyes with his cuffed hands. "Could you please tell me what's going on? The other officers weren't very helpful."

"I'll be happy to tell you," McCaffrey said cheerfully, "but first I need you to tell me everything you've done this evening." He looked up at the small green light in the corner of the room to make sure their conversation was being recorded. The prisoner looked for a moment like he was going to object, but then he closed his eyes and bowed his head. "Would you like an aspirin and some coffee?"

"Yes, please." McCaffrey knocked on the window and relayed the order. He then leaned back in his chair and watched the suspect. He had learned long before that silence was the most useful tool in interrogations. Conversations initiated by prisoners were almost always fruitful, but Johansson said nothing. He sat with his eyes shut and his hands in his lap until the door opened and a styrofoam cup and a small packet containing two Tylenol were set down before him. He thanked the guard and fumbled to open the foil packet with trembling hands. It dropped to the floor and McCaffrey reached down and opened it for him. He took the pills with a sip of coffee and then started to talk.

"Tonight we had a big party at the studio. We had just closed the biggest contract in our history and I invited about two hundred people to celebrate." He paused for a moment, as if he were having trouble remembering. "I was seated at the head table on the dais...I was supposed to give a speech. I wanted to thank everyone who had made the movie such a success."

"This is a porn movie?"

"Yes."

"Did you make the speech?"

The prisoner thought for a moment. "No, I don't think so." His voice faded and he started fiddling with one of his buttons. McCaffrey searched for another way to jog his memory.

"What did you have for an appetizer?"

"Excuse me?"

"What did you have for an appetizer?"

"Um, we had those little fishes...fresh anchovies...marinated in olive oil and garlic. Some fried calamari too. They tasted good with the wine." He looked up at the detective. "I definitely had wine."

McCaffrey pulled the pill bottle out of his pocket and handed it to him. "Does this look familiar?" The suspect took the bottle in his right hand and studied it.

"Yeah. I've been having back problems. My doctor prescribed this to me yesterday."

"Did you take any this evening?"

"A couple right before the party."

"It's not smart to mix painkillers and alcohol, Mr. Johansson." McCaffrey took back the pill bottle and tapped it lightly against the table. "Do you remember what came after the appetizers, Mr. Johansson?" The suspect concentrated on his answer, eyes flicking side to side as if he were trying to capture some fleeting image. "Do you remember the main course?"

"No... yes... lobster and steak. But I didn't eat it. I felt sick and went back to my office. I had to go to the bathroom..."

"Did you get sick in the bathroom?"

"I don't know."

"Was there anyone else in the room?"

"I don't remember."

"Do you remember what happened in your office?"

He sighed and leaned over the table. "No. Could you just tell me what happened?"

"Well, Mr. Johansson," he held the suspect's eyes and watched his reaction closely, "you were found passed out on the sofa with a bloody fraternity paddle in your hand and a dead woman on the floor next to you."

"My God." Johansson bent over as if someone had hit him in the stomach with a two-by-four.

"Not much of her face left, I'm afraid."

He raised his head slightly and whispered. "Who was it?"

"The security guards seem quite certain that her name was Jade Delilah." He watched as Johansson's head sunk below his waist. He slipped all the way to the floor, crouching on his hands and knees before emitting a visceral groan and spitting a clot of yellow bile on the detective's shoes. For a few moments, he panted like a dog, then he wiped his mouth with the sleeve of jacket and retched again. When he stopped shuddering, he spoke in a raspy voice, eyes still fixed on the floor.

"I need to talk to a lawyer."

# VII

# THE HISTORIAN

S tanley and Angela pushed the musty bed in the Van Nuys motel room as far as they could into the corner. To their mutual disgust, the sliding foot board popped a dead cockroach up out of the carpet. Stanley got a tissue, scooped it up, and plopped it into the toilet. "That was gross," he heard as he flushed the critter down.

Angela surveyed the pale square of carpet revealed by the moving bed, closely inspecting it for more vermin. "I wonder how long it was there." Although the hotel chain had a solid reputation, judging by its tired furniture and mummified bug carcasses, the franchise in the San Fernando Valley was clearly below the national par.

"Who knows? Just be glad we're not staying here." Despite the events of the previous night, he was hopeful that the interviewees would still show for their scheduled slots. The police had detained the entire banquet group for several hours while they took brief statements and recorded everyone's identity. Angela had been without her purse, so Stanley had vouched for her and promised to bring her to the local police station with proper identification within forty-eight hours. Back at the hotel, they had watched the news, but had learned little more than Jade Delilah was dead and a "person of interest" was in custody.

Stanley created an interview area in one corner of room, a small table with water and soft drinks next to the chair where his subjects would sit. He would face them, alongside a digital video recorder on a black tripod. Angela could monitor the audio from her perch on the bed.

"What time is it?" She asked.

"Almost ten. Layla should be here any minute."

"If she's coming." He sensed that the death of Jade Delilah might cause a huge stir in the porn world, but how that would affect his project was far from clear. If the women failed to show, his whole career might be a casualty of Jade's murder. He avoided thinking about the prospect of a baby on the way and a termination letter from the university in his mailbox. "Let's do a quick sound check."

"Four score and seven years ago…one, two, three… testing, testing…I love a parade…" While the professor babbled, his wife set the levels on the audio monitor and then made sure one more time that the chair occupied the center of the camera's visual field.

"That should do it." She sat back on the bed and looked in the folder that held the interview schedule. "First up, Ms. Layla DiBona." She sighed and put down the papers. "My god, why not just call yourself Loose-Legs McHarlot?"

"Come on," he chided, "she seemed very nice last night. You said that she was very articulate." Until the scream from the back of the banquet hall, he had enjoyed himself immensely. He would have sworn that his wife had been having fun too, but at the hotel afterward she had intimated that the crime was a karmic comment on both the evening and his research project.

"Okay, fine. I just hope she's wearing a shirt this time." She grabbed a bottle of water from the mini-fridge and sat back down on the bed. "Wasn't there some other profession you could have chosen to study?" She asked. "What's wrong with realtors? Most of us are women."

"Entirely too sexy," he replied with grin. "You couldn't trust me alone in the room with them."

"Ha, ha."

"Actually, I considered it a couple of months ago, but most agents are really independent contractors. Most realtors aren't technically employees of anybody, so the cross-profession comparisons wouldn't have been parallel."

She sighed in response. "Okay, but can I just say that I'm not looking forward to this."

He was about to peer out window when he heard a sharp rap on the door. "Right on time."

He opened the door and let in a somber woman who extended her hand and reintroduced herself as Janet Stephens, known to the video world as Layla Dibona. She was casually dressed in a pair of lightweight khaki trousers and a modest knit blouse. A pair of Ray Bans were pushed deeply into her thick, blond hair. She wore little makeup and no jewelry, except for two small diamond studs in her ears. Only the lines around her eyes and the slight wrinkles on her neck gave away that she was in her late thirties.

"I'm so glad you could come!" He said with genuine enthusiasm. "Especially after last night." She nodded noncommittally and sat down in the chair obviously reserved for the interviewee. "Did you know Jade well?"

"Pretty well," she replied after a moment's hesitation. "We never did a scene together, but it's a pretty small community and she's been busy the last few years."

"Do you know who the police have in custody?"

"No," she shook her head, "all I'm hearing is wild rumors."

Stanley waited for more explanation, but she did not seem interested in hashing over the night's events. "Why don't we get started?" He gestured to Angela. "I'm not sure I mentioned last night that my wife is my audio-visual expert."

"Hi." The women said simultaneously.

He explained the confidentiality agreement and consent form that permitted the interview to be used only for anonymous research purposes. She perused it briefly and then signed. "I hope you'll be able to give us a full two hours," he said. "I don't know what Don told you to expect today."

"Two hours!" She waved her hands frantically. "But I've got to be back to the set of *Granny Love 4* by eleven!"

Stanley opened his mouth, but no sound came out. Angela's eyes flicked between the actress and her husband. They were both suddenly aware of the whizzing of traffic outside the motel window.

"That was a joke!" The starlet broke the awkward silence with an exasperated cry. "Don calls me the porn historian, but I'm not that old for chrissakes!" She laughed, and the couple joined in nervously. "Don't worry, I'll stay here as long as you like." She sat down and smoothed the top of her pants. "It's about time someone took a serious look at this industry."

Stanley picked up his yellow legal pad, nodded at his wife and began:

INTERVIEWER: Could you tell us your age and place of birth?

SUBJECT: I'm thirty-eight years old and was born in Marina Del Rey, California.

INTERVIEWER: How long have you been making adult films?

SUBJECT: Since about 1991. Yeah, almost seventeen years now. Christ, that's a long time.

INTERVIEWER: Unusually long?

SUBJECT: Oh yeah. The average career is about eighteen months, maybe two years, max. But I've always been lucky; I was one of the first contract girls.

INTERVIEWER: Meaning?

SUBJECT: Okay. These days girls like Jade Delilah, Genna Lynne, me, for example, do one year contracts with a studio. We make a set number of films per year for a regular salary. Plus, we get some percentage of sales if we're on the DVD cover. That was totally unheard of in the old days.

INTERVIEWER: When would that be, the 'old days'?

SUBJECT: The seventies. That's when porn really took off in a big way. Sure, there were always stag films. You know, the kind of crap your father would watch at an Elk's Lodge bachelor party. No plot or anything, just some choppy scenes of naked bodies banging away. But after *Deep Throat* in 1972, you had what might be called porn's 'golden age.' *Deep Throat* was shot for peanuts, but it made over a hundred million dollars. Then, you had a series of bigger budget movies like *Behind the Green Door*, *The Devil in Mrs. Jones* and *The Opening of Misty Beethoven*. Hard to imagine now, but they showed this stuff in regular theaters in suburban malls, just like any other movie.

INTERVIEWER: [laughs] My father once admitted after a few beers that he and my mom went to see an x-rated version of Cinderella. Apparently the wicked stepsisters were pretty damn wicked.

SUBJECT: There was a lot of curiosity, but it died down pretty fast, and after a bit of a lull people got VCRs and the industry switched to much lower budget video productions. The seventies were the golden age because the movies were shot on film, just like Hollywood productions. Some of them are really quite beautiful. Video just can't give you the same quality.

INTERVIEWER: It sounds like Eden Studio is trying to start a new golden age.

SUBJECT: That's the goal. If Eden can get a movie on mainstream screens, it'll have the money to starting shooting on film. I don't know what will happen to *Babes* now that Jade is dead.

INTERVIEWER: But right now video productions are still the name of the game? Why's that?

SUBJECT: It's so much cheaper. You can make a video for, say, twenty thousand, forty thousand tops, and then distribute it directly to stores or online. For a successful one, the profit margins are pretty huge.

INTERVIEWER: What about porn on cable television?

SUBJECT: Cable TV started getting seriously into porn toward the end of the eighties, but because of obscenity laws, channels couldn't show everything, you know, an erect penis, pop shots, or any sort of penetration. Then, a couple of years ago, the Playboy Channel finally started showing movies with blow jobs and vaginal sex, but only after eleven at night in certain markets, and still no cum shots or anal. Even so, it opened things up. So, you have cable creating this huge market for movies where people are actually screwing on camera, but you couldn't have close ups of where the action's at. This forced production companies to change their focus.

INTERVIEWER: In what ways? Don't you just do the same thing but tell the cameraman to shoot from a different angle?

SUBJECT: It's not that simple. First, you need better actors. If the camera can't be focused constantly on people's crotches, it's going to be on their faces a lot more. There's more dialogue, so that puts pressure on the director to make a movie with some semblance of a plot or maybe a bit of humor. And some cable channels, say, Playboy, like to think of themselves as being "classy," so they're going to be interested in showing more profession-al-looking stuff. And the women have to be better looking. With all the extra face time, these girls can't look like goats anymore.

Some of the best movies I've made have been aimed at the softer core cable market. In a regular porn film, you have to contort your body into some pretty uncomfortable positions for the camera to catch what's going on. Plain old missionary just doesn't show much, so you're doing a reverse cowgirl hanging from a forklift with a camera about a foot away from your pussy. Not very sexy.

INTERVIEWER: So, for you personally, sex is better on cable?

SUBJECT: Yeah, less gymnastic sex is definitely better sex, but you still gotta to be suspicious of women saying they have orgasms while filming.

INTERVIEWER: What about the internet? I'm kind of surprised that it hasn't wiped out the adult film industry. You can see almost anything you want for free online.

SUBJECT: Speaking from experience? [laughs] Think about it. You can read almost anything you like on the inter-net for free, but the book industry's still alive and kicking.

Same with the news. There's all sorts of news online, but people still get the *LA Times*. The internet just expands the size of the overall market. Adult films are definitely not dead.

INTERVIEWER: So the internet is overrated?

SUBJECT: I didn't say that. The internet has had a huge impact. I mean Pamela Anderson's and Paris Hilton's x-rated home videos paved the way for the mainstreaming of pornography. It's very telling they weren't ostracized. Far from it! Without Pamela and Tommy Lee, we sure wouldn't be seeing Jade Delilah on MTV. For some reason, exposing yourself on the internet is somehow more acceptable than starring in traditional porn. Maybe it's because more people have been exposed to it through the internet. You don't have to walk into the dirty book store anymore to buy *Hustler,* or show your face at the video store to get an adult movie. You can surf the web in total privacy with complete anonymity. More than anything else, that's what's mainstreaming porn.

INTERVIEWER: Would you say that *Toys in Babeland* is the culmination of the evolution of the industry that you've been observing?

SUBJECT: Eden would certainly like it to be! They've shown, at least, that you can treat talent fairly and with respect. People who work there like the place. You should talk to girls from other studios, though. You'd get a distorted impression from just focusing on Eden. There's still plenty of sleazebags out there. God knows, I've worked for enough of them.

INTERVIEWER: Do you ever feel exploited?

SUBJECT: Of course. You're in an industry where men who never show their asses are making the real money. And you know, sometimes you don't feel like getting up at seven in the morning and having sex with two guys you've never met before. But I felt exploited when I was a secretary too. My boss treated me and everyone else like crap, and we barely got paid a living wage. All work is exploitation as far as I can tell. At least at this point, people like Jade and me have a little bit of control...

INTERVIEWER: How did you get into the business?

SUBJECT: Like everyone else! [laughs] I answered an advertisement to be a "figure model" at Olde World Modeling Agency in Los Angeles. I was a bit of a rebellious kid and got kicked out of the house when I was eighteen. I worked as a receptionist for a while and in a department store, but all I could afford was a tiny apartment in a crappy neighborhood that I had to share with two other people. I knew figure modeling meant nude modeling, but I've never been ashamed of my body and didn't see the harm in making some easy money.

INTERVIEWER: A lot of women would react to that prospect with, uh, some trepidation.

SUBJECT: And that's why they don't do it! More power to 'em, but when I pictured myself doing it, well, it just didn't bother me. If I'd still been at home and worried about my parents, I might not have done it. But that's the last thing I was thinking about back then.

INTERVIEWER: What do you parents think now?

SUBJECT: We're very close. They usually don't bring up my career, but if I do, they're comfortable with it. It took a long time though.

INTERVIEWER: Did you start doing movies right away?

SUBJECT: No, that came later. I did nothing but photos for a couple of years but all my new friends were in the industry. There's a lot of overlap between the magazine trade and the video trade. Anyway, my boyfriend at the time suggested that I try doing adult films.

INTERVIEWER: That seems kind of odd. Why would he want you to have sex on camera with other men?

SUBJECT: You know, I think he was the one who really wanted to be the star. Maybe he thought he could ease his way into the business? Maybe he was screwing vicariously through me? All I know is that once I did a couple of movies he started calling me a whore and very soon he was an ex-boyfriend.

INTERVIEWER: Why did you stay in it then?

SUBJECT: Why not? The money was good. I liked the people I was working with. They were the only family I had at that point. I had already taken the plunge. Why not continue? It was just a job.

*　*　*

Three hours later, the young couple locked up the room behind them and walked down a flight of sticky metal stairs to the parking lot where their rental car sat baking in the sunshine. Layla had been an enthusiastic respondent, happy to fill in some of the gaps left open by the sparse academic literature on pornography. Stanley doubted her level of introspection was typical, but she was a valuable first informant.

"Well, would she have jumped my bones if you weren't in the room?" He asked with a grin as he opened all four doors of the car to let the heat out. His wife looked at him across the roof of the vehicle.

"She was pretty professional," the Angela admitted grudgingly. "I can't see how she does what she does, but at least she didn't act sleazy." She put her hand on the seat to check its temperature and then sat down. He joined her and turned the air conditioning on full blast as they headed to lunch at a Mexican restaurant they had spotted on the ride to the motel that morning. "I guess you would have been okay by yourself," she conceded.

He nodded and squinted at the sign in the distance. "Don thought everyone would be flattered and try to impress us. We may bring out the professional side in people rather than the sleazy side."

"Maybe." She thought for a moment. "She's still pretty intimidating, though. Even dressed conservatively, you can tell she's got a killer body, and you sit there thinking…" She paused again. "But she was interesting. I'll give her that."

"Definitely, but I doubt everyone is going to be like her. Don admitted he was throwing us a couple of ringers at the beginning. When we get down to the last round of interviews, it's going to get pretty boring. It always does." He pulled into the restaurant parking lot. Technically the storefront eatery was walking distance from the motel, but taking the car avoided an unappealing trek through crowded parking lots.

He looked over as he parked the car. "Did you notice that Layla was more analytical about the industry and the market than about herself? She skimmed over the personal questions."

"Yeah," Angela replied, "but I think you can read between the lines pretty well: She thinks having sex on camera is work and claims not to feel degraded while she's doing it, but the public's attitude towards it pisses her off." She put on her sunglasses as she got out of the car. "Her response to your feminist question was telling. She was pretty insulted by the notion that she doesn't have free will in making decisions, that she's some kind of victim."

"You're probably right, but I can't ask book reviewers to look between the lines," he explained. "I need juicy quotes."

"Then you're going to have to ask better questions. For good quotes, you need to get people going."

"Like how?"

"We saw that movie yesterday." She paused for a moment while a waitress sat them down and then continued when she was out of earshot. "Ask some specific questions about the kinds of scenes we saw: What were you thinking the first time you did a scene with a woman? How long does it take to get prepared for a bondage fantasy? Does your jaw get sore from going down on a guy for a half hour?" She giggled. "Does size matter?"

Stanley realized she was right. It had been a good first interview, but he would have to be less prudish if he really wanted to get the information he needed to write a good book. He looked at her and grabbed her hand. "I'm glad you came."

# VIII

# THE FREUDIAN

"Sweetheart, could you check the audio from this morning and make sure that the levels were right?" Stanley sat down and browsed through his notes from the first interview, adding additional questions in the margin of his yellow legal pad while Angela donned a pair of headphones and listened to the playback. A large *burrito de carne asada* with extra guacamole was rumbling ominously deep in his gut.

"Sounds fine." She took off the head set and sipped on the soda refill she had saved from lunch. "How much will it cost to get the audio transcribed?"

"A small fortune, but the grant covers it." He heard a soft knock on the hotel room door. "Are you ready?"

He opened the door and greeted Kristy Page, a young brunette who had sat across the table from them the night before. His formal handshake and introductions seemed to amuse her. She plopped down in the interview chair and grabbed a bottle of water from the end table. "Don told me you're an old friend from college. Where did you guys go to school?"

"University of Virginia."

"Cool."

"Speaking of Don," Stanley added, "have you spoken to him since last night? I can't get a hold of him."

"No," she shook her head vigorously, "but he must be wrecked. Jade was not only his biggest star, but he had a serious thing for her." Johansson had said Kristy was twenty-three, but she looked much younger. She was petite, slim-waisted with a small pert bust. If she had implants, they were only a modest addition. Her thick hair was cut in a stylish bob that emphasized her high cheekbones and deep blue eyes. There was a freshness about her that Layla might have had ten years earlier. She managed to make her simple outfit of blue jeans and a t-shirt seem dangerously sexy.

"Don told me that you went to school too."

"Oh yeah, I did two years in the psych program at Cal-Irvine before I started working for Eden."

"Do many actresses have an education?"

"Well, Nina Hartley has a nursing degree, and I heard Sharon Tyler went to graduate school somewhere, but most of the girls just have high school diplomas, if that." She bit her lower lip and tried to come up with some more examples then shrugged her shoulders and took a sip of water.

Stanley nodded at Angela who clicked a button on the side of the camera. "Why don't we get started?"

* * *

INTERVIEWER: Could you tell us your age, and place of birth?

SUBJECT: I'm twenty-three years old, and I was born in Milton, Wisconsin.

INTERVIEWER: How long have you been making adult films?

SUBJECT: About a year.

INTERVIEWER: How did you get into the business?

SUBJECT: Well, I came to Los Angeles to go to school, and my sophomore year I met this girl in one of my classes. Her boyfriend had dropped out and was running a soft core website featuring college girls, mostly just college-age girls as it turned out. She asked me if I wanted to make five hundred dollars for a weekend of getting my picture taken. She showed me the website. It was really nicely done, no banner ads like "SoCal Sluts Spreading for You!" or anything like that. Just a site for guys with a particular girl-next-door type of fantasy. I figured, what the heck, it's easy rent money, so I went. The photographer was really polite and easy to work with, so I continued to do it periodically.

INTERVIEWER: Did you see this as a big step?

SUBJECT: I was a little worried about my mom finding out, but I figured the chances were pretty remote. But of course they always find out! I didn't think my dad would mind, given the amount of porn he consumed when I was growing up. So, if he objected he was going to look like a prime hypocrite.

INTERVIEWER: Is that necessarily so? Couldn't he enjoy his porn without wanting his daughter to do it? He might have had a vision of these women that didn't fit his image of his daughter.

SUBJECT: Probably. He's not talking to me right now, so you may have a point.

INTERVIEWER: Do you wish you hadn't done it?

SUBJECT: [Silence] I don't know. I like the respect that I'm getting from people in the industry. And if *Toys in Babeland* goes nationwide, everyone's going to know who I am. Have you seen it yet?

INTERVIEWER: No.

SUBJECT: It's an excellent movie! I've got one super hot girl-girl scene in it and a lot of dialogue. I don't think that this kind of opportunity would have happened any other way. I'm having a lot of fun, so I guess I regret my dad's attitude more than I regret my decision.

INTERVIEWER: How did the transition from soft-core to hard-core happen?

SUBJECT: About a year after I started, the website offered me triple my normal pay to give my boyfriend a blow job on camera. By this time, my folks already knew, so I figured what the hell? For ten minutes work, I made the biggest paycheck of my life. It was more than I made in a month as a lab assistant in the Psych Department.

INTERVIEWER: So, it really is all about the money for you?

SUBJECT: [Laughs] You have no idea what a loaded question that is. Every girl you talk to will tell you that they're in it for the money, except for the ones who pretend money is only incidental and say it's all about the 'great sex.' In one sense, of course, it is all about the money. I wouldn't work for free. The real question is what sort of personality traits lead you to accept the work in the first place. That's the juicy one.

INTERVIEWER: Well?

SUBJECT: Okay, here's what two years at Cal-Irvine gets ya! Seriously, I don't think that there's any single personality type in porn. You've definitely got one set of girls who are just plain rebellious. They've got issues with their family, with their high school, with their jobs, with society in general. Doing adult videos is basically a big "fuck you" to the world. Then, when they get inside the business, they meet a bunch of other people who also consider themselves rebels. Like some of the producers see themselves as spitting in Hollywood's face. Anyway, for the first time they're working with like-minded people, and they're getting a lot of attention and pats on the back. For some, it's essentially their first taste of adult approval. That hooks them more than anything.

INTERVIEWER: I've heard the word "family" used more than I thought I would.

SUBJECT: It's weird, isn't it? But for some it's the most normal family they've ever had.

INTERVIEWER: Would you put yourself in this category?

SUBJECT: No. At least not according to my therapist! He says I've got a sexual fixation. He says I'm reenacting the psychosexual dynamics of my childhood. He says I feel comfortable having sex on camera because it validates my sense of self.

INTERVIEWER: Um, could you put that in layman's terms?

SUBJECT: Well, he says that video sex is a fetish for me. Supposedly I don't have sex on camera because I'm horny, but because it releases tension from my childhood. When I fully understand this, he says, I'll no longer want to make adult movies.

INTERVIEWER: Do you believe it?

SUBJECT: I think he's half right. I was a sexually precocious kid. I wasn't molested or anything, but I started having sex with my boyfriend when I was fourteen. And I do find something satisfying about being primped for hours by a stylist and makeup artist and then being the center of attention on camera. I get pretty excited on the set. On the other hand, I don't think that self-awareness affects people's behavior much. Think about the guy who likes brunettes wearing stockings and garters. According to Psych 101, this guy's mother's a brunette and he saw her in stockings and garters as a child. But guess what, you can explain all this to him and he'll still like brunettes in lingerie! And who cares? It's a harmless fixation.

INTERVIEWER: I read where guys who get off on pictures of women peeing probably spent a lot of time hanging on their mother's knees as toddlers as she sat on the toilet.

SUBJECT: Exactly. And so what? Let them get off on pee pee porn. No one's getting hurt. I had a feminist professor who tried to prove to us that all porn was about violence. I think it's way more about fixation. The pee pee porn guys are not fantasizing about hurting anyone. They're getting some kind of comfort.

INTERVIEWER: Would you want to generalize this to performers as well?

SUBJECT: (pause) Good question…I don't know. You see, I've met a lot of control freaks out there too. There's definitely a subset of women in the industry who've been dominated by men their whole lives. Making a man come provides a temporary sense of control, of being in charge for once. And if you're a porn star, you can magnify that feeling by a couple of thousand, because that's how many guys are whacking off to your video! And, of course, getting into the business reproduces both the problem and solution. It's still a very male dominated industry and there's plenty of shithead managers and boyfriends out there ready to latch onto you. So, if you've had an abusive or manipulated background, then the porn scene can be very familiar. You can rapidly oscillate between being controlled and being controlling.

Of course, some people just need money for drugs. But that's begging the question too. There's a whole lot of women with drug problems who don't go out and shoot porn.

INTERVIEWER: Do you see any commonalities in all these personality types?

SUBJECT: I see a lot of people desperate for a sense of security. The business does provide that to a certain extent. Everybody knows everybody else, and there's always a shoulder to cry on when things go wrong. But it's a pretty sad and dysfunctional kind of family. That's why I've tried to keep my friendships with people outside the industry. That's hard, but it's worth it. Whatever sense of security you get from being in the business comes at the cost of long-term stability in your life. You can forget about having a romantic relationship with anyone outside the business. It never works. I mean never. I have less real sex now than when I was in college.

INTERVIEWER: Is anyone in the business because of a conscious career choice? Like: I could be a banker or a porn star...hmmm, I think I'll be a porn star.

SUBJECT: Nice! When that happens, you'll know that porn has been truly mainstreamed! I don't know. Television now certainly teaches kids that shaking your booty in a man's face is a normal thing to do. Paris Hilton has her own television show, for god's sake! *Girls Gone Wild* videos are advertised on regular television channels. Maybe the generation growing up now will think porn is normal. On the other hand, there's something pretty reactionary about those MTV rap videos. I find some of them really demeaning, so maybe it's all just a step backward. I don't know. When it comes to sex, things are always pretty complicated . . .

* * *

Stanley looked at his watch as the young actress said goodbye and left. To his delight and surprise, she had talked for over ninety minutes. Two interviews down and one to go. He walked to the bathroom and splashed some cold water on his face. "I saw a Starbucks a couple blocks from here," he yelled to Angela. "Do you want something? We've got a thirty minute break."

"Nah. I'm going to stay put." She watched him leave and then stood up and stretched. She checked the quality of the two recordings that she had just made and then popped a new memory card in the machine. Satisfied that they were ready for the next girl, she sat down where Kristy had been and opened a bottle of sparkling water. She stared into the digital camera and wondered how hard it would be to tell two strangers the intimate details of her life. Probably like falling off a log if you had sex on camera for a living. She brushed her hair back and addressed the camera.

"Hi! I'm Sandy Sweetcheeks and I just did a scene with three Chippendale dancers and a large cucumber." She rolled her eyes and took another sip of water. The interview with Kristy had been both easier and harder than the one with Layla. As a former student, Kristy was a more familiar and engaging personality. But she also oozed a more immediate sex appeal than Layla. Just being in the same room with the young college dropout had made her feel stodgy and matronly.

She sighed. If they did three interviews a day, then they would be done in two weeks. She wondered if she could convince Stanley to stay a couple of extra days to do some tourist stuff. Visiting Disneyland would be a lot of fun. Her best family vacation as a child had been to Orlando. She and her brothers and sisters had run wild for three days, trying out every ride and attraction a half a dozen times. Playing tourist would be fun, not to mention that a couple more nights in the hotel might lead more quickly to having kids of their own to take on future vacations.

# IX.

# THE VICTIM

A sharp knock on the door interrupted Angela's reverie, and she peered through the peephole to see who was there. An impatient middle-aged woman stood in the hallway looking at her watch. Angela cracked open the door.

"Can I help you?"

"I'm Susan Jenkins. I have an appointment with Professor Hopkins." She looked past Angela for a sign that she was in the proper place. "I hope I have the right room."

"This is it. Come on in." She introduced herself and offered the woman a fresh bottle of water. "Stanley just ran out to get some coffee. He'll be back in a moment. We weren't expecting you until three thirty."

"Traffic was lighter than I thought." She looked to be somewhere in her early forties, tall and slim, with thin lips and large brown eyes. She wore a long print skirt and a white blouse buttoned almost to the top of her neck. Unlike the first two interviewees, it was difficult to imagine her performing. "I hope this isn't going to take too long. I've got to get back at work this afternoon." She looked at her watch again.

"We'll get started as soon as Stanley gets back," Angela replied. "Are you filming this afternoon?"

"Good lord, no! Didn't anyone tell you? I've been out of the business for years now."

"Oh…"

"Aren't you doing some sort of exposé of the porn industry?"

"I don't know if you'd call it an exposé. My husband is studying five different professions, including adult films."

She arched her brow. "I wouldn't call making porn movies a profession. That gives it a dignity it totally lacks."

"I think Stanley uses the term pretty loosely." She tried to change the subject, but could not think how. "We're just collecting data at this point." Much to her relief, she heard a key being inserted in the door and got up to let her husband in. "Susan is already here," she told him, "and I think she's anxious to get started."

"Great." He cast a forlorn glance at the blueberry muffin in his hand. "Let's not keep her waiting."

* * *

INTERVIEWER: Could you tell us your age and place of birth?

SUBJECT: I'm thirty-two years old and I was born in Pasadena, California.

INTERVIEWER: How long have you worked in the adult video industry?

SUBJECT: Like I told your wife, I quit five years ago. Before that, I was in movies for three years and modeling and dancing for five years before that. I worked under the name Sheila Easy.

INTERVIEWER: How did you get into it?

SUBJECT: My boyfriend and I were huge coke heads. He figured that I could make a lot of money as a model, and he was right. I made even more money dancing, but we snorted up every penny.

INTERVIEWER: What did he do?

SUBJECT: In theory, he was my manager. In reality, I was just a way to support his habit. That was the only good thing about doing movies. He couldn't handle me having sex with other guys, so he eventually left.

INTERVIEWER: How did you make the transition into adult videos?

SUBJECT: Make the transition? Like I had any choice in the matter! I'd been modeling for a couple of years. I hated it, but we needed the money. I was in every men's magazine that you can name. Anyway, one day I got sent out for a shoot and I saw a way bigger crew than usual. With most photo shoots, there's just a photographer, a makeup girl, and maybe a light guy. There must have been a dozen people at this house up in Topanga Canyon. I'm looking around trying to figure out what's going on and no one would say anything more than, "Sheila, try the breakfast buffet; it's great." Finally, this guy introduced himself as the director and told me what he expected me to do. I totally freaked out and called my agent.

INTERVIEWER: You didn't want to do the shoot?

SUBJECT: Of course, I didn't. My agent thought that I would be impressed by how much money I'd make, but I said no way. Then, he informed me that he had made a commitment to the production company for three films and that we'd be sued if I didn't go through with it. Well, I couldn't afford to pay a bunch of lawyers to fight it, so I figured I'd grit my teeth and do the movie.

INTERVIEWER: Why didn't you stop with the couple?

SUBJECT: My agent said that he was having trouble getting modeling gigs for me; I needed to keep making videos in order to earn any kind of money. Since I was snorting two to three hundred dollars a day at that point, I didn't really have any choice. My family wasn't talking to me, and my only friends were in the business. They weren't going to help me quit. I was such a fool. I didn't see that they were all just bloodsuckers.

INTERVIEWER: How did you eventually get out?

SUBJECT: I talked to a pastor who finally got me to see how I had been used. I was a very trusting person who had gotten into a business where you shouldn't trust anybody. He helped me to see my years as a porn star as a long black tunnel that I had to emerge from. I wasn't a bad person; I was just forced to do bad things.

INTERVIEWER: What are you doing now?

SUBJECT: I've got a great job at a non-profit agency that works with abused girls and runaways. I've even gotten to do some public speaking about my experiences at fund raising events and on a couple of talk shows. I hope what you're doing isn't going to be some sort of whitewash. This business is pure exploitation.

INTERVIEWER: I can honestly say that we have no agenda. We're just interviewing as many people as we can and collecting their perceptions.

SUBJECT: Well, beware the party line: [raising the pitch of her voice] *I love having sex on camera, especially anal sex! I wouldn't want to be doing anything else. I have multiple orgasms every time I screw on camera.* [back in normal voice] Take everything with a grain of salt.

INTERVIEWER: We certainly plan to.

SUBJECT: What you might want to do is read Linda Lovelace's book, the one where she describes how she was forced to have sex during the filming of *Deep Throat*. For me, that book captures the whole spirit of the porn enterprise. She describes a gun literally being held to her head.

INTERVIEWER: Have you seen anything that extreme yourself?

SUBJECT: Not myself, but it happens! Linda really had to struggle to get out of the business. Me too. If Jesus hadn't plucked me up, I don't know what would have happened. There is no other way to escape. Even if you stop doing movies and take a regular job, until you've found Jesus, you're still doing porn in your heart...

* * *

"That was weird," Angela commented after the interview ended and she turned off the equipment. "Susan said out loud all the things that I've been thinking about porn, but I really didn't like her that much."

"Me neither," her husband replied as he turned off the lights in the room and opened the door for her. "Too sanctimonious by half." He put his arm on the small of her back while they walked down the stairs. "Layla and Kristy are a lot more likeable, even though they're still working."

They got in the car and pulled into traffic. The boulevard leading back east to their hotel was stop-and-go as far as they could see. They crept forward a block before getting wedged behind a delivery truck in front of a strip club. "Stan?"

"Yeah?"

"What do you really think about all this stuff?" Angela understood the need to collect information, she did it all the time for her articles, but the point of the collection was to gain some perspective and then pass judgment. If anything annoyed her about her husband's job, it was the alleged inappropriateness of actually expressing a personal opinion.

"What do you mean?"

"You're always the objective observer, gathering data and writing it up." She turned in the seat so that she could see him more easily. "But you've just spent six hours talking to porn stars in a hotel room: What do you really think?"

"I don't know. What do you think?"

"Stop being such a wimp!" She was not going to let him get away with turning the table. "If you were single, would you sleep with Kristy? Would you ban porno movies if you could? Is there a difference between what happens in a porn video and a club like that?" She gestured with her thumb to the Pink Pussycat Gentlemen's Lounge.

"Would I ban porn?" He skipped over the question about Kristy. "It's been banned at various times in various places and that's never seemed to work. Victorian England was a hotbed of porn even though it was totally illegal."

"That's not what I meant!" She yanked his seatbelt as the car inched forward toward the next stop light. "Do you think pornography is bad?"

"I don't even know what that means," he shook his head, refusing to be pulled into an argument. "I know you disapprove, but I don't see why I have to decide whether porn's bad or not. The first amendment protects most of it, so why do I need to take sides?"

"Don't you once in a while feel the need to commit to a position?"

"I'm not sure—"

"—Stan!"

He laughed as he fended off a playful slap. "Of course I do." The traffic started loosening up a bit and he began to roll forward steadily without having to press the brake. "By the time I finished interviewing carnival workers, I couldn't stand them. I don't think I'll ever go to the county fair again." Choking the devious little carnie bastards would have been even more fun, but scientific detachment forbade such measures. "But I'm not sure that I'd ban carnivals. That just seems pointless."

"We're just different," she concluded after digesting his response. "I'm always wanting to change the world and you're always looking at individual problems. We've had this argument before." She gestured to the right lane to indicate it was moving more quickly. "Alright then, do you feel guilty when you consume pornography?" Then she added with a mischievous grin, "And would you sleep with Kristy?"

He squirmed against the seat. "Look, I don't see why anyone should feel guilty about consuming free porn, but throwing money around in a strip club is clearly a different matter. That's direct support."

"What about paying for the movie we watched?"

He chewed his lip while he considered his answer. "I wanna do some more interviews first. Don might be right about some movies…"

"And Kristy?"

"If I were single, I'd do her in a heartbeat."

"You pig!" She smacked him with the back of her hand.

"Hey," he exclaimed as he finally moved into the fast lane, "you're the one who wants me to take more passionate positions."

In their hotel room, Stanley sat on the bed staring at the television screen. The announcer on the local NBC affiliate had just explained that Donald Johansson, aka Richard Ramrod, had been arrested for bludgeoning to death his top grossing star with a wooden paddle. The reporter added, with a knowing look, that drugs and alcohol appeared to have played a significant role in the crime.

The professor muted the television and tried to decide what was worse, watching a former friend flush his life down the toilet or having the same friend sabotage his own academic career. It seemed unlikely that the interviews would continue now, making it unlikely that his book would ever be finished, making it likely that he would soon be looking for another job. He felt guilty for equating his own worries with Johansson's, but could not help but wonder who else would be affected by the sensational crime.

"I guess it's a dark night for the adult filmmakers," he wondered somewhat absently.

"Or it might be celebration time," Angela replied.

"Huh?"

"Didn't you say that Don was putting a serious dent in the competition's profits? How many of the Women of Eden will want to continue to work for his company?" She turned off the television and stood up. "And surely the distribution deal is dead. No mainstream market is going to touch *Toys in Babeland* now. In some corners, this might be considered pretty good news."

"Maybe you're right." He sat thinking for a moment longer and then grabbed his keys. "Who knows? I'm wiped. Let's just go to dinner and see what happens tomorrow."

# X

# THE SHOW MUST GO ON

The next morning, the young couple arrived early at the interview hotel and sat gloomily reading the *LA Times* account of the murder while waiting for Shalya Devereaux, a young star currently working for Boudoir Films. The *Times* story provided no new information beyond a brief comment from a spokesperson at American Cinema Distribution confirming Angela's guess that the nationwide distribution of *Toys in Babeland* would be put on indefinite hold. Stanley refused to torture himself by looking at the clock, so he read through the front page stories and ploughed through the comics and the sports page before Angela finally cleared her throat.

"She's twenty minutes late."

"Maybe she's stuck in traffic." He snapped the pages of the newspaper back and folded the crossword puzzle into a neat square.

"Well, I'm giving her a few more minutes, then I'm going out and getting us some coffee."

When she got back from her coffee run, she found him alone, pouring over the real estate section of the paper and shaking his head at the cost of even the most modest house in Los Angeles County.

At the one hour mark, Stanley paced and looked through the curtains to see if any likely candidates were headed up to the room. All he could see were waves of heat rising off of the asphalt parking lot. He finally forced himself to sit down and read the part of the paper that he usually avoided: the business section. On the bottom of the first page was a description of the broken deal that Eden Studio had struck with American Cinema Distributors. The deal was newsworthy, the paper explained, because of the nature of the film, not because of the contract terms which were modest by current standards. The story had been filed before news of the murder had scuttled the transaction, but it did contain one new bit of information. Eden Studio was described as "financially troubled," and he was reminded that Stan Matteson had alluded to money problems when he had visited Chimera Studios with Don.

As he finished, he was startled by a knock on the door. Angela got up to open it. It was ten fifty-five, nearly time for the second interview. A tiny brunette wearing tight designer jeans and a sleeveless blouse stood in the doorway.

"Come in!" Stanley stood up and extended his hand with an anxious smile. "I'm Professor Hopkins. This is my wife and audio engineer, Angela."

"Nice to meet both of you. I'm Ginger Porsche." She returned his smile and revealed a perfect set of white teeth. She had a glowing girl-next-door look that spoke of malt shops, picket fences, and chaste kisses at the prom.

"I'm so glad you came," he said with feeling. "Our first interviewee didn't show, and we were afraid that after Don was arrested people might not come."

"It's horrible, isn't it!" Ginger said emphatically as she sat down in the chair. "I was at the banquet with Stacey Ballentine; she's the newest Eden girl. She wasn't in *Babes*, but Don had promised her a starring role in the sequel. Anyway, I still can't believe what happened. I spilled wine all over my dress when Lanie screamed." She spoke breathlessly, as if reporting the latest gossip from her high school. "Hey, didn't I see you guys there too?"

"We were there," Stanley confirmed. "I'm an old friend of Don's from college." He looked at Angela. "It's hard to believe what happened."

"Me too! I've done a couple of videos for Don, and he was about the nicest guy in the business. Never broke his word to anybody. Stacey couldn't believe it either." She took a piece of chewing gum out of her back pocket and popped it in her mouth. The gesture made her look even younger. "Love can make people do pretty crazy things though."

"Love?"

"Yeah, didn't you know? Don had the hots for Jade, but she wouldn't give him the time of day." She blew a small bubble and continued. "Not that she went out with anybody else either. That was part of her mystique, I guess. Biggest bitch in the business. She had no boyfriends or girlfriends; she stayed totally away from everybody. But put her on camera and holy shit! Directors used to tell her to stare straight into the camera during a scene. That's usually a no-no, but she'd just look through the lens and send this *please do me* message straight to the dude watching the movie on his sofa."

"Are you sure Don was that interested in her?"

"He was totally obsessed with her. It must have been hard for him in the editing room, watching her eyes roll back in her head while somebody else fucked her." She shrugged her shoulders. "On the other hand, you better get used to it if you're going to fall in love with a porn star."

He nodded at Ginger and then looked over at his wife. "Why don't we get started?"

\* \* \*

INTERVIEWER: Could you tell us your age and place of birth?

SUBJECT: I'm nineteen and I was born in Whittier, California.

INTERVIEWER: Have the events at the Eden party made you rethink your present career?

SUBJECT: Wow...I don't think so. I mean, bad things happen in almost every kind of job. Even the post office isn't safe! I'm still more worried about AIDS and stuff like that.

INTERVIEWER: Have you ever seen other instances of violence?

SUBJECT: Related to work?

INTERVIEWER: Yes.

SUBJECT: Not really. Unless you want to count jealous boyfriends as part of work. In that case, I've seen some pretty ugly scenes. You'd be amazed how many guys will date a porn star knowing what she does for a living and then at some point turn around and accuse her of being a whore because she's doing a scene and looking like she's enjoying it too much.

INTERVIEWER: And what happens when a guy can't handle it?

SUBJECT: Well, they usually make your life miserable until they finally pack up and leave, but sometimes you'll see girls show up on the set with a black eye. Then the shit hits the fan. It makes the video look bad.

INTERVIEWER: We had someone yesterday who insisted that some directors threaten physical violence to get their actresses to perform. Have you seen this?

SUBJECT: [laughs] You need to go down to Olde World Modeling when they're having a casting call. When you've got that many girls showing up and begging for parts, why the hell would you need to threaten someone?

INTERVIEWER: Have you ever done something that you didn't want to do?

SUBJECT: Sure. Last week, I was giving Stiff Masterson a blow job in *Win One for the Stiffer*, and he's getting all hot and sweaty from the lights and about every thirty seconds I'm getting hit with a drop of sweat off his gross hairy chest right on my face. I'm telling you, it was like Chinese water torture, but he's getting ready to pop, so I don't want to break off the scene. It's times like that when I start wondering whether I should go to junior college.

INTERVIEWER: What kind of other jobs have you had?

SUBJECT: I was working at a department store at the mall when I started doing videos. I used to work at Burger King in high school. Talk about gross! There was plenty of stuff I didn't want to do there either.

* * *

When Ginger left, Stanley consulted the interview schedule while Angela opened up a bottle of spring water. The interview had gone well. Ginger seemed to be one of a new breed of starlets heralded by the acceptance of the Paris Hilton and Pamela Anderson home sex videos. Beneath her bubbly surface was a businesswoman who balanced the costs and benefits of choosing pornography as her profession. He read the next name on the schedule and tossed the paper over to Angela.

"It looks like we've got some time this afternoon to go to the police station, flash your ID and make a statement if you need to." Angela had forgotten to put her driver's license in the clutch she had taken to the banquet and had been put on the police list of people who needed to report in.

"How come?" She put down her water and read from the page. "Two o'clock, Jade Delilah, Eden Studio." She clicked the memory card out of the recorder and stood up. "And I thought this was going to be a vacation. Let's find some food first and get this over with."

While she eased into the drive-thru lane at Taco Tico, he looked at the station address on the card that the police officer had given him and entered it into his wife's smart phone. He stubbornly clung to his old style cell, but he had to admit that some of the apps on his wife's new device were pretty helpful. If the battery lasted longer than twelve hours without recharging, he might be tempted to switch.

He leaned over his wife and told a large plastic head wearing a sombrero that he wanted a quesadilla and a coke. He checked his phone messages, and she grabbed a bag from the take-out window and pulled over into an empty parking space next to the restaurant. She handed Stanley his meal and took a sip from her diet soda.

They ate in silence and he recalled a surreal afternoon spent golfing on the afternoon of 9/11. Once his classes were cancelled, he could not face spending a day at home watching the disaster rerun over and over on the television, so he had detoured to the university golf course. The links were packed with like-minded escapists, none of whom said a word about what had happened in New York City earlier in the day.

He looked over at his wife and saw her take a bite and then make a face. "You should've known better than to order the Road Kill Taco."

"It's not that," she replied when she was done chewing.

"What? Are you nervous about talking to the cops?"

"Not really." She set the food down on her lap. "But I saw something at the banquet that I need to tell the police about."

"What?"

"You know how I was watching people during dinner? I noticed Don lean over and whisper something in Jade's ear. About five minutes later, I saw him get up and leave. And then Jade left a couple of minutes after that."

"I'm sure a lot of people saw them leave the dais." He wadded up his wrappers, stuffed them into his empty cup and jammed it in a paper bag.

"Yeah, and others probably saw him whispering to Jade too, but I still need to tell the police." She grimaced and took a sip of her drink. "It makes me feel kinda slimy. Isn't that stupid?"

"No," he explained, "I get it. If you had to testify, it would make you part of a sleazy story carried on every network and cable news channel." He reached out the window and tossed his garbage into a cactus shaped bin on the side of the parking lot. "If you think *you* feel queasy, don't forget who supplied him with the murder weapon."

"Oh Christ, you don't think we'll have to come back here for the trial, do you?"

"I doubt it. Would you take this case to trial if you were Don's lawyer?"

With Stanley giving directions, Angela got the rental car to the station in less than twenty minutes. It was a stylish new building made of light colored brick and tile. Only the phalanx of police cruisers parked in front gave away that it was not a public library or an office complex. She parked behind the building, and they held hands as they walked around to the lobby. They passed through the metal detector one at a time and asked the guard for directions.

He pointed down the hallway to the left. Police officers, civilian employees, and lawyers bustled past them as they searched for the room. Once there, a female officer reached for the witness list and asked them their names.

"Professor Hopkins?" She gave Stanley a curious look. "We've been trying to get a hold of you for hours. Hang on. Let me check with the detective." Stanley looked over at his wife and shrugged his shoulders as the officer spoke on the phone. When she hung up, she sent Angela further down the hall and asked her husband to take a seat.

"Do you know what this is about?"

The sturdy blond officer shook her head. "All I know is that the prisoner has been asking for you." She looked over his shoulder and nodded to someone behind him.

"Professor Hopkins?" A tall man in a dark brown suit was walking toward him. He was about fifty years old, broad-shouldered with graying hair. His ruddy face looked incapable of any expression other than disapproval. "I'm Detective McCaffrey. Do you have any idea why Mr. Johansson has been so insistent on seeing you today?"

"No, sir." He normally never called anyone 'sir,' but the detective's demeanor seemed to demand some kind of honorific. "Don's an old friend from college. We just renewed our acquaintance when my wife and I came out to Los Angeles to do an academic study of adult film stars."

McCaffrey raised his eyebrows, but offered no further comment before leading him out of the room and down another hall past a security check point. The holding tank looked more like a prison than a police station.

"We would have transferred him to the county lockup by now, but we've got a little bit of an issue," he offered cryptically. "Were you at the banquet the other night?"

"Yes, my wife and I had a table at the back."

"Did you see either the victim or Mr. Johansson leave the dais?"

"No. At some point I noticed Don was no longer up there, but I didn't see either of them leave. Angela saw him whispering to Jade before he left." McCaffrey nodded and made a brief notation in his note pad. They passed through another metal detector and walked to a small interview room. "Do you know what this is about?" He had to pass through so many doors, he felt like he was in the opening credits of an old *Get Smart* episode.

"Someone will be waiting outside. Just yell if you need help." With that admonition, McCaffrey opened one more door and Stanley saw Don Johansson seated behind a table, hands and legs shackled.

The prisoner looked up with fevered eyes and a grim smile. "Boy, am I glad to see you."

# XI

# HAPPENSTANCE

Angela sat in the waiting room wondering how long the police would keep her husband. To her surprise, the interview with Officer Greene had taken the better part of an hour. Several other people had seen the porn director whisper to Jade before he had left the dais, so her story confirmed what the police already knew. The officer had taken far more time asking how she knew the suspect, why she and her husband had come to Los Angeles, and how the fraternity paddle had come to be in the suspect's possession. He took notes slowly and deliberately as she spoke. When he looked up, his judgmental squint told her that decent people do not get mixed up in the murder of a porn star.

"So, your husband took the bat out of the attic and brought it to Eden Studio as some sort of a thank you gift?"

"That's right, officer. He was grateful to Mr. Johansson for facilitating the interviews."

"So, when we finish fingerprinting the paddle, we're likely to find your husband's prints on it too?" This question took her aback, but she realized it was likely that both their prints were on the murder weapon.

"I suppose. You might find mine too. I think I touched it before Stan left." He looked at Angela as if witnesses did not usually confess to having their fingerprints on murder weapons. When he was done, he gave her his card and asked her to call him if she remembered anything else. She walked back to the lobby feeling every bit as tainted as she had feared.

Stanley stood and stared at his former friend. The producer seemed to have aged ten years over night. The wrinkles around his eyes were no longer just laugh lines, but deep creases of pain and confusion. The professor sat down across the table and wondered what he should say. Despite the circumstances of the crime, his first impulses were civility and sympathy. *Nice lobster at the party. Do you think it's going to rain tomorrow? Did you really do it?*

"Thanks for coming." Johansson gasped with relief and leaned toward his visitor. "You've got to help me."

"Help you?"

"Yes." The prisoner looked exhausted, yet his eyes were burning brightly. Stanley wondered, just as he had days before, whether this intensity was a sign of fierce intelligence or some sort of unhinged mania. "You're the best hope I have left."

"Don, what are you talking about?"

"You're the only one who can get me out of here. You've got the smarts to—"

"What the hell are you talking about? Don, have you talked to your lawyer yet?"

"My former lawyer, you mean?" He gave a bitter little laugh. "Oh yeah, I've talked to him. The guy comes in here, we talk for a while, and then he explains how after some maneuvering we might be able to plead the charges down to second degree murder or manslaughter. He's a public defender burn-out with a caseload of two hundred felonies. Two hundred! How much time do you think he's going to spend on a case where his client is found holding the murder weapon?"

"Public defender?" Stanley sat straight up in his chair and asked skeptically. "You were talking to the public defender?"

"Yeah. I suppose I shouldn't be so hard on him. I'd think I was guilty too, if I were him." He leaned forward and rested his elbows on his knees.

"What does your own attorney say? Why are you even talking to the public defender? Why haven't you called in the dream team?" Stanley waited for an explanation.

"That would be nice," came the wistful reply. "My attorney told me that once I pay him the seventy-five thousand that I currently owe, he'll be quite happy to help. But there's no chance of that. I'm leveraged up to my eyeballs. Without the money from the distribution deal for *Babes*, Eden Studio is bankrupt. And so am I."

"What about your house and car?"

"Both rented." He took a deep breath. "I gambled and lost. The kind of pictures that I wanted to make, the kind of studio that I wanted to run…well, it's a very expensive proposition. I needed the influx from *Babes* to pay off my debts and show investors that my business model can work. I was going to take the studio public sometime next year." He clenched his fists and ground them into his thighs. "Now, regardless of what happens to me, Eden Studio is done."

"I'm sorry, Don." He could see the desperateness of his friend's situation. His life was as messy as a laundry basket in a nursing home. On the other hand, if he had killed Jade Delilah, then he deserved whatever he got. "I see." Stanley finally put two and two together. "You've got no choice but the public defender. And he, uh…doesn't inspire much confidence."

"That's not my only choice." He looked up and stared hard at his friend. "I've fired him. Tomorrow at the arraignment, I'm going to exercise my right to represent myself."

"Are you crazy? You don't know anything about the law!"

"Hey, I watch *Law and Order* every week." He gave an ironic snort. "But I'm not counting on going to trial and outwitting the prosecutor. The real killer has to be caught before the case ever gets to trial."

Although the evidence pointed to the man sitting right before him, Stanley played along. "How are you going to find the killer when you're stuck here?" It occurred to Stanley that the public defender probably had the right idea about trying to plead to a lesser offense. With the prime suspect found passed out, evidence of premeditation might be hard to come by. He may have worked summers in corporate firms, but criminal law and procedure were his best subjects in law school.

"That's why I need your help." Johansson's request sounded as casual as if he were asking to borrow a pencil. "You can help me do some digging." He leaned forward and pleaded with his friend. "I can't afford a private investigator, and you already know some of my employees and competitors. You've studied the industry. You're a skilled interviewer, and you have a law degree. Shit, interviewing people is your profession. I can't think of anyone else better qualified to figure out who did this."

Stanley was too shocked to object immediately. Even if he were comfortable with the insane proposition, which he most assuredly was not, this did not seem like a crime requiring much research. He studied the prisoner and tried to see even a single hint that his friend was not guilty. He resisted the conclusion that the tears running down the face of the accused were exculpatory.

"Don," he let him down slowly, "you've got to think this through more clearly. You need professionals to help you with this mess. Isn't there some way you could raise the money?" Tears didn't prove anything, but Stanley hated to see anyone look so hopeless.

The prisoner sat, shoulders slumped, drained of the energy that had animated him just minutes before. "My parents disowned me. My competitors are not going help me out. It'd just make them look bad, not to mention that it's not in their best economic interest."

"Don't you have any friends?"

"Apart from you?" He managed a weak smile. "Stan, any of my friends who have enough money are in the business. To all outward appearances, I just killed one of their own. I don't think they'll be organizing fundraisers for my defense anytime soon."

Stanley sensed that he was right. A notorious pornographer accused of brutally killing a beautiful woman was unlikely to generate much sympathy anywhere. He wracked his mind for another way to convince Don that the plan to use a sociology professor as a criminal investigator was preposterous. "Was the public defender really that bad? You said yourself, from an outside perspective, getting the charges pleaded down to a lesser offense would be a rational strategy."

"I didn't do it." He waited for Stanley to meet his gaze. "Look at me," he insisted. "I didn't do it."

He refused to look away, holding the professor's eyes for a long moment. This is crazy, Stanley thought. He's probably a sociopath who can lie more convincingly than regular people can tell the truth. Nonetheless, the pleading brown eyes begged to be believed, and he cursed the gene that made it so hard to say no to his parents, siblings, teachers, colleagues, wife and friends. He was determined to deny the crazy request, but Don's abject declaration of innocence demanded that Stanley at least hear the full story. He felt a sudden and unexpected resurgence of an ancient love for the law and asked his friend what had happened.

\* \* \*

Angela was standing and stretching when Stanley finally returned, her posterior sore from two hours on the unforgiving wooden seats in the waiting area. She jammed a nearly finished paperback into her purse as he walked slowly toward her, hands in his pockets, pensively biting the corner of his lip. Of one mind about escaping the station as quickly as possible, they slipped out of the room and the building without a word.

"They sure kept you long enough," she put a concerned hand on his shoulder once they were in the car. "What the heck did they want?"

"Huh? Oh, I only talked to the detective for a couple of minutes." He was looked out the window back at the jail. He rapped the glass with his knuckle before replying. "I spent the whole time with Don."

"Are you kidding me? Is that why the cops were looking for you?"

"Yeah. He wanted to talk to me."

"But why?" She did not like the thought of him alone with the man who had bashed Jade Delilah's face into an unrecognizable pulp. "That doesn't make any sense."

"Probably not. Didn't we see a donut shop around the corner when we drove in? Let's talk there. I need some caffeine."

In true California fashion, they drove the two blocks down the street and parked on the shady side of the familiar franchise. The business was decorated in bright pink and green, normally a garish affront to Angela's aesthetic sensibilities but now a welcome relief from the oppressive atmosphere of the police station. Apart from the young Indian girl behind the counter and an elderly man reading a newspaper, they were alone. She resisted the urge to order a Bavarian cream donut with her coffee and gave herself a mental pat on the back.

When they were finally seated in a window booth, with iced coffees in hand, Stanley recounted the bizarre meeting with Don. She listened intently and with increasing disapproval.

"Don claims that he was starting a new muscle relaxant and pain killer for his back on the night of the party. He can't remember exactly how many glasses of wine he had, but he began feeling woozy and nauseous on the dais, so he went back to his office. He remembers opening the door but nothing else until he was being hauled away by the security guards."

"Well, that's convenient." She leaned back in her chair and crossed her arms. Her own reconstruction of the crime was quite different. Don had whispered an invitation to Jade to come talk in his office. He came on to her there and she rebuffed his advances once again, maybe offering a nasty insult to his manhood. In a drunken rage, he had given in to his first violent impulse, and the result was a dead porn star flat the floor.

"The memory lapse is not necessarily convenient for him," Stanley explained. "If he had seen someone else in the room, he could point the finger at them."

"So, he says he's innocent, even though he has no memory of what happened?" Sometimes her husband could be truly dense. "Isn't the most generous explanation, even if you believe his story, that the drugs and booze pushed him over the edge?"

"Pain killers, muscle relaxants, and alcohol are all depressants, Angie. Passing out is just as possible as rage, especially with someone like Don who's not naturally a violent person."

"But the first story you ever told me about him was violent! He beat up your frat brothers over that girl." Getting her husband to admit the obvious could be a challenge sometimes.

"That was righteous anger, not homicidal rage, and that story is fundamentally about treating women with respect, not killing them. Before last night, I would have thought that he was incapable of committing this kind of crime. Why should I change my opinion now?"

"Well," she explained as if he were a third grader, "maybe because he was found next to a dead woman with a bloody bat in his hand." Stanley was silent, and she checked out the traffic backing up on the boulevard before turning back to him. "Do you really think there's a chance in hell that he didn't do it?

"I don't know, but he wants me to help him find out."

"Find out what?"

"Who killed Jade Delilah." She searched for any sign that he was joking and saw none. He drained the last bit of his coffee and leaned back. "He wants me to find the real killer."

She laughed. "Did you tell him to look in the mirror? Or maybe he should ask O.J. for help." He did not respond to her barb, so she reminded him of some facts that he conveniently seemed to have forgotten. "Are you seriously thinking about helping him? Don't you remember what Ginger Porsche told us? He was in love with Jade but she wouldn't give him the time of day. If there's a more common motive for murder, I'd like to know what it is. Did he admit to you that he loved her?"

"Yeah," he answered, "he said he loved her and that she didn't love him. He said she had some problems in her childhood that needed working through before she could really be with any man."

"Don't you think that's an odd thing to say about a porn star?"

"I don't know. Maybe 'being with someone' means loving them. Maybe she drew a line between sex and love." He shook his head and wiped a coffee drip off the table with his napkin. "Anyway, he didn't get into her problems, whatever they were. He didn't hate her because she rejected him. He was absolutely convincing about that. By the time he was done talking about her, he was bawling like a baby."

She bit back a sarcastic comment. One of her roommates in college had been abused by a boyfriend who later wept outside their door begging for forgiveness. Guilt and penitence explained many a fit of sobbing. "So what are you going to do?"

"I don't know, Angie." He looked out the window and paused for a moment. "He wants me to be his investigator in the case. He's representing himself because he's broke and doesn't trust the public defender. He said I'm his last chance to find out what really happened."

"You've got to be kidding me. He must still be high." Then she saw something frightening in her husband's eye. The same kind of look he sometimes gave an expensive sports car that they really could not afford. "You're not thinking of doing it, are you?" Something in his eyes gave away the temptation. "But what about the book?"

He offered an explanation that sounded rehearsed. "The book project would provide pretty good cover for talking to people. You know the woman who discovered the body? She's already on our interview list. I'd have a great excuse to go back to the heads of the other studios and to talk to Jade's friends and family. We could keep doing our regular interviews but expand them with questions about the crime."

"Alright," she paused to regroup. Emphasizing the book was an obvious attempt to anticipate her objections. "Helping Don would take more than just a couple of weeks."

"You're right. I could end up staying here for the rest of the summer." He was unfazed by the realization. "Angela, you know how I've felt kinda stuck?" She did not want to admit that he had been unhappy, but she had noticed that he sometimes talked about work like it was a grind instead of a vocation. "I've sort of been sliding through life and this has reached out and grabbed me. I know it's hopeless, but I keep thinking about the girl in the frat house."

He traced a circle with a drop of coffee and then looked into her eyes. She looked away. Soul-baring was not something he did often, and it made her uncomfortable. "I just kept playing pool while those guys were going to rape that girl. Don was different. He charged in and prevented me from being an accomplice to a crime." She studied him carefully, unsure how to respond. He shrugged his shoulders. "I don't know if he killed Jade, but I owe him something, even if he did."

"Oh."

"I know what you're thinking," he spoke quickly, "but nothing is going to put the book off schedule. We'll do all the interviews and by the time we have the transcripts back, I'll be ready to write."

"How can you know that?" She shook her head. "You've never done anything like this before. You can't possibly predict how long it's going to take."

"You're right," he admitted, "but I told Don that I start teaching again the second week in August. That gives me almost three months. He understands that if I can't dig up anything by then, I'm going back."

"And the book?" She gave him a piercing look. Over the last two years, his progress had been glacial. It had taken him forever to complete each new section. Freud would have a great deal to say about this book project and his desire to be a professor. "You've got a tenure vote coming up."

"Don't worry." He reached out and touched her hand. "I haven't forgotten."

# XII.

# MACMILLAN AND WIFE

Stanley could not get to sleep. After hours watching thoughts spinning in his head, he turned on the small light beside his bed, found a pen and jotted down some notes on the back of the room service menu. First, he needed to get as much information as he could about Don and Jade during the regularly scheduled interviews. Beyond that, he needed to speak with everyone who worked in the Eden Studio office and also get back in touch with Don's competitors. He would also need the guest list from the party and the various forensic reports from the crime scene which should be forthcoming when Don informed the police of his decision. It would also be a good idea to search the office, although he had no idea what he should look for. At the bottom of the page he drew a number of diverging arrows. In every study he had conducted, the first set of questions and informants always led to secondary and tertiary investigations that were frequently more fruitful than the initial line of inquiry.

He had not been so excited by a project since his study of migrant farm workers had inadvertently uncovered an immigrant smuggling operation conducted by a major agricultural firm. That time he had backed off and kept quiet. The workers had told him that the pipeline to the U.S. was safer and cheaper than paying the typical ruthless coyote to cross the border, not to mention that whistle blowing would have trashed eighteen months of his research. This time, he would be free to take Don's case as far as it needed to go. No mindless IRB committee would be looking over his shoulder monitoring his questions. No panel of external reviewers would ignore a manuscript for six months and then toss it in the garbage. If he really got his teeth into something, he had a client who would want him to chew to his heart's content.

He looked over at Angela before he turned off the reading light. She was worried that he would screw everything up, and she was not being totally unreasonable—there was a danger of getting sidetracked. She had a hard time understanding the motivations of anyone who was not as focused as she was. She was like a laser beam pointed at journalism and a house full of kids, and her tenacity was one of the things he loved about her. She knew what she wanted and was passionate in pursuing it. Where would he be if she hadn't pursued him? He flicked a hair out of her face and she rolled over with a grump. As long as the book kept moving forward, she'd be okay with his new vocation.

\* \* \*

"Who's first today?" Stanley asked as they set up the interview room.

Angela looked at a sheet of paper on the table. "Tracey Savannah—no studio affiliation. Let's hope she comes on time."

He sat down on the bed and looked over the additional questions about Don and Jade he had added. Rather than include them in the formal interview, he decided that raising the murder casually before they started might prompt a more open response. Angela would make sure that the video camera and audio recorder were on the whole time, so he would not have to take notes. As soon as they heard a knock on the door, she flicked on the camera, and he waited until she was seated again to let Tracy in.

"I'm sorry I'm dressed like a slob," the chestnut-maned beauty said breathily, "but I'm working this afternoon, and I always go to the set in a sweat suit. No sense getting dressed up when you're going straight to hair and makeup." She shook

Stanley's hand, and when she turned to acknowledge Angela, he could not help but admire the wide swath of firm, tanned belly revealed by the cut of her outfit. The plush sweatsuit was not made for long distance running. The bottoms were cut low across the curve of her hips and the top barely covered her navel.

"Don't worry," he said honestly, "you look great. And thanks for coming! We were worried that people might not show up after what happened on Wednesday night."

"Wasn't that awful!" Tracey shook her head woefully.

"Were you there?"

"No. I got an invitation—I think everyone who ever made a film for Don got one—but I had a headache and my babysitter didn't show, so I stayed at home. Good thing too. I woulda hated getting stuck there afterward."

"How do you know about that?"

"God, I must have spent half the night on the phone. This is a real close group. I mean, everybody knows everybody, or at least has heard of everybody. The cell networks were probably on overload."

"Were you surprised by what happened?"

"Oh yeah, totally." She started to say more, but interrupted herself to take a quick glance at her cell phone and silence it. "At first, I figured it must have been her manager." Her face looked like she had just bitten into a dead squirrel. "What a total scumbag."

"Who do you mean?" Stanley cast a quick glance at the mirror behind Tracey to see if he could catch Angela's eye in the reflection.

"Well, I don't want to speak ill of the dead, but Jade was one of those bitches who just begs to be slapped upside the head." She seemed oblivious to her choice of words. "And her manager did just that, plenty of times. He's a big time meth dealer who doesn't take any shit from anyone. Some of the girls used to say that it was a good thing her skin was so brown, because it made covering up the bruises easier."

Stanley nodded his understanding and cast another glance at his wife. "So, in other circumstances this manager—what's his name?—would be the logical suspect."

She hesitated and then shrugged. "You could get his name from anybody. It's Chance Geary. And I've never met a bigger turd in my whole life." She spat out the words. "He's hit on, or hit, every girl he's ever met, including me. Made a pass at, that is. He's got about ten girls so strung out that they can barely work any more." She unexpectedly popped a bubble of chewing gem. "He's still a member of some biker gang."

"Why would a big star have someone like that as her manager?"

"God, do I look like a psychiatrist? He latched on to her real early; I know that." She reached over and took a bottle of water. "They sort of fed off each other, and in a lot of ways she's just as hard as he is. I guess she liked having an attack dog close by even if it bit her once in a while. Shit, I don't know."

"And Don?"

She sighed. "Don was like a good ol' golden retriever. I don't understand why he'd do this."

Stanley ran a theory past her, one that would save Don years of jail time if it could be proven. "Someone told me that he was pretty drunk and took some painkillers that night. Do you think he could have hit her accidentally, not knowing what he was really doing?"

She thought for a moment and tugged on her sweat suit. "I don't know. You're a friend of his, right?" He nodded. "You tell me."

Stanley answered her question with a shrug and guided the interview in the familiar waters of his study. Following up on the theme of managers, he discovered a whole new facet of the porn industry. Universally despised, porn star agents were, according to Tracey, the lowest form of managerial life. Each story she told was laced with fraud, betrayal, and abuse. Many of the agents were boyfriends, excited about dating and managing a porn star, but wallowing in insecurity and self-doubt that they covered with cheesy bravado. Most were amateurs, so they seldom got the best deals for their 'clients.' According to Tracey, relationships often ended with the discovery of embezzlement. When confronted, the man would inevitably justify the theft with some uncreative name-calling. She admitted that there were a few good managers out there but insisted that a girl was much better off learning the business quickly and representing herself.

The interview ended with a crisp rap on the hotel room door. While Angela got up to answer it, he thanked Tracey and wrote his cell phone number on the back of his business card. "Call me if there's anything else you think of."

Tracey took the card and bounced over to the buxom redhead that Angela had just let in. "Hi Jenna! Meet Jenna Jay-mes, the Queen of the Pearl Necklace." She gave her friend a quick peck on the cheek. "Have fun, Jen. He's a cutie." With quick wink at Angela, she nipped out of the room.

Stanley hid his embarrassment with a cough and invited Jenna to sit down. Angela signaled with a twirl of her finger that the equipment was still on. He excused himself to the bathroom and stranded his wife with the curvy redhead.

"Hi," she said as she extended her hand. "I'm Angela, Stan's wife and general gofer."

"Nice to meet you." Jenna wore a short, print dress. Its tailored cut emphasized the generous swell of her breasts, barely managing to stay within the range of acceptable daytime attire. Her most striking feature, however, was the teased and tousled hair that seemed to take up half of the room. She smiled. "Are you a professor too?"

"No, I'm just a real estate agent." The starlet looked confused, so she elaborated. "Stanley thought it would be fun if I came out with him and did the audiovisual stuff. After what happened Wednesday night, fun may not be the right word."

"Oh my god, were you at the party?"

"We were sitting at a table in the back. When that woman screamed, I just about had a heart attack." She could see Stanley standing in the doorway of the bathroom listening to how the conversation was going. She took his cue and asked Jenna about the party. She had been there but had not seen anything suspicious.

"Did you know Jade?"

"Well, not really. I worked with her once, but we didn't talk much."

"Did you know Don?"

"Sure, everybody did."

"Do you think he did it?"

"Sure, probably. I mean they found him with the murder weapon, didn't they?"

Struggling with Jenna's curt answers, she tried to come up with a better question. There must be something important left to ask, but she could not put her finger on it. Then she remembered what Tracey had said earlier. "What does 'Queen of the Pearl Necklace' mean?"

Jenna laughed and delivered a response that seemed deliberately calculated to embarrass the uninitiated Midwesterner. "Well, when a pop shot goes just right, the dribbles of cum can look just like a pearl necklace." She traced a wicked line across the top of her cleavage. "It's my specialty."

Angela looked at her husband with alarm, and he strode into the room holding two bottles of mineral water. "Would you like some water, Ms. James?"

"Yes, please." She unscrewed the bottle top and smiled. "Thanks."

"And thank you for coming! These are crazy times, and we appreciate you making time to talk to us. Did I overhear you saying that you knew Ms. Delilah?"

"Sort of. We did a three-way scene together once."

"What was that like? I've heard so many conflicting things about her. One person even suggested that her manager might have murdered her!" He spoke in a confidential tone, as if he were sharing a choice bit of gossip.

Jenna took a drink of her water and ignored the reference to Jade's agent. "Like I said, I didn't know her off the set, but she was an animal on camera. In the one scene we did, she clamped her mouth on me like she was never going to let go. She just kept going and going until I had the most intense orgasm of my life. And before I could catch my breath, she was stuffing me with this guy and rubbing me with her fingers. It was really an amazing scene. When we were done, she just got up and left. Didn't say a word. Me and the guy just shook our heads. It was like getting hit by a tornado."

"That's unusual, I take it."

"Yup," she said emphatically, "most sex on the set is pretty mechanical. As soon as you start to feel good, the director wants you to switch positions again. It can really be a grind, but that time was different. Really different."

"Do you remember who the director was? Was it Don?" He finished his water and set it on the floor next to his chair. "I guess you know that he and I went to college together."

"Yeah, she said that," Jenna replied without glancing at Angela. "Come to think of it, it may have been Don. It would have been like him to let the talent have a little fun."

"Did you like working for him?"

"Well, like I said: Work is work. But with Don it was usually stress free. You knew you would start and end on time. You knew that the check wasn't going to bounce." She settled back in her chair. "It's too bad that Jade's dead and that Don's in trouble."

"What do you think of the idea that Jade's manager may have been involved?" He studied his notes as he asked the critical question.

"When it comes to him, I've got nothing to say."

Stanley could tell from her body language that she would not offer any dirt on Chance Geary. He nodded to her. "Sometimes silence says a lot."

"Sometimes it does."

"Well," he picked up a pencil, "we've only got about ninety minutes left. Could you tell us how you got started in the business?"

\* \* \*

"You are so much better at getting people to talk than I am," Angela said as they lay in bed. They had capped off the long day of interviews off with an expensive seafood dinner and had mostly steered clear of conversation about the case. Despite the fancy meal and their swank accommodations, she was ready to go back to Illinois. After interviewing porn stars, she had a new appreciation for the mundane conversation of her middle-class home buying clients.

"Good interviewing just takes practice," he explained and then barked out a laugh. "Hey, you got her to explain what a pearl necklace is!"

"Woo hoo! Jenna thought I was being judgmental and clammed up."

"Well," he leaned back in the bed and smiled. "Weren't you?"

"Not really," she protested, "or at least I'm trying not to be judgmental of the women. I still hate the business."

"I'm not sure the actresses appreciate that distinction."

"Probably not." She puffed up her pillow and propped herself up. "I'll be so glad when this is over and we can go home. I talked to Nanci today, and she said a family was asking about me. Apparently, they've got a huge house with a pool that they want to sell. We could use the commission."

Stanley grunted and turned on the television to a twenty-four hour news channel. After a story about the wild rescue of some boaters caught in a flooded river, the anchor promised an update on the famous pornographer charged in the death of his bombshell star.

"Here we go," she said, "maybe he's confessed, and you're off the hook."

"Shhhh…" He turned up the volume.

"This morning in Los Angeles," a middle-aged reporter announced in front of the county courthouse, "adult film maker Donald Frisch Johansson pleaded innocent to all charges stemming from the death of Jade Delilah. The killing took place in his office on the night he was hosting an event to celebrate the nationwide release of his newest movie. In a surprise courtroom maneuver, he dismissed his attorney and stated that he would represent himself *pro se*. The judge ordered a psychological evaluation to determine whether Johansson was mentally capable of proceeding on his own. In addition, Johansson requested that the court permit a friend, Professor Stanley S. Hopkins, to conduct the investigation on his behalf." A picture from her husband's biographic page on the university website flashed on the screen. Angela groaned. She had always hated the sheepish grin in her husband's official faculty photo.

"Hopkins is a sociology professor and former fraternity brother of Johansson's. According to our sources, he is currently in Los Angeles interviewing adult film stars for his latest book." The reporter smirked into the camera. "Nice work if you can get it! Back to you, Karl."

Stanley clicked off the television and tossed the remote onto a chair. "This is not good," he sighed. "I thought I could just quietly talk to people and then report to Don what I found out." She turned off her light and put her head on his shoulder. "He must have had to give my name to the judge so the cops would send me the forensic reports." He turned the light off and wrapped his arms around her.

"Well," she offered, "you've had your fifteen minutes of fame."

"That's not why I'm doing this."

# XIII.

# JAILHOUSE BLUES

The unwelcome television report gave Stanley the sense that he had an official role to play. He felt an enlarged sense of responsibility and resolved to spend his evenings questioning witnesses and suspects who were not on the daytime interview schedule. In particular, he wanted to talk to Chance Geary, but before he did anything, he had to pay a visit to the Los Angeles County jail. As he and Angela had been drifting off to sleep, Detective McCaffrey had called and demanded to talk to him and his client the following morning. Angela reluctantly agreed to conduct the morning interviews by herself, and they shared a restless night, both obsessing on what awaited them the next day.

He hit terrible traffic and arrived twenty minutes late to find a stormy McCaffrey waiting for him in the large marble lobby of the county jail. Before he could say hello, the detective turned his back, waved his hand, and led them through the metal detectors and into the lock up. In a small interview room they found the prisoner and a portly man in light weight navy suit who got up and shook McCaffrey's hand.

"Hey Stu," the lawyer said to the detective, "good to see you."

He then turned to Stanley and extended his hand, "I'm Jerry Dermott, Mr. Johansson's lawyer, whether he likes it or not, at least until the judge grants his petition to represent himself." Dermott carried a stack of file folders under his left arm and seemed comfortable in the jail, like a doctor making his rounds on a busy morning. "It's departmental policy for me to be with the suspect during questioning until I'm officially relieved of duty."

Stanley could not see any overt signs of incompetence in the public defender, but Don had not complained about the attorney's skill, just his caseload and lack of zeal. He thought the prisoner was crazy to cast away the lawyer's expertise; he would not want to be without professional assistance in the intimidating atmosphere of the lockup. "Is there any chance that the judge will deny his motion?"

"I doubt it," Dermott explained. "He's sane, and he's got a college education. They let people with way fewer qualifications than that represent themselves." He shrugged his shoulders with a good-natured smile. "And besides, it's his constitutional right."

"Yeah," McCaffrey interjected, "and it's my constitutional pain in the ass. *Pro se*'s don't know what the fuck they're doing, and if you're really this guy's friend, you'll convince him to work with Mr. Dermott here."

The public defender nodded and added. "I'm pretty sure that I could convince the district attorney that the charge should really be manslaughter instead of murder one." Dermott looked over at the detective hopefully. "Right, Stu?"

"When bats fly out of my ass and fertilize the lawn," McCaffrey replied. He looked down at the prisoner sitting quietly in his steel chair and continued slowly. "I don't think we'll have any trouble proving premeditation here." Don flinched at the provocative bluff but stayed silent. He sat with his arms crossed, staring at the wall behind the detective. "Nope, no trouble at all. It seems that Mr. Johansson had a major league crush on his victim. Kind of an open secret, as far as we can tell. And we have a sworn statement by his secretary that he and Ms. Delilah had engaged in several violent arguments in his office. The same office, of course, where she was eventually murdered." He slapped the public defender heartily on the shoulder. "Sorry Jerry, but this is a death penalty case all the way."

"I didn't kill her," Don said through clenched teeth, eyes fixed on the detective.

"Don't say anything," the lawyer warned him.

"I just want him to understand that." He looked from the attorney back to the detective. "He should be out looking for the real killer."

"Sure, O.J.," McCaffrey saluted, "we'll get right on it."

"That's enough, Stu. Why don't we just get down to business?" Dermott sat and the other two men followed his lead. "You've got the preliminary forensics and the medical examiner's report?"

"Here's the crime scene report, but the M.E. won't be done until tomorrow." He pushed a manila folder over to the public defender. "I don't want to ruin the ending for you, but you'll want to pay close attention to the fingerprint evidence which shows Mr. Johansson's prints on the handle of the murder weapon. His prints and his alone."

Stanley scooted his chair closer so he could see the file. "Is it okay for me to read it too?"

"Why not," McCaffrey replied, "there's nothing but the obvious in there."

He digested the report quickly with a tingling sense that he had already found a hole in the state's case. "No prints other than Don's?" Stanley ventured after he finished. "That's odd."

"How so?"

"Well, for one thing my prints should be on there. I carried it from Illinois and handed it to him." He felt a surge of adrenalin as he blindsided the veteran detective. "Isn't that suspicious? Sounds like someone wiped his own prints off the paddle and then wrapped Don's hand around it."

"Ya think so, Sherlock?" McCaffrey responded with a laugh. "Isn't it more likely that your friend polished it up before he put it on the wall? That would be the normal thing to do, and it would explain why we only have one set of prints."

Stanley's face reddened but he did not reply. He saw Don mouthing, *good try.*

The detective continued. "Let's finish up, if we could. Professor Hopkins, you're the main reason we're here today.

Mr. Johansson told the court that you're gonna be his investigator. Now, unfortunately there's no official approval you need to get. In theory, anybody can investigate anything and the prisoner here is entitled to see all our reports, and he can give them to you if he wants." He punctuated his next statement with a pointed gesture at the professor. "But if I'm going to be dealing with you, then you're going to follow some ground rules. First of all, have you ever conducted a criminal investigation before?"

"Not as such," he said after a moment's pause.

"Not as such?"

"I did a semester-long practicum in the criminal defense clinic in law school. That involved interviewing witnesses and helping attorneys during arraignments and probable cause hearings." He had earned an *A* in the course but so had almost all the other students. All of his clients had pleaded guilty except for one woman who did not go to trial until after Stanley had graduated. He had enjoyed the clinic. It had been more relevant and engaging than Estate Tax or Partnership Law. "But I've never done an investigation for someone, if that's what you mean."

"That's exactly what I mean," McCaffrey stated bluntly. "So, you don't really know squat, do you? Well, let me begin your education. First, the law requires I send copies of these written reports and any exculpatory evidence that we uncover in the course of our investigation."

"I'd also like a copy of the guest list and access to Mr. Johansson's office," Stanley added, "so that I can conduct my own search."

"I can fax the list to your hotel, if you give me the number." McCaffrey tossed one of his cards to Stanley who wrote down the name of the hotel and his room number. "But I'll have to check whether we're done in the office yet." He pocketed the card without looking at it. Stanley got the impression that the detective did not like him, but he could only guess whether the resentment had something to do with him personally or just his siding with the defense. Maybe he got a bad grade in sociology in high school.

"Most importantly," McCaffrey continued, "we need to have a little talk about witness tampering. This usually isn't a problem with professionals, but when friends of the accused get involved in an investigation, there's a serious possibility that an interviewer will cross the line from mere questioning to an attempt to influence testimony. If that happens, charges will be filed, and you'll find yourself sitting where your friend is. Do you understand me?" The detective's expression left little doubt that he would love to carry out his threat.

"I think so."

"And this would include encouraging witnesses to be uncooperative with the police." He stood up and nodded at Dermott. "Not that we need any more evidence to build our case. Your client pretty much tied it up in a nice package and gave it to us. Now, Jerry, if you'll excuse me, I've got to go meet with the district attorney." He got up and frowned at Stanley. "Remember what I said."

"Are you sure you're up to this?" The public defender asked the professor once the detective had left the room.

"To be honest," Stanley replied, "I'm not really sure." Despite his doubts, he had a growing confidence that he would uncover more facts than the police, given that they seemed to have stopped looking. "Do you think that I could have a couple of moments alone with Don? There are some things I'd like to ask him about."

"Sure, if that's what he wants." Dermott looked at the prisoner who nodded his head. "Alright, but I wish you'd convince him of the stupidity of what he's doing. Neither of you have any experience in this kind of thing. And if McCaffrey is serious about proving premeditation, he'll ask the district attorney to charge this as a capital case." With that final admonition, the lawyer rose and left two men alone.

"That was pretty intense," Stanley said with a shake of his head. "Are you sure you don't want his help?" Dermott did not seem to be a bad guy. Surely, it would be better to keep him. He looked carefully at Don and tried to crawl inside his head.

"Are you kidding?" the prisoner replied emphatically. "Did you notice how chummy he was with that bastard McCaffrey? What does it say when the cops are encouraging you to hire the public defender? Dermott just wants me to plead guilty to second degree murder and count it as a victory for the defense." With the two other men out of the room, he was much more animated. He leaned forward in his chair and crossed his arms on the table. "Before you and McCaffrey got here, Dermott asked me about the party and about Jade. I don't think he believed a word I told him."

"Did you mention Jade's manager?"

"No."

"Why not?" Stanley gave his friend a puzzled look. "I've only been on the case one day, and Geary's name stands out like a sore thumb."

"So, you know about Chance already?" Johansson looked down at his jump suit and flicked something off the top of his leg. "How'd you find out about him?"

"Tracey Savannah. We talked to her yesterday." Stanley leaned forward on the table and pressed his question. "He sounds like a serious suspect. How come you didn't mention him to Dermott or McCaffrey?"

"Because he wasn't at the party," he admitted with a sigh. "Chance Geary may be an utter piece of shit, but I don't see how he could have done it."

"How can you be sure?"

"Because every security guard in the building was instructed to turn him away if he showed up. In fact, keeping him out was their number one priority. You could go ahead and check the surveillance recordings, but I'd be stunned if you see him make an appearance."

"Surveillance recordings?"

"There's a video camera in the lobby. Anyone who came to the party should be recorded."

"I see." Stanley wrote a note to himself to get copies of whatever the surveillance camera had picked up. He wondered briefly if McCaffrey knew about the recording device.

"You could talk to the guards too, but I can't imagine that he got in."

"But if he did?"

"He'd be a great suspect, wouldn't he?" He shrugged and leaned back in the chair. "The only good thing about being here is avoiding him. He'd kill me if he could."

"Because he was in love with Jade?"

Don snorted. "Love? It was more like pride of ownership. Psychotic children don't like their toys taken away."

Stanley nodded and then took five minutes to sketch out his preliminary plan for the investigation. Even if Johansson killed Jade Delilah, there were still mysteries to unravel. What sort of relationship did the two have? Why did it end in murder instead of a series of nasty text messages? Maybe their story would shed some light on Don's descent into the porn industry. "Two more questions before I go. First, I need somewhere to work from, close to the people I want to talk to. Is there an office at Eden I can use? Space for me and my laptop? It'd also be nice if I could use your secretary to track folks down."

"Good. We've suspended all production, but Miriam is still there answering the phones, watching the server, and filling DVD orders. I'll call her and tell her to set you up."

"You've got access to a phone?" He nodded. "That's something at least." An expression of concern creased the sociologist's face. "Are you doing okay in here? You're not getting, uh, hassled too much, are you?"

The disgraced movie mogul managed a wry smile. "As long as the Eden supply of soft core posters and autographed celebrity panties holds out, I'll be fine. I'm having Miriam send my cellmate something almost every day. With him on my side, I've got no worries." There was an unexpected twinkle in his eye. "I've been hinting at a role for him in my next film."

# XIV.

# PAGE TURNERS

Ellen McCaffrey sat at her computer and put the finishing touches on Jade Delilah's autopsy report. After a third proofread, she sent the document to the printer in the secretarial pool and told her assistant to bring it back for her signature. While she waited, she checked her agenda and cursed the bad luck of drawing her ex-husband on a case once again. Ever since the divorce he had been hypercritical of her work, so she labored to make sure that every sentence was clear and unambiguous, no infinitives split and no modifiers dangling. It was ironic. Had Stuart decided to pursue his original plan of becoming a high school English teacher, they would probably still be married.

Her assistant returned with the three page report, and Ellen sat down to scan it one final time. The attacker's fury startled her again with undiminished force. A blunt instrument, almost certainly the fraternity paddle found in the room with her, had reduced the right side of Delilah's face to a bloody mess of bone and sinew. She had been struck once, probably by a left-handed person, while she was standing. A slicing bruise on the right side of her face indicated that she had hit her head on something with a sharp edge while she fell to the ground. A coffee table lay between Jade and the sofa in the suspect's office, and the mark was consistent with a hard fall against it. After she lay sprawled on the carpet, the assailant struck her several more times, obscuring any evidence of the angle of the first blow that might have provided a clue to the assailant's height.

The victim had been in excellent physical condition when she was killed. Apart from two small silicone implants, unusual in a woman whose natural bust measurements would have been at least 34D, and some uterine scarring probably caused by a case of chlamydia, the examiner could find nothing out of the ordinary. The toxicology report showed a low level of alcohol in her blood and trace levels of methamphetamine, neither in quantities likely to impair her judgment on the night of the murder. She had not had coitus within twenty-four hours of her death.

She signed the report and put it in her 'out' box. Stuart was going to have to be satisfied with a report that described no physical evidence of the suspect's involvement with the victim: no gouged skin underneath her fingernails, no tell-tale semen providing evidence of the murderer's DNA. She had found a short blond hair caught on a ring on the victim's left hand, but given the description of the suspect, it would probably not match his dark hair. She could have picked it up at dinner or in Johansson's office. Or she may have struggled with someone and pulled it out of his or her head. The condition of the follicles was consistent with such a theory, but hardly dispositive. Stuart hated loose ends that created opportunities for defense attorneys; he would not be happy to read about the stray hair.

In theory, she no longer cared about what made Stuart McCaffrey happy or unhappy. Their marriage had ended in an acrimonious divorce two years earlier, and with two grown children living on the east coast, there had been little reason to maintain anything more than civilized relations. At fifty-four, she saw little reason to resume dating, not that anyone had asked. She had no idea whether he had found female companionship, nor did she care. In any event, it had not been another woman who put the finishing touches on their marriage. It had been a man.

Earl Ray Curtis had broken into a half-dozen women's homes and tied them up with duct tape before donning a condom and raping them. An anonymous tip had led Stuart to Curtis's car, where he found a roll of tape similar to that found on the victims and a used Trojan of the sort commonly advertised as being "ribbed for her pleasure." The suspect's evasive responses to the detective's questions and his failure to establish an alibi for any of the nights when the crimes were committed left Stuart with no doubt that he had arrested the right man. Unfortunately, Curtis had worn a ski mask during the assaults, so no victim could identify him. The district attorney was unwilling to prosecute the case in the absence of more direct physical evidence of Curtis's guilt. When the suspect was released without being charged, he had smiled at Stuart and taunted him, "You've got no chance, asshole."

Two days later, the body of Melanie Smith was found bound with duct tape in her apartment. She had suffered an asthma attack during the assault and had suffocated. Ellen was assigned to perform the autopsy. Although there was ample evidence that the victim had been brutally raped, there was no semen in Smith's vagina. The perpetrator had worn a condom. After telling his wife everything he knew about the case, Stuart had convinced her that Curtis was the perpetrator, but nothing he said could convince her to "find" semen inside the victim's vagina. Stuart offered to supply his wife with a sample from the used condom he had found in Curtis's vehicle. He even brought it to her, assuming that she would be willing to bend her professional ethics to prevent future assaults.

When she refused, he exploded. The contemptuousness of his response had damaged their relationship more profoundly than an affair ever could have. She was an utterly worthless, pencil-pushing bureaucrat, an irresponsible disgrace to her gender. He disappeared for a week, and when he returned, their life together was one extended recrimination. He refused counseling and after a month moved out again. Marriage to the moody detective had never been easy, but this was the last straw. She filed for divorce six months later.

Divorce, of course, seldom cleanly severs all contact. At least once a month, she would be assigned an autopsy and see that the detective in charge of the case was Stuart McCaffrey. She was polite, and when he was not correcting her spelling, so was he. She had to agree with the description of their relationship he had once offered to a colleague, "We're civil to each other for the sake of the corpses."

*  *  *

Stanley met Angela for lunch, got a brief report on the morning's interviews and then dropped her off before driving directly to Eden Studio. What should have been a thirty minute trip took almost an hour and a half. With every rise in the highway, he expected to see signs of some horrific accident causing the delay, but all he ever encountered was the glint and glare of a sun-drenched serpent of vehicles stretching for miles before him. The longer the drive took, the longer the to-do list in his head grew. By the time he pulled into the Eden lot, he was desperate to get started. Miriam greeted him with a look of annoyance and led him to a small back room.

He gave her his most winning smile, which was received like bad news from an oncologist. "Could you make appointments for me with the heads of Boudoir Films, Chimera Productions, and Janus Studios? Evenings would be best, but any time will do as long as it's soon." She stared at him a moment before reaching down and writing herself a note. "Also, could you get me the number of Chance Geary, Jade Delilah's agent?" She nodded her recognition of the name but displayed no other emotion. "I'll call him myself."

Stanley surveyed the room. It was drab but functional, possessing none of the amenities of the studio head's office. A dead philodendron occupied most of the space on the top of a gray metal desk while a phone and fax machine sat on a battered credenza. The office was windowless, but offered a distracting view of at least two hundred DVD's stacked on a bookcase across from the desk. He picked up one at random. *Spicy Girls III* featured Jade Delilah and four other multi-ethnic beauties dressed as the sexiest all girl pop group of all time. He grimaced at the thought of what had been done to her perfect face. While he was reading the fax number to the McCaffrey's voice mail, the door opened.

"Here's Geary's number," Miriam said as she pushed a pink message sheet across the desk. "And here's a key for the office. It's the master for all the rooms in the building. Mr. Johansson insisted that I give it to you." She started to go, but he stopped her with a quick question.

"Were you here the night of the murder?"

The secretary seemed bemused. "I was invited to the banquet, of course, but I didn't attend. I was home watching television with my son." She crossed her arms and stared down at him. "As a general rule, I don't socialize with anyone from work."

"Why not?"

"Well, I don't want to sound judgmental, but these aren't the sort of people I want to spend my time with." She sounded very judgmental despite the disclaimer. "I only work here because Mr. Johansson pays me more than I could make elsewhere. My son is in college and he needs help with his tuition."

"So you're not a big fan of Mr. Johansson's movies?"

"Not hardly," she frowned and moved toward the door, "nor the people who make them."

"Do you think that Mr. Johansson is responsible for Jade's death?"

"That's an interesting way to put it." She brushed a piece of lint from her jacket. "I have no idea whether he killed her or not, but I'm quite sure he's responsible for her death."

"How so?"

"Isn't it obvious? Don't you think that without the porn industry and Eden Studio, she'd still be alive?" She turned and started to leave the room. "Now, if you'll excuse me, I think my phone's ringing."

When Miriam left, he leaned back in his chair and promised himself to ask about the arguments she had heard between Don and Jade, but in the meantime, he stared at the slip of pink paper in his hand. What was the best way to confront a man deemed too dangerous to be allowed to enter Eden Studio the night of the party? Nonetheless, he needed to know whether Chance Geary had a credible alibi, which reminded him that he needed to review the video logs. He dialed Miriam's extension, but it was busy.

He clicked the receiver, dialed the number that Miriam had given him, and got a voice mailbox instructing him to leave his name and number. After explaining vaguely that he was involved in the murder investigation, Stanley left his Eden number and his cell number and stated that he needed to talk as soon as possible. After a second try at Miriam's line, he walked down the hall to see her in person. By the time he got to her desk, she was off the phone.

"You've got an appointment this evening with Brian Mulkahey at Boudoir at eight, and tomorrow afternoon with Stan Matteson at Janus at three. I'm still trying to get a hold of Milton Barkley at Chimera." She handed him the two message slips.

He mentioned the video monitor of the lobby entrance and asked about the recordings. Looking around the room, he noticed a small camera suspended from the ceiling.

"The cops took the recordings the morning after the banquet."

"Did you make copies first?"

She looked at him like he was crazy and shook her head. He went back to the office and realized that he would not have time to pick up Angela and also make his interview with Mulkahey. As he called and told his wife take a cab back to the hotel, the fax machine started humming and printing out the forensic reports. He said a quick goodbye and eagerly began to read the hard evidence that had been collected from the victim and the crime scene.

The Medical Examiner's report printed first. Stanley did not need a medical degree to understand the severity of the injuries to Jade Delilah's face and head. A note attached to the front of the report stated that the photos of the victim would be sent to him by mail. The written description was nauseating enough; he was in no hurry to see any pictures.

The report's final section contained the findings relevant to the circumstances surrounding of Jade's death. In an ideal world, Stanley would have ordered an independent analysis of whether the killer really had been a left-handed person of indeterminate height, but Don's funds were severely limited and the report appeared quite professional. If her head was repeatedly bashed as she lay on the floor, it was likely that the impression made by the initial blow would have been totally obscured. Stanley was struck by the violence of the attack. It spoke of rage, uncontrollable anger directed at a hated enemy. He had a difficult time attributing such savagery to the man he thought he knew.

The toxicology results were less interesting. Given his knowledge of Chance Geary's drug dealing activities, Stanley was not surprised to learn that a trace of methamphetamine had been found, but the mention of a short blond hair snagged on the victim's ring caught his eye. Even if the killer had not left this evidence, it would be something to shake Detective McCaffrey's smug demeanor. He wondered if the police would try to identify the source of the stray hair.

He ignored the problem hair for a moment and picked up the forensic report. Jade had been found lying on her left side, with her back against the coffee table separating her and the sofa on which Don had been found. Given the blood pooled on the carpet, the report concluded that the body had not been moved after it fell to the floor. Several blood and tissue fragments had been discovered on the wall behind the sofa, indicating that the initial blow had been struck on the right side of her head with a ferocious follow through. More blood and tissue were located within a radius of carpet close to the victim's head, scattered by the downward blows. Blood traces were also found on the coffee table. There were a couple on the top of the couch several feet farther away, but none on the couch cushions.

He processed the implications of the splatter pattern. Could Don have been lying passed out on top of the sofa cushions, thus shielding them from blood spatters? He flipped to the section of the report analyzing the suspect's clothes and discovered that two tissue fragments had been found on the front of Don's shirt along with blood stains on his shirt sleeve. This evidence was consistent with Don having been laid out unconscious on the sofa, oblivious to the bludgeoning as it occurred. It also supported the police's conclusion that he had himself wielded the weapon and got splashed with blood in the process. Still, the lack of blood on the sofa cushions was something. It did point away from the McCaffrey's assumption. Oddly, Don would be better off if the attack had been even gorier, with the police finding a blood-soaked couch except for the outline of Don's body.

The report also noted that hair and fiber evidence had been collected from every area in the room. It detailed what had been found and where, but drew no conclusions as to relevance. Detective McCaffrey had already announced the report's most damning evidence. The only fingerprints on the murder weapon, lying directly beneath his hand and in between the sofa and the coffee table, were Don's. Either he did it, or he was framed. That much was clear. But as much as Stanley wanted to believe that his friend was innocent, he had trouble imagining some other killer who at one instant was utterly consumed by rage, but in the very next was calm and collected enough to wipe the fraternity paddle clean and wrap Don's hand around it.

He looked at his watch. He had just enough time to call the detective before he left to interview Brian Mulkahey.

"Detective McCaffrey," Stanley offered in a respectful tone. "Thanks for sending over the reports so promptly. They're extremely helpful."

"Yeah? I expedited them. I figured the sooner you got them, the sooner you could convince your friend to plead."

"Well," he ventured, "given the evidence you've collected, I don't understand why you'd think that. The hair alone points strongly away from Mr. Johansson, as do the lack of blood spatters on the sofa cushions. Wouldn't you expect more blood to have fallen on the couch if he hadn't been lying there during the assault?" There was something in McCaffrey's smug tone of voice that made him want to slap the cop down whenever he had the chance.

"Uh, huh, and I'd also expect a lot of blood on his shirt if he were just motionless on the couch during the murder." McCaffrey laughed. "Wait 'til you get the photos. You can see how the spray pretty much peters out by the time it gets to the sofa. Nice try though."

"What about the hair," he exclaimed, "how do you explain that?"

"I don't have to. She probably picked it up in the party room somewhere. With one hundred fifty gussied up porn stars eating dinner, there's gonna be a lot of stray hair floating around."

Frustrated by McCaffrey's unshakeable assumption of Don's guilt, Stanley's first impulse was to argue. But he forced himself to breathe and imagine the cop was his older brother, a born bully and stubborn as a stump. In that conflict, strategy had usually defeated bluster. He recognized his first missteps with the detective but did not back down. "Given your assumption about the hair, I'm sure you won't mind checking it against everyone at the party."

"Excuse me?"

"Have you gathered hair samples from everyone at the party to see whose hair it is?"

McCaffrey paused for a moment and measured his answer. "No, that would be a waste of departmental resources."

"Looking for the killer…a waste of resources? That won't play too well with the jury. A suspicious hair is found clutched in the hand of the victim and the police don't even bother to follow up? Even when they have a list of everyone at the party?" He envisioned himself making the closing argument at trial. "Detective, that might fly in Minnesota, but we're in Southern California, land of O.J. and Michael Jackson."

Silence on the other end of the line and then a quiet growl, "I'll think about it."

"You should do more than think about it—"

"—I said that I'd think about it. Now, if you don't have any more ridiculous requests, I've got a pile of paperwork to finish. Good evening, Professor."

Stanley cradled the phone in his hand with the dawning realization that he had won his first small victory. He tried to remember a moment in his academic career that felt as good. Having an article accepted by a journal was a good feeling, but the review and resubmission process took so long that the final approval years after writing always felt anti-climactic. Getting the rare brilliant paper from a student was a good feeling too, but he suspected that the quality was probably due to the student's talent and hard work rather than his teaching. Whatever they were, academic joys were esoteric joys. It was more exciting to meet someone in combat and, at least for a moment, prevail.

# XV.

# SENSE AND SENSIBILITY

Angela lay on her back frowning at the hotel room television. "Next up, new developments in the Delilah case," the anchor promised for the third time before cutting to a commercial. The murder had put her life in limbo and now the television news was stringing her along too. She should have been tapping on the laptop, putting a humorous face on everything she had seen in LA, but murder was a new topic for her and its impact was too personal for her funny bone to feel tickled. As a picture of Jade finally appeared on the screen, the phone rang and she picked up the receiver in frustration. "What!"

"Hey Angela, it's Max. Could I talk to Stan?"

"He's not here right now." A picture of Don Johansson flashed next to the talking head of the reporter. She tried to turn up the volume but accidently switched the channel to ESPN. "Can I take a message?" She asked as she fumbled with the television remote.

"Just have him call me as soon as he gets back. We have a little emergency here, and I gotta get a hold of him." She did not like the urgency she heard in Max's voice. He was usually cool and casual.

"What's going on, Max?"

He paused a moment. "I don't know if you saw Stanley's picture on CNN the other night, but a top administrator at the university did, and now I'm getting questions about what he's doing in Los Angeles. I've done my best to explain to the Dean and to the President that he's engaged in legitimate sociological research, but all they see is sex." He sighed and she could hear him take a drink. "And to make things worse, the news report says that he's helping with the murder defense of his old college buddy. This is big news here, Angela. Sex sells, even in the Midwest, and everyone wants to hear about the *porn* star bludgeoned to death by her *porn* director in the middle of a big LA *porn* party."

"God, I told him not to do this." She leaned her head back against the wall and rubbed her temple. "He's just showing his loyalty to an old friend. Is that so bad?" Her husband was a brilliant guy, but sometimes he needed a handler. "How much trouble is he in?"

"I spent all afternoon talking to the administration, and I think I've got something worked out. If he comes back now and drops what he's doing, there won't be any negative repercussions, apart from losing the funding for the porn part of his research. The university is mostly concerned about bad publicity. They don't want to see the institution linked to sex, murder, and gore every night on the news. If he comes back now, they'll be willing to forget about it." It was clear from the tone of his voice that Max was sympathetic to the administration's position.

"But what about his book?" She asked in a sudden panic. Stan could not possibly finish in time if he had to start the last section from scratch once again. No book plus no tenure equaled no family. It was a simple equation that started a sickening churning in her stomach.

"Well, let's just say that I'm not totally worthless as a negotiator." Max sounded pleased with himself. "I convinced them to add a year to Stanley's tenure clock. He won't have to come up for tenure until the year after next. That gives him plenty of extra time to finish."

She let out a breath. The plan smoothed out things for Stanley and its logic was inexorable. Max was indeed a good negotiator.

"Max," she said gratefully, "you're awesome! He'll be so relieved." She sat up in the bed and hung her legs over the edge.

"It's been really stressful for him to work under such a tight deadline."

"No problem. I shouldn't have approved this junket in the first place," he said graciously. "Anyway, talk to him and have him call me as soon as he gets back. I want things settled as quickly as possible."

He rang off and Angela found her way back to the news channel, but she had missed the story. It didn't matter now. Stanley and she could now go back home and leave the cesspool behind. Max, good old Max, had saved the day.

\* \* \*

Stanley drove into the lot at Boudoir Productions just as the sun was setting over the Pacific. He could not see the ocean from the parking lot, but he stood for a moment appreciating the orange and purple streaking the horizon. Los Angeles might be hot and dirty, full of people scrambling from one place to the other, but on occasions it was sublime, even from the perspective of a sticky, black parking lot. The door to the building was open, but there was nobody in the lobby, so he walked down a carpeted hall looking for Brian Mulkahey. He stuck his head into the first open room and a young man stuffing DVD's into boxes told him to return to the lobby and follow the other hallway. Stanley eventually found himself outside a door waiting for the florid producer to finish a phone call. He waved Stanley in and motioned for him to sit.

"Yeah, sure," he said into the receiver, "no problemo. I don't know about a contract, but we'll have something soon. Gerry will call you tomorrow. I've got someone here now." He nodded at Stanley. "Yeah, don't worry. I'll call you." He hung up with a smile.

"That was Crystal Ferrari, one of Don's hottest properties," he explained with satisfaction, "totally panicked because production has stopped at Eden. Nobody's signing any checks and nothing's getting made. I've gotten about five calls today from girls who usually work over there."

"So, Don's arrest has been good for business?" Angela's instincts about the fall out of the murder dead on. A major shake up was in store for the industry and those quick enough to take advantage would make a nice profit from the downfall of Eden Studio.

"It's been great." Mulkahey polished his glasses and mopped his bald head with his handkerchief. "Look, I'm sorry Don's in the soup, but it's his own fault."

"So you think he did it?" Stanley watched carefully.

"Yeah, I mean who else? I'm as surprised as the next guy. He always seemed like such a straight shooter, but when you're right obsessed, you're gonna get in trouble. You know he paid Janus over one hundred thousand dollars to get Jade out of her contract so that she could come to Eden?" He shook his head in disbelief. "I know she's hot, but that was fuckin' insane."

"It almost paid off," Stanley countered.

"Almost," the producer admitted with a shake of his head. "Look, on the one hand, I'm surprised that he'd kill her, but on the other, he never really played by the rules. He didn't fit in and he pissed off a lot of people over the years." Mulkahey poked his finger in Stanley's direction and then slapped his desk. "The bottom line is: He just wasn't hard-boiled enough, ya know what I mean? And when he runs into a real hard-boiled chick like Jade, you see what happens."

Stanley felt like he was interviewing a character from a Mickey Spillane mystery, but he was grateful the producer was willing to talk so openly. "How do you think that Jade's boyfriend felt about all this?"

"It pissed him off," the producer explained, "but that guy is always pissed off. He called here last week trying to convince me to hire Jade once her contract with Eden was up. He said he had almost closed a deal with Chimera but wanted to give me a chance to get in on the bidding."

"Jade was thinking of leaving Eden? What did you say?"

"I told him to go fuck himself. He was throwing out ridiculous numbers. I told him she had the best contract in the business with Eden, and that no one else would be stupid enough to match Don's rate, much less top it."

"What'd he say to that?"

"He blew up, shouted that he'd worked out something better with Chimera already and hung up on me." Mulkahey held up his hands palm up, as if to say *whachya gonna do?*

"But he definitely wanted to get her away from Don?" Stanley pushed.

"I know what you're thinking. Geary shopping around his girl just before she gets murdered…look, if you can hang this on that little scumbag, more power to you. Just take your time, okay? Business has never been better." He stood up and offered to lead Stanley out of the building.

"One more question. On the night of the murder, where were you?"

If the pornographer was offended, he did not show it. "I was here making a film until about midnight. You can check it out with the crew if you want. The cops already have."

As Stanley walked out of the building toward his car, he pondered the implications of the police checking out Mulkahey's alibi. Perhaps McCaffrey only appeared to have prejudged Don's guilt. Why check on Mulkahey's whereabouts unless the detective was considering other suspects? Of course, he might just be going through the motions to appear more thorough to a jury. As he turned the key in the ignition, his cell phone rang. He fumbled with it a moment before finally locating the talk button.

"This is Chance." The high-pitched and wary voice did not sound as menacing as he had expected. "I got your message."

"Thanks for returning my call, Mr. Geary." When in doubt, he thought, just be polite, especially when dealing with potentially homicidal drug dealers. He had interviewed some slimy characters for the other chapters in his book. At least two of the carnival workers and one termite exterminator had struck him as sociopaths, if not psychopaths. But they weren't that hard to deal with: just nod your head, seem completely absorbed by everything they say, and never utter a word of disagreement. "I'm investigating the death of your client, Jade Delilah, and I'd like to schedule a meeting with you."

"I've already talked to a detective. Are you another cop?" He spat out the word with disgust.

"No, no. I'm working on Mr. Johansson's behalf, trying to get background information on the victim."

Instead of the explosion Stanley feared, Geary responded with a skeptical laugh. "Are you kidding me? Why the fuck should I talk to you?"

Good question. "Well, I'm trying to find Jade's killer and the more I know about her, the easier that's going to be. I've been told that you know more about her than anyone else."

Geary chuckled through the receiver. "How's this for background information? Don Johansson locked me out of his party and then killed Jade when I couldn't protect her. That help?"

"Look, I understand you're upset. I would be too, but I just need fifteen minutes. I could get a subpoena, but it would be easier for both of us if you'll just see me tomorrow." Stanley had no idea whether he had any right to subpoena anyone, but he could not think of another way to gain leverage over Geary.

The agent pondered the threat a moment and then replied. "I'll be in my bike shop all morning. It's in Las Llaves, on Hortaleza Avenue across from the Taco Bell." Then he hung up.

Stanley's confidence surged. The meeting with Mulkahey had been productive, and talking to Geary would make a good start to the next day's investigation. He would take the interviews and conversations where they naturally led, hoping that he would find someone other than Don at the end of the trail. The task of unraveling the murder had begun to take on a familiar feel. It was not that much different from his usual research, except the stakes were higher and he did not have to produce an irrelevant academic paper at the end of the day. The next day's hunting would be interesting.

\* \* \*

Angela stood packing her suitcase, humming quietly, contemplating sleeping in her own bed after the long journey back. A hot bath would feel good too. Best of all, she could get back to her computer and start writing about her crazy trip out west. The outrageous cast of characters she had met in LA would be good for at least for five or six juicy columns. She specialized in revealing the humor and weirdness in everyday life. One of her favorite columns, a description of an Armenian-Mexican wedding gone awry, had even been picked up by the Morris new service. The porn stars offered similar subject matter. They were both more ordinary and more outrageous than she had imagined. They certainly put the *extra* back in extraordinary. They also put the *whore* back in horrible.

As she checked the closet one last time, she heard a plastic key card slide through door lock. She turned to see her husband, a confused expression registering on his face as he looked past her shoulder to the suitcase. She clicked off the television set and gave him a hug. "Stan, you need to call Max right away." He squeezed her back and then pushed her away gently so he could see her face.

"What's going on?"

"Max called," she explained, "with some really terrible news. The university administration is freaked out about your helping Don and has withdrawn your research grant."

"What!"

"They saw the news reports on CNN." She grabbed his hand as she talked. "They don't want you out here on university money defending a porn director in a sensational murder case."

"But we've still got interviews to do." He shook his head in disbelief and broke away from her grip. "Why should anyone care if I help out a friend at the same time?"

"I think the personal connection actually makes it worse." She felt truly sorry for her husband. He looked unable to catch his breath, like someone had just sucker-punched him. Even though she had had doubts about their impulsive trip to California, the project deserved a better fate. She reached out to him. "Stan, there may be a silver lining. Max said he has convinced the Dean to give you another year on your tenure clock. As long as you come back now, you'll have extra time to finish the book."

"As long as I come back now?"

"Yes, that's why I was packing. I called up the airline, and there's a flight out tomorrow morning."

"So, they take the funding," she watched in dismay as his shock gave way to anger, "and they want me to give up the interviews and the investigation too?"

"That's what he said," she explained. "It's the publicity…the scandal. The university just wants it to go away."

Stanley suddenly shot up and walked across the room to the phone. "Where's his fucking number? Did you write it down?" She shook her head and watched him search frantically for the department head's number on his laptop.

"Stan," she said, working to keep the panic out of her voice, "what are you going to tell him? Don't you think you should calm down first?"

"I am calm," he said in a barely controlled voice. "I'm totally calm, but I'm not going to let a bunch of bureaucrats tell me what to do." He put the receiver down while he talked but kept his hand on top of the phone. "They can pull my funding; that's their prerogative. So what if I have to come up with a couple thousand dollars on my own? But I won't be told that certain topics are forbidden, and there's no way in hell I'm going to be bullied into turning my back on a friend."

\* \* \*

Stuart McCaffrey sat at his desk mulling over the short blond hair that had been found tangled in Jade Delilah's ring. It would be futile to test the hair of everyone at the party. Even if a match were found, that would not prove its owner was the killer.

On the other hand, what if the defense proved that it matched the hair of someone with a record of violence? And what if the same person had no alibi for the forty-five minute period when the murder might have taken place? Any decent defense lawyer would love to play that scenario to a jury. The professor had hit a sore spot. A California jury needed to be convinced three times over before it found a celebrity guilty of anything. He decided to give Ellen a call to see how feasible it would be to do the check. He tried her office first, and then caught her at home in the middle of dinner.

"Ellie? I've got a question about the Johansson case, if you've got a second."

"Not really, but go ahead anyway." When he heard her voice, he imagined her sitting in the kitchen where they had eaten most of their meals together for twenty-five years. Hearing irritation in her voice was better than not hearing her at all.

"Johansson's investigator saw the note in your report about the strand of hair found on the victim's hand, and he's asking me to follow up on it. Normally, I'd tell him to go, uh, screw himself, but he understands how it might look to a jury if we don't do anything to try and find a match." He swished a couple of ounces of cold coffee around in a chipped ceramic mug. "How hard would it be to run a DNA test on one hundred fifty people?"

"We wouldn't have to do that. We could eliminate ninety-five percent of the people with just a microscope. If you collect samples and bag them, it wouldn't take us that long. You'd only need to run DNA on any closely similar strands."

"So you think we should go ahead and do it?" He knew the answer was yes, but since their divorce he had learned that asking her advice sometimes softened the tone she used with him.

"Yeah, it's suspicious, and it's unexplained. I know you're tempted to say that she could have picked up the hair anywhere, but any defense attorney is going to say that she yanked it from her assailant's head."

"Could it have been?"

"Maybe." She paused for a moment. "It would be kind of odd for a hair of that length to remain lodged for so long after the dinner. And while you're in a mood to take advice, I'd have everyone sign a receipt acknowledging that their hair was taken." "We'd do that as a matter of course."

"Yes, but have the officer note which hand each donor signs with. You're looking for a lefty, remember." He almost lied that he had already thought of this, but instead he thanked her for the suggestion. "And one more thing. I don't know what it means, but nobody's come forward to claim the victim's body. I thought you might want to know."

* * *

For a moment, Angela stared completely tongue-tied at her husband. Max had offered an honorable solution to a terrible situation. How could he not see that? He could not torpedo his career out of some misplaced loyalty to a killer. She would not let him. "Just talk to Max. We need to go home tomorrow."

"I'll talk to him, but I'm staying here." The look on his face and the tone of his voice was maddening. He was so busy standing up for his right to do as he pleased that he could not see the impact on anything or anyone else.

"Stan," she spoke to him as if he were a man about to jump off a window ledge, "think about it. They're giving you another year. I know you're upset, but as far as your career is concerned this is just a bump in the road. It's really no big deal."

"No big deal? Don's put his life in my hands. He's rotting in jail waiting to be tried for murder, and I'm the only person helping him. I promised I'd do this investigation, and I'm going to do it."

"Just like that?" Outrage and contempt began to sneak into her voice.

"Just like that. And you know what?" He sat down next to her on the bed, unaware of the volcano of emotions within her. "I think I can do it. It's just like any other research project. You collect all the data you can; you talk to all the people who know something." He touched her hand. "I'm not claiming that I can prove he's innocent. But I can unravel the story." He squeezed. "I can figure it out."

"You're not thinking straight, Stan." She stood up and broke away. "You're not getting this! Call up Max! These guys are not fooling around. Are you willing to lose your job over this? Are you willing to lose everything that we've been working for?"

"I shouldn't have to lose my job because I want to help someone in trouble."

"Well, that may be unfair, but it's the world you're stuck in." She started jamming the remaining clothes in the suitcase, shoulders shaking. He had always been such a pragmatist that this idealistic turn completely blindsided her. She knew that the undergrads drove him crazy and that he didn't like having to crank out an article every year, but he had always seen the massive upside of academic life. What the hell was going on?

"They can't fire me for staying here. This is a matter of academic freedom, and I have a contract."

"Sweetheart," she said with as much sarcasm as sympathy, "they don't have to fire you. If you come up for tenure without the book, then you'll be turned down by the faculty and your contract won't be renewed. They don't have to do anything special." She knew the rules of the game as well as he did.

"Then I'll have to find a way to finish the investigation and the book, even without the extra year." She stared at him with fury. He was completely immune to reason.

"Then you'll do it without me! I married a professor, not an amateur detective." She didn't care if everyone in the hotel could hear her yell. "I'm leaving this fucked up city and your porn star pals as soon as I can! I'm going to go home and sell some houses, because pretty soon that's going to be the only income we have." She turned away from him, threw the rest of her clothes into the suitcase and stormed into the bathroom to collect her toiletries. Stanley sat on the bed staring at the phone. To his surprise, it rang.

"Hello? Yes, I remember. That would be great. Yes, we can talk tomorrow afternoon...thanks." He put the receiver down slowly and sat back on the bed.

"Was that Max?" Angela asked anxiously. If only her husband would just sleep on his decision and talk to his colleague the next day, then he would see reason. She looked up at him hopefully.

"No, that was Layla."

"Layla?" For a moment she was at a complete loss to recall the name. She tried to remember if Max's secretary was a Layla, but then a nasty thought crossed her mind. "Wait, not the porn star we interviewed?"

"Yeah. She's got some ideas about the case that she wants to talk about. She claims Don is innocent." He was afraid to look up and see his wife's reaction. His fear was justified. Angela's eyes were like darting yellow jackets.

"So, you're going to talk with her tomorrow?"

"Yes."

"In LA?"

"Yeah, where else?"

"Where else?" she screamed and picked up her suit case. "How about fucking Neverland with Peter Pan and Wendy, because that's what you're acting like!" With that, she yanked open the door and left. He sat for a while without moving, waiting for her to return. After a moment, he looked at his watch, and it dawned on him that she had just enough time to catch the red-eye flight back to Chicago.

## XVI.

# MACMILLAN AND BABE

Stanley slept fitfully and awoke before dawn. He called home, but Angela had either not yet arrived or was choosing not to answer, and he didn't know what to tell her anyway. The decision to stay in Los Angeles came from his gut, from the sort of impulse that he usually ignored. He didn't want to go back home and interview waitresses or real estate agents or receptionists. He no longer wanted to play it safe and sell his flaccid soul to the concrete monolith of BFU. When he spoke with Angela, he would try to make her understand, but he didn't yet have the words to explain his decision to stay.

He stepped into the shower and let the hot stream of water pound at the tension in his shoulders. Angela had left, and he wasn't sure how worried he should be. The good news was that she was just retreating home. She wasn't threatening to divorce him or move away. The bad news was that he had never seen her so angry. Crazy as it seemed, after ten years of marriage, this was their first major blow out. With no kids, nice in-laws, and adequate money, what had there been to fight about? Affairs? Nope. Addiction and alcoholism? Nah. Who lost the remote? That was more like it. But now they had gone off the rails into new territory. She had chided him for being too objective, but now that he was following his heart, she longed for the return of Caspar Milquetoast. What the hell did she want anyway?

He toweled off and saw there was plenty of time to have breakfast and still make the eight o'clock interview. Before he left, he took out his laptop and emailed Max. Nothing could be gained by deliberately antagonizing the department head or the administration, so he explained that he had gotten the message from Angela and promised not do anything to bring the university into disrepute. No interviews with the media, for sure. And he would not seek reimbursement for any of the expenses that he incurred. He was continuing with his research and hoped to be done with the book in a timely fashion. He clicked "send." If it took Max a couple of days to track him down, so much the better.

When he got to the interview room in the Van Nuys hotel, he saw that Angela had downloaded the previous afternoon's interviews. It was still early, so he played the first interview with Nikki Ferrari on his laptop while he waited. He sat on the edge of the bed as an attractive, light-skinned African American woman answered Angela's questions about the now infamous party and Jade Delilah's death. She had been there as the guest of a friend and had never worked for Eden Studio or with the victim. She knew Don only by reputation and had no opinion of the incident except to complain how she had been inconvenienced by the police.

He heard a knock on the door, missing the question that provoked Nikki into a tirade about "booty-ass shakin' MTV whores." He hit pause and opened the door to a voluptuous blond wearing a tight black sweater and short leather skirt. She had high cheekbones and lush ripe lips, but her eyes were red-rimmed and bleary.

"Hello, I'm Professor Hopkins. You must be Linda Simi?" He shook her hand and gestured to the empty chair in front of the tripod. "Please come on in and sit down. Thanks for coming so early in the morning! Would you like some coffee?"

"No thanks, I'm still pretty wired." She crossed her legs and showed a pulse-quickening amount of thigh. He wondered whether her energy came from cocaine, crystal meth, or just youthful adrenaline. "We had a late shoot last night and then went out clubbing after. I came straight here from Sunset Strip."

"Then extra thanks! You must be exhausted."

"Nah, and I gotta work later this morning anyway." She looked around the room with a distracted air. "What do you want to know?"

Stanley began with the usual questions about the night of the murder, but learned nothing new from Linda who grew quickly bored. The only time she showed any animation was when he asked her about Chimera's attempt to lure Jade from Eden.

"I don't know anything about that," she replied, "but I do know that Milton Barkley doesn't like Don. I made a couple of movies with him and thought they were pretty good, so I asked him about maybe getting some kind of contract deal. You know, like the girls at Eden. Well, he lost his shit and started screaming about Don. He was pissed."

"Do you still work over there?"

"Yeah, you can't afford to be too picky." She suddenly grabbed her breasts. "I thought new tits would take me to the next level, but the doc didn't do that great a job. When I'm on my hands and knees, you can see these stretchy sort of lines on the sides." She balanced one against the other, frowned and asked, "Do you want to see?"

"No, no." He shook his head vigorously. "That's alright. I'll take your word for it."

He decided to pursue the topic and plowed ahead with questions about the role of plastic surgery in the porn industry. After an enlightening discussion of optimal breast and lip size, the interview ended, leaving him fifteen minutes to collect himself before Tia Rosa arrived for the second and final session of the morning. He wrote up his notes and decided to truncate the upcoming interview so that he could catch Chance Geary at his bike shop before lunch. As it happened the interview petered out naturally due to the Latina's limited English skills. He managed to get rudimentary information about her work experience in porn, but she was a newcomer to the business, had no sense of the players, and thus could shed no new light on the murder.

Once he had ushered Tia out of the hotel room, Stanley grabbed a note pad and hopped in his car. Las Llaves, where

Geary had his bike shop, was only a couple of miles away, but he had no idea how long it would take to get there. His stomach rumbled as he drove past a dozen fast food places and he promised himself a roast beef sandwich once he was done talking to the victim's agent and boyfriend.

Geary's business shared a battered storefront with a pawn shop and a liquor store in the middle of a neighborhood dominated by signs in Spanish. He parked the car and decided to watch the shop for a few minutes, half expecting to see massive, tattooed bikers leaving with suspicious cellophane envelopes stuck in their boots, but no one appeared in the ten minutes he sat watching. All he learned was that he would never have the patience or the bladder for a real stake out. When he finally entered the shop, he saw no customers, just a wiry white mechanic in overalls with a long greasy ponytail bending over a Yamaha.

"Mr. Geary?"

The mechanic looked backward toward him. He was thin, bordering on emaciated, with a peculiar gaze that reminded Stanley of Charles Manson. How had such a creature managed to bed one of the most desirable women in the world?

"Yeah?" The nasal voice was wary and unfriendly.

"I'm Stanley Hopkins." He took a step toward the crouching figure with an extended hand. "We spoke on the phone yesterday. Thank you for agreeing to talk with me."

"Yeah?" He stood up and wiped off his hands with a filthy rag. "You threatened me with a subpoena." He muttered and tossed the rag to the ground, but instead of walking over to shake Stanley's hand, Geary got on the Yamaha and started it with a kick. He revved the engine a couple of times and then turned the bike off. For the rest of the interview he sat firmly in the leather seat, cocky and belligerent. "What do you want?"

Given the hostility in the biker's voice, Stanley decided to start with something relatively safe and asked him why the director of Eden Studio would kill one of his biggest stars.

He reminded the biker that the act was financial suicide, but Geary was not impressed with the contradiction.

"Because she wouldn't sleep with him. He got fucked up and when she said no, he went crazy and killed her." He rubbed a blemish off the leather seat of the motorcycle. "Happens all the time."

"But his business?"

"Fuck his business. Junkies will do anything. They'll kill their own mothers if you ask 'em." Don was not a junkie, but Stanley guessed that arguing with the rat-faced mechanic about the fine points of analogic reasoning was an unproductive idea.

He asked whether Don's attentions toward Jade had provoked any jealous feelings, but his only response was a hostile glare. Stanley was now glad of the bike underneath Geary. If the suspect decided to rush him, it would take him a moment to get off, giving the professor a head start on his flight out the door. "Come on. You can't have liked the guy." Geary wouldn't bite. Frustrated, the professor jumped to the most important question. "Where were you the night of the party?"

"I'll tell you what I told the cops." He patted the Yamaha's gas tank. "I was right here working."

"Did anyone see you?"

"Maybe a couple of people."

"Could I have their names?"

All he offered was a smug smile. "Ask the cops." He reached down with his left hand and made an adjustment to the engine, then he fired it up again and revved it for a minute. When the engine died down, he looked up with disappointment to see that his visitor was still there. "One last question, dick head. I'm a busy man."

So, this is how high school bullies end up, Stanley speculated, stuck in a grimy routine of beating their girlfriends, selling drugs, and straddling a shiny artificial penis. "So Chance," it felt good to let his contempt show and abandon years of professional constraint. "Did it make you feel like a tough guy to hit Jade?

Because looking at the size of you, it must have been a pretty even fight." He balanced on his heels, ready to turn and flee if things got ugly.

For a moment, Geary looked like he was about to jump off the bike, but he settled for strangling its handlebars in a knuckle-whitening grip. A bitter blast of a laugh blew past his lips, "The bitch loved it. She wanted it rough, dude. She wouldn't have even looked at a pussy like you." He pulled a packet of cigarettes out of his pocket and rapped it hard against his knuckles. "Now, get the fuck out of my shop."

Stanley obliged without looking back, resolving to check the video logs to make sure that Geary had not managed to slip into the party. Thankfully, the law required McCaffrey to be forthcoming with the names of Geary's alibi witnesses. There must have been some way for the little psychopath to get into that office. What a huge favor he'd be doing society if he put a weasel like Geary away for life. Sounds like a legitimate goal for a sociologist, he decided as he drove away.

Stanley arrived back at the hotel ten minutes before the third and final interview of the day, a post-lunch meeting with Athena Portia. Afterwards, he had a three o'clock appointment to talk to Herb Matteson at Janus. Athena knocked on the door fifteen minutes late and at first seemed in a hurry to get through the interview, but she quickly warmed to the young professor.

"Can I see Don Johansson as a killer?" She repeated one of his first questions, seeming to give it serious thought. "You know, I can sorta see it." Athena was an athletic-looking brunette with a head full of dark curls and compelling brown eyes who had a career as a personal trainer ahead of her when she stopped making movies. The other starlets had found it difficult to imagine the director murdering his top actress. Stanley put down his pen and listened.

"Don and I were lovers for a while, maybe three or four years ago, when I was just doing modeling, and I saw him lose his shit a couple of times."

"Did he ever hit you?"

"No," she admitted, "but he'd break stuff and punch the wall. It was pretty scary, but he never hit me."

"Was he like that often?"

"A couple of times." She paused for a moment and studied him. She had a kind face that added an intriguing edge to her sex appeal. "I once saw him throw a laptop through a window when it wasn't working right." She dropped her eyes and studied the floor. "If he ever got really mad at somebody…" She looked up and shook her head. "I don't want to speak ill of the dead, but Jade was not exactly the easiest person to get along with."

He paused for a moment and digested the new information. He got himself a bottle of water and asked whether she wanted one. "Ms. Portia, do you mind if I ask why you and Don broke up?"

"He didn't want me in the business. When I started making movies, things fell apart pretty quickly. It was too bad. I really liked him. He was one of the good guys…"

Stanley mulled over the interview as he drove to Janus Studios. Until his conversation with Athena Portia, he had successfully pushed to the back of his mind the fact that the most likely suspect in the case was his former fraternity brother. He intended to ask Herb Matteson too whether his former partner had anger issues. Unfortunately, a mixture of drugs, alcohol, and passion remained the best explanation of how Don could have killed his favorite star.

Stanley arrived on time at the converted bowling alley that housed Janus Studios and was led by Matteson's flirty secretary back to his office. The producer sat behind his desk with his feet propped up. He invited Stanley in with a wave but did not stand up to shake his hand. They made small talk for a few minutes until Stanley asked whether Donald Johansson had a violent side.

"Yeah, he'd definitely go off on occasion. He couldn't abide a fool, so he'd sometimes shout at people, slam things to the ground, that kinda thing. Mostly, though, he was hard on himself. He fucked up an edit really bad once, wasted about five hours of work and got so pissed off that he pushed a monitor over.

That was about a thousand dollars right down the toilet." He smiled. "That pissed *me* off."

"Can you see him taking his rage out on someone else?" He watched the producer's reaction to the question closely. "Like Jade?"

"Nah." He thought about the question a moment longer. "Not if he were straight."

"Did you talk to him the night of the party? How did he seem to you?"

"He seemed fine to me, but I just saw him at the door. I didn't talk with him at all afterward. I was little jealous, to tell you the truth." Stanley found it hard to imagine the relaxed figure before him had once been at odds with Don over the level of sadism in their movies. If Matteson could hide that side of himself so easily, what else might the affable director be hiding?

"Could others have been jealous enough to want to sabotage Eden? Brian Mulkahey told me yesterday that Chimera felt threatened by Don." He was surprised to see the director struggle with the question before cautiously explaining what he knew about the rival studio.

"I'm only telling you this because you're Don's friend," he said confidentially, twisting a large turquoise ring on his left hand. "Barkley tried to get me interested in some scheme to freeze Don out of the nationwide video distribution chain. He said he wanted to convince our distribution people to market only movies made by Chimera, us, and maybe Boudoir. I don't know how he thought he could pull this off, but I told him to forget about it."

Stanley leaned forward in his chair and asked for more details about the process of off-line video distribution. He had assumed that studios sent their product directly to sex shops and video stores around the country.

"There's always a middleman," Matteson explained. "We take a lot of orders from individuals right off the website, but we have to rely on a distributor to get our goods to local outlets." He ignored an incoming phone call and waited for the ringing to stop before he continued. Stanley studied the awards covering the walls. He looked at the dates and saw that all of them had been earned when Don was still there. "They make a huge profit, more than we do, in fact."

"How come?"

"Well, part of it is because they bear the risk of obscenity prosecutions. Do you know how *Miller v. California* works?"

Stanley flashed back to his First Amendment course the second year of law school. *Miller* had established the infamous "community standards" test whereby an image might be legal in one jurisdiction and illegal in another depending on the standards of the people who lived there. Matteson explained how *Miller* worked in practice.

"If you sell a video depicting a blow job in some Mormon hellhole in Utah, then you're going to jail because you'll have exceeded the tolerance level of that local community. In New York City, you can sell almost anything short of kiddie porn." He explained how the distributors navigated these treacherous waters and decided what sort of material could be sold in which places. "When they make a mistake, they're the ones who pay for it. To make a long story short, the distributors take a big slice of the pie to bear the risk."

"I see." The legal decision had essentially organized an entire market. "So Barkley was going to convince the distributor not to deal with Don's product?"

"That's what he claimed," he answered with a shrug of his narrow shoulders.

"And you were too loyal to go along with the idea?"

"Too loyal and too scared." The director paused and frowned, taking a moment before continuing. "This is the part you can't repeat. You've probably read something about mob connections in the porn business? Well, most of the rumors are pure bullshit, at least as far as production goes. I've never seen any kind of mafia influence on any set in the valley. We do what we want when we make movies." He made an emphatic motion with his hand. "But I suspect the mob still has its fingers in distribution, left over from when all porn was illegal and they were in charge of the black market. Suffice it to say, I keep away from these guys as much as possible. They scare the shit out of me, and I just let 'em make their money. Live and let live, you know."

"You didn't want to get in bed with them and Barkley," Stanley concluded with an understanding nod of his head.

"Exactly. These are the last guys in the world I want to owe a favor." He ran his fingers through his hair and smiled. "I do watch *The Sopranos*, you know."

Stanley laughed, asked a few more questions, and learned that Barkley had approached Matteson a few weeks before the announcement that *Babes in Toyland* would be shown in mainstream theaters.

"One last question. Did Barkley mention that Chance Geary was involved in his plan in any way?"

"Nah, but it wouldn't surprise me. They knew each other and that little fuck is so dirty I wouldn't wipe my feet on him."

Stanley laughed again and gave the director his card in case he thought of anything else that might be relevant to Don's case. He said goodbye and made his way out of the studio and back to the car. Talking with Milton Barkley had suddenly risen to the top of his to-do list, and he hoped that Miriam had managed to arrange an interview. As he drove past the endless strip malls back to Eden, another thought entered his head: Why not have a look around the murder scene? McCaffrey thought the forensic team had completed its job, and he had the pass key to the office building. If he waited until later in the day when everyone at Eden was gone, he might dare to slip past the crime scene tape.

Stanley pulled in to Eden Studio after grabbing a quick sandwich and found that Don's sullen secretary had already left, but on the walk back to his temporary office he discovered that he was not entirely alone. In the room next to him, an acne-scarred teenager was busy stuffing oversized envelopes with DVD's. When the professor waved a greeting, the young man pulled off his ear phones and introduced himself as Jerry. He asked Stanley if he had locked the front door. The kid warned him about the neighborhood and informed him that the security guards had abandoned their posts when they found out that no more paychecks were coming.

"What about you?" Stanley asked. "Aren't you worried about getting paid?"

"Nah, Miriam pays me cash every night before she goes. It's a pretty sweet gig. I sit here all night filling orders." He pointed to a storeroom full of DVD's and promotional goods as he spoke. "And then get paid the next morning." He winked. "But don't tell the tax man."

"I won't," Stanley promised. But I will tell your boss, he thought. Don might question how his secretary got the cash to pay the kid for his nightly duties. Once the clerk left, Stanley sat down and sorted through the notes left on his desk. A pink form told him that McCaffrey had called, and a yellow sticky set the time for a lunch appointment with Milton Barkley the next day. The last message was to call Janet Stephens. He wracked his brain for a moment, and then remembered that Layla DiBona had introduced herself by that name before their interview several days earlier.

He called McCaffrey first and found him at his desk finishing up the day's paperwork. The detective told him that hair samples would be taken from everyone who attended the party on the night of murder. He also mentioned that no one had asked to pick up the victim's body for burial. This was uncommon, he explained, even in cases of indigent deaths, but it was almost unheard of with well-off and well-connected victims. Stanley pondered the information. Don had no money to take care of Jade's burial expenses, and Chance Geary was unlikely to be charitable. But where was Jade's family? He had not asked a single question about the victim's family, and the foolishness of the error reminded him that he was still a rank amateur in the detection business.

As he considered his omission, he heard a faint tapping on the front door and looked up to see if Jerry would answer it. Seeing no sign of the kid, he walked into the lobby and saw a smartly dressed blonde standing at the door.

Janet Stephens, aka Layla Dibona, followed him down the hall to his office and sat down with a smile. The middle-aged actress was dressed conservatively in jeans and a blouse, similar to the ensemble she had worn the first time they met, but she had added a turquoise choker to her long tan neck, and a more generous swell of bosom now peeked through the v-shaped opening of her silk top. "I dropped in this morning to collect my mail and Miriam complained that Don had given you an office here. I've been trying to get a hold of you."

"How did you know that I was here this evening?"

"I was driving by on the way home, so I pulled in to check. I saw the rental car and figured it might be you." She fingered the stone in the choker and smiled again. "I want to help with the investigation."

Her expression was serious and her body language confident. Of all the people he had interviewed, she had struck him as the most intelligent and self-aware. He had seen one of her films too; she was a surprisingly good actress. He pushed away the steamy memory of a pool boy bending her over a deck chair and asked why she wanted to help.

"Because Don's my friend." She folded her hands in her lap and stared down at them while she spoke. "Everyone's decided he's the killer, but he's the most decent person in this business, and I can't stand seeing him slandered by every news show in the country. His reputation is destroyed and so is his business." When she looked up, he could see tears glistening in the corner of her eyes. "You're the only one standing by him and I want to help."

She quickly regained her composure and ran through a laundry list of reasons why her former employer was incapable of murder. Her arguments were consistent with Stanley' own personal experience, as long as he conveniently forgot about the fingerprints on the murder weapon and the stories of Don's temper.

The possibility of taking on a partner was tempting. After his wife's defection, he needed help badly, and Janet was a true insider with a wealth of knowledge about every facet of the industry. "I'm not sure." He sent up a trial balloon. "Maybe we can start with a question that's been buggin me. Tell me what you know about Jade Delilah's background."

She dabbed her eyes with a tissue and considered the question. "Nothing at all, I'm afraid, but I have a pretty good idea how to find out."

# XVII

# SEARCH AND SEIZURE

"We just need to break into Don's office," Janet explained to the surprised young professor. Don's door was insubstantial and a quick flick of her credit card might suffice to open it up for inspection. A look at Jade's personnel file would give him all the information he wanted about the dead porn star. Hell, Don had probably filed away his love letters to her.

Her new partner looked doubtful about the plan. Although he was handsome, and maybe even had some sex appeal underneath his god-awful choice of 'professor chic' apparel, his goggling at her plan made him look more like Don Knotts than Magnum P.I. She placed her hands on her hips and stared him into submission. With a sheepish look on his face, he produced a key to the office in an upraised palm.

"Come on," she urged, "don't you want to see the room where it happened?" He eventually nodded his head and then went down the hall to make sure the Eden envelope stuffer was still distracted by the death metal noise rumbling in his ear phones. She watched him and nodded her approval. He had a nice butt which the worn corduroys showed off nicely. With that kind of raw material to work with and a no-limit credit card, it would only take a couple of hours at the Armani boutique in Beverly Hills to make him presentable in the LA circles that counted.

He returned with a conspiratorial nod of his head and together they padded down the blue carpet into the lobby.

The door to Don's office was immediately on their right, crossed by a large X of crime scene tape. He stuck the master key into the lock, turned it without touching the doorknob with his fingers, and pushed the door open with his elbow. After he flipped the light switch on with a tissue, they ducked underneath the tape and found themselves just five feet away from the blood stained-carpet where Jade had been found. Well, well, she thought, they really do use white chalk to draw around dead bodies.

He edged his way farther into the room and motioned for her to follow. She held her hand over her mouth and nose. "That's a lot of blood."

"Christ! It stinks," he replied. "I'm gonna open up a window." He walked behind Don's big wooden desk, turned the window handle to the right and pushed outward. Nothing happened. It was locked tight. He turned the handle back to its original position, and the window pushed out easily and let in a blast of warm dry air from the back parking lot.

"Fuck me!" He muttered. "The window was open." She knew immediately what he was thinking: Even if security were perfect at every door on the night of the murder, someone could still have snuck in through the unlocked window. "Come here," he waved her over. "Do you think it's big enough for someone to crawl through?"

She put her hand on the small of his back and leaned over his shoulder. "As long as they're not a Sumo wrestler."

Stanley pushed the drapes back and looked into the parking lot, trying to imagine it as the killer's entry point. She made a quick check for fibers that might have caught on the window sash but saw nothing. She wondered aloud if the window was open the night of the murder.

"I don't know," he replied. "I don't remember the report saying anything about it." He promised to ask McCaffrey if the forensic team had found the window locked or unlocked and then turned his attention to two wooden filing cabinets standing against the wall to the left of the desk.

After fumbling with two small keys, he finally opened the drawer marked "personnel." The files were ordered alphabetically by first name, beginning with Abby Lane and ending with Zephyr Breeze. "I saw this on porn websites too; it's always by first name."

"It's not like the phone book," Janet responded.

"I suppose," he speculated as he leafed through the files, "that actresses are treated like girls because children do as they are told. If you call someone Ms. Jameson instead of just Jenna, she's not as likely to jump into bed with three ugly dudes."

She hesitated to credit his academic speculation, but experience told her that he was probably right.

"Here it is," he exclaimed, "*Jade Delilah (Lily Walker)*." He pulled the hanging file folder out, swore and then turned it inside out to show it was empty. "McCaffrey must have taken it. He has to let me see it eventually, but I wanted to talk to her family before he did. I wonder what else is gone." He looked around the room.

While he was trying to guess what had been taken, she took a closer look at the file drawers and saw one labeled *18 U.S.C. ' 2257*. Here was a chance to prove her usefulness. She bent over, well aware of the impression her tight jeans were likely making on him, and explained the law that required legal documentation of the age of everyone who appeared in an adult film. Don would have to keep proof of age for all his actresses, including Jade, and it was highly likely that the cops had not bothered to cross-check.

She pulled the drawer out and stepped back to let him have the satisfaction of plucking out the file if it were still there. "Jade's label said Lily Walker, right?"

While he searched for the right file, she took another quick look into the personnel drawer. Just as she feared, her own folder was empty. The police had decided that her file was worth taking too.

"Here it is," the professor announced. He opened the file and found a single sheet of paper containing a photocopy of

Jade's driver's license with a handwritten name and address scrawled underneath listing "William Walker" as Jade's emergency contact. He scrutinized her license photo before handing it to Janet. "Damn. The DMV can make even a porn star look like a terrorist."

She smiled. "Do you think William Walker is her father?"

"Maybe. It'll certainly give me one more person to talk to who knew Jade." He handed the folder back. "Why don't you thumb through the rest of the files? I'll see if I can find anything interesting in the desk and credenza."

"What are we looking for?" She asked as she copied the information and refiled the paper.

"Hell if I know," he admitted. "The cops have already done all the fingerprinting and fiber collection, so I guess we're looking for anything that tells us something about Jade or Don or their love lives or whatever." He shrugged. "A signed confession from Chance Geary would be nice."

They spent the next two hours combing through the office. He started with the credenza and discovered that it was used as a general repository for DVD's, adult film awards, framed pictures, and obsolete software. Apart from the fact that most of the videos starred Jade Delilah, he found nothing remarkable. Neither did he find anything that looked like evidence in the small refrigerator next to it. The desk was somewhat more promising, if only because of the enormous number of papers stashed in its drawers. He never would have guessed that Don could be so disorganized. In the left side drawer he found receipts from lunches and dinners, sometimes with the names of his fellow diners scribbled on them. He put those from the most recent three weeks together in a small pile on top of the desk. In the middle drawer, he found an assortment of office supplies, a map of Los Angeles County, a stick of deodorant, a set of keys, and a collection of business cards. He flipped through the cards, which consisted mostly of equipment vendors, agents, and production people. He was about to put them back when the card on the top caught his eye. It was from a lawyer, but not someone practicing entertainment law or some other specialty that might be relevant to the owner of an adult film studio. The card listed the name and address of Deborah Spellerburg, Women's Justice Project, UCLA School of Law. On the back was written the time and date of the Tuesday immediately before the party.

He gazed down at it for a moment and then put it with the receipts he had saved. "Did you find something?" Janet asked from her station at the file cabinets.

"I don't know. A card that might be worth following up on." He looked over as she slowly picked her way through the files. With Jade's file gone, he doubted that she would find anything interesting, but the job needed to be done. He watched her move gracefully about the room, then looked away and vowed to think of her in the same chaste way that Inspector Thomas Lynley thought about Sergeant Barbara Havers.

"Did you find anything interesting in the files?"

"Plenty," she said, "but nothing relevant. I feel like a peeping tom. He's got everyone's STD records in here, but nothing has anything to do with Jade. It's just personnel files, tax records, and business contracts, jammed in with some stock photos and stuff related to various ads and trade shows."

Stanley tackled the final drawer and found little more of interest. If there were anything relevant, the police had taken it. They were undoubtedly focused on proving premeditation, so anything bearing on Don and Jade's relationship was gone. He would have to contact McCaffrey and arrange for a time to sift through whatever had been collected. As Stanley helped Janet finish with the files, they heard a car pull up outside the open window.

"Shit!" the professor whispered and touched the porn star's arm. "Shut that drawer and let's get out of here." They rushed toward the door, and she reached out to turn off the light. "No! Whoever it is will see it go off and know we're here. Just get to my office." They ducked under the tape, shut the door, and sprinted down the hall. He barely had time to close the door before someone entered the lobby.

"What do we do?" she whispered in his ear.

"Stay here 'til we know who it is." He forced himself to be still, and she pressed her cheek to his shoulder, holding him tightly. A moment later they heard faint footsteps and the jangle of keys coming down the hall. The intruder passed their hiding place and continued to the storage room.

"Was it just the stock boy?" Before he could answer, he heard voices coming from the room and he cracked the door slightly.

"It's Miriam!"

"What's she doing back here?" The actress held her lips close to his ear as she spoke. Her breath was warm and cigarette tinged.

He shook his head and waited for the conversation down the hall to end and shut the door quietly. After footsteps passed his door, he cracked it again and saw Miriam standing in front of Don's office. She entered and closed the door behind her. "Let's get out of here."

"Are you crazy? She'll see us!"

"Not if we leave while she's still in Don's office. Let's go!" He led her quickly down the hall, through the lobby and out the front door. After a quick look around to see if there was any convenient cover, he jogged over to the dumpster in the parking lot. "We can watch from here."

Stanley poked his head around the corner of the rusted metal bin. Janet stood behind him with her hand over her nose, trying to minimize the stench from the garbage. He saw Miriam emerge from the building carrying a flat object in her left hand. She walked around the corner and got in her car without so much as a suspicious glance at her surroundings.

"Now that was interesting."

"What did you see?"

"I think she was carrying a file folder."

They stayed hidden until the car pulled out of the parking lot and sped away to the east. They waited a moment, then made their way back across the blacktop. By the time they reached

Stanley's car, he had a short-term plan in mind. "Do you still want to help me out?"

"Absolutely," she exclaimed, "I haven't had this much excitement in years."

This was something he had never expected to hear from a porn star. "Then let's get something to eat." He looked at his watch. "It's almost midnight and I'm starving. We can talk and make a plan for tomorrow."

"I know just the place." She walked to her car. "Follow me."

Janet led them to a cozy Mexican restaurant in North Hollywood where the menu was full of items unavailable at the typical taco stand, including her favorite goat fajitas and the corn smut tamales. The waiter took their order and brought them a round of beers with some guacamole and homemade chips. She asked Stanley what they were going to do the next day.

"Okay, here's a possible plan for tomorrow. In the morning, I'd like to track down William Walker. Then, I've got lunch with the head of Chimera Productions. In the afternoon, I need to make some phone calls and start going over the video logs." He let out a sigh and stabbed at a chunk of avocado in the dip. "I also eventually need to see Don and ask him about Miriam, not to mention talking to McCaffrey about what was missing from Don's office and the open window. There's also that business card that needs to be checked out."

"What do you want me to do?" A sincere gratitude lit up his face. He really was adorable. If she were the mothering type, she might have been quite turned on, but sincerity and earnestness were traits that she appreciated more in her banker or her brother.

He hesitated a moment and then replied. "You remember the hotel room where we interviewed you two weeks ago?" She nodded. "I'd like to meet you there early in the morning and show you how to do the actress interviews for the day. I've been starting the interviews with questions about Don and Jade and the murder." He took a long gulp of his beer. "I think talking to women in the industry is key, and I've already gotten some leads. It would be super helpful if you could keep the interviews going."

That made sense, she supposed. He needed background information, and having her play Oprah would undoubtedly keep his own book project chugging a long. He promised to give her a script of questions and asked her to focus on getting information about Jade's sleazy agent and Milton Barkley, the head of Chimera.

"Wait a minute." She reached into her purse for a pen and a piece of paper to take notes. "You think there's a connection with Barkley?"

"He really wanted to see Eden fail and was trying to get Jade back to Chimera, maybe with Geary's help. He paused as the waiter dropped an aromatic plate of food in front of them. "Even more interesting, Stan Matteson told me that Barkley was involved in a conspiracy to freeze Eden out of the national video distribution market. Stan decided not to join, but he thought Barkley might go to extremes to hurt Don."

The professor was quite the imaginative little bulldog. Clearly, his theory was to muddy the waters so badly that the jury might entertain some doubt despite the physical evidence. She was impressed. Her feelings about Don were an oscillating, twisted mess, but she did not want to see him executed for a crime that he did not commit. She asked the professor if he had any other suspects.

"Well, for obvious reasons I'm pretty curious about Miriam." He looked suspiciously at a plate of blue tinged corn, but nodded in appreciation when he sampled the tasty fungus growing on it. "What does anyone know about her? And before you arrived tonight, I learned something from this Jerry dude who works back in the store room. She's been paying him cash to fill orders at night. Now, Don has no money. He can't even pay the security guards anymore. They've all been let go, but she's paying cash to the envelope stuffer."

"Do you think she's ripping Don off?"

"She could be skimming off the top of the mail order sales or running her own little business while the boss is locked up. Either way, she was pretty hostile the one time I questioned her about the murder. So, anything anyone knows about her would helpful too."

They sat in silence for several minutes and savored the meal. If the professor was nervous about having dinner with a porn star, he did not show it. The meal was all business, quite a contrast to her first dinner at the restaurant with Mötley Crüe drummer, Tommy Lee. He was the one who had introduced her to the place, and his agenda had definitely not been professional. When the check came, she slipped two twenties under the bill and told him that he could pay next time.

They had brought both their cars to the parking lot, and before driving off, they set a time for their meeting the next morning. The night was cool and a soft breeze blew through the valley. Neither was in a hurry to leave and Stanley filled the silence with one more bit of information. "I can show you the forensic reports tomorrow, but in case you're wondering, according to the Medical Examiner, we're looking for a lefty, maybe one with blond hair."

"Don's got dark hair," she replied. "Is he left-handed?"

"He's ambidextrous. I remember that from playing softball with him in college. I don't know if Detective McCaffrey knows, but I'm not about to tell him."

She rewarded him with a conspiratorial smile and a squeeze of his right bicep. "Thanks for letting me help." She kissed his cheek, slid into her bright red Mini Cooper and drove away.

# XVIII.

# A DAY OF PROBING

S tanley groaned in bed, unable and unwilling to object to the hands and tongues running over his body. Temptation had arrived moments earlier, when Janet and her friend Mia had come into his hotel room, arms around each other's bare waists, smiling lasciviously.

"This is the guy I told you about," Janet said to the voluptuous redhead at her side. "Isn't he a cutie?"

"Oooh, yeah," Mia purred as she crouched next the naked young professor and traced a finger down his stomach. Her green eyes beckoned as she licked her glistening red lips and reached down to touch him. "Mmm, a real cutie."

He moaned and watched with increasing excitement as Janet kissed her friend deeply, tongue slowly flicking from lip back to tongue. He could feel Mia's fingers tighten around him as she too fell under her friend's sway. Janet then moved her face closer to his and whispered seductively in his ear, "What do you want, baby? We'll do anything you want." Mia's ministrations rendered him incapable of verbal response, but Janet kept repeating the question in a smoky voice. She kissed him on the mouth for the first time and he arched his back. Mia gave a throaty laugh.

"Do you want her?" she whispered in his ear. He nodded his head and moaned again. "You gotta say it. Do you want her, Stanley?"

"Yes." She propped herself up on her elbow and gave him a commanding look. "Yes," he said desperately, "I want her." Janet lowered her face to his and kissed him as he felt Mia lower herself on to him. She moved slowly up and down, purring her pleasure and then squealing, "oh god, oh god, oh god, oh god," as she writhed on top of him. Stanley held on for a moment, but it was too much. He arched his back and screamed. With a final shudder, he lay back and received one last tender kiss from Janet. When his lips reluctantly left hers, he lay amidst a ruinous tangle of sheets.

Stanley shifted in bed and felt the sheets stick unexpectedly to his stomach. No way, he thought, not since high school. He gingerly lifted the top sheet, wiped himself off with disgust, and pushed it to the foot of the bed. By the time he made it to the shower, the details of the dream were already fading, but he recognized the scenario from the movie he had watched in the hotel room with Angela. As he scrubbed away the guilt of unconsciously cheating on his wife, he filed away a fact from the fantasy that he should have noticed earlier. Janet, like many other people, had short, blond hair.

When he got out of the shower, he went straight to the phone and dialed his home telephone number. The answering machine, once again. Angela had left a brief message the night before, asking that he not call too late. He had gotten back from his dinner with Janet after midnight Pacific Time, so he had waited. Now, it was more phone tag. That may not be a bad thing, he thought. She'll have more time to calm down, and he'd have more time to show that he was not on a wild goose chase.

He got dressed, grabbed a surprisingly fresh hotel donut, and arrived at the interview motel five minutes early. Janet was already waiting, parked in the space closest to the stairwell leading up to the room. She smiled when she saw him and stepped out of her car.

She wore a conservative twill skirt and matching jacket. Her tan silk blouse was buttoned all the way up to her neck and closed off at the top with a small cameo brooch. She asked him if her attire was appropriate for an interviewer.

"Absolutely." He pushed images from his dream out of his mind. "You look lovely." They walked side-by-side toward the building and he could not resist asking, "You mean this isn't your normal workday attire?"

"Not usually," she laughed and then grinned wickedly. "Although I did play a very naughty secretary in this outfit once." Knowing the penchant in porn titles for juvenile puns and double entendre, he wondered whether the movie she referred to had the word *dickation* in the title. As if reading his mind, she gave him a mischievous look as they arrived on the landing. "It was a parody of *Nine to Five*, so you can probably guess the title…"

Stanley unlocked the door and thought for a moment. "Oh no, not *Sixty-Nine to Five?*"

"Oh yes! You've got a future in the business, Professor." She looked around the room, taking inventory of the equipment. "God, especially with this setup here…if you knew how many rooms like this I've worked in." She sat down on the bed next to camera, her expression inscrutable. "Well, show me what to do."

He gave her a rundown of the equipment, and she grasped the technology easily. She slipped the notes she had taken at dinner into the yellow pad of Stanley's interview questions and asked to see the day's schedule. "Veronica, Aja, and Vanessa. This shouldn't be too bad. I've worked with two, and I've met Aja. Veronica might know something about the situation at Chimera. She's done most of her work there, I think."

While they finished setting up, he asked her about the banquet and her relationship with Jade. She had not seen anything of interest at the party and readily admitted that she did not have a good relationship with Eden Studio's hottest property.

Before he could explore her opinion of Jade, his cell phone rang, and a quick glance at the number told him it was his wife. He waved and left the room to take the call outside. It was a short conversation and ended before he could finish a single round of pacing across the parking lot. She wanted to know when he was coming home. He didn't know. Had he talked to Max? No. Would he reconsider his decision? Not yet. When he sensed she was about to hang up, he blurted out that he loved her. But the overture was met with a disapproving humming noise and a curt goodbye. So much for the cooling off theory, he thought as he tossed the phone into the car.

The problem was that they were both legitimately entrenched in their opinions. They both thought that they were absolutely correct, but unlike most marital disputes, the validity of their positions would soon be empirically verifiable. If Stanley wrote a book and caught a killer, then he would win. If he stained his reputation and lost his job, Angela would be proven right. He needed to find a way out of the win-lose scenario before the shit really hit the fan.

He crawled slowly into his car and with some effort managed to turn his mind to the first item on his day's agenda. Talking to William Walker better be more productive than dealing with Angela.

The address at the bottom of Jade's proof of age sheet took him just over the line from Los Angeles into San Bernardino County. California Bell directory assistance had no record of a William Walker at the address, so he entertained no great hope of meeting the man face to face, but he hoped neighbors might be able to provide a clue to his whereabouts. And if Jade had grown up in the neighborhood, then he might learn something about her too. He drove along Route 66 and easily found the cross street he was looking for. He continued along a busy commercial thoroughfare, noting an increasing number of liquor stores, strip clubs, and shabby hotels. If Jade had grown up here, he felt sorry for her. Small brick houses baked in the sun, their weed-choked lawns conveying a message of neglect and resignation.

One more turn and he slowed down to read house numbers. Many were obscured or simply not posted. He finally spotted two small houses marked Twenty-two fifteen and Twenty-two nineteen. Number Twenty-two seventeen, the address he was looking for, was presumably the one in between. He pulled into the driveway but a chain link gate prevented him from getting his car completely out of the street. There was no traffic and only eighteen inches of the bumper stuck out, so he parked.

He walked a couple of paces down the sidewalk to the front gate, trying to determine whether the house, like both of its neighbors, was guarded by a dog. A Pontiac parked inside the fence was so battered that it only minimally signaled someone might be at home, so he shook the fence and coughed loudly. When no guard dog came leaping out, he opened the gate slowly and walked tentatively to the front door, ready to hightail it back over the fence at the first hint of a growl.

He stood on the cracked concrete porch and looked around at the cinderblock bunkers that passed for houses. Being a door-to-door salesman in this neighborhood would totally suck. The doorbell did not work, so he rapped hard with his knuckles. Two dogs immediately began barking and scratching the inside the door. A moment later, he heard a voice scolding them, and a man in his early thirties looked out warily. "Yeah?"

"I'm sorry to bother you," Stanley began, "but I'm looking for a William Walker. He used to live at this address."

"I'm William Walker." He was a muscular and attractive man whose appearance was marred by a Neolithic forehead and a sullen look. "And I still live here, as far as I know." He made no move to invite Stanley into the house.

"Nice to meet you!" He replied with feigned enthusiasm. "Directory assistance had no phone number for you at this address, so I thought you must have moved."

"I just have a cell." His eyes narrowed and one of the dogs behind him emitted a low growl. "So, what do you want?"

He cleared his throat. "I'm an investigator working on the murder of Jade Delilah, and your name is listed as the emergency contact on her paperwork at Eden Studio." The scowl on Walker's face deepened, but Stanley plowed ahead. "We're looking for leads in the case and I wanted to talk to you about her."

"Who's we?" The dogs started barking again, and Walker cuffed a Rottweiler/Doberman mix hard on the back of the head and told it to shut up. Its glare suggested that it would definitely enjoy making an early lunch of its master's visitor. When Stanley made eye contact with the mongrel, the bad tempered rumble in its chest deepened. The professor forced a smile and focused his attention on Walker.

"I'm the chief investigator for Don Johansson, Ms. Delilah's employer who is currently being held in connection with her murder." He tried to keep his tone conversational and engaging. "We've been having trouble tracking down Jade's family. In fact, her body is still lying unclaimed at the county morgue."

"A private investigator? That figures." Walker gave a sarcastic laugh. "The fucking lazy-ass LAPD haven't been out here yet, but a civilian has no problem finding me." He shook his head and snorted. "I wouldn't work with those LA clowns again if they doubled my salary."

"You're a police officer?"

"San Bernardino County Sheriff's Office." That explained the barrel chest and massive forearms, but it did not explain his relationship to Jade. "What do you want to know?" The cop demanded. "Make it quick. I've got a shift starting soon."

"Well, first of all. How did you know the victim?" Afraid that the door might shut at any moment, he went directly to the heart of the matter. "What can you tell me about her background?"

Several emotions crossed the police officer's face in a flash, but he settled on anger. He spoke in a measured, menacing monotone. "I'm her husband. That's how I know her. And there aren't any relatives to talk to. Her parents are both dead. She's got a sister somewhere in Oxnard, but I haven't seen her for years. You want to know about her history? Well, join the fucking club." He snorted and shook his head. "She said she had a turd for a dad and never said much about her mother or her sister."

"What was her maiden name?"

"Lily Sharperson, but she wasn't much for telling the truth. I met her at one of the strip clubs on the highway."

"Mr. Walker, when did you two separate?"

The officer looked at him like the answer was obvious. "When she became a whore." Stanley was stunned by the vehemence of the reply. The estranged husband grew impatient waiting for another question and reached for the door knob.

"Wait!" Stanley exclaimed, "Are you going to claim the body?"

"No, bury her yourself," he spat and then slammed the door shut. The erstwhile investigator was left standing on the porch wishing he could get more out of the angry cop, but the dogs started barking madly and he hurried back to the car.

On the drive back to Van Nuys, he considered Walker as a possible suspect in the killing and realized once again that he needed to examine the video logs of the Eden Studio lobby as soon as possible. If Chance Geary or William Walker's face were on the recordings, then he could narrow his focus. As it was, the suspects were proliferating at an alarming rate. He had no desire to add a bitter cop husband to a list that already included a sleazy drug dealing manager, a do-gooder porn director and all his unscrupulous competitors. He looked at his watch. There was just time to stop at the studio for an hour before meeting Milton Barkley for lunch.

Stanley went straight to his office with only a passing wave at Miriam who was busy at the photocopy machine behind her desk. A policeman had delivered copies of the lobby surveillance recordings the previous afternoon, and he plugged in a television and found a DVD labeled 17:00-22:00 on the date of the murder. The DVD should contain the faces of all who entered the building during that time, except for someone who may have entered through the window in Don's office. He watched for forty-five minutes, fast-forwarding much of the beginning, but he saw no sign of either Geary or Walker. Then, as he watched large numbers of people arriving for the dinner, he caught a glimpse of Jade Delilah entering the building on the arm of a distinguished looking mid- dle-aged man. He froze the screen and studied Jade's companion, but he didn't recognize him. Another player unaccounted for, he winced. Perhaps Janet could make an identification.

A quick look at his watch told him that he needed to get moving. Stanley had not met Milton Barkley on his porn studio tour, and he wondered how he would compare to the other studio heads, Brian Mulkahey and Stan Matteson. It was a short drive to Chimera which he found on a cul-de-sac off Friar Street. It was the most heavily guarded of all the studios. A black-suited man with a silver ear piece stood at the front door, while another guard sat in the lobby. Once his identification was checked, a shapely young receptionist led him to a large modern office where a buffet was set out on a linen tablecloth.

"Mr. Barkley said to make yourself at home. There's plenty of food." She accepted his thanks and left him alone in the office. The walls were covered in abstract art, with no sign of movie posters or starlet glamour shots. Framed photos on the credenza behind Barkley's desk showed him in restaurants or on golf courses with a number of recognizable athletes and rock stars. Resisting the temptation to snoop in Barkley's desk, Stanley gravitated to a pile of shrimp sitting in a bowl of ice and had just popped one in his mouth when a vaguely familiar face in a tailored Italian suit stepped into the room and introduced himself as the owner of Chimera Productions.

Stanley wiped his hand and swallowed quickly. "Nice to meet you, sir. Thanks for taking the time to speak with me." He gestured to the table and tried to determine where he had seen his host before. "The food's great."

"Thank you," he replied, "we've got the best caterer in the business. In fact, I once had a girl tell me that she'd be willing to screw a horse just for the lunches." He laughed, and Stanley recognized where he had seen him before. He had accompanied Jade as she arrived at the party on the night she was murdered. "We try to set the standard here at Chimera in every way. Please, serve yourself."

Stanley fixed himself a crab salad croissant and sat down across from Barkley in a comfortable, overstuffed chair. "As you know," the professor explained, "I'm helping Don with his investigation. Right now, we're learning everything we can about Jade to figure out who had a motive to kill her."

"I don't know who would want to hurt her," Barkley replied before he popped a shrimp into his mouth. "She was a charming and beautiful young woman."

"What about her agent, Chance Geary?"

"Now, why would Chance want to kill Jade? She was his meal ticket." He shook his head in disbelief.

"It wouldn't be the first time a jealous man did something stupid, Mr. Barkley." The producer was altogether too slick and confident. "The people that I've talked to tell me he's a drug dealer with a very nasty reputation."

"Sure," he conceded, "Chance is ambitious and rather rough around the edges, but I'm sure that he wanted only the best for Jade." Taken aback by the nonchalant dismissal of his prime suspect, the professor temporarily lost his train of thought. He took a bite of his sandwich and regrouped.

"What about William Walker?" He watched carefully for any flicker of recognition. "He's a cop in San Bernardino County who claims to be Jade's husband. Have you ever met him?"

"William Walker? No, I don't think I've ever heard of him. Jade may have mentioned an estranged husband once, but I certainly never met him." He calmly picked at some calamari, looking more like a partner in a white-shoe law firm than a porn mogul.

"Do you think Don did it then?"

"Of course he did." Barkley reached over and put his empty plate back on the buffet table. "But not for the reason everyone thinks. You see, the day before the party, I convinced Jade to come back to Chimera. I presume that she made the mistake of telling Don that his hottest property was leaving Eden. Toss in his crush on her and you have a recipe for disaster." Barkley seemed mildly amused by the whole situation.

"Have you told the police this?"

"Of course. It's certainly relevant to their investigation, don't you think?" Stanley envisioned the smug look on the director's face as he handed the police Don's motive on a silver platter.

"Do you have any proof that she was leaving Eden?" He tried to regain some momentum and wipe the self-satisfied expression off Barkley's face. If he had just rehired Jade, he should be more upset by her death. But then again, the benefit of losing Eden as a competitor may have been far greater than the benefit of adding another star to his own stable. "Or is it just your word that Jade was joining you?"

"We hadn't put anything in writing yet, if that's what you mean." He shook his hand dismissively. "This is an industry where handshake deals are still common."

"Is it also an industry where someone might collude to exclude one of his competitors from a national distribution market?"

"Excuse me?" The producer looked curiously at his interrogator. "I'm not sure I know what you're talking about."

"I can't reveal my sources, but I've heard that you've been conspiring to cut Eden Studio out of the national video distribution chain. If you're working to destroy Don's business, it makes me wonder what you might be willing to do to succeed." For a moment, he thought he had shaken the producer's calm demeanor, but Barkley brushed him aside like an annoying insect and responded smoothly.

"Professor Hopkins, I have never conspired to cut my good friend Don out of any business, and I find your suggestion that I meant him harm to be quite offensive." He wiped his mouth on his napkin and stood up. "Now, if you'll excuse me, I need to get back to the set."

"No problem," Stanley said as he put down his plate, regretting the fact he had lost control, but realizing he had little to lose in antagonizing Barkley further. "I was watching an interesting piece of video footage from the surveillance cameras in the Eden lobby. I saw that Jade was your date to the party on the night she was murdered."

"Nice, Professor," he said with disdain as he opened the door to let his guest out of the room. "Jade called me and asked for a ride to the party, and I was happy to accommodate her.

Make of that what you will. Detective McCaffrey did not seem particularly impressed by the revelation. Now, if you'll excuse me, I've got work to do." He led Stanley to the lobby and nodded at the security guard before striding back down the hall. Stanley watched him for a moment, trying to measure whether Barkley's brusqueness was evidence of arrogance or guilt or both, but then he felt the pressure of a hand on his back and was guided gently to the exit.

When Stanley got back to Eden, he sat down in front of the video monitor and continued to watch the parade of characters who had attended the party, but his mind kept drifting back to his talk with the head of Chimera. It had been an amateur performance at best and reminded him of other interviews with executives that he had botched. He could coax great information out of everyday workers, but guys in suits sometimes flustered him. He was going to have put on his big boy pants if he wanted to get anything useful out of people like Barkley.

He watched Janet arrive unattended at the banquet in her shirtless tuxedo and saw Don greeting the guests crowding into the lobby. Then, he saw Angela light up the screen, to his mind every bit as sexy as the stars who preceded her. He hit the pause button and thought about calling her, but the chill in her voice that morning deterred him, and he decided to send her a bouquet of flowers instead. He pressed play again and the crowd in the lobby thinned out until only the guards remained. Toward the end of the recording, two or three figures he did not recognize exited the building and then one entered. To his surprise, he recognized the one who entered late. She paused as she took a puff of a cigarette before extinguishing it in an ashtray and walking back to the party. He checked the time imprint on the recording—her appearance was within the time frame when the murder would have occurred.

How could Janet have entered twice when he had not seen her leave? He worked back through the DVD and found no sign of her ever having left the building. He forwarded to the end and saw no one else leave the building until the video log showed a commotion among the guards and then the police rushing in several minutes later. The screen went blank and he reached for the telephone.

"McCaffrey here." The detective's voice was even more brusque than usual.

"It's Stanley Hopkins. Do you have a second?"

"No."

"Could we meet tomorrow? I've got some questions."

"How about eleven tomorrow morning, at the jail? I need to check in on your friend, and I'll squeeze you in." Stanley thanked him and got around to the real reason for his call.

"And could you check and see whether the officers on the scene noticed whether the back window to Don's office was open when they arrived? It was open yesterday."

"Did you go into the office?" McCaffrey demanded immediately.

"No!" Stanley improvised, "you could see from the back parking lot that it was cracked open."

"Don't bullshit me." To his surprise, the detective laughed. "But it doesn't matter; we're done in there. Poke around all you want. Just don't take anything."

"Don't you think it's important that the window may have been open the night of the murder?"

"No," he laughed again, "but I'll ask the team. We're dotting all of our i's and crossing all of our t's on this one. 'Til tomorrow, Sherlock." With that, he hung up, and Stanley wondered what to do next.

He poured himself a cup of coffee from a pot located in a small alcove and decided to reread the crime scene forensic report one more time. It did not reference the open window, but the section on fibers listed a purple tuft that had been taken from the window frame. His planned to request a test of the fibers found at the scene against the clothing worn by all of the guests at the party and guessed the police would not greet the idea with much enthusiasm.

As he was finishing with the report, he heard a rap on his door, and Janet walked in and sat down. She looked excited, and he delayed asking about her mysterious double entrance the night of the party.

"How did it go?"

"Really well, I think. Veronica and Vanessa each went the full two hours. Aja had to leave a little early but we got through all your questions." She smiled. "It was fun. I just pretended I was a talk show host. Veronica even admitted that she doesn't have twenty-seven orgasms every time she does a scene."

"Great!" He hoped Janet could provide an innocent explanation for her double entrance at the party. Without her, he could not help Don and finish the book interviews at the same time. "Did you find out anything relevant to the investigation?"

"I think so. It's a great way to start the interviews, by the way. Everybody wants to talk about the murder. It really gets 'em going." She pulled her notes out of a small black purse. "Well, first of all, it turns out that Aja was pretty close to Jade. They weren't super tight, but they've got the ethnic thing in common." Janet was confident and professional; maybe she'd do better with suspects like Milton Barkley. "Anyway, Jade told her that she was going to drop Geary as her agent when she went back to Chimera." Stanley imagined the mechanics fury at losing his girlfriend and prime source of income at the same time.

"Had she told him yet?"

"I don't know, but Jade was afraid of what he might do when he found out."

He leaned back in his chair and processed the information. It dovetailed nicely with what he had learned earlier from the head of Chimera.

"There's more, too." She flipped a page in her notebook and added excitedly, "Vanessa hooked up with Chance before Jade did."

"Are you kidding me? The guy's a weasel. What do these women see in him?" His exasperation was genuine and personal.

He still had vivid memories of the swaggering louts in his high school who inevitably dated the most attractive girls.

"Well, with Vanessa, it was definitely the crank. He was her meth connection until she got into rehab, and she was probably his connection to the business. Anyway, according to Vanessa, while they were together he threatened to kill her at least twice."

"Why am I not surprised?" He layered on the sarcasm. "Did she say why?"

"He thought she was stepping out on him. She said he was insanely jealous. She was totally terrified of him. I think that was part of her going into rehab, to get away from him." She put her notes back in her purse and crossed her legs.

He told her about the fibers that had been found by the window and wished he could run an analysis on Geary's clothes. But if the agent had paid a visit to the Eden office, then how had he have known that Don and Jade would be there? He thought for a moment and ran a scenario past Janet. "Let's say that Chance knows he's not welcome at the party, so he prowls around trying to find a way in. He finds the window cracked, or maybe he jimmies it open, and then waits in the dark. He can't be sure that Don will come in, but maybe he's looking for something in the office or maybe he's just planning to trash the place."

"Or maybe he's waiting for the right moment to pop out and crash the party."

"Sure," Stanley acknowledged and continued. "He didn't bring a weapon, so he wasn't planning to kill anyone that night." He closed his eyes briefly and envisioned the scene. "So, he's sitting waiting and much to his surprise, Don stumbles in and passes out on the couch. What do you do when your nemesis falls right into your lap? It throws him off guard for a while. He waits and wonders what he should do, but before he can decide, his woman comes in, clearly anticipating a private rendezvous with the other man. He loses his temper and goes nuts. Somehow, he has enough presence of mind after killing her to wipe the handle of the fraternity paddle for fingerprints and slip it into Don's hand."

She nodded her head. "That story makes as much sense as Don killing her, but we've got nothing to place Geary at the scene."

*Unlike you*, he thought. He debated once again whether to raise the issue of her double entrance, but decided again to wait. Instead, he abruptly stood up, "I'm totally starving. Why don't we hash through this over dinner?"

# XIX.

# JADED

At six o'clock the following morning, Janet congratulated herself for ordering only a small tuna salad the night before. Her workout would go slightly easier having avoided the thick steak and Belgian fries that she had really wanted. She leaned against an outside wall at her gym and took a deep drag on a cigarette. Exercising would go smoother still if she stopped smoking, and she told herself, as she automatically did with every cigarette, that she'd quit in two years, max—once she was done with the business. Even so, smoking was better on the hips and thighs than the chocolate sundae she'd rather be sucking on. But in a couple of years, hell with it; she'd just let the thighs and hips go. But not quite yet, not for a couple years more.

She heard the annoying clank and squeal of a garbage truck working its way down the street, and absentmindedly rubbed her temple where a headache was just starting to tap. As the smoke curled up around her, her eye caught the flouncing, sashaying approach of two teenage girls leaving the all-night diner next door to the gym, carelessly strolling arm in arm. As she watched their approach, she remembered being seventeen herself, beautiful and knowing it, reveling in the exhilarating realization of the effect her body and her looks had on men. Hell, on *all* people, really. The girls were so young and effortlessly gorgeous that it never occurred to them that some women actually had to work at it, that their own older selves would have to work like mad if they wanted to keep the magic alive.

As the girls passed the garbage truck, the middle-aged man swinging the cans allowed his eyes, and then his entire head to follow their every step as they approached and then passed. Once he'd seen both the front presentation and their tight little asses swaying in unison, he glanced up at the driver with a smile and a rueful, appreciative shake of the head. The girls giggled, added a little extra bounce to their walk, but carried on without breaking stride. Janet watched them and reflexively evaluated their attributes and flaws. The short one was cute, with great hair and eyes, but her hips and thighs were already beginning to saddlebag. This was the best she was ever going to look. Better grab a boy now, darlin' and hopefully one that will be pushing a pen behind a desk rather than some garbage worker a year before his back goes ZAP and he's stuck on the couch yelling at his wife to bring him more PBRs and another oxycodone and to keep them damn kids *quiet* for chrissakes. If she didn't start working on those thighs soon, or snag the smart guy, she'd be in trouble, because she sure didn't look smart enough to catch 'em with her amazing wit and intelligence. The taller one, though, she had a cunning look about her that made her the alpha for sure. Good legs, small boobs, but they're round and firm…she's definitely more aware. Would she be interested in doing a few photos?

As her eyes followed the girls' movements, she absently ran her hands down her own hip and outer thigh and decided she needed to kick up her regimen on the Stairmaster, maybe another fifteen minutes twice a week. Only for another two or three years, though, then *that* particular torture-fucking-machine would be the first thing to go, right before the smokes. She envisioned physically lifting the hated beast up in her bare hands and smashing it through the gym's plate glass window, and watching it crash and tumble down the manicured embankment, maybe taking out a couple of Porsches or Beemers in its wake. She shook her head and snuffed out the cigarette. Even though there were a dozen trodden butts littering the landing, she reflexively looked around for the skinny phallic ash can. She would no more throw a used butt on the ground than wear black granny panties under a pair of white skinny jeans. Discipline, old damn habit, was a constant companion and the only way to survive on top, no matter what the business was.

As she walked around to the front of the gym, the mechanical roar of the garbage truck stopped, and a low, slow whistle followed in the sudden silence. A small, satisfied smile curled one side of Layla's glossy lips. Yeah, definitely in three, four years she would toss the cigs after the Stairmaster and just let herself go. Five, tops.

At the end of dinner, Stanley had asked her to reschedule the interview set for the following morning and to instead track down Jade's sister in Oxnard. If the sister were no longer there, or if she were married and no longer going by Sharperson, then it was going to take some professional leg work to find her. When Janet had gotten home, she had gone straight to her computer and searched for Sharperson in the Oxnard online white pages. She got two hits: one for a Samuel T. and one for a Rebecca. She then did a Google image search of both names, but none of the pictures in the results looked anything like the exotic Jade Delilah, née Lily Sharperson. Resolving nonetheless to call the two Oxnard hits first thing in the morning, she brushed her teeth, slipped on a shapeless gray t-shirt and fell into bed.

She got back from the gym and learned that Oxnardians were early risers. Neither Rebecca nor Samuel were at home at 7:30 a.m., so she left messages and sat back down at the computer to find a private detective. Stanley probably did not have the money to reimburse her for the expense of hiring a private eye, but her bank account was healthy, and she was intrigued by the possibility of learning Jade's secrets. As she was searching for online ratings for investigators, the phone rang and a cheerful female voice introduced herself as Rebecca Sharperson.

"I was in the shower when you called," she explained breathlessly.

"Thanks for getting back to me so quickly." Janet grabbed a pen and note pad and pushed her laptop to the side. "My name is Janet Stephens and I'm looking for the sister of a woman named Lily Sharperson. I don't know the first name, but I was told that she lived in Oxnard, or at least used to live there." She dooddled an abstract pattern of overlapping circles and squares while she talked. "I started with the white pages and found you."

Silence on the end of the line and Janet wondered whether the woman had hung up. "I have a half-sister named Lily," she replied cautiously, "but I haven't seen her for a while. Who did you say you were again?"

"Janet Stephens." She considered the possibility that Rebecca had not heard about the murder. "I'm a research assistant for Professor Stanley Hopkins—"

"—is she okay? Are you with the police?"

"No," she spoke calmly at the tide of anxiety rising on the other end of the line, "we are definitely not with the police."

"You're not with her husband, are you?" She spoke with determination. "I already told him that I didn't know where she was. And even if I did, I'd never tell that pile of shit."

"No, wait, don't hang up!" Janet scrambled to put together a story that would keep the young woman on the line. "I'm a friend of your sister and we need to talk. Is there anywhere we could meet? I just need a little bit of your time."

A pause. "There's a Denny's on the 101, just past the last Camarillo exit."

"Could you be there by nine thirty?" Sharperson promised to be there, and Janet hurried to get ready, plotting a course in her head that would avoid the worst of the morning traffic.

As she drove down the highway, she thought about the tidbits of information that Stanley had learned about Jade from her husband. No shock that little Jade had gone to Stripper College before graduating to porn. Strippers were a nasty lot, angrier and bitchier than the girls who started off as models. Society might not see any difference between posing for a magazine and taking off your clothes in a room full of men, but those who thrived in the raucous world of strip clubs were simply tougher, and usually more damaged, than the girls who took the plunge in private, with a little lingerie and a discrete photographer. Strippers liked controlling men in a club, not just teasing and baiting, but grabbing their balls, metaphorically, of course, and squeezing hard. Dancers were into revenge, not seduction. She hated pinheaded speculation on why women became porn stars, but she had to admit that strippers were knee-jerkers, reacting to times in their lives when they couldn't control their men.

She popped onto the Ventura Freeway at Hidden Hills and made her way west between the hills and canyons that signaled the northern edge of the Los Angeles. She pretended that Thousand Oaks and Westlake Village did not exist and looked off toward the Santa Monica mountains whenever it was safe to take her eyes off the road. Once past Casa Conejo, she got another nice dose of green before dipping down into the Santa Rosa valley. It was noticeably warmer in the valley below, so she rolled up the windows and switched on the air conditioning for the last few miles to the Denny's.

By 9:30 a.m., most of the breakfast crowd had cleared out and only a couple of tables were occupied. Janet looked around and saw a mousy blonde sitting in a booth at the back, dipping down her head slightly to blow on top of her coffee. She looked up and responded to the newcomer's wave with a hesitant smile. Janet walked over and shook her hand warmly. "Thanks so much for meeting me."

She sat down across from the woman and decided to ditch her plan to ask some quick questions before mentioning Jade's death. Rebecca Sharperson's face was utterly guileless. She was significantly older than Jade, probably in her early thirties, but looking even older due to the lack of flair in her frizzy hair and Wal-Mart clothes. There was something of her sister in her striking blue eyes and her nose and jaw, but nothing of the sullen smolder that was Jade's trademark.

"Rebecca." She took a deep breath. "I'm sorry to have to tell you that your sister is dead." Janet saw the head drop and the shoulders sag and hurried to get it over with. "She was killed last week."

The woman stifled a sob and Janet reached into her purse for a tissue. She did not completely break down but wiped her eyes and blew her nose. She looked profoundly sad, but not completely surprised. "Did her husband do it?"

"We don't know yet." She handed over another tissue. "Haven't you seen the television reports?"

"The television?" She sniffed and looked confused. "I just got back from Vancouver. I was doing a Native American jewelry course in British Columbia for a week." She held out a beautiful obsidian ring and bent back her collar to reveal a matching necklace. "I make and sell jewelry, you know." She blew her nose and corrected herself. "Of course, you don't know."

"You must be the only person on the west coast who doesn't know that Jade Delilah was killed at Eden Studio last week." She reached over and covered Rebecca's hand. "I'm so sorry."

"Jade?" She paused for a moment. "A stage name?"

Janet waved at a waitress and ordered a cup of coffee and a refill for her companion. "Why don't you tell me what you know about your sister over the last couple of years, and I'll fill you in with what I know."

The jewelry maker splashed her coffee with cream and poured in a packet of artificial sweetener. She seemed oddly comfortable telling her story, almost relieved that the inevitable last chapter had finally been written. "I last saw Lily about two years ago. She was planning on leaving her husband—"

"—William Walker, the cop?"

"That's right." She took a sip and continued. "She wanted to borrow some money to rent an apartment and get away from him. I knew that she'd never pay me back, but I was so glad that she was leaving him that I gave her what she needed. He called me a while later, asking where she was, but I wouldn't tell him. He was really pissed. He called her a whore and said she was making porn movies. I called him a liar, but he sent me some nasty internet link to prove it."

"Did you know that she worked as a stripper before that?"

She sighed and accepted more coffee from the waitress. "How else do you meet a winner like William Walker?" She shook her head. "Yeah, I knew. She said that she was just earning enough money to go back to school, but I never believed her. She burned through her cash as fast as she earned it. That's why she needed to borrow from me."

"And that was the last time you saw her?"

"She basically disappeared. I assumed that she was dancing or making movies or whatever and that she'd eventually show up on my doorstep." She grimaced and wiped her eyes with her hand. "Now I guess she has." She straightened up and pushed her hair back out of her eyes. Despite the frizz and the unflattering jacket, she was quite attractive. She had a long sleek neck and captivating eyes when she lifted them from the table. "How did you know Lily?"

"We worked for the same studio; Eden Studio, that is. It's the best, not that that's much consolation, I suppose." If Jade's sister was surprised, it didn't show. "We were at a large party together at the studio when your sister was found beaten to death."

"I heard about that when I was waiting in the airport. I was sitting behind the monitor reading a book." She shook her head and moaned.

Janet paused for a moment and took a small yellow pad out of her purse. She doubted that she would forget anything that Rebecca had to say, but the gesture of professionalism might make the interview easier. "My friend, Don Johansson, has been accused of killing her, but he didn't do it. In fact, he was in love with her. I'm working with the investigator in his case to find out all we can about Jade, to find out who might have wanted to hurt her."

"William is the obvious one. He used to beat her." She nodded her head at the logic of her assertion. "That's why I was so glad when she left him."

"Have you ever heard of Chance Geary?" The victim's sister shook her head. "Milton Barkley? Miriam Wilhoit?" She mentioned several other names of people in the industry that Jade worked with or knew.

None of Janet's prompting bore fruit. Rebecca Sharperson really had little clue about her sister's life. "I'm sorry. Like I said, I hadn't heard from her in two years."

"I know it's probably not relevant, but could you tell us a little about Lily's background?" She spoke gently, conveying the understanding that she might be intruding on private territory. "Everyone at Eden knew her, but no one had a clue about who she was. She really was pretty mysterious."

"She's was always like that. Even when she was a baby, she hardly cried." The memory of her little sister evoked a rare smile. "She'd just stare up at you with those gorgeous eyes."

"You're older than her?" The fact was clear but politeness demanded the initial question. "You said on the phone that you were half-sisters."

"That's right." She finished her coffee and then pushed it away. "I was ten when she was born. My father had divorced my mother and moved to Seattle a couple of years before that. My mother remarried an Indian surgeon named Vikram Chandrasekar, and Lily was born on their one year anniversary."

"Are your mother and her husband still in Oxnard?"

"No," she said quietly, "they died in a car accident last year." She reached into her purse and pulled out a picture of a very attractive fifty-something couple sitting down at a formal dinner. Jade's mother had beautifully styled short, thick hair and was wearing a black dress that showed off generous décolletage. Her husband was even more striking, a dashing Indian version of Sean Connery. "They look happy, don't they?"

"Absolutely."

"It's just a good picture." She slipped it back into her purse. "I keep it because my mom looks so beautiful. I should just cut him out."

Janet nodded and considered where to go next with her questions. The line between relevance and mere curiosity was blurry. "What was your stepfather like?"

"I was nine when they married, and quite frankly, I barely got to know him. Vik was establishing his practice and was never home. And whenever he had any time off, he'd go back and visit relatives. When he was around, he was very reserved. Cold and distant, but not abusive. Other than the obvious reason, I never could understand what my mom saw in him." An elderly couple walked in the restaurant and the waitress began guiding them in the direction of Janet and Rebecca's table. The actress warned her off with her eyes and a slight movement of her head, and the threesome altered course.

"What about Lily?"

"I don't know," she said carefully. "She was about eight when I left for college, so we were never super close, but she was a cute kid and really smart. I figured she'd end up as the cheer-leader/honor society type, but somehow she went off the rails." She shook her head and sighed. This was a story she had tried to puzzle out unsuccessfully many times. "I don't know what it was, but there was so much tension in the house that I just stopped visiting. My mom would come up to see me at school or over here in Oxnard after I moved." She looked up hopefully. "They were living down in Orange County then, so maybe it was just the suburban drug rebellion thing."

"Do you know for sure that she was using drugs?"

"I know that she smoked pot because I smelled it on her a couple of times, but so does every other high school kid in California. I really don't know what she was doing." The restaurant was almost deserted and Rebecca spoke freely, spinning her ring around her finger and trying to work out how her family had disintegrated. "All I know is that she started running away from home when she was around fifteen and finally made it stick when she was seventeen or so. I remember because my mom called me and was crying because she had dropped out of high school. Vik refused to talk about it and wouldn't let my mother mention her name around him."

The waitress came over and laid the bill on the table. Janet reached for it and put it underneath her coffee mug. Rebecca continued without prompting. "I really should have done more. But their house...it just wasn't my home, you know? I did put Lily up for a couple of weeks, but she left and moved in with some boyfriend. I'd hear from her occasionally. She actually invited me over to her house after she got married, but it was as fucked up as my mom's." She started to cry again. "I guess I'm a pretty shitty big sister."

"No, you're not." Janet reached over and squeezed both her hands. "There was nothing anyone could do for Jade." She almost mentioned the sheer destructiveness at the core of her sister's personality but there was no reason for her to know how vicious her sibling had become. "It sounds like you were there for her when she needed you. That's all you can do."

"I guess so," she replied doubtfully. Janet asked a few more questions, but there seemed little more to learn about the household Jade grew up in. If there were any secrets, they probably died with the handsome couple in the photograph. Rebecca pulled out her pocketbook, but Janet refused her offer to contribute and brought the bill to the counter. The grieving sister went to the bathroom, and they met a few minutes later on the sidewalk outside the foyer.

"There is one more bit of bad news," Janet said as they walked to their cars. "No one has claimed Lily's body. It's still with the county." To her surprise, Rebecca brightened a little.

"I can do that for her, at least," she said with sudden determination. "I won't leave her alone."

Janet gave her a brief hug and got into her car and wondered idly who would come and deal with her own corpse. At one time she had thought Don might have taken care of her, an old man shaking with emotion as he scattered her ashes to the wind. Not happening now. And her family certainly wouldn't do the job. Her parents were long out of the picture and her sister's Mormon husband allowed no contact with her profligate kin.

She pulled out of the parking lot and headed back to meet Stanley. Regrets were for fools. She had the life she wanted. Porn was not the problem; even conventional businessmen stared into the abyss sometimes. She shook her head, turned on the radio and let the Beach Boys welcome her back to LA. She watched the valley spread out before her. Maybe someday a nice academic like Stanley would take apart her body and dissect her life for the sake of science.

# XX

# FIFTEEN MORE MINUTES OF FAME

Ellen McCaffrey stood exhausted over her microscope. Her eyes could barely focus after examining one hundred and seven different hair samples over a two day period. Normally, she would have assigned the work to her technicians, but one was out with the flu and another was having a baby, so she popped into the lab whenever there was a break in her hectic schedule of autopsies, crime scene visits, and report drafting. So far, she had identified five donors whose hair required DNA testing to see if a match could be made with the strand found tangled in Jade's ring: Alexia Genoux, Matt LeHunk, Chrissie Nubile, Janet Stephens, and Rock Tower. When given the list of names, her ex-husband volunteered that only Stephens had signed the donor consent form with her left hand.

Given the savagery of the attack, she reconsidered the likelihood that a woman could have committed the murder. With enough adrenaline, with enough rage, it was possible. On the other hand, Donald Johansson's toxicology report lent some support to his claim that he was too stoned to have killed the victim. His blood sample had not been taken until several hours after the murder, but it had tested positive for alcohol and a pain killer/ muscle relaxant. His story gained credibility when she examined the pill bottle found in his pocket and saw that the prescription had been filled for the first time just two days before the party. He may well have been unfamiliar with the drug's side affects.

Were the levels high enough to incapacitate him? This is what the police wanted to know. Stuart's face had gone dark at her answer. Johansson's physical state could not be determined within a reliable degree of certainty, she had explained. There were enough drugs in his system to make him woozy, but she would have to know more about his liver and kidney function before she could opine further. The detective had also pressed her about behavioral side effects of the drug and alcohol together. On that topic, she had been a little more helpful. The combination could possibly be destabilizing; it could significantly lower inhibitions which, at the wrong time and in the wrong person, might facilitate violence. Or it might just cause someone to pass out. He could have been walking a fine edge of consciousness, mobile and dangerous, or just shuffling like a zombie.

Her ex-husband's reaction to her analysis reminded her why they had divorced. Nothing kills a relationship as quickly as contempt, she thought. What was the point of being so resentful of the inevitable muddiness of reality?

\* \* \*

Angela held the long box of dark red roses in her arms and decided it would be extravagant to throw them in the trash with no one around to witness the gesture. Besides, the flowers had worked, at least a little bit, and she was no longer quite so angry. The attached card read: *Don't worry. Everything will be alright. I love you!* She was still worried sick, but it softened her heart to know that her husband was thinking about her, even in the midst of his idiotic windmill tilting. She was arranging the blossoms in a vase when the phone rang.

"Oh hey, Nanci." Her friend and fellow realtor had already heard the story of her trip to Los Angeles. They traded pleasantries for a couple of minutes before Nanci came to the point of her call.

"I've decided to have a pool party a week from Friday," she explained. "Summer's here, and I'm afraid we can't wait for your husband to come home before we have some fun. Promise me you'll make it?"

She did not feel like socializing in the slightest, but her friend continued to pressure her. Nanci had been very understanding, almost too understanding, since she had gotten back to Illinois. Once she had sensed Angela's frustration, she had taken her side against Stanley, enthusiastically seconding all of her emotional attacks on her husband. Nanci was divorced, and she seemed to think that separation was the natural result of conflict. What the young writer wanted to hear was that she was blowing things out of proportion and that everything would be alright.

"Just because Stanley's in Los Angeles hanging out with porn stars doesn't mean that you can't party a little," Nanci insisted. "Besides, everybody wants to see you. You've developed quite a mysterious cachet."

"Yeah, that's me alright," Angela laughed. "An alluring enigma."

"Hey," Nanci replied, "I don't know anyone else who hangs out in sleazy hotel rooms with her husband and adult movie stars! Inquiring minds want to know! And beyond that, you'll have an opportunity to lobby Max on Stanley's behalf. He's already RSVP'd."

She thought for a moment. She had no desire to talk to anyone about what had happened in Los Angeles, but if there were anyone who could salvage Stanley's career, it was Max. Anger welled up inside her again. Why did she have protect her husband as if he were some sort of wayward child? "Alright, I'll come. What do you want me to bring?"

* * *

The professor arrived at the county jail two hours before his meeting with Stuart McCaffrey. He had wanted to spend some time with the accused murderer, but ended up twiddling his thumbs in an empty interview room for almost an hour. A taciturn guard finally pushed the handcuffed prisoner into a seat across from him with no explanation for the delay. Stanley waited for him to leave before saying anything, and after the usual warning against physical contact, the door slammed shut.

He was dismayed at how the days in jail had started to wear on Johansson. The clean-shaven, confident theologian of porn was fading away, and in his place sat a scared, middle-aged man who looked like he had not slept in days. Regardless of what the man had done, he cut a pitiable figure, and he immediately inquired whether any progress had been made.

"I think so." Stanley decided to lead with the most hopeful line of inquiry. "Chance Geary is looking more and more like a prime suspect. It seems he was conspiring with Milton Barkley to get Jade to move back to Chimera, and at the same time Jade was planning to dump him as her agent and presumably as her boyfriend, which might explain why Barkley took her to the party."

"He took her to the party?" Don looked stricken. The thought of Jade on the arm of his chief rival was a bitter pill to swallow. "I saw them walk in at the same time," he said, his voice cracking, "but I didn't know they were together."

Stanley reached over, touched his friend's forearm, and tried to emphasize the positive side of the revelation. "Jade's screwing Geary over gives him a serious motive. Until now, we've been wondering why he would kill his best and only client. Jealousy and anger are pretty powerful motives."

"But he wasn't at the party."

Stanley explained that the office window had been left open and the killer could easily have slipped in. He watched hope and confusion creep into the prisoner's face.

"You mean he could have hid in the office without anyone knowing?" Don looked up and truly engaged his investigator for the first time. "But how would he know that Jade would come there?"

Stanley then reconstructed the murder scenario he and Janet had spun out the day before. "He could have been waiting to crash the party when you and Jade just stumbled in."

"So, he was there when I passed out?"

"Maybe."

"Jesus."

Stanley let him digest the information. It was pure speculation, but Don looked like he had seen a ray of hope. One nagging question needed answering, however. The director had never explained why he had called his favorite star into his office in the middle of the dinner party. Stanley posed the question as nonchalantly as possible.

"It was the next movie," Johansson replied. "I wanted to show her the script for *Toys in Babeland II* and promise her a cut of the profits once it was released."

An ugly thought crept into the professor's head. If Don had spoken to Jade in the office about the sequel, she might have told him that she was leaving Eden for a rival company. Not welcome news to get at a celebratory banquet. "You didn't tell McCaffrey this, did you?" It would not take the detective long to put two and two together and find a motive in Jade's rejection.

"Nah," Don smiled weakly. "I advised myself to plead the Fifth Amendment."

Stanley then summarized the interviews with the rival studio heads and with Chance Geary. The prisoner nodded as he listened, plainly appreciative of all the leg work done on his behalf. Don agreed that neither Mulkahey nor Matteson made very good suspects. When Stanley mentioned his meeting with William Walker, the prisoner interrupted.

"You talked to Jade's ex-husband? How did you find him?"

"He was listed as her emergency contact on the proof of age form Janet Stephens and I found in your office. The cops had taken her personnel file, but Janet suggested we look in your legal records." He paused. "Did you know that Jade was still married?"

"She told me she was divorced." He spoke quietly while he scuffed at a crack in the yellowed linoleum floor and then looked up at Stanley as something registered in his mind. "Did you say Janet Stephens was in my office with you?" Stanley explained the role she had been playing in the investigation.

"And she's been helpful?" Don asked doubtfully.

Stanley described her role the previous day, and Don started to say something, but thought the better of it. "I'm glad she's decided to help. She's one of the smartest people in the business, and she knows everybody." He took a deep breath and his voice caught. "You've done a lot in a short period of time, Stan. I really appreciate it. I don't know what I would do without you."

Uncomfortable with his friend's display of emotion, Stanley plowed ahead and asked how well Don trusted his secretary. The professor felt like every question was stripping his friend bare of those he had trusted, but he couldn't help it. It wasn't his fault that Jade was a turncoat and a liar and that Miriam was probably ripping him off. He laid out what he had seen: the nighttime video shipments and the cash payments she was making to the kid in the back room. He also recounted her late night visit to Don's office.

"She went into my office at midnight and took a file? Are you sure?" Don looked incredulous. "That's totally bizarre. I did tell her to keep filling orders. That income is the only thing keeping the creditors at bay, but there's nothing in my files she needs to see. All she's supposed to do is take the orders, fill them, and keep sale and inventory records."

"Did you tell her to make it a cash operation? Could she be skimming something off the top and doctoring the records? That's what occurred to me when the kid told me she was paying him in cash every night. She might be disgruntled enough to skim some cream." He wished he could think of some way to tie her to the murder. Jade Delilah's spectacular death at the party had effectively finished off Eden Studio as a player in the adult video world. The judgmental secretary would not mourn the demise of the porn factory, but that did not seem sufficient motive for a murder that would cost her a job.

"Miriam is so straight laced, I have a hard time seeing her stealing from me. But you never know, I suppose." He closed his eyes and slumped back in his chair. "Nothing makes much sense since they threw me in here."

"You mean captivity hasn't been spiritually enlightening?" Stanley queried with a grim smile. He could not avoid feeling a wave of affection for his embattled friend. He was convinced that even if Don had killed Jade, it was a barely conscious act spurred by drugs and alcohol, an act inimical to his true nature. The thought of McCaffrey asking for the death penalty was outrageous.

"No," Don shook his head. "I'm afraid it hasn't." He gave his friend a thoughtful shake of the head. "The Apostle Peter and Dietrich Bonhoeffer managed to turn incarceration into a religious experience. Hard times brought them closer to God, but I haven't learned the trick yet. I'm still in the scared and bitter stage." He managed a smile as the guard entered and put an end to the interview. "But then again, Saint Peter never had a skinhead for a roommate."

\* \* \*

Stuart McCaffrey stood waiting in a small office outside the jail's confinement area. He made a point of checking his watch as the clueless academic entered the room. He was not really late, but the detective liked to rattle the enemy whenever possible. He asked the young man to sit down in the only chair in the room, while he perched on the edge of a battered wooden desk looking down from above. "What do you want?"

"Did you ask about the office window?"

"Yeah." The detective had talked to the team on the scene, as well as the forensic specialists, and was surprised that the professor had discovered something of possible consequence not listed in the official report. "The window was unlocked when the first officers arrived on the scene."

"So, someone could have gotten in without showing up on the surveillance record?"

"It's theoretically possible." He shrugged his shoulders, minimizing the finding's significance. "If someone had wanted to sneak into the room, kill the victim, frame her not-so-secret admirer and then escape unseen, he might have been able to do it. Do you have someone in mind, professor?"

"How about Chance Geary?" Stanley charted out the drug dealer's possible motives and opportunity. "He was losing Jade to Milton Barkley at Chimera Studios and was enraged over her betrayal."

This was, in fact, interesting news. McCaffrey nodded his head as if he had heard it all before, while making a mental note to follow up. Geary's meth-head alibi witness was not quite iron-clad. "Then why not kill Barkley," he queried, "if he's the one stealing Geary's girlfriend."

"The goal was to punish Jade. I think Don just came in handy as someone to pin the murder on."

"And you've got some proof of this?"

"Your report mentions fibers found by the window. Why don't you get samples from Geary's clothes and run some tests?" The expression on the supplicant's face was earnest and expectant. Fuck me, thought McCaffrey, this guy believes that the police are at his beck and call. The same suggestion from a real lawyer or investigator might have lit the fuse of his quick temper, but he let the poor guy down easily.

"If we have a reason to suspect Geary beyond his charming personality, we may be able to get a warrant to search his house. But right now, we don't have shit to take to a judge. You're going to have to find something yourself." He savored the look of frustration on the amateur's face. "Is that all you've got?" He looked at his watch, pushed himself off the desk and walked toward the door. "Because I need to talk to your friend for a bit."

"Have you ever heard of William Walker?" Stanley blurted out. "Did you even know that Jade Delilah was married?"

Score one for the professor, McCaffrey mentally chalked up a point. The detective had been planning to spring the news later, but now was as good a time as ever to wind up the defense. "Sure. He's another turd pancake. He used to be with the LAPD until he got caught beating a gang-banger to death with a baseball bat. He should have gotten a medal for that one, but instead he was forced to resign and got picked up by San Bernardino." He could not resist exiting with a sly wink and a mock home run swing. "Now Walker's someone you might think about looking at."

Stanley sat in the small room alone, pondering the detective's hint that Walker might be a viable suspect. He knew that the police needed some sort of individualized suspicion before they could conduct a search, but he dearly wished that the full wardrobes of Chance Geary and William Walker, and for that matter those of Miriam Wilhoit and Milton Barkley, could be checked against the fibers found on the window. Don was probably the only person whose clothes had been analyzed, and he gave himself a mental kick for not asking if the fibers mentioned in the report had come from the prisoner's clothing. He tried to disentangle the evidence he had already collected from the evidence he still needed to obtain. The last thing he needed was one more suspect, but he resolved to check out William Walker further, even if the detective was just waving a red herring.

Stanley had forgotten about his meeting with Janet, but she came up to him immediately after he exited the back of the jail. She was wearing a light-colored chemise, and he could just make out the outlines of a black bra underneath. She moved as fast as her tight miniskirt would permit and grabbed his arm. Before he could ask her about the morning interviews, she pulled him close and whispered in his ear as a small crowd gathered around them.

"The press has been waiting for you to come out. I overheard one of the cameramen say that they got a tip you were here." He looked at her with alarm. A press interview was the last thing he needed, but when they turned the corner, at least three cameras were pointed directly at him.

"Professor Hopkins, how is your investigation going?" A young man in a dark suit shoved a microphone under his chin. "Could you give us an update?" When he did not respond, a young Asian woman pressed him further. "Do you have any evidence that Donald Johansson is not the killer?"

"Would you like to make an announcement to our viewers? Twenty million people will be seeing this tonight." He looked at the identification badge of the energetic woman who had just spoken and saw the logo of one of the major news networks. He searched for an escape route, but he and Janet were being squeezed together in a dense knot of reporters and cameramen. With no way out, he offered a curt response in the hope they would then disperse.

"Neither I nor my client have any comment at this point in time. We do not want to jeopardize our investigation." He tried to make eye contact with as many people as possible. "We have no comment." But before he could push his way through the crowd, a burly cameraman whispered to one of the reporters.

"Professor Hopkins!" the reporter shouted. "Is it true that you are dating Janet Stephens, the famous porn star?" Suddenly everyone was pressing in even closer as the cameraman confirmed that the stunning woman at his side was the star of over one hundred adult videos.

"No!" He stared into the hungry faces and realized that he would have to violate his short-lived "no comment" policy. He spoke in firm voice. "Ms. Stephens is aiding me in the investigation. No ones knows the adult film industry as well as she does—" this claim drew some snickers "—and her help is invaluable in tracking down leads."

Before he could stop her, Janet interjected, "Don Johansson has been a close friend for years, and there's no way he committed this crime. We're going to prove he's innocent."

A flurry of questions followed, but Stanley refused to comment. He put his arm around Janet, ducked his head, and bulled his way through the crowd and toward the parking garage. They were dogged with questions all the way back to his car, and he did not feel they had escaped until he slammed the Taurus' door in the face of a particularly persistent woman from the *LA Times* and had put several blocks between themselves and the courthouse.

"Shit!" he shouted as he pounded his hand against the steering wheel. "Shit, fucking shit!" Janet straightened her hair in the visor mirror and then glanced at Stanley who was still chanting. "Ho-ly fuck-ing shit."

"That was annoying," she agreed and flipped the visor back in place, "but it wasn't that bad, was it?"

"You don't understand," he replied with another slap to the wheel. "If anyone at my university sees this, a truckload of shit is going to hit a massive turbine fan." He shook his head and imagined Max Kurland and the University president reviewing a recording of the interview. How long would it be, he wondered, before he got a call ordering him to come back to BFU?

"I don't understand. You sounded fine." She smiled and patted him on the thigh. "You've got a nice face for television."

"That's not it," he explained. "The University doesn't want to be associated with this stuff. They don't want the publicity, and they've already yanked the funding for my research. They don't want to sponsor porn star interviews, much less an investigation of a porn star murder. I'm basically fucked."

Janet shook her head slowly and watched the cars in front of them merge onto the freeway. "Only if you care about what other people think," she counseled in a steely voice. "Only if you're afraid to do what you need to do."

# XXI

# TANGLED WEBS

S tanley drove down the freeway for five minutes before he realized that he had no destination and that Janet probably had left her car back in the parking deck. Just when he was starting to feel a little competent in the investigation, he felt reality's steel-toed boot in his rear end. He had been making progress, or so he thought, but McCaffrey was still playing him for an amateur. He had little doubt who had leaked his presence at the jailhouse to the press.

He glanced over at his partner, but she seemed unconcerned.

"Where to now, boss?" The confidence in her voice helped him regain his focus. He needed to check out Geary's and Walker's alibis but he couldn't proceed without making a call to McCaffrey begging for the information. He was not in the mood for another confrontation with the detective, so he decided to pursue the lead that had been sitting in his front pocket for three days. He took out the business card taken from Don's desk the night of the search and scanned it quickly. "Do you know how to get to UCLA?"

"Sure. Just take U.S. 10 west back to the 405 and go north. It's basically in between Sunset and Wilshire. Really nice neighborhood, not like Southern Cal."

He asked her if she had gone to school at either place. It was easy to imagine her as a student, either as a serious sociology major wearing blousy sweaters to mute her curves or as blonde bombshell who was the darling of some raucous fraternity. She seemed to appreciate the compliment but shook her head.

"I've talked to student groups at both," she explained. "The psych departments hold a regular forum on human sexuality." She laughed and kicked off her heels for the duration of the ride. "It's kind of fun; they treat me like the ultimate sex authority."

He turned to her, arched eyebrows indicating this was a reasonable assumption.

"I'm an expert in technique, not sex," she said cryptically. "They should probably be talking to some happily married old couple, not me."

"So you're a closet monogamist?"

"No, not me," she laughed. "That boat's already sailed, left the harbor, and got lost in the Bermuda Triangle." She looked like she was going to say more but changed the subject. "Who are we going to see at UCLA?"

He handed her the card and speculated aloud on its likely significance. Law schools often ran free clinics for their students to get practical experience. For some reason, the accused murderer had an appointment the day before the killing to meet with the head of UCLA's free clinic. Stanley had forgotten to ask about the appointment during his visit to jail earlier in the day and now seemed like a convenient time to learn why Johansson had needed pro bono legal advice.

Stanley also needed to deal with one more loose end: Janet's multiple entrances into the Eden Studio lobby the night of the banquet. As nonchalantly as he could, he described what he had seen on the video recording and wondered how she could have entered twice when there was no record of her having left. Unfazed by the question, she reached into her handbag and pulled out a packet of light menthol cigarettes. "Do you mind if I have one?" He shook his head, and she cracked her window so that most of the fumes would be sucked out of the car.

"In the middle of the party I decided that I wanted a smoke. You remember where we were seated? There's an emergency exit right behind the back curtain. If you've worked at Eden, you know you can light up just outside. The place is littered with butts." She took a deep drag and blew it out the window.

"Anyway, the door slipped shut before I could prop it open, so I got stuck outside and had to walk around the building to the front door."

He was tempted to ask whether anyone could verify her story, but she was not a suspect, and keeping her trust was his only chance to complete both the investigation and his book. He glanced quickly over to see if his question had shaken her and resolved to check behind the exit door for cigarettes butts when he got back to Eden. She poked her half-finished smoke out the window, and he changed the subject to her search for Jade Delilah's sister.

"Oh shit! I did better than that!" She reached over and touched his arm. "I talked to her." Her sunglasses slipped and she pushed them deeper into her hair.

She explained how she had tracked down Rebecca Sharperson in Oxnard. "Well, I suppose the most important thing was that she just assumed that Jade's husband did it. He was abusive, and when Jade left him he tried to track her down." She kept talking while signaling with her left hand that he should change lanes to avoid exiting prematurely. "But that was two years ago. She really doesn't know anything since then. Did you see Walker anywhere on the recording?"

"No," he replied, "but he could have come in the window."

"Like Geary."

"Like anybody." He checked his rearview mirror before turning his attention back to Janet.

She recapped her conversation with Jade's sister and added her insights into stripper psychology. "I mean, it's no surprise that someone who starts working the clubs at eighteen is not very happy at home. Rebecca didn't know for sure if Jade had a serious drug problem."

"What about the father?" He did not want to add yet another suspect to the list, but anyone who had a serious conflict with Jade needed to be looked at.

"I don't know...he might have abused her, but Rebecca didn't say. I don't think she knew."

He looked over at her and shook his head. "I mean can we talk to him?"

"Oh." She shook her head and pointed out the upcoming turn. "No. He died last year along with Jade's mother."

Stanley took the first exit for the massive UCLA campus and drove aimlessly for a few minutes before he realized a casual drive-by sighting of the law school was unlikely. When he saw a security guard, he stopped and got directions to the northeast corner of the university complex. After fifteen minutes of missed turns, he finally saw the handsome red brick law building and found a place to park. Janet slipped her heels back on and they made their way across a green commons to the law school's front entrance. For Stanley, the walk among the stately buildings of the university gave him a weird sense of déjà vu. By summer's end, he would be back at his job and Los Angeles would seem a million miles away.

The receptionist in the lobby told him where he could find the law clinic, and the professor and the porn star were soon walking down a long hallway sparsely populated by students attending summer school. They soon found a door stenciled "UCLA Law School Civil Clinic" and asked a student where Deborah Spellerburg's office was. They found her in a small, windowless space in the back of the clinic. Stanley knocked on the open door and introduced himself and his companion.

"What can I do for you Professor Hopkins?" The attorney was a chunky brunette whose serious demeanor was rendered even more severe by a pair of rectangular black glasses.

"I'm the chief investigator for Donald Johansson who, as you may know, is currently under arrest for the murder of Jade Delilah." He saw the attorney nod. She would have to be under a total media blackout not to know the names of the players in the murder case. He took the business card out of his pocket and handed it to her. "I found this in Mr. Johansson's office and was hoping that you could tell us something about your meeting with him."

"Mr. Johansson came in twice, once briefly to set up an appointment, and then again, on the day before the murder." She pushed her glasses back against the bridge of her nose. "But I'm afraid that's all I can tell you."

"Attorney-client privilege?" He expected this unwillingness to talk and had formulated a plan in the car. His least favorite professor's course on legal ethics would finally prove not to be a waste of time. He nodded understandingly and scanned the books lining the shelves in her office. Virtually all in some way were concerned with family violence and domestic abuse. He asked her what she did at the clinic.

"I run our protective order program. Our clients are primarily woman seeking to escape an abusive relationship. We find them shelter and help them navigate the system to get a protective order. We've helped over four hundred women in the five years since the project started." Stanley nodded his appreciation.

"And you supervise law students involved in the process so they can get hands-on legal experience?" Luckily, his own law school practicum had been in the criminal law clinic.

"That's exactly right," she beamed.

"What's odd," he said, furrowing his brow, "is that I can't imagine someone abusing Don. He's a powerful guy." He gave the attorney his best look of puzzlement. "Do you get a lot of male clients in here?"

"Oh, Mr. Johansson wasn't a client," she readily clarified. "He came on behalf of someone else."

"So he wasn't a client." He paused for a moment, as if to digest the new information. "Then, there shouldn't be any attorney-client issues, should there?" Before she could object, he added. "And my guess is that the person whom he was trying to protect is now dead and no longer covered by any privilege."

"He didn't give me a name." She was wary but made no attempt to shoot down his theory. He had interviewed subjects like her before. People whose initial instinct was always to say nothing, but who then quickly opened up to a non-threatening questioner who seemed to understand their predicament. He told Angela about a carnival worker that he had interviewed: "He put the *confide* back in *confidential*."

"Ms. Spellerburg, one of my client's employees was living with her agent, a violent methamphetamine dealer named Chance Geary. He is associated with a biker gang and was known to have beaten her on several occasions. That actress's name was Jade Delilah."

"She was also my best friend," Janet added, her small voice cracking ever so slightly. Stanley gave her a quick look, but managed to hide his surprise at the blatant, but helpful, lie. The attorney, however, accepted the emotional statement at face value. Friends of domestic abuse victims were probably frequent visitors to her office.

"Since Don was not your client," he pleaded, "and Jade is now dead, we were hoping you might be able to tell us about your meeting with him."

"I guess I can," she said as she shuffled through a stack of files on her desk. "But why don't you ask Mr. Johansson? You did say you're working for him, right?" She pulled a file from the stack and held it in her hands while she waited for his answer. Stanley panicked for a moment, but he had spent years improvising with an astounding variety of interviewees.

"More precisely," he explained, "we are working with Mr. Johansson's attorney. In the course of preparing his defense, we need to check out everything Mr. Johansson has told his lawyer. As I'm sure you know, not all defendants are completely forthcoming, and it's our job to prevent any nasty surprises at trial. So, we'd like to compare his version of the story with yours."

"Of course," she said. "Well, our meeting was not terribly long. Without using Ms. Delilah's name, he told me basically the same story you did about the abusive meth dealer. I told him that we needed to talk to her directly, but that if she came by and asked for emergency shelter, we could probably arrange it. Then, we could help her obtain a protective order to keep her abuser away. We're very proud of how rapidly we respond to crisis situations. If you don't act quickly, the consequences can be horrible." Janet sniffled at the attorney's last statement, and the sturdy brunette handed her a tissue. "Mr. Johansson said that

he would bring her here on…" —she looked at the file— "…
June 25th."

"The day after the party," he said.

"And two days after he spoke with me," the attorney added.
"I even penciled in a slot on my schedule."

Stanley needed time to think. He asked her if she could
remember any details of her conversation, but she had little more
to offer. He thanked her for her help and wrote out his contact information, asking her to call if she remembered anything
else. Stanley and Janet were soon walking quickly down the law
school corridors and back to the car. They did not speak until
the doors of the school closed behind them.

"Don't you think it's odd that she never mentioned calling
the police?" Janet asked as they walked down the sidewalk away
from the building. "I mean, I got the distinct impression that she
hadn't. I was wondering why you didn't ask her about that."

"Goddammit!" He slapped his forehead. "Because I'm a
moron."

"We could go back and ask her," she suggested as they
stopped in the middle of the law school courtyard.

He considered heading back to her office but then turned
and walked to the car. He would talk to the attorney again after
he had asked his client why he had failed to mention the meeting. The day before Jade's murder, Johansson was out trying to
protect her, not plotting to kill her. The evidence was clearly
exculpatory, so why hadn't he said anything about it?

\* \* \*

When Angela arrived home after a fruitless afternoon of showing
a new BFU administrator several unsatisfactory homes, she
popped a frozen bagel into the microwave and sat down with
a glass of sparkling water. The Hopkins's house sat in a large
neighborhood south of the university. The subdivision had once
been farmland, but it had been thirty years since the last ear of
corn had been harvested there, and now Ash and Poplar trees

raised their branches well over the rooftops. The house was a brick split-level ranch with an unfinished basement that could be converted into two additional bedrooms and a bathroom when the need arose. The microwave dinged and she brought her snack to the leafy patio behind the house, but the mosquitoes were out in full force and she settled for eating in front of the television. When the news hour began, she got up and went down to the basement. In the middle of the floor stood an arc-flex exercise machine where she worked out whenever she got too depressed by the throngs of fit young things that strode around the BFU campus and made any woman over thirty feel dumpy.

As she puffed through her work out, she remodeled the basement in her mind's eye, picturing what could be done to make it an inviting and cozy place for kids. She was the fourth of seven children raised in a middle-class suburb of Chicago and had shared a bedroom with her older sister, Valerie, and then later with her younger sister, Hannah. It was a raucous, joyful, messy house, and sometimes the solitude and orderliness of life with a routine-loving academic nearly drove her bonkers. Having children would change that for the better, but it would be the final disaster for her figure. Nobody's stomach ever really survived pregnancy, but she didn't care. Swapping the arc-flex machine for playpens and train sets and noisy ping pong and foosball tables was a more attractive fantasy than flexing perfect abs in a quiet house.

Back upstairs, she sat through several commercials and was then confronted with a reporter who stood on the steps of the Los Angeles County jail and announced that Stanley Hopkins, Professor of Sociology at BFU and chief defense investigator for Donald Johansson, had just finished introducing his new assistant, porn star Layla DiBona, to the media. Angela watched her husband on the screen, standing with his arm around the sexy blonde. When he was asked about his relationship with the infamous porn star, her glass of water went splashing to the carpet. Stanley's face turned crimson as sputtered out an answer: "Ms. Stephens is aiding me in the investigation. No one knows the adult film industry as well as she does, and her help is invaluable in tracking down leads."

She had called him two nights earlier at a very late hour and had gotten no answer. Her stomach folded itself into a nauseating ball. Stanley might not actively pursue a sexy porn star, but that didn't mean he couldn't be seduced by one. He was easy-going by nature, a pleaser, someone who might have a hard time insulting a beautiful woman by saying "no." She was fairly certain that he had never cheated on her, and lord knows how many opportunities he must have had with his students, but could a young co-ed turn on the charm with the same intensity as a veteran of dozens of adult films? Angela turned off the television and got a towel to blot up the spilled water. As she entered the kitchen, she noticed the phone laying next to Stanley's flowers in the middle of the table and impulsively dialed his cell phone number. It rang ten times, but no one picked up.

* * *

"Where to next?" Janet had slipped her shoes off again and leaned back in the passenger seat. Her skirt rode up to the middle of her tanned thighs, and she tugged it down as she turned toward him. He looked at her and inadvertently caught a glimpse of some scenic cleavage. He wondered if any scholar had ever had a research assistant like this one.

He focused back on the highway and went through his mental punch list. He needed to track down the alibis and there was still an evening interview he wanted Janet to do. "Let's stop at Eden on the way back to your car," he suggested. "Maybe you'll see something on the surveillance recording that I missed."

"Back to Eden?" she said. "That's easier said than done."

He groaned and remembered the quote from Genesis that he had seen in Don's office, "*And Adam and Eve saw that they were naked and were ashamed.*"

"Typical Donald," she sighed. "He thought his style of porn would melt away America's puritan sense of shame. He really believed that if people no longer thought sex was dirty, we'd all live together in harmony."

She did not sound like she bought into his fairy tale version of porn, but then why did she continue? She was intelligent, hard working, and funny. Clearly, she could be successful at any number of different careers. He had not asked her any questions about work since the formal interview in the hotel room, and he wondered whether she might open up now that they were companions in the same hopeless enterprise.

"I hate to disappoint," she replied when he finally popped the question, "but the truth is pretty boring. Like I said in the interview, I fell into this by chance when I was young and my family situation wasn't very good. I stayed in it out of inertia: plenty of pats on the back and plenty of money."

He turned off the freeway and headed down the boulevard in the direction of Eden Studio. The power of inertia in job markets could not be underestimated, but her longevity was striking and set her apart from her peers in a way that suggested something beyond inertia. He understood Don's way of thinking about the business. The porn director had a theory, why shouldn't the porn star? She couldn't be as facile as she pretended.

When he asked about her philosophy, Janet let go an irritated chuff of air and looked out the window as she spoke. She looked annoyed with herself for answering. "Look," she finally explained, "Don's right when he talks about the level of shame in society, but he's too much of an idealist. He's never going to change a thing about this country. You need to stay on the level of the poor ashamed slobs that I meet at conventions and DVD signings. They're all over the place. They watch my movies, get themselves off, and they feel good."

She shrugged her shoulders and continued to look straight ahead. "Pleasing the audience is what this business is all about, just like regular movies. I do it well and I am appreciated for it." He wished he could study her more closely instead of fighting the traffic on the boulevard. "All these slobs are pathetic, and the industry is pretty pathetic too." She gave a harsh little laugh. "But when you get right down to it, we're all pathetic, right?"

He pondered his own career path, considered his present situation, and then nodded his head.

# XXII.

# CAST FROM EDEN

As Stanley and Janet drove within a couple of blocks of their destination, a siren screamed and a large fire truck roared past. In the distance, a plume of dirty smoke obscured the immediate horizon, and they were only able to drive another hundred yards before the line of cars in front of them came to a complete halt. Stanley turned on the radio and surfed through the bandwidth but heard no news of a fire snarling traffic in the San Fernando Valley.

"You don't think it's the studio, do you?" Janet reached down and slipped on her shoes.

He rolled down his window and tried to see around a delivery truck. Up ahead, a dozen emergency vehicles and police cars blocked the street in both directions. Behind them, rush hour traffic had backed up as far as he could see. He motioned to his partner and they slipped between the disgruntled drivers and walked toward the conflagration until there was no doubt that the main office of Eden Studio was engulfed in flames.

Two firefighters manned a hasty barricade at the edge of the parking lot keeping a crowd of gawkers at bay, but Stanley and Janet pressed close enough to see that Don's office was a total loss. The fire had blackened the lobby and angry orange flames spewed from the director's office window. As he surveyed the scene, Stanley recognized a reporter from his debacle at the court house and shielded his face, but the newsman was too busy talking to the nearest fire fighter to notice him. The professor whispered to Janet to stay where she was, and he slid along the barricade to catch the conversation. The reporter was asking whether the fire was a case of arson.

"Probably," the white-haired official shouted over the din. "This one started up way too fast to be something electrical, and I always get suspicious when there's no one in a building. Apparently, it's recently abandoned, and that's always a tip-off for arson." After listening to the rest of the conversation, Stanley worked his way back to his partner and pointed them away from the barricade with a tip of his head. As they walked back to the car, he told her what he had heard.

"That's crazy! It's a good thing we went through Don's office when we did." She paused for a moment. "Wait. Did you have anything valuable in there?"

"The surveillance DVD's and the police reports, but I can get duplicates from McCaffrey. I've got to talk with him tomorrow about getting Geary's and Walker's alibis anyway. Thank god I've got my notes and my laptop in the car." He checked in the back seat to make sure his file folders were still there along with his phone.

"Someday I'll remember to carry this thing with me," he mumbled as he checked his missed calls. He saw one from his wife and vowed to call her later that evening.

"I wonder who set the fire?" Janet asked as the cars around them slowly pulled U-turns and drove away down the boulevard away from the fire. "Do you think it's a coincidence?"

"If it is, it's a helluva big one."

For the next two hours, they fought through a malicious traffic jam back to the parking deck of the county jail, collecting their thoughts along the way and organizing a plan of attack for the rest of the week. The fire, they concluded, was not much of a set back. Nothing irreplaceable had been lost and any clues uncovered by the police investigating the arson would probably lead away from Don, unless he had hired someone to burn it down to collect insurance money. By the time they got back to her car, Stanley was starting to feel a bit more like Sam Spade again. The trip to UCLA had been productive, as had Janet's visit to Oxnard. He was uncovering important clues that had eluded LAPD's finest.

He followed Janet's directions to the location of her Mini Cooper and pulled past it on the mid-level of the courthouse parking deck. She gathered up her purse and cast a quick glance in the small mirror on the visor above her head.

"Would you like to come back to my place and have a drink before dinner?" She spoke in an offhand manner as she flicked back a stray hair from her forehead. He suppressed a lascivious image conjured by his subconscious, but knocked it back like a whack-a-mole. *Sex.* How could he maintain a professional façade all day long and have it disintegrate with a simple invitation? Janet's suggestion was surely innocent, but his face turned red anyway. After having seen her alter ego in action on the hotel's pay-per-view, there was simply no way to keep certain images at bay. He looked up and wondered if she could read his thoughts.

"Thanks, but I need to get back to the hotel and call Angela." He managed to sketch a wave before pulling too away a bit too sharply and heading back to the hotel.

As he entered the darkened room, he noticed a red button flashing on the telephone. He debated calling home before checking the message, but he pushed the button first and heard Max Kurland's voice telling him to call as soon as he got in. Any conversation with Max would interest Angela, so he dialed his colleague's number first.

Max thanked him for calling back and took a moment to gather himself. "Stanley, I've got bad news. The administration had a complete heart attack when they saw your press conference this morning—"

"—it wasn't a press conference, goddamn it!" His voice filled with anger. "And what the hell do these people do all day? Watch fucking CNN?"

"No, they don't watch television all day," Max explained. "But they do get recordings from a news clip service of anything that mentions BFU, and your connection with the university is prominently featured in all of them. As far as the world is concerned, BFU is paying for you to hang out with a beautiful porn star and get an infamous killer out of jail. Trust me, this perception is at odds with the image that the university would like to project. In fact, the President has already been contacted by several major donors and at least two state senators."

"She's not going to cave in is she?" He expected his friend's liberal leanings to be gravely offended by any decisions made in response to political influence.

"No, the president decided to suspend you *before* she heard from any of these people," he said. "I cannot even begin to describe how pissed she is! You are suspended without pay for an indefinite period of time, and I've been told to tell you not to bother applying for tenure." The assistant professor heard his department head take a deep breath. "Look, I'm sorry, Stan. I feel partly responsible, but I did warn you to come home last week. If you had done that, this never would have happened."

Stanley's first impulse was to sue the university. Surely, it lacked the power to dismiss him for helping out a friend, but his tenure situation had been precarious even before he came to California. Even if he finished the book, a positive vote by his colleagues was not assured. Given the publicity surrounding Jade's murder and his defense of her boss, he doubted the final chapter of his book would ever be considered serious scholarship. Suing the university would tip no one's vote his way. "Shit, Max," he finally sighed. "What should I do?"

"Okay, here's the deal." His colleague answered more quickly and definitively than he expected. "I calmed the President down a little and then suggested a compromise. She's not wild about this, but if you leave California right away, she'll announce the suspension and then quietly lift it at the end of the summer so you can teach the fall and spring semesters. You have to agree, however, not to put yourself up for tenure. She wouldn't budge on that, but you can use the year to look for a position at another school. That'll be a lot easier to do if you're still employed."

His voice softened for the first time during the conversation. "I'm sorry, man, but that was the best I could do."

"Thanks, Max."

"So, I'll see you in the office tomorrow?"

"Let me think about it."

"Are you kidding?" The department head did nothing to hide his exasperation. "What's there to think about? If you come back, finish the book, and go on the job market, you'll find a job somewhere. If you get dismissed, you're history."

He weighed Max's words against his commitment to help his jailed friend and was suddenly too tired to carry his end of the conversation. "I just need some time to process this." An auditorium full of two hundred bored undergraduates flashed through his mind and he hung up without a further word.

Stanley got up from his seat on the bed and began pacing the length of the narrow room, wondering what he would say to Angela. How do you explain to your wife that you've just been fired? How do you explain that you're tempted to stay in Los Angeles despite the consequences? His brain told him he should cave in and go back home, but he had to admit that after just a couple days of investigating the murder of Jade Delilah, the thought of crawling back into his academic shell seemed unbearable. As an undergraduate, he had slid effortlessly into sociology and then slipped into law school and graduate school. He had landed at BFU without ever thinking too hard about whether he wanted to write articles and teach for a living. His other colleagues had amassed enough publications by their third or fourth year to make tenure a certainty. He had cut it close, hoping to finish a project that would put him just over the top, at just the final moment. With a sigh, he sat down on the edge of the bed and teetered.

\* \* \*

Angela lay in bed unable to fall asleep. The image of her handsome husband with his arm around a beautiful porn star was the only thing she could see when she shut her eyes. All it took was a couple of unanswered phone calls to stoke the fires of jealousy red hot. It was not a new emotion. She hated when women flirted with her husband (as much as she liked Nanci, she would never leave her alone with him), but this was the first time she truly feared something might happen. A variety of disturbing scenes flashed through her mind until the phone's jangle jolted her upright and her husband's voice sounded a conciliatory note over the line, "Hey, I hope I'm not waking you up."

"I'm in bed but I'm not asleep." Her anxiety quickly returned. "I tried to call you earlier, but you weren't answering the phone, just like the other night."

"Yeah, I saw. I keep leaving the damn thing in the car." Was he telling the truth? His tone was pretty casual. "How are you doing?"

"Not too good." Her voice caught and she fought back a sob. "I saw you on the news tonight."

"Did you talk to anyone at the university?"

"Huh?" She shook her head. "No, what are you talking about? I haven't spoken to anyone. I've just been sitting here wondering why my husband is on news traipsing all over Los Angeles with some whore." The last word felt good to say out loud.

"Honey, you remember meeting Janet." He scrambled for a reasonable explanation. "She was our first interview, and she sat with us the night of the party. You know she's not a whore! She's just an old friend of Don's who's helping the investigation." He was trying to make the ridiculous situation sound like a mundane research project. "It would have been stupid to turn down her help. More importantly, she's taken your place in the hotel room—"

"—what?!"

"—to finish the interviews, in order to finish the book, darling!" The tears began flowing in earnest now. "I understand what a shock it must have been to see us on television, but it wasn't a real press conference. I was talking with a detective at the County Jail and got totally blindsided by reporters as we were leaving." She took a deep breath and blew her nose. "You need to trust me. There is *nothing* going on between us. I love you more than ever, sweetheart. I *need* you more than ever too."

After a few more minutes of reassurances, she finally stopped crying and decided that life would be simpler if she chose to believe him. "I know nothing's going on," she sniffed, "but do you know how embarrassing it is to see your husband on television being asked if he's screwing a porn star? I can't even go out of the house tomorrow."

"I know," he sympathized. "It must be horrible. I wouldn't want to see you on television with Brad Pitt."

"Johnny Depp."

"Whatever." He paused and she felt the hairs on the back of her neck start to tingle. "Sweetheart? I got a call from Max Kurland today. Apparently everyone at the university was watching the news too."

"Oh, my God."

He took a deep breath. "The president went ballistic, and she suspended me indefinitely without pay. Apparently, I can forget about getting tenure too."

She felt both tears and anger surging together. "I told you to come home with me! If you only had the common sense God gave a squirrel, you would have bolted from Los Angeles the first time Max called." She blew her nose savagely. "So we're fucked...we're totally fucked."

"Maybe not totally." She heard a monumental sigh rumble all the way from the west coast. "Max did work out kind of a deal with the President. He says she'll reinstate me for the fall and spring semesters, if I agree to come home right away and promise to not to go up for tenure."

She understood immediately what this meant. "So, you'd have a year to finish the book and look for another job." She tried not to get overly excited by the lifeline they had been thrown. "That's better than nothing! You'll be able to find something. It might even be good to move some place new and put all this stuff behind us. I just want this all to be over…" She dabbed at her eyes with a tissue and tossed it onto her nightstand. "When should I pick you up at the airport?"

He took a moment to respond. "Late afternoon, probably. I'll call you tomorrow with the flight number and the time." She tried to put herself in his shoes, to imagine what he must be thinking, but it was too hard. It was like getting a call from Pinocchio from a phone booth on Pleasure Island.

"Good night, honey," he said quietly. "I love you."

"I love you too."

One quick call and he was booked on a morning flight back to Illinois. He would be home in time for a late dinner. He sat on the edge of the bed and rubbed his temples, already preparing a speech of explanation to Don. He was still rehearsing, flat on his back in his shirt and pants, when the alarm rang the next morning.

# XXIII

# JAILHOUSE ROCKED

When Stanley arrived at the Los Angeles County Jail, the night shift was ready to go home. He was as tired and unshaven as they were, and in sympathetic weariness they showed him directly to his client. The disheveled professor was led down a dimly lit hallway to a sour smelling interview room. He slumped into a chair and rubbed his blood-shot eyes, still without any idea how to break the news that he was giving up and going home.

When Don arrived moments later, he sat down and folded his cuffed hands in the lap of his loose-fitting jumpsuit. "What's up?"

The disgraced professor stumbled through the story of the 'news conference' and his conversations with Max and Angela. His explanation unraveled in a series of non-sequiturs and apologetic rambling. Eye contact was impossible, and the erstwhile investigator spent much of the time staring at the concrete floor. To his surprise, when he finally looked up, his friend was nodding his head with a smile that looked both sincere and stoic.

"You need to go back to your wife, Stan." There was more understanding in his friend's voice than he deserved. "It's the right thing to do."

But it's not the right thing to do, Stanley thought, it's the coward's way out. It's the path of least resistance once again.

"This isn't an ordinary crisis in your career or in your marriage," the prisoner continued. "You're in almost as much trouble as me, but at least your situation is fixable." He reached out his hands and touched his friend on the knee. "I've had a lot to think about since we talked yesterday. After you left, the detective came by hinting that they might not charge me with a capital crime."

"Well, that's good news, at least." Stanley admitted.

"The catch is that I have to plead guilty to second degree murder."

A wave of outrage surged through the sociologist, but when he was done railing at McCaffrey, the LAPD, and the whole American criminal justice system, he did not see his anger mirrored on the face of the accused.

"Think about it." Johansson shrugged his shoulders. "My career is over and my business is bankrupt. And unlike you, I don't have a pretty wife to go home to. Jade is dead. I'd be out in about ten years or so. I'm no Solzhenitsyn, but it wouldn't have to be an unproductive period in my life."

Stanley plowed on unaware that convincing someone to chance the death penalty might not be good advice. "Sure, Saint Paul and M.L.K. did some good writing when they were locked up, but they had a lot of support on the outside. The porn community is going to hang you out to dry if you confess. You'd be alone in there." The director nodded but said nothing

Stanley insisted that Janet could carry on the investigation without him. She would do an excellent job. The prisoner should at least accept her help and not cave in to the police pressure so quickly.

"I'll think about it," Don replied without enthusiasm. "I'm glad she's been a help."

The conversation was suddenly over, but Stanley was stuck in his chair. He had received the prisoner's blessing but still felt like a traitor. He despised himself for needing reassurance that his cowardice was acceptable. The man who would soon go back to his cell seemed calm; the man who would soon be walking free was in turmoil. He could think of nothing comforting to say, so he struck off wildly in a new direction. "Why didn't you tell me about your visit to Deborah Spellerburg at the UCLA legal aid clinic?"

"How do you know about her?"

"I found her business card in your desk." Don seemed more upset by the question than by the news he was losing his chief investigator. Stanley described the trip to UCLA and explained that he knew about the plan to get Jade a protective order. Don slumped in his chair, bereft of the confidence he had displayed just moments before. "Why didn't you tell me about this? Right before the murder you were out trying to protect Jade from a violent boyfriend. It's great evidence!"

The prisoner did not respond. He closed his eyes and tilted his head, struggling with some internal demon. When he finally spoke, his voice was quiet. "It's not as good evidence as you think." He looked apologetically at his friend. "I did go to the lawyer because I was worried about Jade. Chance was becoming more and more violent, and it seemed to me that she had to get away. For her own safety, she needed to leave him. It tore me up every time a makeup artist told me about covering up her bruises." He paused for a moment while he tried to compose himself. "I admit that I wanted her to myself, but you can't blame me for wanting to get her away from him."

Stanley didn't understand why his friend was questioning his role in what seemed to be a wholly laudable attempt to protect the woman he loved. Johansson wrung his hands and struggle to continue.

"That's what I wanted to tell her the night of the party... about talking to the lawyer, to explain how easy it would be to get a restraining order, how we could get her to a safe place."

"So, you lied to me about why you met her in the office? Why? Getting her to Spellerburg makes you look like a good guy, not a killer."

Don squeezed his eyes tightly together, as if he were in pain. He did not cry as Angela had done the night before, but his voice cracked and his breath was ragged as he tried to keep a flood of emotion at bay. "She told me that she didn't want my help, that everything was just fine. She said that she was sick of me interfering in her life."

There was an awkward silence. Stanley eventually broke it. "She was in denial, I suppose."

"We argued," he rocked forward slightly and whispered. "We said a lot of things, terrible things. I was fucked up on the pills and wine and said stuff that I didn't mean…then we fought. I grabbed her; she slapped me…"

Stanley sat in horror, waiting for the inevitable confession, but it did not come. His friend just sat shaking his head and trying to stifle his tears. "What happened then?"

He replied with sudden vehemence and frustration, "I don't know! I remember some pushing, and the next thing I know I'm waking up on the sofa surrounded by security guards." He shook his head again. "I blacked out."

Stanley wasn't sure what to think. Over the years he had developed a fairly keen sense of who was telling him the truth and who was not. His friend's emotions seemed genuine, but that did not mean he was innocent. Given his condition, he might not be able to remember killing Jade, and his distress could come from guilt just as easily as from frustration and grief. He suddenly understood why Don was considering the deal McCaffrey had offered: He really was not sure how Jade died. The prisoner gave a barely perceptible nod.

"I was angry." His shoulders shook. "I don't know what happened."

Stanley felt the urge to put his arms around the lost man and comfort him, but he could see the guard watching them from the hall and touched Don's hand briefly instead.

The sobbing slowly subsided and the man in the orange jump suit grew quiet. With one final squeeze, Stanley stood up to leave. "I'll talk to Janet before I go," he promised to the bowed head. "You need to know all of your options before you accept McCaffrey's deal." Don gave no acknowledgment that he heard his former investigator's departing words. Stanley knocked on the door to be let out and walked as quickly as he could down the corridor and away from the bars and the guards and the despair.

When he entered the large foyer of the building, he called an excited Angela and informed her that his flight was leaving at noon Pacific time and would arrive in Illinois around 7:00 p.m. eastern time. It was early, but he decided to return the car to the airport immediately. His mood fit more with sitting in a generic departure lounge than wandering around downtown Los Angeles. He was heading out the door when a familiar voice stopped him.

"Professor Hopkins, do you have a moment?" Stuart McCaffrey stepped toward him with a wry smile on his face.

"Not really," he replied. "I've got to be somewhere."

"This will take just a moment." The detective put an arm on his shoulder and led him back behind the reception desk. "There's something that we need to talk about."

"How did you know I was here?" Stanley followed the detective as he peered into the interview rooms that lined the hallway. McCaffrey found an empty one and waved the professor in.

"Whenever someone talks to my suspects, I have a friend who notifies me. It's amazing what you can learn just from the visitors people get." He grinned wickedly. "Now all we have to do is bug the interview rooms, and we'd really have ourselves a justice system." He laughed. "Just kidding, Professor. I'm all about the Constitution."

He could have told the detective that he was off the case, but he didn't want to admit defeat in the face of such smugness. "Hurry up. I gotta get somewhere."

"Two things, Professor; you have to decide for yourself if they're related." He pulled a sheaf of papers out of his the breast pocket of his jacket. "First, the medical examiner has sent hair samples from four individuals to the FBI lab for further DNA testing. I've written their names on the back of the last sheet here. You'll note that one of them is your associate, Janet Stephens." Stanley took the papers and stared at McCaffrey without looking at them. "Second, take some time and read through this stuff. We finally got the report back from the techies who've been going through Johansson's computer. There's wasn't too much of interest there, but they did print out some correspondence between Ms. Stephens and your client. You might find it interesting."

Stanley considered tossing the material back at him in a grand gesture of disdain and then leaving for the airport, but he could not resist a quick glance at the top page. The printed emails suggested that Janet considered herself more than just a friend to Don. He flipped to the second page and the next and the next and saw proof that she was in love with him, pursuing him with fervor that bordered on stalking. Judging from Don's response, her romantic feelings for him were unrequited and her messages were spiked with frustration and anger. Throughout, she railed against "her" or "your lover" or "that bitch," all of which might have been references to Jade, whom she clearly despised but never named. It was hard to reconcile the calm and rational woman who had been so helpful, with the personality on display in the email messages. He set down the papers on the desk and looked at the detective.

This explained the plea deal offered to Don the day before. The new information posed problems for the prosecution. Stanley spoke first, "If the hair turns out to be Janet's, a jury looking at the emails might consider her a suspect." McCaffrey conceded the point with a grimace that quickly melted into his usual stoic expression. "Throw in a medical report that says Don's blackout story is scientifically possible, and you start getting close to reasonable doubt."

"There's still no direct evidence of Stephens' involvement, of course, but you're right about the toxicology report. I'm not too happy about the way it's written."

"Detective McCaffrey," he managed a brief smile at his foe, "you look almost human right now."

"Sorry to disappoint," the detective said as he pushed himself off the desk and he made his way to the door. "You can get the full transcript from my office, but given whom you're partnering with, I thought you'd rather see these sooner than later." He grunted as he left. "Don't ever say I never did anything nice for you."

Nice? Stanley asked himself as he stood in the empty room. The detective had just destroyed a partnership between the only two people working to exonerate his prime suspect. And he was perilously close to convincing a man to plead guilty to a crime he might not have committed. "Nice" was not quite the word that Stanley had in mind. A leaden weight of anxiety and guilt settled itself firmly on his shoulders, and he slumped onto a hard wooden chair in the corner of the room. Given the emails, he could easily imagine a scenario where Janet killed Jade and framed Don. Her absence from the dinner table the night of murder provided her with the opportunity, and McCaffrey's revelations put a nasty spin on her mysterious double entrance to the party captured on the surveillance DVD. He thought back to her story of being locked out of the party during a cigarette break and visualized her smoking in the car while she calmly explained herself. Was she left-handed? Had she lit the cigarette with her left or right hand? Was he turning over responsibility for Don's investigation to the most likely suspect?

* * *

Angela was never late for her period. Ever. Her sisters had warned her jokingly when she was a teenager that if she was ever a day late, then she'd know that she was pregnant for sure. And now it had happened. She was two days late and she thought something was different about her body. An undefinable something tickling her endocrine system whispered that she would be having a baby. She told herself that she was crazy, that you couldn't be this sure, this soon. But cold reason lost the battle to warming hormones.

The timing for a pregnancy was not very good, but she dismissed the difficulties. Stanley would have an entire year to complete his book and find another job. He might not end up at a top school, but she had never met a starving Ph.D. She could work especially hard in the upcoming months to grow the cushion provided by their modest savings. Thankfully, her parents were comfortably well-off and would be happy to help if things were tight for a while. She walked through the house, making plans, unable to let go of the shiver that promised the advent of glorious noise and chaos.

She fingered the telephone, tempted to call her husband but decided that something so important, and possibly uncertain, should be conveyed in person. He was still depressed over his job situation and any discussion could keep until tonight. She looked at her watch. She had a condo showing in an hour, but the property was close by and she had just enough time to hit the grocery store and buy the ingredients for a nice dinner.

As she searched for her keys, the telephone rang in the kitchen. It was probably Stanley calling from the Los Angeles airport. Could she keep her secret? "Hey sweetie," she asked breathlessly, "what time are you getting in?"

His voice was flat and tired. "I missed the flight."

"What happened? Can the airline get you on the next one?" She needed him home. If she had to spend another night alone in the house, she was going to scream. She waited for a response, but the other end of the line seemed dead. "Stan? Are you still there?"

"Yeah," he sighed, "I'm still here." There was another long pause before he spoke again. "Look. I'm going to have to stay here for a little while longer. There's just no way that I can leave right now. I was going to leave the investigation to Janet, but—"

"—but what!" She yelled into the phone, all her emotions coalescing into anger. "If you don't come home today, you'll lose your job for the next school year! Are you crazy? We were lucky that the university was willing to take you back under any conditions. You can't screw this up, Stan!" She tried to say more, but her argument reduced itself to an enraged sputter.

"I know this sounds irresponsible, but Janet—"

"—I don't give a flying FUCK about that slut!" she interrupted him again. "Get home today!" she shouted. "Now! GET ON A FUCKING PLANE NOW!" With the final admonition, she slammed down the receiver and kicked the refrigerator in frustration. A moment later the phone rang again. She silenced it by giving the cord a violent yank and pulling the jack out of the wall. For several minutes, she stalked about the kitchen like a caged tiger, then she screamed out one last obscenity, slumped down at the kitchen table, took a halting breath and started to cry.

# XXIV.

# MOONLIGHTING

J anet sat in the hotel room patting a young starlet on the back and rolling her eyes. Mimi LaRue was the youngest employee of Eden Studio, and it was clear why Don had put her on the interview list. She hadn't started her career at one of the major studios, but had been scooped up at a modeling agency meet-and-greet by a pair of gonzo amateurs. Instead of finding herself on one of the lush sets on the Playboy Channel, she had been dumped at a filthy bungalow in Pasadena where two paunchy middle-aged men had taken turns with her while another had recorded the action on a cheap digital movie camera. She may have consented to the plan, but she hadn't enjoyed the rough handling by either would-be stud. And she really hadn't like being labeled "Our Newest Jizz Slut" on their website the next day.

How naïve can you get? Still, cash was cash, so she stuck with the bottom feeders of the industry for several months until she came to the attention of that epic collector of lame ducks, Donald Johansson.

Mimi wasn't nearly as attractive as someone like Jade, but Don gave her a chance and she made the most of it. She could actually act, which counted for something with him, and when she seemed to (did?) have an orgasm on screen, she looked like a volcano about to erupt, earning her nickname "Screaming Mimi." Her girlish looks probably boosted sales too. She had just been asked to attend her first DVD signing when Jade Delilah's murder put an end to Eden Studio.

She was crying in Janet's arms, partly for financial reasons and partly because the interview had dredged up unwanted memories of her first weeks in the business. Janet gave her one last perfunctory pat and then handed her a tissue. "Are you okay?"

"Yeah," the slim blonde sniffed, "I'll be alright. I'm thinking of starting my own website, ya know?"

"That's a good idea," Janet agreed. The little trollope just might survive if she cultivated that pragmatic streak. The veteran actress felt an uncharacteristic burst of pity. "Are you okay with people seeing the bit with you crying at the end? I could ask the professor to cut it out if you'd like."

Mimi laughed for the first time that morning. "Right now, you can go online and see me giving two guys a blow job while I'm riding one of their buddies. I'm not worried about a few minutes of blubbing." Mimi gave her eyes one last wipe and left the hotel room with a sniff and a flip of her hair.

Just a couple more days of interviews remained, and Janet had to admit it was kind of fun. Who said she had no retirement options? Ellen Degeneres needed competition from someone living in the real world.

Mimi had been talkative but she didn't know anything about the murder. She'd heard about Don and Jade, and had witnessed a quarrel between them, she but hadn't attached any significance to it, even in retrospect. As with the other interviewees, not a word had been said about Janet's own relationship with Don. The police must have sniffed out something, however, because a cop had called two days earlier asking for a second hair sample for DNA testing.

At least the first girl interviewed in the morning had told an interesting story about Chance Geary. Tiffany Imperial (she recalled an old advertisement: "Imperial Margarine: The Best Spread") was a leggy, red-headed meth-fiend who admitted to calling Geary repeatedly the night of the murder looking to score some dope. His failure to answer was notable, according to Tiffany, because he was totally reliable. If he had no supply, he always had a friend who did. She was still pissed at him for not returning her calls, several of which had been placed within the time frame of the murder. Tiffany's story proved nothing, but any bit of evidence that pointed in Geary's direction was surely welcome.

\* \* \*

Stanley trudged slowly down the steps of the jail and stood in the middle of the sidewalk, waiting for divine guidance. He saw the parking garage on his right. There was still time to hop in the car, drive to the airport and catch a flight home. A group of teenagers jostled him as they passed by, and a middle-aged man in a suit bumped him with his briefcase before turning up the jailhouse steps. This is not the best place to ponder his future, he decided, as another suit brushed past him. A quick glance across the street found a pastry shop offering freshly brewed cups of free trade coffee. He weaved quickly through the traffic, dimly aware that a sane person would have run to the rental car as fast as his legs could carry him.

"Hey, haven't I seen you on television?" A perky young barista narrowed her eyes and scrutinized him.

"Oh god, I hope not," he sighed, a black cloud descending.

"I'm sure I have," she replied as she fetched his coffee and croissant. "I got it! You're the guy representing that porn star, right?"

He looked at her bright young face and saw nothing but genuine excitement. "More or less."

"That's so cool!" She pushed his drink and pastry across the counter. "This is totally on the house."

"That's okay," he replied and looked at her name tag. "You don't have to do that, Glenna."

"But it's policy!" she exclaimed. "My manager says, like, celebrities eat free. He's like: It's good for business." She nodded toward the jail house and grinned. "You'd be amazed at the people I've seen here. I've served Robert Downey, Jr., twice!"

He gave up trying to pay for the food and worried about the state of a country where criminals and their attorneys warranted such youthful admiration. The same country, he imagined, where the *Girls Gone Wild* tour bus can pull into any college town and find volunteers lining up to make out with their sorority sisters.

He took a booth in the corner of the cafe with his back turned toward the window and stared at his cell phone. He sipped his coffee and took a bite of the croissant but didn't get much comfort from the treat or from spinning his cell phone on the polished table. He slapped down his hand on the whirling phone and swore under his breath. He simply could not leave Don alone in Janet's hands. There was no way. He would not be able to live with himself.

There was some relief in finally making a decision. He wasn't just floating around anymore, bumping into whatever came his way and calling it living. So, he took a sip from his coffee and pressed Janet's number on his speed dial. From now on, he would keep her close by, not only to make sure that she wasn't sabotaging the investigation, but to gather evidence of her possible guilt. In particular, the chance to look through her closet for a purple garment to match the office window fiber would be very welcome indeed.

\* \* \*

Janet found Stanley in the corner of the coffee shop across from the courthouse, right where he said he would be. He had sounded tired on the phone, but the guy in front of her looked positively pasty. Usually, he wore a natty jacket, a bit dated by Los Angeles standards, but probably pretty cutting edge garb for the Midwest. Hunched over a cup of coffee and a plate full of crumbs, he looked like Peter Falk playing a suicidal Inspector Columbo. She sat down across from him and cheered him up with the story of Tiffany Imperial's unanswered phone calls to Chance Geary on the night of the murder. For a moment, a glint of interest pierced his exhaustion.

"Did you get any sleep last night?" she asked. "You look totally wiped." He reminded her a little bit of Don, who was prone to mini bouts of depression. "Can I get you something?" She gestured back to the pastry counter.

He shook his head. "Nah, I'm not hungry." He moved the remains of his croissant around with his forefinger and squashed them into a little ball. "The president of the university saw us on the news yesterday and my department head called last night to let me know that I've been suspended indefinitely." He looked up with a stoic smile. "Basically, I'm fired."

She reached over and touched his wrist. "It wasn't anything that I said to the reporters, was it?"

"No," he replied, "you didn't say anything wrong. I think this project was doomed from the beginning."

"Don't say that." She tried to cheer him up. "The book idea is great, and you've got tons of interview material. And you're a real hero for staying here to help Don!" She gave his hands an energetic squeeze. God, he was just like Don: high-minded and hot at the same time. It really wasn't fair. She had to sculpt her body for hours on the evil Stairmaster for what these slobs could generate with a wistful smile and stylish pair of glasses. Society was to blame, or maybe it was just the forbidden fruit thing. She had wanted Don and couldn't have him. He had been immune to her charms which made losing him to that bitch Jade all the more in-fucking-comprehensible. She wouldn't make the same mistake with the handsome young professor. But there he sat, pushing back a shock of dark hair, just like Don always did, agonizing whether some decision was right or wrong.

She looked into his face. "You're doing the right thing. Don't let the bastards get you down."

He looked at her like he was trying to figure out a particularly tricky crossword puzzle. "Well, they've already got me down." He took a sip of coffee and made a face that told her it had gone cold. "The question is how to finish up the investigation and get some resolution. I left a message with McCaffrey a while ago asking for the names of Geary and Walker's alibi witness. I figured we'd pay Deborah Spellerburg another visit while we're waiting for him to call back. We also need to track down Miriam and see if she wants to talk about the fire yesterday."

"Do you know where she lives?"

"No," he replied, "but I remember her last name is Wilhoit. It stuck in my head when we were introduced. I grew up with a bunch of Wilhoits down the street from me in Chicago." They got up from the table and walked outside into the bright sunshine.

He suggested that they start off with another visit to the UCLA attorney, and she offered to drive. A light breeze blew off the ocean and she couldn't help but notice the sharp-edged day glittering around them. It was a perfect afternoon in Los Angeles, cool and clear, with a slight tinge of salt in the air. She walked directly to the most eye-catching car on the street, the bright red Mini Cooper convertible with custom rims and a white leather interior, license plate 4PLAY.

She put the roof down with the push of a button and slipped on a pair of Armani sunglasses. In the coffee shop, she had been an unremarkable addition to the decor. Once in the car, it had taken nothing more than a flick of a finger through her hair and a sidelong glance in the review mirror to regain the glamour that had been temporarily hidden. Stanley seemed not to notice. Over the previous week, she had caught him (when he thought she wouldn't notice) staring in frank appreciation of her figure. Now, he sat and stared straight ahead, wind whipping through his thick dark hair as they made their way back to Westwood.

As they drove to the law school, Stanley revealed that Don had invited Jade to his office during the party to offer her Spellerburg's protective services.

"Did he say why he lied about the new script story earlier?" Normally Don was scrupulously truthful. "It doesn't make much sense."

The professor was silent for a moment. "Not really. Maybe he didn't want anyone to know that she was the battered-woman type?" He shrugged. "It *is* a pretty pathetic story. Don said he couldn't convince her to leave Geary."

"He was worried about admitting failure?" That made sense in the context of a cocktail party but not a murder investigation where he was the target. "I don't buy it."

She wondered if her partner was telling her everything as they walked from the UCLA parking garage to the law school. He opened the front door of the building and let her in. Something smelled bad about the story. Then again, it was typical of Don not to think straight when Jade was involved. How could someone so rational act like such an idiot? It should have taken a woman with curves *and* brains to attract the philosopher king of porn, but one sleek brown body had been plenty. If that wasn't a betrayal of his most precious principles, she didn't know what was. "Do you think he's telling the truth?"

He shrugged but said nothing more as they made their way to the legal aid clinic. When they arrived, they found Spellerburg wearing the same drab pantsuit as she had the day before. If she's trying to live anywhere near Westwood on an academic salary, Janet thought, she's lucky she can afford to buy any clothes at all.

"What can I do for you, Professor Hopkins?" The woman motioned for them to sit down.

"There were just a couple of questions that we forgot to ask you yesterday." He pulled a chair closer to her desk. "Thanks for seeing us."

She looked at her watch. "I've got about half an hour. What do you want to know?"

"Quite frankly, we're curious why you didn't take your information to the police. I mean, Don's visit here seems pretty material to the investigation." Stanley posed the question in an offhand way that minimized the risk the frumpy young attorney would take offense. "Surely you considered it?"

"I did," she admitted immediately, "but I thought the police would show up and interview me. I figured that Mr. Johansson would bring it up as part of his defense and then I would be asked to describe our conversation. No one came, until you two." She paused for a moment and polished her glasses while she formulated her thoughts. "And there was something else that I was trying to work through. Sometimes we have men come through here posing as friends of abused women. They're trying to find out where our safe houses are, or they're abusers getting some sort of creepy kick out of talking about what their girl-friends are going through. Quite frankly, I wondered whether Johansson might be one of those guys. He was acting kind of strange, and he said something that raised a red flag with me."

"What was that?"

"Well, he said that he was a victim too. Believe it or not, a lot of abusers see themselves as victims, as victims of their girlfriends' shortcomings or as victims of their girlfriends' imaginary lovers. When he said he was a victim, I started to wonder whether he wasn't one of these creeps that I told you about, especially in light of the eventual murder."

"I think I understand," he replied after thinking about her story for a moment. "You didn't want to go to the police with an exculpatory story because it might get a potential abuser and murderer off the hook. On the other hand, you didn't want to get someone in trouble on your intuition alone."

"You see the problem," she admitted. "And trust me, the police are not very good at parsing these fine sorts of distinc-tions." She leaned back in her chair. "Working this job, I'm afraid, has done little to increase my respect for the Los Angeles County police department."

"I'm not a big fan myself," he replied with a smile that made Spellerburg beam. Damn, the little professor was getting pretty good at this. "When Don said he felt abused, did he mention anyone in particular?"

Janet watched the attorney closely and saw that she was tempted to answer. "If he really were a victim and had asked for my help with his own problem as opposed to someone else's, then I couldn't tell you. Attorney-client privilege attaches in that situation." She stood up and apologized, but she had no more to say on the matter. Stanley thanked her again, and they left the clinic.

"What now?" Janet's question hung in the air as they walked back to the car. It was late afternoon and the campus was almost empty. The few students that she could see were heading home for the evening.

"Since we're still waiting on McCaffrey, why don't we try to track down Miriam Wilhoit's address?" He sat down on a bench in front of the parking garage, and she lit a cigarette while he pulled out his phone and checked an online directory. "That would have been too easy," he said. "Maybe we can find her son. She said they were tight for money, so they might be living together."

"It's worth a try," she replied. "The only time I ever saw her smile was when she was talking about her kid."

"Do you know his name or where he was going to college?"

"I have no clue. Definitely in LA, but there are dozens of schools he might be at."

"Sounds like Google time to me. Do you have a laptop? We could find somewhere with WiFi."

"I've got a better idea," she said as she opened the door to the Mini. "Let's swing by and pick up your car, then head back to my place and use my computer."

# XXV.

# A STIFFIE

Janet lived in a small Spanish-style condominium complex several miles west of the UCLA campus. Her stucco townhouse was one of a dozen clustered around a spacious courtyard with a large sparkling fountain splashing warm, glazed tile and generously landscaped with bougainvillea and hibiscus. She opened the heavy, wrought iron gate at the main entrance with a magnetic key card and checked her mail while Stanley admired the view. "This is amazing."

"It's a lot nicer than my old place."

"Do you rent or own?" The query was gauche, but he was curious and she seemed to take no offense.

"I own it. Most people lease, but between my website and some good luck investing, I was able to finally buy something."

"Congratulations," he replied. "It's a lot more than just 'something'."

She led him to a corner unit that featured a small balcony on the second floor overlooking the courtyard. Two potted lemon trees stood in the arched entryway on either side of her door, and they added a gentle scent to the already fragrant space. When she waved him in, he could see more ceramic tile set among polished hardwood slats running through the ground floor.

Her heels clicked sharply as she walked into the kitchen and pulled out a bottle of white wine. She tilted it in his direction with a smile. "Would you like a glass?"

"Yes, please." While she poured, he looked with envy at features in her kitchen that he would never be able to afford on a professor's salary: solid cherry cabinets, a professional grade, six-burner stove, a huge double-doored stainless steel refrigerator, and thousands of dollars worth of copper pots and pans hanging from a wrought iron ring over a glossy quartz island in the center of the room. "You must love to cook."

"I like to cook, but most of this stuff only gets used by caterers when I have a party." She handed him the glass and led him down a hallway that began where the kitchen and dining room flowed into each other. A marble bathroom stood on one side with a large bedroom on the other. It seemed to be the only bedroom on the ground floor and he assumed it was hers. In the closet, perhaps, was a purple sweater whose fibers might match those found on Don's office window by the police.

She entered a small room at the end of the hall and sat down in front of a teak desk. A large monitor and a keyboard were set on top, while the largest CPU he had ever seen sat on the floor next to it. She looked up from the keyboard and saw him checking out the computer. "Welcome to the home of *laylaxxx.com*. There's my server, and if I bring up this window right here, it will tell us that…forty-two clients are currently logged on. We store about thirty thousand jpeg files and one hundred full length digital movies in the memory, all ready for download any time of day or night."

Sitting down had forced her skirt high on her thighs, and from his vantage point over and behind her, he admired the view without being caught staring. The proximity of thousands of images of her in various states of undress, wearing who-knows-how-many styles of lingerie and bondage gear, having sex in every position described in the Kama Sutra and beyond caused an undeniable stirring. He flashed back to high school on warm spring days when the sexiest girls in his class squirmed and giggled in their halter tops and miniskirts. He scrambled for a safe image to cling to.

"Have you ever visited the website? There's a free tour for non-members." She clicked on the URL at the top of the screen and started typing. "It's one of the slickest sites in the business."

"No!" he fairly shouted. "I'll check it out later."

She turned and looked up at him. "Don't worry, Stanley," she said with an amused grin, "I'm just going to Google." She finished typing and let him sit down in her seat. As he searched, she stood next to him and leaned down to see his results. She turned her face toward him, so close that he could feel her breath on his ear. "What's your plan to find Miriam's son?"

He could feel a bead of sweat forming on his forehead. A few more moments like this and he would not be able to stand up without acute embarrassment. He poured his concentration into the search for Don's secretary. "Okay, let's find an online list of American colleges and universities." He entered his search terms and found several websites providing comprehensive lists of institutions of higher education in the United States. After browsing through a couple that provided only alphabetical listings, he finally found one organized geographically. "I'll cut and paste a list of all university and college URL's in Los Angeles, and then search for "Wilhoit" in their student directories. There shouldn't be all that many; it's not a very common name. Then we can make some calls and track down the right one."

"Sounds like a plan." She stood up and watched as he pasted the initial set of web addresses into a spreadsheet. "While you're doing that, why don't I make us something to eat? It's already past six."

"Great. I'm starving." He felt her hands give his shoulders a gentle squeeze as she wished him luck and left the room.

He waited a moment and then turned to watch her walk down the hall, but his gaze, for once, was not voyeuristic. He wanted to make sure that she would be completely out of sight when he slipped into her bedroom. He felt a twinge of guilt at planning a deliberate invasion of her privacy, but she had not been honest with him. She had been hiding the extent of her relationship with Don, and also her feelings about Jade. The weight of her deception more than offset the wrong of a quick peek in her closet.

He went through two student directories and paused. All he needed was two minutes to spot something purple hanging in her closet, grab a fiber and then sneak back to the desk.

The chair squeaked loudly when he got up, and he waited a moment to make sure the sound had not alerted her. Then, he crept silently down the hall, listening carefully for the reassuring sound of clattering pots as he slipped into her inner sanctum. A large, four-poster bed sat in the middle of the room, parallel to a large curtained window. The entrance to the master bath was located through the wall opposite the bed, next to an old fashioned wardrobe whose open doors revealed a large plasma screen television. On either side of the bed sat small end tables, one covered with books and another with a half-finished bottle of water, a pair of reading glasses and an alarm clock. Stanley saw the closet on his left, and he pushed the French doors open wide with a quick look back over his shoulder.

The closet space extended at least fifteen feet deep and it was too dark to perceive distinctions between the black, dark blue, and purple clothes hanging there. He stuck his hand along the closet wall and found a light switch that quickly filled the space with a soft fluorescent glow. Before him spread row after row of dresses, skirts, pants, sweaters, shirts, lingerie and a separate section for outfits that could only be costumes for Janet's more fanciful roles. At the far end of the little room, filling the wall from floor to ceiling, were over a hundred cubicles housing everything from tennis shoes to outrageously high heels. He goggled for a moment at the immensity of her collection and then quickly started to scan the rows of shirts and sweaters running parallel above and below.

He spotted two purple sweaters on the right side of the closet and pinched off a small sample from each. Then he spotted a purple wool skirt and realized that once his inspection was over, he would have a pile of little tufts in his pocket with no idea which garment they came from. He was anxiously working his way through the left side of the closet when he heard a large crash from the kitchen accompanied by a shriek. He froze for an instant, then he shut off the closet light and ran to the bedroom door. Just as he was about to stick his head out into the hallway to see if the coast was clear, footsteps approached and he heard her cursing her clumsiness.

He spun around in a panic and quickly surveyed the room. The bed was too low to hide under, so he ran back into the closet, shut the door, and peered out from behind the linen curtains that covered the glass of the French doors. A moment later she entered, holding the stained front of her blouse away from her skin with both hands. She stood next to the bed, carefully undoing the buttons and letting the garment slip off her shoulders to the floor. She looked in the direction of the closet for a moment, but instead of going inside to grab a new top, she picked the soiled blouse off the floor and walked into the master bath.

Here was a chance to escape. One quick move and he could be down the hall happily typing away when she emerged, but when he peeked past the curtains and saw her filling up the sink with water, he saw the large oval mirror above it provided a perfect view of the closet entrance. If he opened the door to leave, she would see him as she stood soaking the garment. Go to the toilet, he urged her. If she sat down and relieved herself in the corner of the bathroom, he could slip away without being spotted. He watched her squeeze the shirt a couple of times in the soapy water, but she made no further move.

With the stain safely soaking, she wiped her hands on a plush towel hanging next to the mirror. She straightened up and slowly arched a kink out her back before grabbing a brush and running it vigorously through her hair. When she was satisfied, she touched up her lipstick and strode back into her bedroom. He was ready to retreat into the corner of the closet and seek shelter behind a wall of dresses when she stopped and pulled out the top drawer of the wardrobe.

He sighed with relief as he watched her consider a colorful knit top. She slid the drawer back in and examined herself in the full length mirror attached to the back of the bedroom door.

She shifted her weight from one foot to the other as she unfolded the sweater, and he could not take his eyes from the movement of her body. A low-cut, blue bra supported full, round breasts, and beneath it her stomach was flat, with hips flaring out at precisely the place he found himself staring when confronted by mid-riff bearing co-eds on campus. Layla gave a little shimmy as she slipped on the garment, and he felt himself respond involuntarily.

He adjusted his trousers and assessed his chances. If she went back to the kitchen, then he would be home free. If she decided to check on him in the study, he could bolt across the hall to the guest bathroom and pretend to be washing up for dinner.

She paused for a moment in front of the mirror and undid the top button of the sweater. She stood to the side and checked the view, pushing her breasts up slightly with her hands, then frowning and buttoning up again. As she reached for the door, she took one last look in the mirror and pursed her lips. Something was not quite right. She smoothed the sweater against the skirt and returned to the brightly lit bathroom to make a final decision on the outfit.

They look great! He beamed a mental message across the room. They look fabulous together! But Janet shook her head and slid her hand to the zipper on the side of the skirt. It fell to the floor, and Stanley saw a lacy pair of panties that matched the light blue of her brassiere. When she bent over to pick up the skirt, he nearly gasped aloud, but the joy of peeping ended abruptly as she spun out of the bathroom and strode toward the closet to find a skirt to match her new top.

Stanley scrambled to the very back of the clothes rack. Some of her longest dresses hung in the corner, and he made himself as small as possible behind a drape of fluffy chiffon for-malwear. The doors to the closet opened, and he held his breath, holding his body absolutely still. If the light were turned on, he could not escape being noticed. Through squinting eyes, he saw her step into the room and reach straight for the upper rack of skirts across from him. She had a specific item in mind and made no move to flip on the light switch. He watched nervously as she reached for the garment, plucked it off its hanger and left the room without a glance toward his hiding place. She shut the closet door. Only then did he exhale, pausing a moment before slipping out. As he emerged from the dresses, he was surprised and dismayed to hear a popular tune playing. She wasn't going to sit in her bedroom and listen to the stereo, was she?

Then, Stanley recognized the music, and in horror he reached into his pocket to silence his cell phone. As he fumbled with the cursed device, it fell to the floor, and he was just picking it up when the doors to the closet opened and the bare-legged porn star stood staring at him first in astonishment and then in anger.

Time then slowed down for Stanley and instead of panicking he stood outside himself and in a calm, almost leisurely fashion, he began formulating a plan. By the time he straightened up, phone balanced in his hand, he thought he had found a way out.

"Hello? Stanley Hopkins here." He put his free hand on his hip and answered the phone in a nonchalant pose. "Yes, Inspector McCaffrey?" He tilted his head as he listened to the detective's message, daring to make eye contact with, and then nodding at, the fuming Janet as he pulled out his pen and took notes. "Alright, terrific." He paused again and nodded coolly. "I got it. And could we meet tomorrow afternoon?" He wrote a bit more on his pad before saying goodbye and snapping the phone shut authoritatively.

When he looked back up, Janet had her arms crossed over her chest, flashing eyes demanding an explanation.

"Well," he explained with a savior faire that belied the tight situation, "that was McCaffrey. He's given us the name of Geary's alibi witness." He tapped the note pad meaningfully with his pen. "Some meth head in West Hollywood. It doesn't sound like it's going to be hard to track her down."

She stared at him for a second, ignoring his reference to the next day's work schedule and interjecting with menace, "What the fuck are you doing in my closet!"

He aimed for apologetic rather than totally ashamed, "I'm so sorry! I should have asked you before looking in here, but I just knew that this was going to be fabulous." As he spoke he gestured expansively with both hands, "and I was totally right. This is amazing!"

He saw confusion mixing with her anger and quickly continued. "Look," he explained as if he were quite embarrassed, which was not hard to play, given the admission he was about to fake, "you've meet Angela. I've been married for ten years and I'm straight as, well, a really straight guy…but I've always loved women's clothes. I used to dress up in my mom's stuff when I was just a kid, and I've got my own little closet at home full of hose and dresses and stuff." He saw Janet's eyes widen.

"Oh Angela knows! Thank God she read all those Dear Abbey posts on how cross-dressers aren't gay." He gave a little lop-sided smile. "I mean, she thinks it's a little weird, but she's gotten used to it. It even kinda spices things up once in a while, if you know what I mean."

"You're a cross-dresser?" The confusion had faded toward suspicion, still spiced with a generous serving of outrage. "Are you fucking kidding me?"

"But that's no excuse for me just barging in here without permission!" He shook his head, ashamed of having given in to impulse. "I'm like a kid in a candy shop sometimes. You're always *so* put together with your wardrobe that I just knew this closet would be amazing." He shook his head. "God, I'm just like the little kid and the proverbial candy jar. I really am sorry. It won't happen again."

"You didn't put anything on did you?" The mere thought threatened to pop the eyes out of her head.

"No!" He looked appropriately horrified. "I would never stretch out your clothes! I swear, I just wanted to look at them."

Stanley had learned long ago in the middle school playground facing down the local bullies, that making himself ridiculous threw people off guard and derailed their anger. Sure, now a beautiful porn star wearing only her panties and a tight sweater thought he was a transvestite, but she had no clue as to the real reason for his intrusion and when she finally had time to think it over, she probably wouldn't stay all that pissed off at a minor league pervert who merely longed to check out her dress collection.

She shook her head as she could not quite take in the situation, then she stepped to the side and spoke in a voice filled more with exasperation than rage, "Could you just get out of here?"

He walked immediately across the hall into the bathroom and shut the door. The figure in the mirror blew out a sigh of relief and then splashed some water on his face and toweled off. He leaned against the sink, wondering what to do with the pile of purple fluff in his pocket and how to make the best of Janet's new image of him.

When he emerged, he peeked in the bedroom and saw that Janet had dressed and gone back to cook. For a moment, he considered finishing his exploration of the closet, but instead he returned to the study and worked dutifully at the computer until he heard a voice calling him to dinner. He walked with some trepidation down the hall and into the dining room where he found a large bowl of pasta primavera sitting in the middle of an elegantly set table. A half-empty bottle of white wine flanked the food, and a second full bottle stood in a marble cooler beading with moisture. He was pouring himself a glass when she appeared with a salad bowl in one hand and a basket of garlic bread in the other.

"Can I help you with anything?"

"No, this should do it." She sat down and gestured for him to do the same.

He thanked her for preparing the meal, and they sat down to eat in uncomfortable silence. After a couple of bites of the pasta and a generous sip of the wine, she looked up at him and spoke.

"In the pantheon of shitty things people have done to me in my life, what you did might seem pretty minor, but you've got to understand how much I like my privacy. When you're most intimate business is a commodity, you really treasure the scraps of privacy you get." She looked up at him with deadly seriousness, willing to put the closet episode behind her if he showed any comprehension of her point. "Just don't do anything like that again. Understood?"

He nodded. He knew when to just shut up.

She lifted her glass again and twirled a bite of the pasta on her fork. "Why don't you tell me some more about your book? Not just the porn parts," she said with the merest glimmer of a smile, "but the whole project."

Unfortunately, the book was being written by a different person in a different life. The "whole project" barely seemed interesting anymore. He had wanted to show that most people in most jobs held the same sorts of attitudes about work: they hated their bosses for the same reasons, smoked pot before work to cope with the same kind of stress, fantasized about their co-workers equally as often. When he tried to explain it to Janet, the whole idea sounded like a waste of time.

As they finished the second bottle of wine and opened a third, most of the awkwardness had disappeared. Self-doubting, cross-dressing professors and porn stars had some common ground, and both of them realized that for different reasons their present careers could not last much longer. Alcohol made them optimistic that something interesting would present itself.

"You know," she admitted, "I like this interviewing stuff. There's got to be room on cable somewhere for a sexy, edgy talk show. I could run circles around Dr. Ruth."

"Hey, I'd watch. That's for sure."

"What about you? Are you going to find another teaching job somewhere?"

"No way!" He slapped the table a little too hard. Ever since he'd come to Los Angeles, he had enjoyed using bits and pieces of his law degree more than being an academic. "I could open up a celebrity law practice in Hollywood." She laughed. "I don't know…but I need to think of something. The clock's ticking."

"Yeah, for me too," she said. She picked up their plates and carried them into the kitchen. "Do you want to go out and get some dessert?" She stuck her head out while he picked up the bread basket and the bowl of pasta. "I don't have anything sweet in the fridge."

Stanley stood up and had to steady himself. "I don't think driving a car is a good idea right now."

"Me neither," she admitted as they finished clearing the table and piled the dishes on the kitchen counter. "You know, if you can't take us to Ben & Jerry's, then you certainly can't drive across town to your hotel." She bent over to put the plates in the dishwasher. "We could call you a cab, but that would mean stranding your car here." She stood up and dried her hands with a towel. He tried in vain to decipher the look in her eyes. "Or you could stay here."

It really was the most sensible alternative. "You're sure you don't mind?"

"Not at all," she said as she tossed the towel in the sink. "I'll show you the guest room upstairs."

He watched her flex and sway as she walked up the stairway and he almost reached out to touch her as her skirt swished before him at eye level. When they got to the top of the stairs, she led them to a cozy room overlooking the courtyard and turned down a woolen Navajo blanket covering the queen size bed. He could not decide what looked more tempting, his hostess or the beckoning refuge for his weary, wine-sodden bones.

"There you go," she said as she pulled down the comforter. "You'll find fresh towels and stuff in the bathroom." She straightened up, put a hand on his shoulder to steady herself and whispered in his ear. "Good night."

\* \* \*

On the other side of Los Angeles, the phone in Stanley's hotel room rang shortly after 11:00 p.m., at 12:30 a.m. precisely, and a little before 3:00 a.m. Angela made a final attempt at his cell phone before she went to bed, but it went straight to voice mail.

# XXVI.

# EXIT STRATEGIES

Janet was sitting at the kitchen table, scraping a cup of non-fat yogurt and sipping coffee when her overnight guest made his way downstairs. She had already spent an hour on the exercise bike, run a virus scan on her server, and checked the status of her online brokerage account. She offered him something to drink.

"Coffee's fine." He took the cup, poured in plenty of cream and sugar and sat down with a sigh. "Thanks for letting me stay." He blew across the top of the hot liquid and took a small sip. "If I had driven, I might have ended up spending the night with Don."

"Or worse."

"Or worse," he confirmed. He took another sip and then scanned the headlines of the *Los Angeles Times* spread out on the table. "I've been thinking about today. This is it for the interviews, right?"

"Right," she said, "just two this morning, plus a couple to reschedule later, if you want."

"Could I work here tracking down Miriam while you're doing the last couple of interviews?" He grabbed an orange from the basket on the table and unpeeled it. "We could pack the equipment afterward, have a quick lunch and then track down Geary's alibi witness in West Hollywood."

"Porn stars in the morning and meth heads in the afternoon," she replied. "Sounds like a plan." Scruffy and unshaven, the young professor had a bit of a Hugh Grant sort of air, basically charming and trustworthy. Surely it was safe to leave him home alone now that he had learned his lesson.

She finished her coffee and saw she was running late. She grabbed her purse and pulled out a spare key to the condominium. "Make sure to lock up when you leave." She tossed it to him. "And don't stretch out any of my dresses!" His strangled protest brought a smile to her face that lingered halfway to the hotel.

The first interviewee was an old friend, Singelica Hotte, a tall redhead who claimed unequivocally that Don could never have committed the crime. Janet had always admired her friend's long legs, but those thighs weren't quite as thin as they used to be. The new boob job was probably meant to draw attention away from the slippage further south. "There are a hundred people in the business more likely to kill Jade," the redhead argued. "He's the nicest guy in the valley. I'd even be a character witness. I don't care what anyone else thinks."

"You might care if no one hired you afterward," Janet replied. A studio like Chimera would surely resent someone working the wrong side of the street.

"Fuck that," spat the veteran of over one hundred videos, "I'm almost done with porn anyway. Next week is my last shoot; then I'm going out on a farewell dancing tour."

"I've heard that one before," Janet replied doubtfully, "maybe even from you."

"I'm serious this time. The money stopped going up my nose a long time ago, and I'm gonna retire. You know my partner, Sarah? We're going back to Pittsburgh, where you can get a house for a tenth of what it costs here. Then, I'll go back to school, or open a business or something."

"You'll probably end up owning a strip club," Janet laughed.

"Yeah, maybe." The redhead shrugged her shoulders and pulled a pack of light cigarettes out of her purse. "But I sure as hell won't be dancing there."

Despite the scripted questions, the conversation kept coming back to retirement and life in the outside world. Janet paraphrased a question she once got from a psychology student at USC: "You say you want to quit. Aren't you too fucked up now?"

The thirty year old actress laughed. "Well, fuck you too!" She tapped out a cigarette and contemplated the question as she lit up. Janet looked at the no-smoking sign on the back of the hotel room door, shrugged, and lit one herself. "Well, I've never gotten any bad STDs, and I haven't fucked up my sex life. Sarah and I are still cool, but we do live in this weird cocoon. Regular people don't understand what we do. They think we're perverts or ignore us. It's really hard to think about living out there," she jerked her thumb out the window, "or Pittsburgh or wherever, and chilling in the 'burbs with the Stepford Wives. Even before I did my first film, I didn't belong out there and it's way worse now." She took a long drag on her smoke. "You cross over a line when you do porn, and I don't know if you get to cross back."

Janet nodded her head. Rejoining society was a pipedream, and what would you find when you got there? The brief fantasy of giving it a shot with Don, the two of them quitting and living like some normal couple, was now as dead as Jade Delilah.

"You know," Janet ventured after a moment's pause, "the professor who's doing this research says that people in most jobs feel the same way, like no one really understands what it's like to, say, work in a factory or wait tables. No matter what kind of work, you get stuck and end up cut off from people not in that world." She smiled at the expression on her friend's face. "Of course, maybe he's full of shit."

"No," Singelica protested, "I like that. My dad worked in the steel mills in Pittsburgh, and when they shut down, he was totally lost. He and his friends spent all their time sitting around, drinking and talking about their old shitty jobs. I thought they were fuckin' crazy, but the mills really were a world of their own. Once they closed, I don't think the old guys ever fit back in."

"Well, try not to end up like your father," Janet said.

"Don't worry," she laughed. "That's always been goal number one."

The two women shared another cigarette while they waited for the next interviewee to knock on the door, but Stiffany Lotz never arrived. Singelica looked at her watch and gave Janet a brief hug goodbye. The novice interviewer straightened up the room and organized the pile of digital memory cards sitting on the coffee table next to the bed. Each one was in a Ziploc sandwich baggie labeled with the name of the girl interviewed and date. She could see that Angela and Stanley had talked to eight women. She was familiar with all of them and had worked with most: Kristy, Dominique Wilde, Jenna Cartier, Sasha Likova, Allura Benz, and Katie Silver. A nice cross-section of some of the more prominent stars of the last five years. One name, however, stood out like a sore thumb. Sheila Easy had quit making movies more than five years earlier and hit the talk show circuit to expose the evils of the porn industry. What was she doing there?

Curious, she popped the card into the camera and played the interview on the small screen in her hands. As she watched it, she became more and more angry as the self-proclaimed victim of porn repudiated the industry that had financed her soapbox.

"You lying bitch," she shouted at the camera as Sheila recounted tearfully how she had been forced to have oral sex. "I saw you film yourself doing it with a fucking German Shepherd!" Sheila had been willing to do anything with anybody (correction: any mammal) at any time. Now the poster girl for decency, she had conveniently forgotten what she had been eager to do for money. Janet watched the recording to the end and shook her head. Did the former star really believe what she said or had she just improved her acting skills?

Don had a catch phrase for what she had just observed: Linda Lovelace Syndrome. The seventies porn icon had found Jesus in the nineties and suddenly acquired amnesia about the years before *Deep Throat*. Over the protests of her peers, she had convinced millions of people on nationally broadcast talk shows that she had been forced to perform sex acts with a gun to her head, a detail conspicuously absent from her first two autobiographies. While other porn tycoons accused her of lying to get publicity, Don had another theory. He was convinced that she really believed what she said. Her religious conversion was genuine, and her new self simply could not be reconciled with her old self. The mental conflict, he argued, was too great. The former Linda had simply ceased to exist.

Sheila showed many of the same signs. In some ways, the ex-star was a perfect suspect, with one swing of the bat destroying an image of her former self and bringing down a cornerstone of the porn empire. Except that she had not been present at Eden Studio on the night of the murder. But neither had Chance Geary, as far as anyone knew, and Stanley was still pushing him as a bona fide suspect to the LAPD. There was no reason not to push Sheila too.

# XXVII

# A STIFF

The pile of purple fuzz grew steadily on the top of Stuart McCaffrey's desk. The detective looked up at the demented professor who was pulling his pockets apart for yet more lint. He had seen many things in his career, but he had never witnessed a criminal investigator, even an amateur one, hand over what might be evidence of a colleague's guilt. He motioned for Stanley to sit down.

"Let me get this straight." He pointed to the little purple mountain. "You pinched these off clothes you found in the Janet Stephens's closet?" He looked up. "I probably shouldn't ask this, but how did you get into her apartment?"

"She let me in," he replied. "I spent the night there."

"Of course," commented the detective, upgrading his opinion of the professor from annoying twerp to devious bastard. "And what do you want me to do with it?"

"I assume that you'll want to examine the fibers and see if they match those left on the window sill in Don Johansson's office the night of the murder. If you've got mysterious fibers sticking to an obvious escape route, they should be tested against the clothes of one of your prime suspects."

"My prime suspect is locked up in the County Jail," McCaffrey replied laconically. "Do you even know which fibers come from which garment?"

The professor had clearly anticipated this objection. "No, I couldn't really catalog them, but if you get a match, wouldn't that be grounds for a warrant to search her house?"

The young man stated his case matter-of-factly, but he had a point. Since the evidence had come from her house legally from a non-police source, a match could get them a warrant for a complete search of the residence. "Probably," he replied cautiously. "I'll talk to the forensic people."

Stanley nodded with satisfaction and turned to leave. "Wait," the detective said, "wait a second." Seeing this new side of his adversary made him curious. "You really want to get your old friend off, don't you?"

"Yeah." The professor paused for a moment and then elaborated. "But I'm at the point where I'd just like to see justice done. Someone brutalized Jade Delilah, and whoever did it should go to jail. If it's Janet, then she should go. If it's Chance Geary, then he should go. And if it's Don," he added with a shrug of his shoulders, "well, then he should go too."

"Even your friend?"

"Yeah, even him."

"You're sounding like a cop now." The detective baited him.

"Not really." He offered a decent comeback. "The police don't seem all that interested in finding the killer." He pointed at the pile of fuzz on the desk. "It seems like I'm the only one looking for the truth."

McCaffrey parried the attack on his work ethic with a wave of his hand. "Don't worry, we'll run the tests. We'll know about Stephens' hair in a couple of days too."

"One more thing." The professor paused by the door and fired off one last question. "What have you heard about the fire at Eden Studio?"

"Arson," the detective replied. "Started in the one of the storage rooms." The information elicited no sign of surprise. The guy was cool; he had to give him that much. "And if you run across Don Johansson's secretary during your investigation, tell her we'd like to speak to her. She seems to have disappeared."

After the meeting with McCaffrey, Stanley went straight to the hotel interview room. Even without stopping to shower and get new clothes, he was an hour late. By the time he arrived, Janet had packed the equipment and tidied up the room.

"Sorry!" He grabbed an armload of gear. "It took me a while to work through all of the college websites."

"Don't worry about it." She picked up the tripod and a metal case and followed him down the stairs to the car. "Stiffany Lotz never showed, so I had time to contact some of the girls you interviewed before the murder. I made a couple of calls and watched Sheila Easy's interview too." She set her load on the pavement next to the car. "There's something not right with that girl."

"What do you mean?" He flipped open the trunk.

"Well, for one thing, she's a liar. No one ever had to stick a gun to her head to make her do anything." She put the items in the trunk and walked back to the room with her partner. "Have you ever heard of Linda Lovelace Syndrome?" As they took a quick look around the room to make sure that nothing was being forgotten, she described how Sheila seemed to be in denial about her past. "We should at least find out where she was at the time of the murder."

He shrugged. "Why not? The more the merrier...we can talk with her again after we track down Geary's alibi and find Miriam." He shut the trunk. "That's all of it. Follow me back to my hotel. It's not too far."

Before they drove away he looked up at the chipped green door of Room 204. When he had first driven up with Angela, they had been hopeful about the book project and dreaming of tenure and a big raise back at BFU. Now, the book seemed pointless, their marriage was rocky, and his academic career was in shambles. On the other hand, he was making progress on a hopeless murder case, and a beautiful porn star in a bright red convertible was following him on the way back to his hotel room. He failed to find an adequately phlegmatic comment to make on the turn of events.

They arrived at the door of his room just as a Latina housekeeper was shutting it. He let them both in and slid open the door to his closet. "Just give me a second to change."

"Let me see the address of Geary's alibi witness and I'll figure out how to get to her place." Janet sat down on the bed.

He pulled a piece of paper out of his pants pocket and handed it to her.

"Is there a phone number?" She asked.

"Nope, McCaffrey just gave me the address and name: Mary Modriani." He took a lightweight suit off of a hanger and headed toward the bathroom.

"Wait a minute," she said. "You gotta rethink the outfit."

"How come?"

"Because I know where this place is." She shook the paper. "It's basically a slum full of addicts and whores, and you definitely don't want to stroll in there looking like a narc." She gestured to his suit. "Do you have any jeans or a t-shirt?"

He threw a pair of worn jeans on the bed and then searched through his suitcase. He grinned and held up a brightly colored t-shirt that read, *I survived Sociology 101 with Professor Hopkins*. She laughed. "Sorry, but you need to look more like a pimp, not a geek. Don't you have just a plain white t-shirt?"

He pulled a wrinkled one from underneath his pillow. "I've got this, but I've been sleeping in it for a week."

"Perfect," she said. "Now, get dressed and slick your back hair like a mean motherfucking whoremonger!" He did as he was told and stared at the unfamiliar image in the mirror. The t-shirt fit him snugly and showed off a decently trim waist and muscular chest. He had no brilliantine to comb into his hair, so he used a dab of body oil from the wicker basket next to the sink. Hopefully, pimps and drug dealers in the twenty-first century looked like characters out of *Grease*.

When he stepped out of the bathroom, he stopped worrying about his own appearance—all eyes on the street would undoubtedly be glued to Janet. She had unbuttoned the side of her skirt past mid thigh and knotted her shirt just above her navel. A thick smear of blood red lipstick on her mouth and dark shadowing above her eyes completed the transformation from respectable, early middle-aged woman to jaw-dropping streetwalker. She pulled a pair of dark hose out of her purse as he stood dumbfounded.

"Voila," she stood up and gave a sexy shake, "instant whore!"

"Oh my god," he gasped.

"You look pretty good yourself." She took his arm with an amused smile and led them out the door. "Now, let's go find Ms. Modriani."

As they drove to East Hollywood, he told her about his search for Miriam Wilhoit's son. After spending several hours on the internet, he had discovered eight Wilhoits currently in college in the Los Angeles area. Five were girls. He got the local phone numbers for the remaining three and called each that morning, but none had answered. Presumably, Stanley, James, and Samuel Wilhoit were all in class at UCLA, USC, and Belle Meade College respectively. Before he left the condominium, he checked the phone book for addresses. The only listing was for Samuel, with an address in Belle Meade. The others, he presumed, either lived in dormitories, making them unlikely candidates for harboring the missing secretary, or were unlisted for some other reason.

"Should we stop by Belle Meade this evening, on the off chance that Samuel Wilhoit is Miriam's son?" As she sat, the slit in her skirt extended almost to the side of her panties. He kept his eyes firmly fixed on the road as he nodded and answered.

"Good idea," he replied. "We've been focused on Geary, but Miriam's a good suspect too. First, she hates the porn industry. Second, she may have been cooking the books at Eden. And third, she surely knew about Don's back window. At worst, we need to press her harder about what went on the day of the murder, not to mention what she knows about Don and Jade's relationship."

"In some ways, she's at least as plausible as Geary and Sheila Easy," she agreed.

"Sheila?" He looked over when she spoke, and got a distracting eyeful of the diamond stud and pendent set in the button of Janet's firm belly. "I know you think she's crazy, but is she really that strong a suspect?"

Janet pulled out a cigarette and cracked open the window. "She might be. Anyone who's that erratic and hates the porn industry that much has the motivation."

"Motivation, maybe. But what about the opportunity? Surely, she didn't attend the party."

"Probably not, but it's still worth checking out." She took a drag and blew the smoke in a narrow stream that was quickly sucked out the window. "Anyone could have gotten in that window."

"I suppose." He looked cautiously around him as the neighborhood grew seedier. "How much farther do we have to go?"

She gave him directions as they drove past several blocks of pawn shops and liquor stores. It seemed to him that half the people on the street were pushing shopping carts, while the other half looked ready to sell drugs, buy them, or knock him over the head to get money for some. Hookers too, he thought, when he spotted a tall woman in a tiger print miniskirt leaning against the corner of a building. "How do you know this neighborhood?"

"I lived here when I first came to Los Angeles. I had no money, and this is about as cheap as it gets."

He looked at her and offered his sympathy.

"And the answer to the hooking question is 'never,'" she added, "just so you don't have to ask."

She pointed her finger at a dingy, two-story, cinder block building on their immediate right. "That's it, number two fifty-one. Find a place to park wherever." This was easier said than done. Many of the spaces were filled with cars that looked like they had been abandoned, while other spaces were saved with garbage cans or stolen cones with stenciled lettering proclaiming "Property of the Los Angeles Public Works Division." The paint on the curbs in front of the derelict businesses and apartment complexes was so faded that it was impossible to tell where it was legal to park. About three blocks past Modriani's apartment, Stanley spotted a space in front of a crumbling flop house.

"What do you think?" He was less concerned about the legality of the spot than the casual menace of the two muscular Hispanic men standing in front of the building.

"Go for it," she replied as if the guys were uniformed doormen instead of crack dealers. His first attempt at parallel parking failed and he had to pull out and try again a second time. A tricked-out Eldorado honked at him as he struggled to squeeze the front end of the car into the space. Janet stepped out onto the curb while he waited a moment for the traffic to pass. When he got out and locked the car, he avoided making eye contact with the two characters who had been observing his parking debacle. He worked his way around the car, put his hand on Janet's bare back, and strolled away as casually as possible. Her skin was cool and his fingers curled easily around her waist.

"Hey! Joe NASCAR!" The shorter of the two men shouted. Stanley paused for a moment but kept walking. "Hey! I'm talking to you." This statement carried enough latent violence that he stopped and turned around. Both of the men sauntered toward them. "Does Jorge know that you're working a woman on this side of the street?" His blood ran cold. If he were alone, he would have considered running, but Janet spoke before he could concoct an answer.

"Don't be talkin' to my bitch like that!" she yelled. "You need to keep straight who's working who on this street." Stanley turned red with embarrassment. She ignored him and continued. "Now if you guys like his ass," she offered, as she spun him clumsily around, "we might be able to arrange something."

They made faces like she had just offered them a turd sandwich. "That's okay, chica. He's not our type," the taller of the two laughed. "But you come back alone later, and maybe we can party."

She laughed back at them as if she were considering the offer. "Maybe later guys. I've got business to attend to now." She slapped Stanley playfully on the backside and guided him away down the sidewalk. The two men whistled loudly, but did not follow.

"Was that really necessary?" he whispered as soon as they were out of earshot.

She looked at him with a skeptical grin. "And just what was your plan?"

"Okay, okay," he acknowledged her street smarts with a smile. "I was planning on using a bit of wicked Kung Fu to take them both out, but it was nice of you to save the taxpayers their hospital expenses."

The building listed on McCaffrey's paper looked like it had been a small hotel at some point in its recent history. It was constructed with the same courtyard design as Janet's upscale condominium, but the resemblance ended there. The doors were battered and dented, and most had extra deadbolt plates screwed in above the door knobs. Torn and stained curtains hung from less than half the windows, and the only sign of green was a lopsided rubber tree plant leaning against one of the corners.

"What a dump," he said as he scanned the doors for the apartment number.

"It's a lot like the place I used to live in."

"My condolences." He turned around and looked over his shoulder. "It's up there, on the second floor." It took them a moment to find the stairs behind an unmarked door in a squalid vestibule. A rusted chain hung from the bottom rail of the stairs where a bicycle had once been attached. A used condom had been tossed in the corner of the stairwell, and the tattered carpeting on the steps stank of urine and stale cigarette smoke.

They emerged into the sun again on an exterior walkway overlooking the courtyard. Modriani's room was immediately on their right. As they approached her door, they could hear high decibel heavy metal music playing inside the apartment. He looked at Janet and then rapped on the door firmly with his knuckles. When there was no reply, he pounded with his fist to make himself heard over the din of the music, but the only door that opened was the neighbor's.

"Are you friends of hers?" A skinny brunette who looked to be no more than seventeen stepped warily onto the walkway.

She was holding a fussy baby in her heavily tattooed arms. "She's been playing that same fucking CD over and over since last night. I've been pounding on the walls, and I've called the cops twice, but they never came." She vented her frustration. "I mean, this is like totally fucked."

The fact that she did not blink an eye at their clothes spoke volumes about the apartment complex and the neighborhood. "She's not answering for us either," Janet said. "Maybe she's not home."

"Then why would she leave the stereo on?" the girl asked peevishly, but with a burst of insight she answered her own question. "Maybe she's too stoned to notice. Could you guys go in and turn it off, maybe?"

Stanley had no desire to break into Modriani's apartment without permission, and to demonstrate the futility of even attempting, he shook the door knob and started to say, "It's not open." But to his surprise, the door swung in and the music doubled in volume. He looked at Janet, and she encouraged him to continue with a nod.

He stood in the doorway, and she squeezed next to him and looked over his shoulder. The living room contained a tilted and torn sofa that looked like it had been salvaged from the curbside garbage pick up. A television stand stood across from it, but there was no set, just a rectangle of dust marking where it had once stood.

"Mary?" he called out loudly and then shouted. "Mary?"

There was no answer. He could hear the little brunette's voice behind him. "Could you please turn off the music? She's nice when she's not fucked up. I don't think she'll mind." He doubted the tattooed young mother had legal authority to let them into the apartment, but he wanted to see into the bedroom. He nodded his assent and walked in with Janet. The music grew incrementally loud as they approached the bedroom door and then practically blasted them to the floor as he pushed it open.

"Oh my god," Janet gasped as she looked into the room and saw the nude body of a young woman sprawled across the bed. Stanley stood frozen in place. He had been in the presence of exactly two dead bodies in his life, and the waxy forms of his aunt and his grandmother lying respectably in the local funeral home had not prepared him for the tableau set before him.

The woman, presumably Mary Modriani, lay on her side along the edge of the bed, the bicep of her left arm underneath her head, elbow and wrist cantilevered palm up toward the door. An angry red puncture wound marked the crook of her left elbow. Her other arm was cocked back awkwardly behind her providing a counterbalance that kept her from tipping onto the filthy carpet that covered the room. Although lank and greasy hair covered most of her face, Stanley could see that she had bitten through her lower lip in a spasm that left her teeth clenched in a grim and bloody rictus. Death had not come easily. The evident cause of the tragedy was scattered on the floor: a cigarette lighter, a tab of unfolded tinfoil, a spoon, and a syringe with a broken needle.

The neighbor girl tried to push past them to see as well, but they barred her way and guided her out of the apartment. "There's been an accident," said Stanley, "probably better for the baby not to see." The baby had fallen asleep despite the loud music, but the point was made. The girl acquiesced, and all three were soon standing together again on the landing. "What's your name?" he asked her.

"Lauren," the woman said, her eyes darting back into the apartment.

"I think Mary is dead, Lauren." He expected to see more of a shock in her eyes, but she had apparently seen more of the world than he had at seventeen. "I'm going to go back inside and check."

"And could you turn the music off?"

"Huh?"

"Could you turn the music off," she repeated, irritation with the thumping bass line more pressing than the horrific news that her neighbor was dead.

Stanley nodded and went back into the apartment. Careful not to disturb the crime scene, he walked over to the bed and put his fingers on Modriani's cold, exposed neck. He could feel no pulse, nor see any sign that she was drawing breath. If the compact disc playing over and over again through the night were any indication, she had been dead for hours. Without touching anything else, he took two steps to the night stand where the boom box stood blaring and reached for the off switch. He almost put his finger on it before he realized that he would be leaving his own prints on the device. He took a tissue out of his pocket and reached for the switch again, but he was afraid that he might erase someone else's prints. He backed off and considered what to do. Finally, he bent over, took hold of the middle of the power cord with the tissue and yanked the plug out of the wall socket. The music stopped instantly and he felt himself relax for the first time since they had arrived in the neighborhood. He took one last look at the death scene and walked out into fresh air.

Janet caught his eye as soon as he emerged, and he shook his head to let her know Geary's alibi witness was indeed dead. "I'm gonna call McCaffrey." He pulled his cell phone out of his pocket. "He needs to see this." He dialed the number and waited while the woman answering the phone looked for the detective.

"Lauren," he asked, "can we wait in your apartment until the police come? It may take them a little while to get here." She nodded her head slowly, for the first time showing suspicion that the slicked down pimp and the beautiful whore were not who they appeared to be. He thanked her and then the detective's voice was suddenly on the phone. Stanley gave a brief rundown of the scene in the apartment and told him they would be waiting next door. "No, we won't touch anything," he assured the cop before hanging up.

Lauren's apartment was sparse, but relatively clean. She at least was still fighting the battle against dirt and vermin that Mary Modriani had lost. The three adults sat around a small table next to the kitchenette, while the baby slept soundly in a cracked yellow carrier on the floor. "Did you know Mary well?"

"Pretty well." She was about to say more, but bit her lower lip instead. "Who are you guys anyway?"

Stanley looked at Janet. He let her answer the question. "We're private investigators, Lauren." She looked directly at the girl and explained the situation in a disarming and gentle way. "We've been hired by a man who has been wrongfully accused of murder. We think that Mary's meth dealer might be the real killer, and we wanted to talk to her about him."

"Her dealer? She has at least three."

"A guy named Chance Geary," Stanley elaborated. "He's a white guy with dreadlocks and a spider tattoo on his arm." He saw a flash of recognition on the girl's face. "Do you know him?"

"I've seen him a couple of times. He rides a motorcycle." From the matter-of-fact tone she used, he concluded that she did not know Geary well enough to be afraid of him.

"Have you seen him recently?" She hesitated, and Janet took over the questioning.

"Did he come by here yesterday?"

"No," the girl replied, "at least I didn't see him. He came by last week though. Mary asked me if I wanted to party with her. She said she was doing a favor for him and he'd given her a shitload of new stuff."

"Did she say what kind of favor?"

"Nope, just that he owed her big time."

The baby began to stir and the young mother gathered her up and disappeared into the bedroom. Stanley and Janet sat working through the implications of Lauren's tale while she dealt with the child. After fifteen minutes, they heard a loud rapping at the apartment door. As he got up to open it, the young mother emerged from the bedroom.

Stanley asked her quickly. "Was Mary right-handed or left-handed?"

"What do you mean?" The girl seemed confused by the simple question and startled by a further round of knocking on the door.

"When she shot up, did she use this hand, or this hand?" He mimicked the act with both arms and she pointed to his left.

"That way," she said, closing her eyes to visualize a scene she had witnessed before. "She used that hand."

He rewarded her with his most winning smile and turned to answer door. When he opened it, McCaffrey stepped in and took a hard look at the professor and the porn star, both still dressed to blend into the neighborhood. Stanley stood with his hands on his hips, one tee shirt sleeve rolled up as if to carry a pack of cigarettes. His partner was showing more leg than a Rockettes' Christmas show, and the diamond in her navel sparkled faintly.

"Hopkins? Stephens?" He looked from one to the other and shook his head. "I don't even want to know." He grunted in disgust, "I don't even want to know…just show me where the body is."

# XXVIII.

# A STIFFED STIFFY

After her husband's decision to stay in Los Angeles, Angela avoided her friends. The last thing she wanted was pity for her inability to win her man back from a dazzling porn star. She tried to believe Stanley's protestations of fidelity, but there was no reason why other people watching him and Layla DiBona on their television screens should trust him. She spent as little time at the real estate office as possible, meeting her clients only at the homes she was showing. Thank goodness for Nanci. Her friend had been privy to the Los Angeles debacle from the beginning and managed to share her disappointment about Stanley without speculating aloud about where he was spending the night. But when Nanci called to remind her of the dinner party, there was no way she could agree to come.

"I'm just not up for it, Nance," she tried to explain. "The last thing I want to do is talk about Stan with anyone but you."

"Look, you can't stay inside forever. And besides, everybody's going to assume the worst if you stay at home all the time. The thing to do is show up with a smile on your face and jump into the pool wearing your lovely Land's End one-piece like there was nothing wrong. That's the best way to shut up the gossip."

"I don't know," she wavered. The thought of facing a dinner party was still traumatizing, even if her friend was right about putting on a bold face.

"And don't forget," Nanci said, "Max is going to be there. There's nothing to lose by asking him if he can do something more. Maybe he could get the administration to relent if Stanley really proves this guy is innocent."

"Maybe." Angela had her doubts about whether anyone could prove Don Johansson innocent given the circumstances of the case, but she had to admit that her husband seemed to be doing okay. As much as she wanted him home and back on track, she could see that he had talent for ferreting out information. He was a loyal bulldog armed with a Ph.D., a law degree, and tons of experience talking to all sorts of people. If anyone could exonerate Johansson, it was him. She could also reluctantly understand why he liked flexing his muscles on a bigger stage than the BFU. But now was not the time to be tilting at windmills and hanging out with porn stars. It was time to come home, find a new job, and start raising a family.

"Come on! I'm making Margaritas."

Nanci knew her weak spots. Angela laughed. "Okay. I'll come, but I'll probably leave early."

"No problem! I'll see you around seven."

The night was warm, and Angela sat on her back patio listening to the sounds of children playing flashlight tag in the neighbor's yard. A little girl shrieked as she dove under a bush to escape a beam shining out of a dilapidated tree fort, and for a moment, the pitch of her voice harmonized with thousands of invisible cicadas and tree frogs chirping in the summer air. Too soon a chorus of mothers' voices was cued, calling their reluctant children home to bath and bed. She sipped a glass of sparkling water and listened as the sounds of her childhood faded in the dusk. Nanci's party had started an hour earlier, but she had not been able to draw herself away from the precious interlude between dinner and children's bed times. She might have sat all evening, gently cradling the tiny secret in her belly, but as the sounds around her reverted entirely to insect, amphibian, and dog, she finally got the courage to stand up and make her way to Nanci's party.

When she arrived at the house, she walked to the side gate to avoid the gauntlet of guests milling about Nanci's front room. Socializing would be less painful in the obscurity of the swimming pool deck. She unlatched the gate and found the pool empty except for the Millers, a dentist and his elementary school teacher wife who lived next door. Talking with them might be boring, but not too embarrassing. She walked along the pool toward them, but they seemed so engrossed in conversation that she left them alone and gave in to the temptation of the clear blue water. She wore her suit underneath her skirt and blouse, with her Speedo serving as a modest, albeit snug, foundation. With a quick jerk at her colorful wrap, she plunged into the water without even checking it with her toe.

Despite the warmth of the air, the water was cool and she swam furiously to the far end of the pool until she got used to the temperature. She felt so unexpectedly refreshed when she reached the edge that she immediately turned and swam back, quickly completing twenty laps before she stopped in the shallow end on the steps that led down from the pool deck. She looked up at the house and could see a dozen people chatting and drinking in the kitchen. Several more were sitting in the living room, but she had no desire to join them. Swimming and maybe talking with the Millers was about all the excitement she wanted. Eventually, Nanci would make her way outside and take her Margarita order. With a drink to hide behind, she could probably survive the evening.

As she sat observing the other guests, she heard a splash. A muscular figure started swimming toward her, and a moment later Max Kurland surfaced next to her and wiped the water from his eyes. He was ten years older than Stanley, with thinning hair and a crooked smile, but he had kept himself in shape, and she could not help but notice his broad shoulders and powerful chest glistening in the soft light of the summer night. She reflexively pushed her hair behind her ear.

"Hi Max," she greeted him tentatively, unsure what to say to the man who had been unable to save her husband's job.

"Hi Angela," he slid through the water and sat next to her on the submerged steps. "I'm glad you could come! I'm sort of co-hosting this party with Nanci."

"I don't know how long I can stay." She was not wholly comfortable with the warm body pressing against her side, but it wouldn't be friendly to slide away. "I'm not feeling too social tonight."

"Well, I don't blame you. It must be tough with Stan still out in California." He touched her arm. "I was really hoping that you'd be able to convince him to come back here. Quite frankly, I don't understand what's running through his head sometimes."

"Me neither," she admitted. She looked at their reflection in the water and shook her head. "I tell myself that he's just being loyal to an old friend, but he sounds so obsessed whenever I talk to him."

"Same here."

He sounded so regretful that she took a chance and broached the subject of her husband's status at BFU. "Max, if he were to prove that Don Johansson didn't murder that girl, would the university consider taking him back?"

The administrator let out a reluctant groan. "I doubt it. It's not just a question of the president having her head up her ass. Stanley's in trouble with the department too. About a third of the people, like me, are cheering him on, but the rest are either pissed off or jealous. Even with a completed book and no Los Angeles frolic, he was going to get some resistance. At this point though, I can't see him getting through our committee, even if the president were willing."

She turned her head away and tried to absorb the news. It seemed impossible that her husband would have to find another job and that they would soon be moving away from their home and friends. Her anger bubbled to the surface and she slapped the water, sending a spray into Max's face. "Sorry! I'm just so pissed at him right now! I can't believe he's still out in California! How can he be so goddamn clueless?" She stared at him, a fellow member of the incomprehensible male tribe, hoping for some sort of explanation. He just shrugged his shoulders.

"You look like you could use a drink." He lifted himself out of the pool. "Nanci's made a batch of killer Margaritas. You want me to get you one?"

She gratefully accepted and made her way out of the pool while he fetched the drink. A pile of fluffy towels was stacked on a table next to some deck chairs, and she dried herself off. Wrapped in two fresh towels, she lay back in one of the recliners and sunk into the warm summer night. The Dalai Lama, she thought, could probably embrace uncertainty and find some sort of inner peace amidst the turmoil of a missing spouse and a sudden pregnancy, but she had never gotten the knack of suspending her connection to reality. It was the biggest difference between herself and Stanley. She was Type A, linear, focused, always working on a plan. He was intuitive and trusting of a future that he never quite took the time to map out. They had often teased each other about their differences, but the joke seemed a lot less amusing now.

"Here you go," Max handed her the Margarita and sat down next to her. "Just what the doctor ordered."

"Thanks." She raised her glass to him and sipped the drink. She had always liked her husband's good-looking department head, and the conversation ebbed and flowed pleasantly until Nanci called for him to help fix another batch of drinks. Angela declined the invitation to come inside and remained in the shadows, safe in the recliner, barely denting her drink but feeling increasingly relaxed and sated. Moments after she set her half-empty glass on the tiled deck, she slipped over the edge of consciousness and fell fast asleep to the chirping of grasshoppers and the quiet hum of the pool filtering system.

"Wake up sleepyhead!" Angela awoke to find hands on her shoulders and Nanci's smiling face inches away from hers. The strong smell of tequila on Nanci's breath worked like smelling salts to rouse her. "Rise and shine!" The teetering hostess stepped back and pulled her colleague up out of the chair. Nanci was wearing a black bikini with long ties hanging down from her slim hips, and Angela wondered for the umpteenth time whether

her friend's breasts were real or not as she came to her feet and brushed against them. They were simply too full and perfect for someone with her delicate Asian frame. She could hardly blame Max for sidling up next to Nanci and putting his hand around her waist. He also seemed a little drunk.

"You missed the whole party, darlin'! But you looked so peaceful out here that no one could bring themselves to bother you."

"What time is it?" Angela got up and put on her skirt. She felt her suit; it was completely dry.

"A little after midnight," Nanci giggled as Max's hand slid from her waist to her hip. His pinky finger ran back and forth over the knot that was holding on her bikini bottom and finally tucked itself comfortably underneath it. "You really conked out. Do you want a ride home?"

She thought about it for a moment. She did not feel like walking, but neither of her friends looked quite ready to drive. On the other hand, the ten blocks home were entirely residential and no one else was likely to be out. "Sure, thanks." As Angela walked to the gate, Nanci put her arm around her and kissed her on the cheek.

"Thank you so much for coming!"

"All I did was have a drink and fall asleep! I didn't even talk with the Millers."

"It's okay," the tipsy hostess explained. "My best friend in the world came to my party when she really didn't want to and that's awesome." Nanci lurched against her and *awesome* came out a bit slurred.

Max walked ahead and unlocked the doors of his luxury sedan with a flourish of his remote entry device. Nanci crawled in the back seat with Angela who immediately buckled herself in. Nanci ignored the seatbelts and scooted over next to her friend. She put her head on Angela's shoulder and whispered in her ear, "Max is gonna get lucky tonight." Angela suppressed a laugh as Max backed the car out of the driveway. Nanci lurched against her as the car went over a curb and giggled. "Very lucky!"

"How many Margaritas did you have?" Angela whispered and then repeated the question aloud to divert the salacious direction of the conversation.

"I don't know," her friend giggled some more. "Just a couple." Nanci had always been able to cut loose at parties, and Angela envied her lack of self-consciousness. She was acting a little silly, but why shouldn't she have a good time? Why not make the most of a handsome man and have some fun? The car traveled the distance to Angela's house without further incident, and when they arrived, Nanci asked if she could come in and use the bathroom. "I really gotta go," she said urgently as she skipped past Angela at the front door. Max followed them halfway to the house and Angela waved him in.

"Would you like a drink? Glass of wine, maybe?" They wandered into the living room and she wished that Nanci had not put in her head the image of her and Max romping in bed the rest of the night.

"Sure." He plopped down on the sofa with a sloppy grin.

She went to the kitchen and discovered that the wine bottle in her refrigerator was nearly empty. After a brief search for the corkscrew, she opened a new bottle and pulled out two small cans of sparkling water for herself and her tipsy girlfriend. Any more alcohol for Nanci and she wouldn't even remember her impending night with Max.

When she returned to the living room, she discovered Nanci curled up next to her boyfriend, kissing him passionately. He was still wearing his loose fitting bathing trunks, and she could see the results of Nanci's ministrations push against its fabric like a tent pole. She turned around, but Nanci's voice froze her in her tracks.

"Don't go!" Before she could answer, Nanci was at her side, hugging her tightly around the waist. "Don't you want to come over and have some fun?" She moved sidled behind her friend and kissed her on the neck, "I'm pretty sure he's got plenty for both of us." She glanced down at the evidence bearing up her daring claim.

For a moment Angela wavered, struggling with an imagination that served up a spicy tableau on her king size bed. A faint *why not* echoed in her head as Nanci's hands unwrapped her skirt. Then, a different set of images: Stanley giving in to the same temptation, in bed with two beautiful porn stars satisfying all his fantasies. With a sudden jolt, she understood what he had been dealing with in Los Angeles.

"No," she said firmly. "I don't want this." Max gave her a sour look, as if the ménage à trois had been promised as a sure thing. "Please go."

Nanci stepped back as her friend's skirt dropped to the floor, and Angela quickly gathered it up, apologizing to her guests. "I'm sorry, but you guys really need to leave." At that moment the spell was completely broken. Max looked ridiculous instead of handsome, and Nanci looked more like a sloppy drunk than a siren. When he got up muttering a curse, she begged them one last time to go and then fled to the hallway bathroom, locked the door, and leaned against it breathing heavily. Had life gotten so settled and boring that this sad scene had constituted temptation? She was surprised at herself—not a nice surprise—and for a moment understood how Stanley might face the perils of sedateness and lack of vocation. She had to go back to California.

She decided to stay in the bathroom until they left, so when she heard the telephone ring, she didn't move. It rang twice and then stopped, and few moments later, she heard the front door slam. She slumped forward with her hands on the sink. After reviving herself with several handfuls of cold water, she looked up into the mirror and two things came immediately to mind: *I need to book a ticket tonight and, boy, is work going to be awkward.*

# XXIX.

# THE GREAT DIVIDE

As Stanley and Janet drove away from the crime scene, the professor ran his fingers absentmindedly through his hair and then shouted an expletive. He cursed and held a glistening oily hand in front of him for the rest of the drive unwilling to slime the steering wheel or his clothes. "Is there any way we could stop by my room before going back to your car? I gotta get this shit out of my hair." He cast a quick glance in the mirror. "Jesus, I look like a pimp from *Happy Days*."

He took a shower and then drove his companion to the hotel where the interview sessions had concluded that morning. After retrieving her car, they headed to a nearby steak house for dinner.

During the meal, he watched Janet carefully and wondered whether she was as resourceful and balanced as she seemed on the surface, a clever woman whose character had survived a punishing business, or whether she was a legitimate suspect in the murder of Jade Delilah. Her role that afternoon pointed in the first direction, but whenever he admired her poise and self-control, he reminded himself of the obsessive and out-of-control emails she had sent to Don. Regardless of whom she really was, he wanted to keep her close, where he could keep both an eye on her and exploit her skills in the hunt for more information.

"Let's figure out an agenda for tomorrow," he suggested over a mammoth t-bone. "Given what we saw this afternoon, I'd like to track down Geary and see if he has any comment on the death of his main alibi." He mashed down his baked potato with a fork and covered it with butter, salt, and pepper. "Do you know why I asked Lauren whether Mary was right or left-handed?" He mimicked the death pose of the young meth addict. "She was lying as if she had been shooting into her left arm. I'll bet right-handed people usually inject into their left arms. If she were left-handed, like Lauren said, I'm wondering why she didn't use the other arm."

"Maybe she alternated arms?"

"Maybe," he shrugged.

"Or maybe someone else injected her?" She took a sip of wine. "I've seen it more than once, I'm sorry to say."

"That crossed my mind too. Given Lauren's story about Mary's stash of free meth from Chance Geary, you might be on to something." He cut a thick piece of steak. It was a nice metaphor for the investigation, something juicy from which to take a satisfying bite and have a thoughtful chew.

"I've got a question," she asked as she finished her flank steak salad. "When you went into Mary's bedroom, did you see any of the meth that she bragged to Lauren about? I mean, there weren't too many places to hide stuff in that shithole."

He thought for a moment. "Uh, uh. Maybe it was under the bed?"

"The bed was flat on the floor."

He nodded. "That's a good question for McCaffrey tomorrow, whether the cops found any more drugs there." The detective had made it clear that he wanted to see both of them bright and early to talk about the discovery of Mary Modriani. "Someone could have taken the stash, I suppose; even Lauren."

"Maybe."

"Or maybe a greedy prick like Chance Geary came back to claim it." He wiped a drab of grease from his chin. "We'll talk to him tomorrow and try out that Wilhoit address in Belle Meade."

As Stanley drove back to his hotel, he decided to call his wife. At this point, even a fight was better than no contact at all. In fact, an argument would show that she still cared. In ten years of marriage, they had never spent such a long time apart, and he found himself cataloging the things about her that he missed: her eyes, her fierce intelligence, her sense of humor, the soft cascade of her hair. He slid over into the slow lane, reached over to his cell phone and speed-dialed his home number, but there was no response. Was she screening his calls? He tried her cell phone, still no answer.

As he drove, he turned on the radio and rolled down the window. The night air was cool and the music filled him with the sort of melancholy that's familiar to teenagers but gets halved every year after age twenty. Old pop lyrics held deep meanings and when the Thompson Twins started belting out *Hold Me Now*, he fell back to the days in college when he had no clue what he wanted to do but didn't care, back to the early days with Angela when he watched her sleeping form for hours, unable to believe she was really there next to him. Once again, he was filled with a sense of risk and uncertainty, and once again, improbably, he was not paralyzed but filled with a strange sense of anticipation and desire. His career was in tatters, his wife was unwilling to speak to him, he was cruising around the streets of Los Angeles fighting the deep thunder of rap music with eighties one-hit-wonders, yet the yearning fit him like a spandex unitard.

When he got back to his room, he brushed his teeth and called Angela unsuccessfully again, this time from the hotel land line. Determined not to give up, he found a movie on the television and called every half hour on the theory that he would either irritate her into picking up or send a message of devotion through sheer repetition. As the movie was ending, he called home one last time and finally got a voice on the other end of the line. A man's voice. He hung up immediately and looked at his watch. It was just after midnight in Illinois. He stared at the phone, his heart sinking. What the hell was Max Kurland doing in his house?

* * *

Ellen McCaffrey sat at her desk studying a fax sent by the state pathologist in Sacramento. She rubbed her neck with her left hand and contemplated transferring to a jurisdiction where she did not have to routinely pass along bad news to her ex-husband. The detective, clinging to Don Johansson's guilt like a rabid pit bull, would not be thrilled to hear that the hair caught on Jade Delilah's ring belonged to Janet Stephens. Stuart had bragged about sowing discord in the defense camp by revealing that the actress had sent desperate email messages to the suspect in the weeks before the murder. Her ex-husband did not seem to take very seriously the possibility that the woman might actually be involved. He would have to rethink his position once he read the report. And one thing was certain: he did not like rethinking his positions.

His mood would only get crankier when he read the preliminary report on the death of Mary Modriani. The initial toxicology screen from the hospital showed a shocking level of methamphetamine in the system of the painfully slim young girl. Her blood also contained high levels of a depressant found most commonly in over-the-counter sleeping pills. Most meth deaths were not true overdoses, but were caused by the victim's anaphylactic reaction to the toxic mix of impurities found in a drug usually cooked up by amateurs in make-shift labs. Other deaths involved human bodies worn to a complete and fatal exhaustion by long-term abuse. Mary's case fit neither scenario. She had injected a lethal dose containing five times as much crystal meth as she had probably wanted, unless she had planned to commit suicide.

This was curious. Mary's right arm bore the track marks of an experienced user, someone unlikely to make an error of that magnitude. Her suspicions deepened when she looked at the picture taken at the scene. The body had been sprawled out on the bed on her *left* side, her spike and spoon lying on the floor underneath her limp left hand. Yet, the vast majority of injection scars were on her right arm. Probably a strong lefthander, Mary had almost never used her right hand to give herself a fix in her left arm. After years of dealing with heroin overdoses, she knew what this meant: someone else had wielded the syringe. Addicts often became ambidextrous over time, but they still preferred to use their dominant hands. Therefore, when their friends injected for them, it was inevitably in the lesser-used veins of the dominate arm. Had someone else given her the fatal dose? Had she crashed from days of speeding with the help of some sleeping pills and then been shown the way to her maker by a third party?

Ellen did not have to determine responsibility for the death, just its proximate cause. Legal questions, thank god, were for coroners and juries. Unfortunately, the job of conveying her findings and suspicions to her ex-husband fell on her shoulders alone. Before she picked up the phone, she forced herself to remember some of the good times they had spent together during twenty-five years of marriage. She would not let his present bitterness mar the memory of the years when she had felt her prettiest and most alive. She fed the papers into the fax machine with a sigh and then dialed his number to give him the news.

\* \* \*

Janet and Stanley had been summoned to McCaffrey's office to discuss the death of Mary Modriani. So far, their meetings with him had been in random interrogation rooms or public spaces. The actress had little interest in seeing the detective's inner sanctum. She stood in the hallway outside of his office waiting for her partner to arrive for the morning meeting, not at all tempted to knock on the door and begin her day with a private interview. The detective reminded her of her elementary school principal, a hawk-faced sadist who would call her into the office and silently stare at her until she confessed to drawing boobs on little Mary's t-shirt or playing doctor with Jimmy in the shrubs. Stanley's presence next to her would deflect the homicide cop's soul-searching gaze. Unfortunately, when she saw her partner walking down the hall, he looked in no shape to defend anyone. Hair uncombed, shirt wrinkled and only half tucked in, eyes bloodshot, he shuffled down the hall like a homeless bum.

"What happened to you?" She walked over and pushed the tail end of his shirt down the back of his pants. "You look like you've been on a bender."

"Just a little insomnia," he mumbled. "That's all."

"Well, be on your toes. McCaffrey was pretty pissy yesterday."

"I'll be okay." He pushed past her and pounded on the detective's door.

A snarl bade them enter, and she followed him into the brightly lit room. McCaffrey's work space was a jumble of battered filing cabinets and cardboard boxes covered with stacks of paper, some of them yellow and crumbling. The man himself sat behind a chipped, wooden desk eating a Danish and sipping muddy-looking coffee. "Sit down." He motioned to a pair of chairs separated by a tower of files that until recently had probably perched upon them. "Why don't you two tell me what you saw yesterday?"

"At Mary Modriani's apartment?"

"No," he replied sarcastically, "at the Dodger's game."

"Alright," Stanley replied with insufficient energy to acknowledge his antagonist's wit. "We went to talk to Geary's alibi witness, but when we knocked on the door, no one answered." He shrugged his shoulders and sat up a little straighter in his chair. "We could hear music inside and banged on the door again. At that point, the neighbor girl, Lauren something-or-other, comes out and says that the music's been playing all night. She asked us to turn it off, so we try the door and, lo and behold, it opens. We take a peek in and call out, but we can't see anyone, so we go in."

"Criminal trespassing?"

"If it is," he snapped, "then fucking charge us and get us a lawyer because we're done talking."

"Don't be so touchy," he smiled. "You thought someone inside might be in trouble; it's a legal excuse. What next?"

"We went as far as the bedroom door without touching anything. Then, we saw her lying on the bed and got out of there."

"But you went back in right? That's what Lauren something-or-other said." He tapped his fingers on his desk, took a sip of coffee and made a face at his cup.

"Yeah, the music was starting to drive me crazy too, so I went in and grabbed the middle of the electric cord with a tissue and pulled it out. I didn't touch any other part of the stereo."

"Did you touch the victim?"

"The victim?" Stanley looked up curiously. "I touched her throat to see if she had a pulse, but I didn't move the body." Some of the tiredness seemed to lift. "Why do you say victim?"

"Because the preliminary forensic report speculates that someone else may have injected her. I have my doubts, but that's what it says. She just looks like another dead junkie to me." He handed him a copy of the report. "And oh," the graying detective added nonchalantly, "I got this one too; the report on the hair caught on Jade's ring the night she died." He scrutinized the report like he was reading it for the first time and looked at Janet. "It says here that the hair belongs to a Ms. Janet M. Stephens."

She could feel the eyes of both the detective and her partner. So, that's why they took hair samples from everyone at the party. Her hair on Jade's ring...she knew how it must have happened. Jade had slapped her hard on the side of the head and a strand must have caught on the ring. That's what happens when you call someone a fucking bitch-whore for seducing your man and stealing the lead in the biggest porn movie ever made: you get slapped hard.

"I brushed past her several times that night," she explained calmly. "We were friends. It doesn't surprise me that one of my hairs ended up on her ring." She gave him a taunting smile. "If you think I did it, why don't you let Don go?"

"Don't tempt me, sweetheart. For all I know, you two are in it together." If he felt any frustration at failing to get a bigger reaction it showed only in a slight tightness at the corner of his mouth. He seemed uninterested in following up his revelation with any questions and sat quietly waiting for her to say more.

"We've got a question for you." Janet ignored Stanley's stare and changed the subject. "Did you find a large stash of methamphetamine in Mary's room when you searched it?"

The detective paused for a moment. "So, Lauren told you that story too? We searched the place high and low and couldn't find any sign that she had recently struck the druggy mother lode. But if she had, anyone could have come through the unlocked door and taken it."

"Or maybe her connection came back to retrieve it after he killed her," she suggested. "Did Lauren tell you that Chance Geary was dealing meth to her?"

"Yeah, but why would Geary kill his own alibi witness? The guy's not a Mensa candidate, but he's not that stupid." His tone was dismissive. He was sure he had all the answers and her anger flashed.

"There are a lot of reasons for him to kill her, especially if she was willing to lie to establish his alibi. What if she changed her mind? What if she were blackmailing him? What if she was planning to leave town before testifying? We're talking about a violent guy with a short fuse."

The detective was unimpressed. "We can play the '*what if*' game all day if you want, but I'd rather rely on hard physical evidence." He smirked and looked down at the report identifying Janet's hair.

"Fuck you, McCaffrey."

He glared at her for a moment and then turned to Stanley, "Oh, by the way, we don't have any results yet on the purple fuzz that you collected from Janet's closet. So, we don't know if we have matches for the fibers caught on Johansson's window sill."

Janet's stoic facade crumbled. Stanley had not been in her closet fantasizing about cross-dressing. He had been collecting fiber samples trying to prove that she was the killer. She glanced over at him, but he ignored her and glared furiously at McCaffrey who sat immobile behind his desk watching with amusement the effect of his revelation on the defense team.

"Was I not supposed to say anything, Professor?" He grinned. "I thought maybe you were trying to prove her innocence or something."

"Go to hell," he responded and slumped back in his chair.

With a tremendous effort, she collected herself. "Am I free to leave, Detective?" Out of the corner of her eye she could see Stanley glancing at her.

"For now."

She slipped past the tower of papers separating herself from her former partner and paused at the door. Stanley remained seated, head pressed back against the chair. She almost felt sorry for him. "You're on your own now," she said, then shut the door and left.

Her heels clicked unevenly down the marble hall to the elevator. She pressed the down button and waited for the old-fashioned brass doors to open. For the first time, she felt like a target of the investigation. Even McCaffrey's obsession with pinning the crime on Don would not prevent him from looking hard at her motives and whereabouts. She fought back a tear of rage, and as the elevator traveled down to the lobby, she determined to fight back. I'm not the only suspect, she thought as she ran her fingers through her hair and touched up her lipstick in the shiny reflection of the elevator's glass covered walls. Maybe the cops could be pointed back in the direction of Chance Geary or Sheila Easy.

* * *

Stanley looked at the detective with as much contempt as he could muster, but he had no comment clever enough to cut him down to size. He finally stood up in disgust and brushed against the pile of files on the floor. "You should watch her carefully," McCaffrey suggested with one eye on the wobbly paper tower.

"Now how the fuck am I supposed to do that? She's not going to let me anywhere near her." The detective had cost him both a helpful partner and the chance to monitor a prime suspect. He looked down at the mountain of files, gave it a gentle push with his knee, and watched hundreds of papers cascade over the stained linoleum floor and under McCaffrey's desk. "Oops," he said to the red-faced detective as he turned smartly and strode out the room.

# XXX

# SEPARATION ANXIETY

Stanley's disastrous call home the previous night put him in the perfect mood to confront Chance Geary. Angela was the only woman he had ever loved, and her betrayal left him with nothing more to lose on his nightmare trip to Southern California. He had dated a couple of girls in high school, none of them for long, and none of them had graced him with anything more than a goodnight kiss. His two relationships in college prior to Angela had been tepid affairs on every level, but when she fell into his lap, everything changed. He had never ceased to wonder why someone so lovely and intelligent had become interested in a studious young boy who had stimulated no positive response in the first thousand women he had met. Now his ultimate fear had been realized and as a result, a skinny, drug dealing, woman-hating, white-boy Rasta shithead was going to get a lot tougher questioning than he expected.

He drove down the freeway toward Chance Geary's bike shop grinding his teeth and cursing the traffic that made a mockery of the posted speed limit. He flipped on the radio to divert his attention from the emotion churning in his gut, but when he tried to find a station, the sound system went into channel-surf mode, and he spent the rest of the drive listening to rotating snippets from every station on the dial. The audio chaos fit his mood. After a half hour of inching forward and stopping, he finally exited onto the broad boulevard that led to the motorcycle shop. When he got there, he suppressed the desire to rush in and strangle its owner. Instead, he sat and waited for ten minutes until the last customer had left and he knew his quarry was alone.

When he walked in the front door and saw Geary lying on the floor working on a big Harley, he knew instinctively what he had to do. Rushing over to the bike before Geary knew he was there, he pulled it down on the mechanic's chest. As the meth dealer gasped for breath, he kicked a large wrench out of his hand, walked calmly to the door, locked it, and turned off the lights so that passers by could not see in.

"Get…this…off…of…me," Geary pleaded as his assailant stood over him, arms crossed on his chest.

"No," he said as he put his foot down on the bike and stomped.

A wheezy rattle sputtered from Geary's lungs. "You fucker," he whispered as he struggled to lift the bike with his unpinned arm.

"I may be a fucker," Stanley hissed, "but you're just plain fucked." He crouched down next to the biker and stepped on the wrist of his free arm. "I need to ask you some questions, and if I like the answers, we'll see about getting this bike off of you. Understand?" Geary replied by trying to spit in Stanley's face, but he missed and was rewarded with the weight of a heel grinding down hard on his wrist.

"I know you killed Mary Modriani," he said quietly. Geary shook his head, and Stanley responded by picking the wrench off the floor and hitting the biker viciously on the elbow. The crushed mechanic made little noise; the rigid tendons in his neck spoke for him. "No lying now, my friend. Just listen to me. I know that you killed her. I just want you to confirm why. She didn't buy any meth from you the night of Jade's murder, did she?" He was rewarded with a barely perceptible nod. "So, she promised to lie in return for a nice big stash of your shit, right?" Another nod. "And then she got uncooperative didn't she? She tried to blackmail you or threatened not to testify or something stupid like that, didn't she?" Another weak nod. Geary was on the verge of passing out, so Stanley slapped his face.

"Very good. See how nice talking about our problems can be?" He walked across the shop, picked up a small crowbar, and put it under the bike. "Now, we need to talk about Jade for a little bit." He lifted the bike up an inch and the prone figure took a series of gasping breaths. The color in his face gradually faded from purple to red. "If I like your answers, then we'll keep things just like this. If I don't..." He relaxed the crowbar and Geary grimaced.

"Okay," he said, lifting the bike up again slightly, "tell me about how you got into Don's office and killed Jade."

"I didn't." He lowered the bike. "I swear," he gasped. "I didn't do it."

"Then who did?"

"I don't know!" Blood-tinged spittle appeared on his lips as he choked out his denial. "Johansson probably. He was crazy about her." Stanley scrutinized him closely, but could not tell whether he was lying.

"Where were you the night she was killed?"

"I got an alibi..." Stanley lowered the bike, partly in response to the lie, and partly as payback for Mary Modriani's death. "Not Mary... Miriam... Wilhoit."

"Don's secretary? What the fuck do you have to do with her?" He adjusted the crowbar so Geary could speak more freely. "How is she your alibi?"

"She came here the night of the party. I was here all night, like I told the cops."

"Why would she come to see you?"

The shop owner took several raspy breaths. "She's been ripping off Eden, making copies of movies and filling orders without entering them on the books." He wheezed his story in a halting voice barely above a whisper. "Me and Jade knew the kid she hired, and we figured out her racket...since Jade starred in half the videos she sold, we told her we deserved a piece of the action ...the old bitch was afraid that we'd rat her out, so she agreed. She came here that night to deliver our cut." The story had the ring of truth to it, or at least part of the truth.

"Why didn't she tell the police she was here with you?"

"Are you kidding? Why would a middle-aged slag drive to a bike shop alone in the middle of the night?" Stanley studied the writhing biker. "Besides, I can't find her. She's disappeared."

The initial adrenalin rush of the attack had subsided and the professor was losing his stomach for interrogation. He doubted there was much more information to extract, so he grabbed the Harley underneath the seat and with a grunt slid it off the crushed body. The biker tried to roll onto his side, but his cracked ribs made it too painful. He lay on his back like a flipped turtle, panting a series of shallow breaths.

He looked up with luminous yellow eyes. "You're dead, motherfucker. You're fuckin' dead."

Stanley picked up the wrench and swung it at Geary's crotch, stopping just before he emasculated him. Then, he grabbed the biker by the throat and pushed his head hard against the floor. A simple threat would ensure his safety and dig at McCaffrey at the same time. "Listen to me, you little fuck face. You think I came here on my own? The LAPD sent me here to do their dirty work. If you or any of your friends come anywhere near me, Detective McCaffrey will personally show up and stick his night stick so far up your ass that people will think you're smoking a wooden cigar." With that, Stanley slammed Geary's head against the floor, stood up, brushed his pants off and walked to the door. As he unlocked it, he saw Geary clutching his arm. He waved with mocking smile, wished the groaning man a nice day, then left the shop, walked over to his car, and retched in the parking space next to it.

\* \* \*

Janet sat in the car and drummed her nails against the lacquered surface of the burled walnut steering wheel. The more she thought about the recently concluded interview with McCaffrey and Stanley, the more pissed off she got. Had the veteran cop just been trying to bust up a team that was shaking his preconceptions, or did he really fancy her as suspect? Was he working on some theory to snag her and Don in his sticky little web, or was he just bluffing? To make matters worse, Stanley's betrayal hurt more than she wanted to admit. There was nothing sexual about her attraction to him, but that made it worse. She had enjoyed talking to him, being treated as an equal by a real intellectual. He wasn't a bad actor either when he needed to be. Damn the devious little prick and his purple fuzz.

But now what? She could not just sit still. She did not want to just let McCaffrey take control and keep grinding down his narrow road. And that meant keeping on the job, pushing on Geary's alibi, finding out more about William Walker, and maybe figuring out how to turn Sheila Easy into another viable suspect for the cops to chew on. She pulled out her smart phone and reading glasses and decided to pursue whomever she could locate first. After fifteen minutes of googling and about a dozen phone calls, she was stymied on Geary and Walker but she had managed to track down Susan Jenkins, aka Sheila Easy.

She was surprised to learn that the ex-porn queen turned anti-porn crusader was still in the same small Malibu beach house she had occupied during her years as a video star. It should have been filled with some pretty disturbing memories for someone seeking to forget her past. Janet herself had done several scenes there, one in which she played a photographer filming Susan being doubly penetrated by two guys playing lifeguards while she sucked off one of their friends. If those walls could talk, Janet thought, the professor would have to put an entirely new chapter in his book.

She cruised up the coastal highway west of Los Angeles, trying to figure out what to say to Sheila, barely aware of the sun-drenched countryside rolling past. Ultimately, this whole fucked up scene was Jade's fault. Without her siren-song, without her raw ambition, the world would look completely different. Don's weaknesses would never have been exposed, and maybe they would even be together. And instead of stumbling about in people's closets looking for a killer's sweater, the young professor from Illinois would be happily interviewing porn stars with his wife.

And where would you be, she wondered, pulling out a cigarette and screwing it into her mouth. Certainly not seeking an audience with a lying nut job. She contemplated pushing down on the accelerator and riding Highway 1 all the way to Washington State. It would be easy to disappear, empty her accounts and live off-line in Costa Rica or the Dominican Republic, but as the turn off to her Malibu destination approached, she knew she was no more able to escape southern California than to quit smoking or to wear an outfit from the Martha Stewart collection at Wal-Mart.

Janet pulled in front of a two-bedroom redwood bungalow whose entryway was level with the gravel drive, but whose beachside end needed the support of long cantilevered timbers to keep from sliding down to the ocean. A new Toyota was parked in the sun, but when she pushed the door bell, there was no answer. She used a side walkway to access the back deck, but could not see Susan through the sliding glass doors that led into her living room. She scanned the beach for her former colleague. Several solitary women were walking in the distance in both directions, so she sat patiently on top of the steps that led to the sand, wondering how to elicit the sort of information that would interest a hard-boiled cop like Stuart McCaffrey.

Half an hour later, a middle-aged woman in a paisley sun dress made her way slowly up from the beach. Susan was not recognizable until she got to the base of the stairs. Janet had seen her recently in the interview made by Stanley and his wife, but the ex-star must have spent hours on makeup and her hair. Without primping for the camera, she looked dowdy and shapeless, with a mousy tangle of wind-blown hair framing a blotchy face. She reached the base of the stairs and looked up.

"What are you doing here?" She showed no surprise at the unexpected guest, greeting her as if she were a Jehovah's Witness rather than an old acquaintance.

"Hi Susan! You remember the interview you did with Professor Hopkins for his book a couple of weeks ago?" Janet stood up and spoke brightly, trying to dispel the suspicion that showed on the woman's face. "He asked me if I could talk to you and ask some follow-up questions."

"Why you?"

"Well," she dissembled quickly, "he's hired me as a research assistant."

The immediate response was a skeptical laugh. "So, you've decided to go straight, huh? Are you having trouble getting roles or did you finally wake up and smell the coffee?" She pushed her way by Janet before she could answer. Susan slid open the glass door. "You might as well come in. I've gotten enough sun for the day." She sat down on a padded wicker couch without offering her guest anything to drink or eat. "So, what do you want to know?"

Janet sat across from her in a matching rocker and spoke confidently. "Well, a lot has happened since the professor spoke to you. In particular, we were wondering if you had any thoughts about the murder of Jade Delilah?" She took out a pen and a pad of paper from her purse.

"The wages of sin are death." Susan gave her a bland smile. "That's my thought. That's what happens when you sin again and again and fail to change your life."

"I've known a lot of sinners who haven't gotten bludgeoned to death with a fraternity paddle." Janet didn't care whether being provocative was a good strategy or not; she just wanted to wipe the smirk off of Susan's pale, pasty face.

"Some people pay for their sins earlier than others, but eventually everyone pays, either now or in hell." She spoke with utmost confidence in the wisdom of her message.

"Do you think Don did it?"

"Of course he did," she responded. "A woman who tempts a man is bound to become his victim."

"Do you really believe that?" She put down her pen and looked up. "Then it's a wonder there are any porn stars left alive."

"Like I said. Everyone pays eventually, even you, Layla." Susan spoke her stage name as if it were a dirty word. "I'll bet you have a nice place to live, but where are your children? Where is your husband? Can you even go shopping without wondering whether the guys in the checkout line will recognize you?"

Janet answered the last question in her head: if you don't dress up like a whore when you shop, no one recognizes you. Instead of arguing, she changed tactics and gave her best dramatic sigh. "You're right about the house and kids. Until I get out of the business, a family is not going to happen."

"It's never too late to turn around, Layla," the former starlet's voice became more animated. "I've started a survivor's support group that meets every Wednesday night in Malibu. You should come."

"I'll think about it," Janet replied with apparent earnestness, successfully managing to keep any trace of contempt out of her voice. "By the way, were you invited to the party where Jade was killed? I know you used to work for Don, and he still respects you. That's why he put your name on the interview list. I thought he might have given you an invitation."

"He did, and I tore it up." She sat primly on the sofa. "I'm not a hypocrite."

"So, what did you do that night instead?" She phrased the question as casually as possible.

Susan took a moment to answer and a wary tone entered her voice. "I'm not sure it's any of your business, but I stayed at home and watched television." Janet stole a page from her elementary school principal's book and just stared at her host until she spoke again. "I stay in most nights and read or watch TV. *Survivor* was on that night."

Janet sat with her for another half hour, listening to more judgment being passed on her profession. When Susan began to repeat herself, Janet stood up and changed the subject. "The professor wanted me to search for anti-porn books or websites that he should mention in his book. Most actresses aren't as critical as you. He'd like to acknowledge your position and include some links."

Susan seemed pleased by the request and reached over the arm of the sofa to uncover a copy of the Bible hidden under a pile of magazines. She declared triumphantly, "This is the only thing he needs to refer his readers to. There's no better anti-porn book anywhere."

Janet nodded knowingly and fought back the temptation to ask about King David's steamy peep show of Bathsheeba bathing, Salome's dirty dancing, or King Solomon's parade of red-hot concubines. "I'll pass that along," she replied as she got up and walked toward the front door.

"No," Susan said suddenly and motioned toward the sliding glass doors. "It's easier this way."

Janet reversed direction and stepped out on the back deck, turning to ask one more question. "Is there anyone who can confirm you were watching television on the night of the murder?"

Susan's face frowned in irritation. "No, I don't think so. It's always just me and the TV." With that, she shut the door, locked it, and pulled the curtains shut.

Janet walked around to her car and sat for moment before she drove off. She could honestly report that Susan hated Jade and all she stood for. McCaffrey would not be overly impressed. If *Survivor* was not on the night of the murder, however, she would have something for the detective to think about.

\* \* \*

Stanley drove past the small bungalow where Samuel Wilhoit resided and saw that he was only a short walk from Belle Meade College. As he had weeks earlier, he wondered how life might have been different if he had chosen to accept the job at the small liberal arts college instead of the research-oriented post at BFU. One thing's certain, he thought bitterly: Max Kurland would not be answering the phone at his house instead of his wife.

As he reversed his direction and parked, he saw a large brown delivery truck pulling into the driveway. He watched a uniformed driver knock on the door and hand a clipboard to a woman who looked a lot like the missing secretary. She walked out of the house and led the young man to the garage where he picked up two large uncovered boxes which contained a number of DVD-sized packages. The driver slid the boxes into the back of his truck, and the two chatted for a minute before he drove away.

Stanley approached the house on foot and walked around to the side of the garage. He peeked in the side window. A gap in a dirty pair of curtains revealed a pile of cardboard boxes partially covered by a tarp. It looked like a substantial supply of DVD's had been taken from Eden Studio before the conflagration had destroyed it. He headed up the walkway to the front door but stopped when he noticed it was recycling day in the neighborhood. At the end of the driveway, a bright green container full of paper, cans, and bottles sat on the curb. He walked over to the bin and was rewarded with the sight of a flattened cardboard box with *Eden* stamped on its side. He plucked the evidence out of the tub, walked up to the house, and knocked on the front door.

Miriam Wilhoit opened the door but slammed it shut when she saw Stanley holding the Eden Studio logo up at eye level. "Ms. Wilhoit!" he sang out. "I just need a few minutes with you."

"Go away!" she yelled. "I don't want to talk to you."

"Ms. Wilhoit. I know what you're hiding in the garage."

"Talk to my lawyer!" He was not going to give her enough time to load up the stash of porn in the back of her SUV and dispose of it. "Get off of my property!" she added when he did not respond.

"Ma'am," he cried out, changing his strategy, "would you like me to call Chance Geary and tell him where you are?" This question was met with silence. "If you'll talk to me, I promise not to tell him or the police about what you have locked up in the garage." After a minute, the door opened a crack.

"You promise?" As she poked her head out, she looked more like the timid next door neighbor from a fifties sitcom than a thief and possible arsonist. She was wearing a faded pink housecoat and matching slippers. Her hair had been recently permed, and she showed a surprising level of deference for someone who had just been threatening him with lawyers.

"I promise." But he had said nothing about revealing her confidences to Don. "Can I come in?"

She led him through a small foyer into a sunny living room at the front of the house and offered him some coffee, but he declined and sat down with her on a faded floral sofa. "Is your son home?"

"No," she replied with alarm, "he's still in class, and he knows nothing about this. Nothing!" Her plea was unconvincing, but he cared little about her son's complicity in the theft. He was merely worried about the complications that might be posed by an overly protective child.

"Ms. Wilhoit, I just spoke with Chance Geary, who is looking for you by the way, and he said that you were paying him a percentage of what you earned from stealing and selling Eden videos."

"Stealing?" she spat out the word with disgust. "If a drug dealer leaves his cash laying around, is it stealing to take some? Can you steal from a pimp? You can call it stealing if you want, but all I was doing was diverting income from a pornographer to a university." She straightened up and puffed out her chest. "I think it's public service. That money went to pay my son's tuition instead of going to a bunch of whores and pimps." She leaned back on the couch with her arms crossed, ready to meet any arguments to the contrary. His lack of interest in the morality of her position seemed to take her by surprise.

"What time did you go to visit Geary on the night of the party?"

"I visited that disgusting shop of his around seven o'clock or so. I left the studio at five, ate dinner out, and then brought him the money." The look on her face told him everything he needed to know about her opinion of Jade's agent.

"How long were you there?"

"Maybe two minutes. I had no desire to chit-chat with him. He's a pig."

"Jade was murdered around 10:30 p.m. Do you think he would have had time to get the money from you and get back to the studio to kill her?"

She looked surprised and then thought for a moment. "Maybe…but I thought Don killed Jade. Didn't they find the murder weapon with his fingerprints on it?"

"Yes," he replied, considering carefully how much he should reveal in the attempt to pry information from her, "but there should have been other prints on the paddle, mine and my wife's, for example. Someone wiped it before Don touched it. Someone else might have killed Jade, wiped down the handle, and placed it in Don's hand."

"That sounds kinda far-fetched to me." She looked skeptical but then a cloud passed over her face, as if she had just seen something indistinct flash in the distance.

"Yeah, but it's a theory backed up by blood tests showing Don could easily have been passed out due to a combination of pain killers and wine." Stanley built up to the most important question. "By the way, where did you go after you left Geary's motorcycle shop?"

"I came back here," she replied, more distracted than offended by the question. "My son was here too. He was studying and I was reading." She shifted in her seat. "Surely you don't think that I had anything to do with Jade's death?"

The previous day, he might have probed gently and used his best manners to elicit information, but he was in no mood to be polite. If there had been a motorcycle in the room, he might well have pulled it down on her. "Why shouldn't I think that, Ms. Wilhoit? I know for a fact that you're a thief, and I have a very strong suspicion that you're also an arsonist. Did you know that a janitor had to be hospitalized after the Eden fire?" He made up the last claim, but she looked appropriately rattled. "In my book, someone capable of criminally endangering the lives of others is also capable of murder, especially when the murder destroys a business that she hates."

"That's nonsense!" she struggled to express her outrage. "I did not burn down Eden Studio! I was right here with my son when that fire was lit." He was about to point out that the official finding of arson had not yet been released to the press when he heard the front door open and saw her son enter the house. He was a surly kid who looked like he would be more at home on the offensive line of his college football team than in the classroom. Miriam stood up. "Sam, this is Professor Hopkins, an acquaintance of mine from work. He was just going."

There was more that he wanted to ask the former secretary, but he realized that she would be unwilling to say anything more in front of her son. He stood up. "I'd like to talk to you again sometime soon."

"I don't think so," she replied as she led him to the door. "I've got a trip planned." A cloud passed over her face again and she drew him aside and spoke quietly as she opened the door for him. "If I were you, I'd spend some time looking at the video surveillance recordings."

Frustrated that the interview had been cut short, he had little patience with her cryptic suggestion. "I've already studied every damn minute of that party DVD."

"Watch the whole day, Professor." She gave him a pensive look. "Watch the whole thing."

# XXXI

# A TRIP AND A DINNER DATE

Angela wanted to get to California as quickly as possible, but she could not get a seat on a flight until the late afternoon. So, while Detective McCaffrey was breaking up Don Johansson's investigative team, she was showing houses to prospective buyers and avoiding the real estate office like it was the center of an Ebola outbreak. The morning passed in a fog as she debated how to confront Stanley when she arrived. Should she accuse him of cheating on her and demand a confession, or should she give him the chance to explain that everything was just a misunderstanding? Should she tell him about the baby right away, or hold that bombshell in reserve? Should she slap him in the face, or fall into his arms weeping? Without knowing whether he had succumbed to temptation or whether he had stood firm, she had no clue what to do. Her anger with him for staying in Los Angeles, regardless of any sexual dalliance, only made matters murkier.

As she packed, she decided to do a little bit of sleuthing of her own. There was no reason why she could not follow her husband around for a bit to learn whether he was a philanderer or just a loyal friend doing his duty. After she packed, she called the hotel where they had stayed and asked for her husband. The desk clerk offered to transfer her call, so she knew that he was at least still paying for the room. Where he was spending his nights might be a different story. She called again later and booked herself a separate room. With a shiver of excitement and dread, she decided that the next morning would find her sitting in a shadowy corner of the hotel lobby (behind a potted plant?) reading the morning paper and waiting for her husband to emerge—or not—to begin his day. She had to know for sure. Until she learned who he really was, she simply could not decide what to do.

* * *

"Susan Jenkins lied to me about her alibi," Janet declared to the detective. It was her second trip of the day to his inner sanctum, but this time she thought she would have the upper hand. "I asked Sheila—Susan—whatever the hell you want to call her— what she was doing the night of the murder, and she said that she was home alone watching *Survivor*." She paused before delivering the news, "*Survivor* was not on that night."

McCaffrey stifled a yawn and leaned back in his chair. "And that proves she murdered Jade Delilah? Do you remember what you were watching on television two weeks ago? I sure as hell don't." He unwrapped a piece of gum and slipped it in his mouth. "Is that all you've got?"

With no physical evidence to tie her to the murder, it was a stretch to divert the detective's attention, but she gave it her best shot. "Look, just go out and talk to her. She told me that Jade deserved to die, for chrissakes. Deserved to die! 'The wages of sin are death': those were her exact words."

"I think that's a quote from the Bible," he replied. "Maybe I'll find my priest and charge him with murder."

"Look," she explained, "you've got a woman who hates the porn industry and a murder that destroyed its biggest studio, stopping the first mainstream porn release in decades. She says that the victim deserved to die and she's lying about her alibi, and you tell me that you're not even interested in following up?"

"Why should I?" He slowly popped a big pink bubble. "I've got someone in the county jail right now who's pleading guilty to the crime you're talking about."

"What?" She was dumbfounded. "Don's pleading guilty?"

"Yup," he replied. "He told me a couple of hours ago that he's willing to enter a formal plea before the judge the day after tomorrow." The detective cocked his head and studied her. "It's interesting what people will do to avoid a charge of capital murder." He gave her an inviting grin while he spoke. "Now if someone else were to come forward and confess, we might forget about Mr. Johansson's offer, but at this point in time, that's about his only hope."

\* \* \*

After his talk with Miriam Wilhoit, Stanley called the detective on his cell phone and drove straight to his office. McCaffrey held the original Eden surveillance recordings, and since the fire had destroyed the copies, he had no choice but to watch it at the police station. The more he thought about Miriam's hint, the more convinced he became that he would see the image of Chance Geary lurking about the Eden Studio anteroom the afternoon before the party. If Jade's agent had managed to get in early enough, he could have hidden in Don's office, waited patiently to kill Jade and then escaped out the back window. He was glad that Janet was not there to watch the recording with him. If Geary was implicated, then he owed her a huge apology.

"Come in!" The detective's voice cut through the frosted glass door like an industrial diamond. "Ah, Professor, you just missed your partner. We had a very nice conversation just a few moments ago."

"What about?"

"Oh, this and that. What can I do for you?" He looked at his watch and pulled his briefcase out from underneath his desk. He packed it with papers while Stanley spoke.

"Like I told you on the phone, I'd like to look at the surveillance recording this evening."

"Why the hurry?"

Stanley hesitated. "I found Miriam Wilhoit. That's where I was this afternoon. She had some interesting things to say. I need to look at the surveillance recording again to check out her story."

"You found the secretary? You know," he conceded with an odd smile as he snapped his briefcase shut, no longer in a hurry to leave his office, "you're really getting pretty good at this." He took out a pen and clicked it. "Where is she? She's currently wanted for questioning in an arson investigation."

"I promised her that I wouldn't tell the police."

"You told her what?"

"Settle down, McCaffrey. I told her that I wouldn't tell *you*. I didn't promise her that I wouldn't tell Don. Given what I've learned about her, I'm sure he'll be happy to rat her out once I've talked to him." He felt no compunction using a promissory technicality to bring in the former secretary, admitted embezzler, and probable arsonist. It would also give Don a chance to score some points with the police.

The detective still looked unhappy. "You'll have to wait a while to talk to him. He's not taking visitors right now." He paused before dropping his bombshell for the second time in an hour. "He's going to be pleading guilty the day after tomorrow, and I think he wants some quiet time to contemplate his sins."

Stanley stared at McCaffrey contemptuously, remembering how the gaps in his friend's memory had undermined his confidence in his own innocence. The thought of the detective taking advantage was repugnant, but the best way to deal with him and his self-satisfied revelation was to ignore it. "When can I see the recording?"

"No comment on the news?" He leaned back in his chair with an expression that momentarily could have been taken for respect. "It seems to me like you're out of a job."

"Has he formally revoked my status as his investigator?"

"No," the detective admitted, "I don't think that he did."

"Then when can I see the recordings?"

A pause. A shrug of the shoulders. "Right now if you want." He stood up and grabbed his briefcase. "Follow me."

The two men walked down a narrow corridor to a cluttered room containing several aging computers and other electronic equipment, including a color television on a black cart. McCaffrey pulled three DVD's out of a filing cabinet. "Here's copies of the surveillance from noon to six p.m., six p.m. to midnight, and midnight to six a.m. I'll tell the sergeant that you're down here and might be staying awhile." He slapped the thin plastic boxes into the stomach of his adversary and headed out the door. "And if he offers you any coffee, don't take it, unless you've got a taste for squirrel diarrhea."

Stanley sat down and popped the first DVD into the machine. It was supper time and he should have been hungry, but his desire to view the recordings was stronger than his appetite. He felt a renewed sense of urgency. He needed to come up with something soon or Don would seal his own fate in less than forty-eight hours.

The first black and white recording began with Don giving a file to Miriam and then leaving the building for the day. Little happened for the next ten minutes, and he looked for a remote control to fast forward through stretches of inactivity. He pushed the pause button on the DVD player itself and engaged in a fruitless search around the room, giving up only after checking every desk and file drawer. He finally resigned himself to sitting close to the cart and manually working the buttons on the face of the machine.

The first two hours revealed a steady trickle of characters wandering in and out of the building. He took a pen out of his pocket and jotted down descriptions: *long hair with dark miniskirt; double-breasted suit with sunglasses; light hair with light pants,* which he later crossed out as each flagged person left.

He paused at the halfway point on the first DVD and rubbed his eyes. No sign of anyone remotely resembling Chance Geary had entered Eden Studio by 3:00 p.m. on the afternoon of the murder. He started the recording again and refocused. Just as his stomach started to rumble, he saw a familiar face pass across the screen. *Dark sweater and dark pants*, he wrote on the paper. He stared at the screen in rapt attention for the next three hours of elapsed time, hardly fast-forwarding at all. The dark sweater and pants had gone in, but had not come out. He rewound the recording back to the precise moment when the suspect entered and cued it up, ready to show McCaffrey. It was almost one o'clock in the morning, and he doubted that he would sleep at all that night. The race was on.

\* \* \*

Angela arrived at the hotel feeling nauseous after a long ride from the airport in a rental car reeking of stale cigarette smoke. It was well after supper, but she had no desire to go out, so she ordered a club sandwich and a salad from room service and sat down in front of the television.

The surveillance of her husband would start at midnight, when she would place a call to his room. She did not want to talk to him, so if he answered, she was going to hang up. The point was to learn something about his nocturnal activities. Then, she would get up early, find a good observation point and see when, if at all, he emerged from his room. The hotel had only one exit, so he would have to pass through the lobby on the way out. If he did not come down by 10:00 a.m., she would check his room. If he was not there, it would be time to hit the warpath.

After she finished the meal, she watched a movie until 12:30 a.m. and when it was over she turned the television off and took a deep breath. Please let him be there, she whispered, but her little prayer, like her telephone call to Stanley's room, went unanswered. She flopped down hard on the bed and fought back a sob, making mental excuses for his late night, concocting innocent scenarios that had delayed his return to the hotel. Her proposed morning surveillance took on increasingly high stakes. If he did not show up, it would be impossible to believe any stories he could offer for not having spent the night in his room.

\* \* \*

Stanley slept better than he anticipated and left an early morning message on McCaffrey's answering machine explaining that he would be coming to the police station to show him something interesting on the surveillance recording. He felt that the case had been cracked wide open, and whether he roused the detective's anger or somehow earned his grudging admiration, he was looking forward to the meeting. By 7:30 a.m., he was showered and ready to take on rush hour traffic. He grabbed a donut from the breakfast nook next to the hotel lobby and strode out of the building with no idea that his wife was sitting in the far corner, peering at him over a copy of the newspaper. Nor did he notice the boxy rental car that followed him all the way to police station.

"Well, if it isn't Inspector Clouseau," the detective said when Stanley walked into his office. "What is it you want to show me today? Got more purple fuzzies?"

"Better than that," he replied with a grin. "I'm going to show you the sweater itself." He motioned for McCaffrey to stand up and follow, "Come on. Let's take a look at the surveillance recording."

As the detective trailed him down the hall, he explained his methodology of keeping track of those who entered and left the building. "I was looking for someone who was recorded entering, but not leaving. Such a person could have hid in Don's office, killed Jade while he was passed out, and left through the back window." He turned on the television and DVD player and immediately hit the pause button. "Imagine my surprise when someone arrives wearing a dark sweater, but never leaves." He started the recording. "You can check it for yourself, but the person you're about to see is never seen leaving the building."

McCaffrey studied the image carefully and then asked Stanley to rewind it. "Let me see it one more time." He shook his head as he studied the figure moving through the lobby. "I give up. Who is it?"

"Susan Jenkins, also known as Sheila Easy during her days as a porn star."

"The chick that Janet Stephens is pushing on me." For once, McCaffrey was taking him seriously. He sat down in a creaky wooden chair in the small media room.

"The very same."

The detective steepled his fingers together and thought for a moment before speaking. "I suppose you'd like me to get a warrant to search her closet."

"You're a mind reader."

He thought for a moment more, and when he spoke, his negativity, for once, did not seem to come from spitefulness. "But what am I gonna to tell the judge? If this were a color recording, there might be a chance of getting a warrant. But all we've got here is a woman in a dark sweater—it could be gray or blue for all we know—who comes into the building and doesn't leave. I've been in that building; there are other exits she might have used."

"Only one that doesn't set off a fire alarm." He explained Janet's smoker's hideaway.

"Without connecting her to the crime in some other way, I don't have nearly enough to go asking for a warrant."

"Are you serious?" Stanley shook his head in disbelief.

"Very serious." He stood up to leave. "Look, you've done good work here. When I first met you, I thought you were a total fuck up, but this is nice." He motioned to the television. "So was finding Miriam Wilhoit and William Walker. But I'm not going to waste my time asking for a warrant that stands no chance of being issued." He turned around just before he left and gave Stanley a salacious smile. "Maybe you could make friends with Jenkins and get a peek at her boudoir?"

\* \* \*

Angela followed her husband into the jail parking garage and waited in a shadowed space several slots away until he returned.

After listening to thirty minutes of news on a public radio station, she saw him walk rapidly to back to his car. He got in, but did not drive off immediately. Instead, he talked on his cell phone for almost fifteen minutes before she finally saw the flash of his brake lights as he backed out of the parking space.

Once on the highway, it was not hard to follow him. Traffic was relatively light, and he had always been a conservative driver, staying mostly in the far right hand lane unless the person in front of him was going at a crawl. He drove north from downtown Los Angeles and eventually exited onto a broad boulevard leading to an attractive neighborhood of Mission-style houses and upscale condominiums.

He eventually stopped in front of a beautiful gated condo community, got out of his car and pushed one of several buttons on a panel next to an ornate wrought iron gate. A minute later, an attractive woman came out and spoke to him through the bars of the gate. Angela had no trouble identifying Janet Stephens. She got a sick feeling in the pit of her stomach when her rival finally opened the gate, gave her husband an enthusiastic hug, and led him back to her home. Angela lowered her head to the steering wheel and concluded that following him around was the stupidest thing she had ever done. Nothing good can come of this, she thought as she slumped back in the seat.

* * *

Stuart McCaffrey slowly walked the six blocks to the skyscraper where the city's forensic pathologists had their labs and offices. Thirty years on the police force had worked two significant and perversely related changes in the aging detective. His instincts had become stronger over the years; the ability to sniff out lies had sharpened. Yet, at the same time, he cared less and less about whether the criminal justice system got things exactly right. Susan Jenkins, aka Sheila Easy, smelled bad to him. On paper, she was just another suspect. The evidence pointed less toward her than to Don Johansson, Chance Geary, or Janet

Stephens, but something about the anti-porn zealot made his nose wrinkle. Did this mean that Johansson might be innocent? Maybe. He would not be the first innocent person to plead guilty to avoid the more serious consequences of going to trial and losing. The detective had ceased dwelling on this sort of injustice long ago, and the hardness made being a cop easier. But he had come to understand that the same hardness had made him impossible to live with as a husband, so he walked across downtown Los Angeles, pensively and purposefully, to talk with his ex-wife.

"Can I buy you a cup of coffee?" The offer prompted Ellen McCaffrey to look up from her computer over her reading glasses. She had never been a traditionally beautiful woman, but her ex-husband liked the way she kept her thick, graying hair cut full around head. Genes from her English mother had helped her face maintain the complexion of a much younger woman, and he wished in vain to see it break into a smile.

"Sorry, I'm totally swamped right now." She looked back at her computer, keeping her hands on the keyboard.

"Can I sit down? I want to talk about the Delilah case for a minute."

After a few more keystrokes, she pushed back from her work station and faced him. "Alright...you've seen the reports, haven't you?"

"Yeah, but I need your intuition right now more than I need forensic science." He patted the folder he held in his hand and sat down in the chair opposite her desk. "You've worked on dozens of murders over the years."

"Hundreds."

"Right." He took a deep breath. "What I want you to do is sit back and imagine the killer. Tell me about the perpetrator. You've always been good at studying a victim and making guesses about the killer. What's your sense in this case?"

He offered her the file, but she shook her head. "The first blow, struck while she was standing, would have knocked her unconscious and disfigured her for life, maybe even killed her.

She was then struck viciously several more times while she lay on the floor unable to defend herself." She closed her eyes and tried to imagine the scene. "This was more than murder. It was an act of destruction. It was an act of hatred and loathing."

"Have you met Don Johansson?"

"No, but I've seen clips of him on television," she replied. "You probably saw the rerun of him on Leno, too."

"Yeah."

"It's hard to see him that angry."

"Maybe," he conceded, "but over the years we've both seen jealousy and frustration turn people into animals." She nodded and for a moment he felt they might be on the same page.

"Lemme tell you why I'm here." He explained Susan Jenkins's axe to grind with the porn industry and revealed her prevarication about what television show she had been watching on the night of the murder.

Ellen seemed unimpressed until he described the image of the anti-porn crusader captured by the surveillance camera wearing a dark sweater. She was well aware of the fabric fibers found on the window sill in the office. "So, you think she might have done it?"

"I don't think anything right now, but I do know that I've got a guy ready to plead guilty to the crime."

"Johansson?"

"Who else?" He looked into her eyes and tried to read her reaction. She didn't blink. She was as sanguine as he about the realities of plea bargaining.

"You know," she responded after a moment's thought, "Johansson's not the only person I've seen on television. I saw an interview with Susan Jenkins on Lifetime a couple of months ago."

"You watch Lifetime?"

She ignored him and continued. "She struck me as being an extremely angry and vindictive woman. Of course, given the stories that she told, I could hardly blame her. But even as a victim, she had a distinctly unappealing quality about her."

She tried to remember more details of the show. "I'm not sure that I know how to explain it."

"Can you see her as Jade's killer?"

"Possibly. She comes off as being a much angrier person than Johansson. I mean, he was really relaxed and funny on Leno. He made me like him despite his profession." She paused again. "It's all just intuition, of course. What I'd rather do is analyze fibers from the sweaters that she has in her closet."

"Me too." He knew that she understood the problem of legally obtaining samples. "But there's not enough here for a warrant."

She erupted into a humorless laugh. "You've never let rules stop you before."

At first he thought that she was going to chide him again for his ethical lapses, but instead she studied the Los Angeles cityscape from her window for a minute before finally turning back around and uttering a huge sigh. "I can't believe I'm asking you this, but how hard would it be for you to get into her house and get some fiber samples?"

He stared at her in disbelief and slowly managed a response. "Unless she's got a really sophisticated alarm system, not very hard."

"Then do it," she said with finality. "Pay her closet a little visit."

"What happened to respecting the law, Ellie?" He waved his right hand in a gesture of acquiescence. "Not that I'm complaining, but our marriage busted up over my request that you forget some evidence rules. Why the change of heart?" He thought he had her, but as usual, she outmaneuvered him.

"Back then, you wanted me to frame someone, jerk face. Now, I'm suggesting you do something that might get an innocent person off the hook. It's not quite the same thing." She leaned back in her chair. "I've never been sure about Johansson."

"Yeah," he admitted. "Your tox report is one reason we can't really ask for the death penalty." When he saw no apology on her face, a sneaky idea entered his head.

"Okay, I'll make you a deal. I'll go over to Susan Jenkins' house, do a quick rummage in her closet and deliver the fibers to you. They'll be inadmissible against her, of course, but if they match the sample found on the window sill, we won't push things with Johansson." He gave her his most winning smile, one that looked more crooked and sardonic than sincere. "But," he emphasized, "you have to go out to dinner with me no matter what the fiber samples show." It was her turn to look surprised. "Baby, if I'm gonna break the rules for you, I should get something out of it."

She frowned at him for a minute before finally relenting. "Okay, but it's got to be French. No cheap Mexican stuff."

McCaffrey got up without another word, nodded his assent to his ex-wife, and went off to reconnoiter Susan Jenkins' house with a lighter heart than he had felt in years.

# XXXII.

# A FORCEFUL CLIMAX

It took Stanley fifteen minutes on his cell phone to convince Janet that she should let him come over and discuss what he had seen on the video. After the third time he apologized for sneaking into her closet, she finally asked him about the recording and let out a shriek when she learned that Susan's image had been captured entering the studio but not leaving it. When he arrived at her condo, she made him explain again exactly what he had seen.

"I knew there was something not right about her." She hugged him hard and kissed him on the cheek. "Are you going to ask McCaffrey to get a search warrant for her house? Of course, if she has any brains, she threw the sweater out a long time ago."

"McCaffrey doesn't think there's enough evidence for a warrant," he said with disgust. "The video is black and white and there's no way to tell whether the sweater she's wearing is purple or some other dark color."

"What should we do?"

He got up and started to pace around her living room, the heels of his black leather shoes tapping out an impatient rhythm on the tile floors. "That's the question, isn't it? We need to be sure about her, because we still have Chance and Miriam to think about. We shouldn't cross a murderer and an arsonist off the list just because of the video, but we definitely have to deal with Susan first. She's our best shot, especially considering that Don's plea is coming up tomorrow."

"Why don't you let me talk to Susan again? She lied to me once before. Maybe I can get her to say something else incriminating." She looked up at Stanley as he passed by the couch. "And stop pacing. You're making me dizzy."

"Sorry." He sat down and pulled up McCaffrey's number on his speed dial, but decided against making a call. "What would you say to her?"

"Well, I could play concerned friend. She invited me to her victim's support group, after all." She gave her partner a brief summary of the meeting with Susan. "I could tell her that the cops know about her entrance into the building the afternoon before the party. Then, we could check out her explanation. I could also tell her that the police are targeting her as a suspect and see how she reacts."

He nodded his head. "Do you want me to come with you?"

"I don't think that'd be a good idea. I think she'll be more likely to let her guard down if it's just me playing the repentant whore." She got up and picked her cell phone off a coffee table. "I'll suggest that we meet for coffee close to her house. I don't want to show up there again unannounced."

He thought about her plan. It had no immediate role for him, so he tried to decide how to spend the afternoon while he waited. Talking to the studio heads again and bringing them up to date might be interesting, but he had no time to track them down, much less follow up on anything.

While Janet set up her meeting, he decided to write up a list of suspects and what had been learned about them. As he outlined the report in his head, he realized that it could have value beyond organizing his thoughts. He could submit it to McCaffrey and show it to Don. By demonstrating in black and white just how weak the case against his friend really was, he might achieve the dual goals of getting the detective to delay the impending hearing and getting his friend to reconsider his plea. Shortly after Janet left, he sat down at the computer in the back office and began typing up a sort of legal brief, a more interesting and compelling document than any he had ever produced in his former job.

\* \* \*

As Janet emerged from her condominium and drove off in her Mini Cooper, Angela was squeezing her thighs tightly together, having suffered through several hours of surveillance without a bathroom break. As the adorable little car drove off without her husband, she decided to take a chance and sped to the nearest gas station. As long as Stanley was waiting for the starlet to return, she figured it was safe to briefly leave her post. When she got back to the condo, she saw that her gamble had paid off. Stanley's car had not moved.

After another hour, she decided to stretch her legs. Her husband had entered a unit, presumably Janet's, in the far back corner of the complex, so no one would spot her taking a short stroll along the street. As she walked, she checked to see if there was any access to the townhouse from its back side. Janet's car had emerged from a narrow driveway on the side of complex, so she walked down the alley and found the garage door that led into the unit where her husband was waiting. It was shut tight, and there was no other exterior door. The only accessible window looked past some lace curtains into a small bathroom. She felt perversely relieved at the privacy offered by the townhouse; she would not have the option of peeping at her husband in bed after the slutty video legend returned.

\* \* \*

While Janet was talking with Susan Jenkins in a quiet Malibu coffee shop and Stanley was drafting a formal report of his investigation, Stuart McCaffrey was jimmying open the patio doors of Jenkins's beach house. He had parked at a surf shop several hundred yards south of her home and walked barefoot across the sand until he found the stairs leading to her back deck. As he sat on the bottom step and brushed the sand from his feet, he scanned the beach for anyone who might have seen him approach. The neighborhood was quiet and no one saw the man in the gray suit jiggling the lock on her door.

It took him less than three minutes to open it and slide the door aside. He took a quick backward look at the empty beach and then walked into the house and looked around. In some ways, it was a typical beach house, rattan sofa, floral pillows and cushions, tile floors, and glass-topped tables, but the motif was disrupted by a cheap cherry entertainment unit with connecting bookshelves. Suburbia meets the beach would not make the next issue of *Home and Garden*. As his eyes adjusted to the shadows, the detective made his way through the living room and into the hallway that led to the front of the house. Assuming that the biggest bedroom was hers, he moved quickly inside and found a small closet next to the master bathroom. He jerked open a set of bi-fold doors and looked at his watch. He had been there for two minutes. It took only another minute to find a purple sweater hanging amid a modest collection of blouses and slacks.

McCaffrey squeezed off a thumbful of fibers from the garment and sealed them in a small plastic lunch bag which he took out of his pocket. Then, he rifled through the clothes on either side of the sweater, checking to see if anything else was worth sampling. Finding nothing, he strode across the room to inspect a large bureau next to the bed. He worked quickly through the remaining drawers, but found nothing more noteworthy than a small pistol. He picked it up and saw that it was a fourth-generation Glock 26, one of the most powerful concealable side arms ever made. As he put it back in the drawer, he heard the distinctive crunch of car tires on gravel and broken sea shells as someone pulled into the driveway.

The detective turned to sprint out of the bedroom but saw that he had left the closet doors wide open. He slid the left bi-fold quickly shut, but the right one stuck and when he yanked it toward its mate, the flimsy panel came off its rails completely and hung awkwardly to the side. A hurried adjustment just made matters worse and the detective was forced to make his escape with the door hanging askew, a screaming confession that the closet had been tampered with. Uttering a curse under his breath, he fled into the living room and toward the back patio as someone entered the house. As he burst through the doors, he realized that unless Susan Jenkins were blind, he would be seen racing across her deck and down to the beach.

\* \* \*

When Susan entered the house, she saw a blur of motion at the end of the shotgun hallway that led from her front door to the living room. Her initial impulse was to pursue, but she checked herself and made a detour into the bedroom where she retrieved her trusty Glock. As she held the pistol up and switched off the safety, she noticed one of her closet doors hanging cock-eyed revealing half of her small wardrobe. Whomever she had seen had definitely been in her room. She turned toward the door, listening carefully for the intruder before she inched her way out into the hall.

She could hear the surf crashing loudly and as she walked with the gun extended into the living room, she found the patio doors wide open. Seeing the room was empty, she lowered the pistol and relaxed a little. The adrenaline rush subsided and she took a quick look down to the beach. The intruder had made a clean getaway. She shut and locked the patio doors and made a quick inventory of her possessions. Nothing of value had been taken in the living room, including a brand new laptop that sat on a stool near the doors. Her digital camera still sat perched on top of the television set. After going through the entire house, she concluded that nothing had been disturbed, except her closet.

Why would someone break into her house to look at her clothes? There was nothing valuable inside. And what a coincidence that she happened to be called off to coffee by that time-wasting cunt Layla while the break-in occurred. She was usually home in the mid-afternoon. She stared at the hanging door and eventually put two and two together. While Layla was asking questions about Jade's murder, her professor friend had been ransacking her closet.

\* \* \*

"Well, tell me what she said." Stanley walked into the living room eager to get a summary of the meeting as Janet kicked off her shoes.

"She denied everything." The weary actress plopped down on a cream-colored leather sofa and propped her feet up on the coffee table.

"Even the video?" He was incredulous. "We've got her on film for chrissakes!"

"She says it couldn't be her. She claims she hasn't set foot in Eden Studio for three years. I was so flabbergasted that I told her I knew that she was lying about watching *Survivor*." She shook her head in frustration.

"How suspicious is she?"

"Pretty damn suspicious now. She wouldn't talk about anything having to do with the murder." Janet rubbed the bottom of her left foot with the big toe of her right foot. "I'm afraid we might have to send you in to raid her closet." She looked up at him. "I hear you have some experience with that kind of operation."

\* \* \*

Susan sat on her bed, fingering the Glock and staring at her closet. Layla had said that she and her partner had spotted her entering Eden Studio the night of the murder. The starlet might be great at faking an orgasm but she was lousy at hiding her suspicion about who had really rid the world of Jade Delilah. But why the hell had they lured her from her house so that the professor could poke around in her stuff? What did they expect to find, a signed confession? A diary entry describing how Jade seemed to crumple to the floor in slow motion? But there was no sign that any likely hiding place in her house had been searched. The professor had gone straight to the closet.

She stood up and walked over to her clothes and a smile creased her face for the first time that day. Fibers. They must be looking for fibers matching whatever had been found in Don's office by the cops. She fingered a blue blouse and then ran her hand down a pair of cream colored slacks. What had she worn to Eden? For the first time she felt a hint of panic tighten her throat. What had she worn? She flipped through her wardrobe trying to jog her memory, but each outfit looked as likely as the next and her attempts to concentrate and pull up the details of that night stuck in the tar pit of her memory.

No worries, she thought as the smile returned to her face. She deserved a whole new wardrobe anyway. She threw the Glock on the bed and grabbed a large garbage bag from the kitchen. Within minutes, she had every piece of clothing and every pair of shoes from the closet stuffed in the bag and closed up tight. She could eliminate whatever evidence Layla had been searching for and then figure out a way to eliminate the slut herself and her plodding lap dog partner.

Susan drove several miles toward Los Angeles before she found a supermarket with a solitary dumpster parked next to its back delivery entrance. She tossed in the bag of clothes and continued toward the city, trying to formulate a plan to deal with her pursuers. She had been to Janet's condo several times before she had escaped the porn business, and she headed in that direction. As she exited the freeway and into Layla's neighborhood, an idea was forming in her head and by the time she pulled up in front of the condo complex, she knew exactly how she wanted to confront the two main threats to her freedom.

She pulled into an open space a dozen yards from the entrance gate and pulled the gun from the glove compartment. When she had purchased the weapon, her agent had taken her out into the desert and taught her how to use the compact 9 mm. She held it in her right hand and clicked the safety off and on twice. The pistol fit neatly in her purse, and Janet wouldn't have a clue she was carrying it. The nosy whore would want to talk to her friend Susan when she dangled valuable clues about who murdered Jade Delilah in front of her pretty nose. She smiled and pressed the buzzer next to the gate.

"It's Susan." She paused dramatically. "I need to talk to you about Jade."

An excited voice crackled over the loudspeaker. "Susan! Of course, come on in."

The buzzer sounded and the gate opened with a metallic click. She pushed her way in, shut the gate behind her, and walked across the courtyard to the corner townhouse. The excited woman stood in the doorway to greet her. Susan entered first and was pleased to see the young professor stand up to take her hand when she entered the living room. He seemed happy to see her too. This was an unexpected blessing. There would be no need to coerce Janet to lure him to her home for a final interview session, a clear sign that her plan was righteous.

"Would you like a drink?" Janet asked. "I've got some wine and also some tea and organic apple cider."

"No. I'm fine." This is almost fun, she thought. She could feel an unexpected strength coursing through her body. These two have no clue that they're not in control. They assume they're directing this scene. They don't realize they're just bit players.

"What did you come over to talk about?" Janet was literally sitting on the edge of her seat on a plump leather couch. The man sat next to her, legs crossed, feigning cool. Susan sat down across from them on an overstuffed ottoman, unzipped purse balanced on her knees.

"I wanted to tell you what happened the night of Jade Delilah's murder." The expression of surprise on their faces was gratifying. Were they sleeping together? Probably. He was a handsome, clean-cut guy, just the kind that Layla would like to seduce and devour. "I went to Eden Studio about three o'clock that day to speak with Don. I thought he might be able to see reason about *Toys in Babeland*."

"To see reason about what?" Janet interrupted.

"About canceling the national distribution deal. The movie was going to change everything. It was going to bring back porn to theaters in every town in America. And nobody was trying to stop it." She deliberately took a moment to polish her glasses. "Instead of exposing Don for what he was, the media was playing into his hands and giving him free publicity. CNN treated the movie like a comedy. And then Leno invited him to talk about it on his show! This was all leading to another so-called 'golden age' of porn." She paused for a moment and waited for them to acknowledge the logic of her concern.

"What did you say to him?"

She shook her head in disgust. "That bitch secretary of his asked me if I had an appointment and then claimed that he wasn't there, so I sat for a while and waited until she left her desk. Then, I walked into his office to talk to him."

"But he wasn't here," Stanley interjected.

She nodded and continued. "No, he wasn't. So, I sat down and waited. I knew about the party and figured he'd come back before it started, but he didn't. I sat there and listened to the party noise in the hallway, trapped in the middle of Sodom and Gomorrah with the voices of the damned on all sides. No way was I going to leave and show my face to that crowd."

"Lot's wife turned into a pillar of salt," the young professor offered.

"She did," Susan said. "I sat quietly behind the desk in his big leather chair, just listening." She smiled. "It was like hearing the buzzing of flies in the deepest pit of hell, but I was not afraid. I sat in the dark and prayed for my deliverance."

Her gaze shifted back and forth from Janet to Stanley. They still have no clue, she thought. The children of Babylon have no clue about their world. She continued her story. "After a couple of hours, the door opened and he walked in. I was ready to confront him, ready to give him a chance to repent and undo the evil that he was planning, but he didn't even turn on the lights. He just stumbled over to the couch and passed out. I sat there wondering what to do next when the door opened again. I spun the chair around to hide before the lights switched on."

Stanley and Janet sat motionless, as though any movement might prevent the revelation of the mystery they had been trying to solve. It was like a movie with everyone waiting for the climax. "I could hear Jade shake him and wake him up. He was groggy but he managed to get something out about an attorney for some problem she was having. She lost her temper and told him that she was leaving the studio."

As much as she wanted to see the expression on their faces when they heard the truth, she stopped short of explaining how Jade had pushed Don back down on the sofa as if he were a rag doll. That's when Susan had turned around in the chair and revealed herself to the quarreling couple. Don was lying back in a stupor and Jade turned her attention to the new presence in the room. Susan had stood up and tried to enlist Jade in her cause, but received only ridicule and scorn in return. The whore blasphemed, called her conversion fake, accusing her of leaving porn because her body had started to sag. The paddle almost seemed to float off the coffee table into her hands as Jade turned to leave the room. A racist epithet had sufficed to spin her around one last time, surprise registering in her eyes a moment before the wood smashed into her slutty painted face.

But, if she confessed, they would guess she had come to kill them. They would resist if they realized that they had nothing left to lose.

"So, I went into the den of lions and what's my reward?" She shook her head vehemently. "You break into my house. You make up stories and you try to get your friend out of jail by putting me in his place." She did not have to feign anger. The rage at the invasion of her privacy was real. The incomprehensible stupidity of those who did not see the righteousness of her cause took her to a place beyond frustration.

"You're playing with my reputation," she explained as she pulled the Glock out of her purse and trained it on the professor's forehead. "Now, I'm going to play with yours."

\* \* \*

From her position in the rental car, Angela had no trouble recognizing Susan Jenkins. After all, she had been the only interviewee critical of the porn industry. What was she doing at the condo gate? She couldn't be there for a threesome. Please don't let it be a threesome! She sat in the car with her stomach doing flip flops, wondering what she should do and cursing her curiosity. Once Susan was let in, the miserable spy concluded that a confrontation with her husband in Janet's townhouse could not be any worse than what her imagination was serving up in the car. She stumbled as she got out and walked back down the alley, but Janet had closed the garage door after her return. She tried to push up the small bathroom window, but it was shut tight.

Frustrated and anxious to have it out with her husband, she walked back out to the street and in desperation tried a ruse she had seen work on a dozen television shows. She strode quickly to the gate and before she could reconsider her course of action, she pushed buzzers at random and until she heard a young man's voice greet her through the speaker.

"Federal Express, package for you…Mr. Carson," she read the name confidently off of the plastic panel and was rewarded with a sharp click as the gate unlocked itself. She stepped in and ran to the vestibule of Janet's townhouse to find her husband. Should she storm in or knock? She hesitated. If she burst into an innocent scene, then she would look like some jealousy-crazed idiot, but if she knocked, then they'd be forewarned.

She pulled her hand away from the door and inched around to the side of the house, to a narrow window that looked into the kitchen. At first, she saw nothing but the big butcher's block in the center of the room, but then she saw a sliver of movement beyond, in the room past the kitchen. Two people on the living room sofa, her worst nightmare coming true.

\* \* \*

"Professor, you need to stand up slowly and unzip your pants." Susan had no intention of shooting her audience as they sat on the couch. Such a scene might lead the police directly to her. A different tableau would need to be staged, one that would force the police to conclude that she was a heroine rather than a multiple murderer. "There you go," she said as he complied reluctantly to her command, "now you're going to get a little taste of what it's like to be a porn star."

She held up her smart phone and pretended to train the small camera on them. "When we get this little video of you two posted on the internet, you'll have an idea what it's like to have someone trash your reputation."

As long as they assumed she was planning their humiliation instead of their death, she figured they would play along. She would direct a little bondage scene where the young professor would pound the veteran porn star nice and hard, leaving little doubt about his savage urges. She would ask him to gag his partner, tie her hands behind her back and lay her on the sofa. When he was positioned squarely on top of her, a bullet to his temple would pin her down, tied and immobilized, pretty throat ready for Susan's elegant tightening fingers. When Layla was dead, it would be a simple matter to move the professor's hands around the strangled neck. When the police arrived, they would lament that the vicious rapist could not have been stopped in time and they would comfort the trembling woman who had shot him. The end game she orchestrated would also seal the fate of the porn director currently sitting in the county jail. Any evidence uncovered by Janet and Stanley would die with them.

"Very nice, professor. Loose boxers are always best." She trained the gun on Stanley and spoke to Janet. "Now, Layla, I think you know what happens next in this scene. You need to go ahead and stroke his cock." The actress hesitated for a moment but complied. She touched him tentatively through his shorts, cupping his testicles with one hand and stroking him with the other.

"Hmm." Susan looked at his unresponsive member. "Let's give him something to look at, shall we? Rip open the front of your blouse." Janet started to unbutton her top button. "No! Rip it! Give him that ravishing *'just fuck me'* look." Janet groaned, buttons went flying and Susan approved of the torn garment that would make the rape look even more real.

The top of Janet's breasts now rose over her torn blouse. Stanley looked away, but Susan forced his eyes back. "Have you ever seen anything quite so nice, Professor? Rumor has it that they're real too. Why don't you touch them for me? Just reach out and touch them." He dragged the tops of his fingers lightly across the swell of her bosom. "No! Grab them hard! Harder! Now, suck him off Janet. Get him good and ready."

Just as she had in so many films, she started to brush her lips gently back and forth. When she felt no response, she took her hand and pulled on the object of her attention, sucking softly at first and then harder as she worked her fingers up and down. "That's the spirit Layla, now you're workin'."

\* \* \*

For a brief moment, Stanley looked down into Janet's eyes and saw something that might have been an apology, a plea for sympathy, or simply fear of what might happen if he did not rise to the occasion as Susan demanded. His first instinct was to step back indignantly and put an end to the ridiculous charade, but the look in Susan's eyes and the menace in her voice forced him to reconsider. She was clearly agitated and mentally unbalanced. What kind of a person forces fellatio at gun point? And what if she were the killer? She had admitted to being in Don's office around the time of the murder. He groaned, not in sexual ecstasy, but in the realization that he was not willing to the take the chance that she was merely bluffing.

He closed his eyes and tried to ignore Janet's increasingly desperate ministrations but the inward turn of his mind just made the sensation more palpable.

He opened his eyes and looked around the room for something that he could use against the demented ex-porn star. The living room drapes were closed, and the only potential weapons, Janet's collection of heavy lucite Adult Video Awards, were just out of reach. As Susan continued to urge him on, he could feel his cell phone banging against his thigh and he slid his right hand, hidden from her view, into his pocket. If he could remember the location of McCaffrey's speed dial, then maybe the detective would overhear and puzzle out the situation. His fingers traced a path along the keypad that hopefully led to the detective's number, either that or the order taker at Pizza Villa was going to get an earful.

When Susan suggested that a tied-up version of Janet might be more stimulating for him, he looked around the room again, trying to find a safe place to rest his eyes, not on his partner's swelling breast, not on the pinpoint eyes of their tormentor. To his astonishment, he saw something by the kitchen and was horrified to see his wife's face in the lower corner of the window, hand over her mouth, a look of horror in her eyes. From her angle, she could not see Susan. All she could she was a gorgeous porn star sucking hungrily on her husband. He opened his mouth to call out, but abruptly choked off his cry when he realized the danger of bringing her to Susan's potentially deadly attention.

He tried instead to signal her with a nod of his head, but Angela picked up on none of his panic. Instead, she ducked her head and disappeared from view.

"Look at Layla, Professor," Susan warned him. "Look at the way her lips are wrapped around that nice cock of yours. Pull up your skirt up sweetie and shake your ass a little bit. There you go! See that, Mr. Professor. That's what you're going to be fucking in just a minute."

"Could you stop pointing that gun at me," he pleaded for the benefit of whomever might be on the other end of his desperate phone call.

"Alright," came the reply, "we'll see if keeping Layla covered instead will improve your performance."

\* \* \*

Angela lowered her head and vomited into the bushes. Her first impulse was to get as far away as possible, as quickly as possible. After ten years of loving and laughing and working together, how could her husband throw it all away? She no longer knew him and as she crouched on her hands and knees, wiping the bile from her chin, she didn't recognize herself either. Pregnant and married to a cheating, unemployed, horny sleazebag. Was this really her life? She stood up slowly and staggered back to the gate, floundering in her own personal hell while her husband approached ecstasy in the warm arms of his new lover. She pushed the gate open and took one step out.

"Fuck you," she screamed hoarsely as she stopped and turned. "And fuck every one of you who can't keep your hands to yourself and your dick in your pants!"

In a blind rage, she reversed direction and ran across the courtyard. If she was going to feel like shit, she was going to let them know that they were no better than pieces of shit themselves. She rattled the front door of the condo and pounded on it, but no one responded. "I know you're in there," she yelled as she darted to the kitchen window, but a quick glance revealed no one. She moved farther along the brick wall and stood outside the living room windows. The curtains were closed, but she knew what lay behind them. "I know you're in there!"

When she got no response, she looked quickly around and grabbed the first heavy object in sight, a ceramic garden gnome with a pointed cap. She took him in both hands and tossed him through the window. When the she got no immediate answer to her challenge, she grabbed the gnome's smiling wife by the apron and sent her through the adjoining window. This toss caused the curtain to part in a shower of glass and she was stunned to see a woman training a gun on her husband.

As in a dream, she could hear Stanley telling the woman to remain calm as she jerked the gun back and forth from him to Janet and then through the broken window. Her husband sounded very confident and reassuring as he tried to convince the woman to lay down the weapon. From her perspective, the three figures in the house looked framed, as if they were on television, and she watched the woman with the gun approach the window with an unexpected sense of detachment.

"Toss your phone in here and come around to the front door," she said, pointing the gun back at Stanley and jerking her hand to the right. "Come inside as quick as you can or I'll blow his head off."

She saw Stanley shaking his head no, while Layla moved slowly back toward a book shelf on the living room wall. Angela stood frozen for a moment and then she saw Layla nod her head urgently. She reached out, placed her phone on the window sill and sprinted around the house to the front door.

\* \* \*

As soon as Angela disappeared from view, Layla snatched the Lucite obelisk she had won at the 2005 Adult Video Awards and threw it straight at Susan's head. The intended target ducked before getting off a wild shot in Layla's direction that lodged in ceiling above her head. Before she could get off another round, Stanley had tackled her, ripped the gun out of her hand and pinned her to the floor. The killer of Jade Delilah put up a frantic struggle but when Layla added her body weight to the squirming figure, she was finally subdued.

Only then did they notice the pounding on the locked door.

"Angela?" Stanley yelled from his position on Susan's back. "Come back to the window."

A moment later, the face of his wife appeared, looking scared, then confused, and finally vaguely amused at the image of her husband and her imagined rival riding a squirming ex-porn star like a tandem bicycle.

He smiled at her and tightened his grip on Susan's wrist as she made one final attempt to grab the Glock. "Could you call the cops, please?"

She nodded, pulled her phone off the window sill and dialed 911. In a calm and almost matter-of-fact voice she described the situation to the dispatcher and promised to let them in at the gate when they arrived. Then, she looked at her husband, and a slightly sardonic look passed over her face. "You might want to zip up before the cops come."

# XXXIII.

# THE TAIL END

Susan began protesting her innocence as soon as the police entered the condominium. She insisted that the two friends of Donald Johansson had framed her in order to get him out of jail. Her story gained early traction with some members of the police department as contradictory statements were filed concerning the incident in Janet Stephens' residence, but all speculation ended when Detective Stuart McCaffrey reported the conversation from Stanley's phone recorded on his answering machine. He also obtained a search warrant for Susan's Malibu home. The elusive purple sweater was nowhere to be found, but through an amazing stroke of luck, he reported finding a small ball of fuzz on the floor of the closet which proved to be a perfect match for the fibers found on the window sill at murder site. As soon as the fiber tests were confirmed, the head of Eden Studio was released, and Susan admitted to killing Jade and assaulting the others, while simultaneously, and unsuccessfully, asserting the defense of reasonable provocation.

Stanley and Angela stayed in California for two more weeks, making themselves available to the police for questioning and enjoying a well-earned vacation. They were sunning themselves by their hotel pool one afternoon when the former professor got word that the former porn mogul was finally back home. He lay down his cell phone next to a cold beer and sighed.

"Don's finally out." He leaned back in the chaise lounge and smiled at his wife who had bought a bright red one-piece

Speedo to celebrate the end of their ordeal. "He'd like to take us to dinner tomorrow."

"He owes you at least that much! You were amazing." The success of the investigation, in addition to her own role in the finale, had completely changed her mind about Stanley's taking the case. "If it weren't for you, he'd still be rotting in jail."

She pushed her sunglasses up on her head, took a sip of her virgin piña colada and looked at him with admiration. "What was the worst part for you? As bad as I felt when I looked in Janet's condo, I can't even imagine what it was like for you."

He shook his head. "Having a loaded gun pointed at me by that nut case was pretty bad, but it wasn't the worst." He reached over and squeezed her hand. "The worst thing was calling home at one o'clock in the morning and hearing Max answer the phone. I'd rather be shot than hear that again."

She squeezed back. "You do believe me, don't you? There was absolutely nothing going on."

"I believe you," he said gravely. And keeping a straight face he added, "But if you're still curious about what it's like to be with a man and Nanci..." His wife reached over and poured her icy drink down the front of his swimming trunks. He jumped into the pool with a maniacal laugh and judged the assault well worth the look on her face.

* * *

The next night, they met Don at an upscale restaurant not too far from their hotel. He looked relaxed and serene as he hugged his friends warmly and sat down in the corner booth with them. The first thing he did was apologize for costing Stanley his job.

"Is there no chance that the university will take you back, given that I turned out not be a vicious killer?" He folded his napkin in his lap and looked seriously at his friend.

"No," he explained, "the President knows that I was a close case for tenure anyway, and she's still pissed off about all the negative publicity that I brought the university. Not to mention that I violated about twenty-seven different human subject rules when I let Janet and Angela conduct interviews without me. They weren't trained or approved, so even if I went back, I'd get totally hammered for that."

"He's got a bunch of resumes out," Angela interjected. "Something will turn up."

"Maybe he should consider being a professional investigator," Don replied. "He's one-for-one with hopeless cases."

Stanley laughed. "I think I'll quit while I'm ahead. Anyway, Janet's at least as responsible for your release as I am." The three placed their orders with a waitress who looked at them as if they were celebrities. "By the way, have you talked to her?"

"Very briefly," he replied, "she's filming something this week for Janus. We're going to touch base later."

Angela, sensing this was an uncomfortable subject, switched gears. "Tell us what you're going to do? For better or for worse, you've had a lot of time to think about it."

"I'm still having a hard time thinking of jail as a contemplative retreat," he laughed, "but being there did help me sort some things out. I've decided to go back to seminary. I'm not a big believer in signs, but I have a feeling that my work in LA is finished."

"Wonderful!"

"And there's no way to salvage the studio?" Stanley asked.

"Miriam actually did me a favor by burning down the place. The insurance money is going to pay off most of the creditors and the remaining ones seem satisfied with taking the rights to *Toys in Babeland*."

"Does that mean it's going to show up in our mall this fall?" Angela asked.

"I don't think so," he shook his head. "With Jade dead and…how she died…" His thoughts trailed off and she finished for him.

"It's not wholesome enough anymore, is it?"

He lifted his head up and managed a smile. "Ironic, isn't it?"

The food arrived and the conversation turned to less weighty matters. They lingered over coffee and dessert, staying together as they walked out to their cars. Before they parted, Don had a request. He wanted to see the interview videos that Stanley, Angela, and Janet had shot. Anxious to put the project behind him, the unemployed academic acceded willingly.

\* \* \*

To Stanley's surprise, Janet too wanted to see the recorded interviews. She came and visited them at their hotel the day before they returned to Illinois. As they sat in the shade next to the outdoor bar, he explained that he had already given them to Don.

"That's fine," she said, sipping a gin and tonic. "I need to talk to him anyway." She had dressed conservatively in a light-weight wool suit. He knew his wife bore her no ill-will, but he was glad that nothing she wore recalled their tawdry last scene together.

"Have you guys not seen each other yet?" He knew a meeting would be uncomfortable, but he was surprised that they had not yet touched base. "I know he'd like to see you. He knows that without you, he'd still be in jail."

"He left messages a couple of times, but I just haven't felt ready." She smiled at Angela and reached over to touch her arm. "I hope you realize how lucky you are to have someone who isn't always chasing after lame ducks."

"What do you mean?"

"It's taken me a while to see it, but I don't think that Don can resist a damsel in distress. I think that's why he got into the business in the first place, and it's certainly why he fell for someone like Jade." She shook her head and laughed softly. "My psychologist says that it would be a bad sign if he were interested in me." She popped a piece of nicotine chewing gum in her mouth. "I'll have to be content with being friends."

"Are you really okay with that?" Angela asked.

"Yeah, I think so."

\* \* \*

Sometimes, after periods of tedious inactivity, changes arrive all in a rush. Stanley and Angela had been back in Illinois for almost four months, watching their savings dwindle to less than two thousand dollars when they received a call from a couple who made an offer on their house. A quick sale would not solve all of their money problems, but it would buy them some more time to continue job hunting. Much to their surprise, Stanley's employment situation began to resolve itself several days later when he spoke with the head of the Sociology Department at Belle Meade College in Los Angeles. The small liberal arts college was less squeamish than the BFU about his recent research. In fact, they thought the publicity would spark student interest in his classes. They wanted to know whether he would be willing to teach for two semesters as a visiting professor, his status thereafter to be determined by the department at the end of the school year. Although the expectant parents doubted they could afford to raise a family in California on a modest assistant professor's salary, the offer was more than welcome.

The following week, Don called from California and told them that he had arranged a big surprise. He offered to fly them down to Los Angeles and ignored their protests that he had no more money to spend on trips than they did. He refused to tell them what the surprise was, but advised them cryptically that Stanley should bring a tuxedo and Angela her most stylish dress. To their surprise, a chauffer met them at the airport in a limousine and checked them into the Wilshire Hotel in Beverly Hills.

The next evening, Don picked them up from the hotel in an even larger limo. The two men wore black formalwear while Angela managed to fit into a blousy black dress that tastefully deemphasized her round belly. As they settled into the soft leather seats in the back of the car, Stanley thanked his friend and then asked for an explanation.

"Janet and I had exactly the same thought about the interviews. We got together and watched them and knew that we were looking at a cultural document of real value." The limo stayed parked in front of the hotel entrance while they talked. "You took a rare snapshot of a misunderstood industry. From most of the women, you elicited the sort of sincerity and genuineness that you almost never see. Others stick to the party line, but that's a true piece of the story too. The cross section of people is amazing and right smack in the middle of all those stories is a murder mystery. You've even got an interview with Susan just after she killed Jade."

He paused for a moment and looked out the window. Janet was waving at them from the hotel steps. She walked over in a strapless red dress and squeezed into the car next to Angela. As the chauffeur pulled out of the circular drive and onto the boulevard, Angela looked at Don and then raised an inquiring eyebrow at Janet, who shook her head discretely.

Don pretended not to notice and continued, "Anyway, Jan and I sat down with all the hours of recordings and edited them into a two hour package. I hired a friend of mine to do some voice-overs, but in the documentary it's mostly you and Janet asking the questions and trying to unravel the mystery of how people find their way into the porn industry and how one of its brightest stars was extinguished."

"You made a movie?" Stanley was flabbergasted.

"Well, it used to be my job after all," he replied with a huge smile. "Besides, it was a labor of love and the least that I could do for someone who gave up his job, almost lost his wife, and damn near got killed trying to save me." The former director became serious for a moment and pulled an envelope out of his pocket. "Look, this may be one of the lowest budget films ever made, but it's gotten some interest on the indie circuit. A good bit of interest actually. Here's what we were able to get up front." He handed the envelope to Stanley. "It's almost six digits."

Angela gave a cry and reached across the back of the limo to give the former porn mogul an exuberant hug and peck on the cheek. "What can we do to thank you?"

He blushed. "Well, if it makes any more money, I think Janet deserves something for all she's done."

"Of course," Stanley and Angela shouted simultaneously.

"And I wouldn't object to a portion of any royalties going to cover my seminary expenses, but I don't want anything more than that." The young couple enthusiastically consented to the plan, and Don opened a bottle of champagne he found in the limo's mini-fridge and added mischievously, "And someone will have to spring for the limo!"

They drove for about twenty minutes before stopping in front of a renovated 1930s theater on the edge of downtown Los Angeles. It took Stanley and Angela a moment to peer out the window and spot the narrow red carpet leading up a flight of stairs past the box office. There were several cameramen and half dozen reporters milling about. When they noticed the limo they walked toward the sidewalk. The young sociologist stared at his friend. "You've got to be kidding."

"Don't you want to see it?" the director asked his former fraternity brother. "I've shown it to the distributor, of course, but this is the official premiere." Don and Janet got out of the car first and held the doors open for the dumbfounded pair of Midwesterners. The director stood between them, with Janet at Angela's side, and they linked arms while they walked past the cameras. It was then that Stanley looked up and saw the theater marquee for the first time: *Death in Eden*. Don started to giggle. "My first choice was *Bad News Bares*, but the distributor made us play it straight."

In the theater, Angela looked around and recognized many of the women they had interviewed, as well as an older couple, the detective in charge of Don's case and the woman pathologist who had testified at Susan's arraignment. As the credits started to roll, she smiled contentedly, put her hands on her belly and whispered to the tiny Hopkins growing inside of her, "Just go to sleep now. I'm not sure you need to hear any of this."